The Horse
You Came In On

Martha Grimes

THE HORSE YOU CAME IN ON

Alfred A. Knopf New York

This Is a Borzoi Book
Published by Alfred A. Knopf, Inc.

ISBN 0-679-42523-3

Manufactured in the United States of America

To

LAURA SCOTT PERRY

a friend in Nickel City

Civilized, and gay, and rotted, and polite.

—F. Scott Fitzgerald, on Baltimore

Contents

Part 1

CIDER ALLEY

2

The girl's name was, ironically, Beatrice. And her skin was pale and her hair red, but not Rossetti-red, not the diaphanous red of the *Beata Beatrix* on the wall before her.

The girl and the boy, even in the face of the immortal paintings that surrounded them, could not keep their mortal hands away from each other. They clung and kissed, regardless of the people nearby who looked at them with vague disgust. They were too self-absorbed to care for anyone else in the gallery and too selfishly young to care that they presented a picture no artist would give a damn to paint. Purplish-red hair and black leather (the girl), a band of purple through brush-cut brown hair and black leather (the boy) suggested they could have been twins; but their groping hands suggested otherwise.

One felt, glancing at these two, that they were not in the grip of worldly or otherworldly passion; not even, really, of lust. Their public display was simply for its own sake, something that would convey to the world that they didn't give a flying fuck for the sensibilities of others, not the ones walking about, or standing to gaze at these marvellous paintings, or sitting near them on the bench.

One such patron of the museum sat nearly shoulder to shoulder with the girl, who was at the moment pronging her tongue into the mouth of the boy and moaning unconvincingly. When she felt the woman slightly behind and to her right, felt the burden of the woman's shoulder against hers, she moved sharply (still tongue-in-mouth with her boyfriend), trying to shrug off the unwelcome burden. The burden, however, grew heavier and heavier as the woman listed farther into the girl's back, until the girl turned and told her to stop it, the stupid old cow.

But the woman, middle-aged, very richly and tastefully dressed, did not stop. Her weight grew heavier, and she might have been seeking refuge for her head on the shoulder of the girl.

"Hey—!" the girl began, wrenching away from the boy. Her movement put a distance between herself and the dozing woman. "La-dy!" she said with searing impatience.

The lady didn't answer, simply fell slowly sideways, onto the bench.
"Bloody *'ell,*" whispered the girl, suddenly rising.

II

Her name was Bea and his was Gabe, and the irony of this was not lost
on Richard Jury, though it must have been on the guards at the Tate
Gallery.

The girl hadn't stopped chewing gum for even a minute. The red hair
was teased and spiky; the black leather skirt barely covered her rump. If
anything, she was the underground version of Dante Gabriel Rossetti's
Beatrice.

It was the boy, Gabe, who was doing the talking at the moment,
though Bea cut across his guttural vowels with her own. " 'Ow was we
t'know, then? Coulda been pissed, couldn't she?"

"Or on the needle," said Gabe, in his worldly wisdom.

Richard Jury assumed these two couldn't imagine the mind's light
flickering out in any other way. Dead, pissed, stoned—it was all the same.

The dead woman had been trundled away on a stretcher across the
polished floor. Her going had been overseen by Inspector Marks of C
Division, who was now talking (and clearly relieved to be doing so) to
Scotland Yard CID, represented by Superintendent Jury. He had got to
the room before Marks and, with the help of the gallery guards, had kept
the people—about a dozen of them—from leaving.

Jury had been in the Tate, coincidentally, to see the Swagger Portrait
exhibit, which was closing. He felt himself to be dull-witted about art and
thought perhaps he could educate himself in the differences between
Reynolds and Gainsborough. More than any other gallery in London,
Jury loved the Tate. And his favorite room was the one he was now
standing in, the one in which Bea and Gabe had made their dreadful
discovery. Rossetti, Burne-Jones, William Holman Hunt, Millais's *Ophelia*—he found them indescribably romantic. The boy and girl had been
sitting on the end of the bench, opposite the Rossetti painting; the dead
woman had been sitting on the side of the same bench, across from the
famous painting of Chatterton.

"Mrs. Frances Hamilton," said Inspector Marks, looking at his notes.
"Warminster Road, Belgravia. She had ample ID—six credit cards,
checkbooks. No driver's license, though."

Why did the address sound familiar? Jury frowned, unable to place it.
He had been standing to one side while the crime scene people and then
the medical examiner took their photographs and prodded the body of
Frances Hamilton. The ME said it was probably a stroke, but he couldn't

1

The blind man smelled something new in Cider Alley, a new scent mixed with the old ones of urine and sweat, beer and whisky, coming from some doorway (he imagined) where a little cluster of men liked to gather. Often when he cut through this narrow street there would be tentative greetings—a tap on his shoulder, a hand on his arm, a shouted hello. He resented and resisted pitying gestures and lachrymose words. For he did not regard himself as on the same level as the other homeless: he had, through tenacity and a sharpness of mind and tongue, held on to his own place for over a year. His spot, his grate. People knew him.

The blind man loathed being approached unless he himself sought help with directions or the time. He refused to fan the pavement before him with a white cane, but he did have a briar walking stick, and he was not averse to using it if anyone started any funny business—or just plain annoyed him.

It wasn't the walking stick but the toe of his shoe that hooked into a pliable, unfamiliar obstacle that nearly toppled him. But he was used to obstacles and had become quick at regaining his balance.

What his foot struck was the source of the unfamiliar smell. He knelt and ran his hand over rough cloth and softer skin.

A man. Fallen, drunk, probably. He felt carefully; his sense of touch was even better than his sense of smell. What he touched was familiar, a kind of rough cross that his friend had always worn around his neck. John-Joy. His fingers ran over, first, the familiar topcoat and then went to the suit jacket beneath. Before he could fight with his conscience, he quickly removed the jacket and exchanged it with his own. John-Joy's was infinitely better; it was fine wool, expensive, and he'd always wondered who would ever throw such a garment in the rubbish. Now John-Joy would wake up, come to, find he was wearing Milos's old gray seersucker. Not the best thing for a night in January. But he could take a joke, John-Joy could.

Or could he?

For drink wasn't the smell. Quickly Milos ran his hand from head to feet. The air was clotted with the smell; he did not have to feel the stickiness on his hand to know.

His tongue, his mouth formed what he knew was an audible cry, though he himself heard nothing. "Police!"

One of his hands scrabbled against the cold stone of the building; the other thrashed with his cane as he put more force behind the word: "Police! Police!"

What surprised people (and he revelled in their surprise) was that, although almost totally deaf, he could speak perfectly clearly. The accident which had caused his gradual loss of sight and hearing had happened only ten years before. If someone trumpeted directly in his right ear, he could sometimes make out what they were saying, but that was the extent of it. He shouted again.

Then he felt a presence; he felt someone there, and he wondered if the someone was joining in his shouts. He told this person he was deaf and that he must go for the police, but there was no movement. He did not know what was happening. He thrust out his hand and said, "Write on my hand!" He felt an arm. "Write on my hand!" he said again. This was his one means of communication. He felt the touch of the other person's finger, but the finger was moving too quickly, the finger on his palm. Stupid bastard! he thought, furious. What did they think he was, a fucking computer? "Slower, slower! I can't understand what you're telling me!" he shouted.

The finger drew the letters "I A M." Then there was no movement, only a rustling. He could feel the other person go down, rise up again, as he himself was forcing breath out and yelling, "What? You goddamned fool! 'I am' *what*? What's 'I am'?" The blind man had never been known for so much as a shred of patience.

The other hand grabbed at his. Now, very slowly, a finger formed the letter "I." Then "AM." Then "POL." There was a pause. Goddamned fool was taking his time—but at least the bastard had the sense not to write home to his mother. "Then ICE."

Angry—Milos was always angry, often mutely angry, always had been, even before the accident—he shouted: "What the fuck's that? 'Ice'? What the hell's that?"

Again, the other hand held his and wrote, more quickly this time: "I AM POLICE."

"Goddamned motherfucker!" shouted Milos. "Why didn't you say that before?"

be certain. The late Mrs. Hamilton appeared to be a middle-aged woman, early sixties, in good health. He could not, until a more thorough examination, tell them more.

"Any of them see what happened?" Jury nodded towards the nervous little knot of gallery-goers at one end of the room. They were being questioned by Marks's men.

"No. Only the two kids. And they didn't actually *see* anything—not until the body slumped. Funny about these kids, how they act like they've seen it all, like nothing can jar them; but just let somebody peg out, let there be an emergency, and they completely lose it."

III

Chatterton, skin like blue ice, lay with his arm draped over the edge of his narrow bed, his fingers barely touching the floor, as if he might retrieve the fragments of manuscript pages that looked, in the painting, like confetti tossed across the bare boards. The pages the poet had torn up before he drank the fatal draught.

The marvellous boy. Wasn't that what someone had called him? wondered Jury. He was sitting on the same bench, in about the same place, that the dead woman had sat little more than two hours before.

Jury had always thought the life of Chatterton to be one of the saddest lives ever lived. At seventeen, most of the kids Jury had run into were shooting up, or joyriding, or else charging on their parents' Barclaycards. It all depended on whether he was operating in W1, SW4, or EC12.

By the age of seventeen, Thomas Chatterton had dazzled the literary world with his cycle of poems. And Jury doubted very much that anyone had really given a damn that the "Rowley poems" were a deception except for Horace Walpole, who'd been taken in by them, to his embarrassment—everlasting embarrassment, apparently. Despair and death by the age of seventeen. Jury shook his head. A life without visible reward, without money, without enough to eat, and then betrayal by his benefactor. Chatterton hadn't even been guilty of literary theft; he'd orchestrated the entire production, imagined the whole thing. What had he done to deserve such an end?

Jury wondered why he of all people was thinking of life in terms of justice. He looked now at the young woman in the Holman Hunt painting, rising from the knees of the lover who would almost certainly abandon her. Jury was particularly fond of the inscription Hunt had painted on the frame: "As he that taketh away a garment in cold weather, so is he that singeth songs to an heavy heart."

He passed the Rossetti; the Burne-Jones; Millais's *Ophelia;* the three-part painting of the hapless end of an unfaithful wife; and the painting, a print of which he held in his hand, of a wife and mother mourning the sailor drowned at sea. *A Hopeless Dawn:* every imaginable shade of gray washed over this painting—the morning light at the window, the waves beyond, the pewter candlestick with its guttered candle, the shadows, the color of the clothes. Their world was one drained of color. He had come back to the point at which he had started his stroll of the Tate, and sat down again on the bench. The death of Chatterton, he supposed, was his favorite. A wall of woe.

He had been on leave for two weeks now, had been to Leeds and decided no, he wouldn't be able to stand permanent removal to Bradford. His next stop would be Stratford-upon-Avon, and after that, Northampton. He was fairly certain Superintendent Pratt would welcome him; provincial CID units were always overworked. And he knew Sammy Lasko of the Warwickshire police would. But of all the men he could imagine working with, the irascible, arrogant, determined Macalvie topped the list. Sitting on the bench in the Tate, he recalled the telephone conversation.

"Exeter? Devon-Cornwall? *Me?*"

"Right three times in a row. That's a record even for you, Macalvie."

"I don't know, Jury. I don't know if you'd fit in. No one else that works here can tell the difference between sexual asphyxiation and strangulation. Pardon?"

This last word was apparently addressed to the owner of the voice that was there with Macalvie, chirruping away in Exeter police headquarters.

"I take it," said Jury, "Gilly Thwaite just imparted one of those two bits of information to you?"

"One of those two bits, yes. So which is right?"

"I'm not there, for God's sake." Jury laughed.

"So what?"

"Is this a test?"

"Sure . . . why not? You want a job here, don't you?"

Jury smiled. "Asphyxiation. Plastic bag over head?"

"Right." Macalvie turned away from the phone again.

Jury heard the already high-pitched voice of Gilly Thwaite—at least, he assumed it was Macalvie's scene-of-crime expert—escalate even more, and then something that sounded like a sideboard falling, and then what sounded like a lot of glass breaking, and then a wail that segued into an awful scream.

"She says hi. Listen, you're hired."

"I was just guessing."

"So was I."

In Exeter, the receiver fell into its cradle. Macalvie's way of saying goodbye.

Jury sighed. If he was tired of London, he must be, as Dr. Johnson had predicted, tired of life.

Chatterton certainly had been.

Jury left the Tate.

3

"I really think, Mr. Jury," said Mrs. Wassermann, pressing her anxious fingers hard against her black bag, "that Mr. Moshegeiian is making a mistake allowing Carole-anne to be in charge of renting our first-floor flat." Her fingers whitened against the black leather, and her face beneath the black hat was pale. Mrs. Wassermann was dressed for one of her rare outings to her cousin's in Bromley. She was about to leave for the Angel tube station. Right now she was in Jury's flat, one of the four in the terraced house, but her eyes were trained on the ceiling—the floor of the first-floor flat in question.

"I wouldn't worry about Carole-anne letting to someone unsuitable, Mrs. Wassermann. You know her—she's fussy."

Carole-anne Palutski lived on the top floor, in the smallest and cheapest of the flats, made still cheaper by her understanding with the landlord; she'd take the management of the empty flat off his hands for a reduction in rent. Mr. Moshegeiian, a Latvian or Lithuanian, was clever enough to realize that if Carole-anne was showing people round the flat, it was a dead cert it would get rented, especially if the viewer was male. But that aside, he would still have succumbed to the blandishments of Miss Palutski.

"And Mr. Moshegeiian is nobody's fool," Jury added.

"Slum landlords never are," Mrs. Wassermann said sweetly.

Jury laughed. "I'd hardly call this place a slum, Mrs. Wassermann." He inspected a sock he was about to stuff into his bag. Hole you could put an elbow through. He tossed it into the rubbish bin. "And Carole-anne's extremely particular." *That* was certainly no exaggeration, although "particular" in this case took on a special Carolinian tincture.

"But that's exactly the trouble, Mr. Jury. Now, there was a sweet young couple just the other evening who came to see it. All the way from Wandsworth. They'd just got married and said it was just what they were looking for. But no. Credit rating not up to snuff, she told me." Mrs. Wassermann looked stricken, as if her own credit rating were snuff-less.

Mrs. Wassermann, who was nobody's fool either, simply wasn't tuned in to the Palutski wavelength. The Palutski wavelength could zap any male between twenty and sixty within sight of those lapis lazuli eyes. But when it came to sweet young couples, Carole-anne passed them by as if she had a white stick and a dog in harness.

Lately, the empty flat above Jury had become Mrs. Wassermann's nemesis, a vast and empty cityscape that was in danger of being overrun by rats and ruffians. Mrs. Wassermann was here all day, pretty much alone, what with Jury gone and Carole-anne keeping her version of a "steady" (meaning, hours that suited) job in Covent Garden: whatever didn't interfere with her novice acting.

The pressing problem now was that Carole-anne wasn't here at night either, hadn't been for the two weeks of the run of the play in Chiswick in which she'd landed a tiny part. Jury had taken Mrs. Wassermann to the opening night, and he (though not she, who believed Carole-anne could do anything) had been surprised to find that the girl could act. Indeed, the girl was the only thing worth watching in an otherwise dreary production that thrashed about like a fish unwilling to be reeled in. She glittered. Jury had met the director and producer that evening, a silly twit who said the production was headed for the West End. Carole-anne said it was headed for the river.

"You throw away a perfectly good sock," said Mrs. Wassermann, who had rescued it from the wastepaper basket. "I can darn this with no trouble at all." She opened her bag and stuffed in the sock. Dolefully, she looked at Jury's suitcase. "And you are going away again." Her tongue clucked.

"Not for long—only a few days. To visit my friend in Northants."

"Ah, yes, the earl. Why does he not visit you?"

"Well, when he comes to London, he usually stays at Brown's. You know, in Mayfair."

Mrs. Wassermann opened and closed the clasp of her bag, growing thoughtful. Then she said, "Just think. Wouldn't it be nice for him if he had, you know, a little pied-à-terre?"

Her eyes were on the ceiling.

4

"I hear you caught the squeal, sir." Wiggins looked up from his paperback when Jury walked into their office.

"Caught *what*?" Jury aimed his mac in the general direction of the coatrack and missed again.

Wiggins tilted his book from side to side in a paperback wave. "That's what they say in the States, sir. In these Eighty-seventh Precinct books they're always saying it. It means the ones who're on rota when a crime gets called in. 'Caught the squeal.'" Wiggins had clearly grown fond of the phrase. "Eighty-seventh Precinct. They're by Ed McBain."

"Well, I wish Ed had caught this one. I'm not on rota; I'm on holiday. If you can call it that."

But the sergeant was not commiserating. He had, after all, just been forced to move into the muster room when the fresh paint was applied here in their office. He was allergic to paint. So it was either the smoke and smells of the muster room or paint fumes. Wiggins's life seemed permanently caught between hell and high water, the devil and the deep blue sea, a rock and a hard place.

"He's very good, sir."

Jury was opening and closing drawers. "Who?"

"Ed McBain. Very authentic background. It's a relief to read somebody who knows how the police really work instead of these detective-story writers who just make up anything that suits them. You really get a feel for American cops here."

"I didn't know you read mysteries." Jury slammed another drawer shut.

"I don't actually, except these ones. I read one and thought it was pretty snappy, so I picked up another."

The phone rang; Jury yanked it up before it had barely finished its initial *brr-brr*. A few "Yes"es and he dropped the receiver.

"The guvnor?" asked Wiggins, not bothering to look up from his paperback.

pounds, Jury had imagined reprisals, in one form or another, taking shape in Cyril's mind.

Cyril sat there and Jury sat there, both of them in their separate ways making plans. Jury thought again about the possibility of a unilateral transfer to the provinces and wondered if he should mention it to Racer. Thus far he had mentioned it to no one. He thought again of Macalvie, of Northants and Superintendent Pratt, of the Warwickshire constabulary and Stratford-upon-Avon. He would stop off in Stratford before going on to Northants.

The fax machine beeped twice and then started humming, and Cyril came to quick attention. Now he was on the desk, stalking the machine. Cyril and Jury watched the paper, listened to the machine spit it out inch by inch. Jury leaned over and read. The fax was from the assistant commissioner. He did not read the message, however; Cyril was on it in a flash, sending the paper fluttering to the floor. Then Cyril looked at Jury and slowly blinked, as if the cat were waiting for any suggestions Jury might have with regard to this fax. Jury shrugged.

Cyril slid down from the desk, caught up one corner of the paper in his teeth, and dragged it across the room to the outer office. At the door he paused and appeared to be scanning the room for Fiona, who, Jury saw, was not there. Probably gone to the ladies' with her sponge bag. Jury moved over to the door to watch.

The fax now lay beneath the water cooler, on the little ledge that held the small paper cup, full of water. The cat did a quick, balletlike turn in the air and knocked the cup off the ledge.

They both stood there watching the water soak into the message, after which Cyril pawed and clawed it around into a soggy ball.

Fiona marched in. "Has that cat been at that water cooler again?" She put her makeup bag on the desk. Her lips were a bright and pearly red, her eyelids winged out in various mutations of blues and lavenders. "And you just standing there?" She picked up the cup and the stringy wad of paper and tossed them both into the wastepaper basket.

II

Racer flipped the intercom switch and barked at Fiona: "Hasn't the AC called?" When she told him no, he switched the object of his spleenish displeasure to Jury. "If you don't want trouble, then you shouldn't be around."

"I'm 'around' because you requested it." If Jury were on the moon, Racer would send a space shuttle.

Jury winced. "No. Fiona. I caught the squeal."

Wiggins sniggered and Jury walked out.

Fiona Clingmore lifted her towelled head from her portable steambath and said, "You're supposed to be on leave, you are. Disgraceful."

"So where is he? I thought he was desperate to see me."

She shrugged her shoulder to indicate a room out of view. "With the AC. That's where he called from. What you been doing on your holiday?"

Is that what they called it? "Been to eleven films in the last ten days. I thought I'd get it over with all at once."

"Whyn't you go somewhere sunny and warm? You're the one ought to be having a holiday on the Costa del Sol, not *him*." Fiona patted some astringent lotion on her face and squinted in her mirror to view the pore damage. "He says he's taking Cyril with him next time he goes to Spain. He saw this animal rights stuff about the disgraceful things they do over there. There was this picture—can you imagine?—where this Spaniard has a cat by one leg and he's swinging him round his head." Fiona clucked her tongue and shook out her hair. "Well, any man that'd doctor a cat's tuna. . . . Poor defenseless animal." She took out her sponge bag.

Jury hunched down in the office chair and watched the poor defenseless animal. The cat Cyril was probably working out some equation in thermodynamics that would levitate him to the top of the water cooler. The small ledge was too tiny to hold him, accommodating nothing larger than a paper cup. One sat there beneath the spout. Jury wondered what fate the cat had in mind for Chief Superintendent Racer that involved the water cooler. Cyril wasn't simply sitting there waiting for Fiona to turn the spout and make bubbles rise. After another moment of staring up at the water bottle, he swayed off towards the chief's office.

Fiona sighed. "He'll be at that fax machine again." She made no move, however, to go in and collect him.

Jury sat down in the chair across the desk from Racer's own swivel chair, occupied now by Cyril, whose head Jury could just see over the desktop. Some of the furniture had been shoved into one corner and covered with dust sheets preparatory to redecoration. In another corner, lengths of ceiling molding were leaning against the wall. It looked like some sort of major overhaul, inconvenient for working, convenient for spending even longer periods of time at one's club.

Cyril's eyes were on the new facsimile machine. Ever since Racer had laced Cyril's tuna with tranquilizers and transported him to one of the

"This Hamilton person's family knows the assistant commissioner. That's what I'm waiting for. Information."

Now Jury was sorry he hadn't read the fax. "So? I know the AC too, but that doesn't mean I'd put me on a case."

"Well, for some reason—don't ask me effing why, Jury—the family wants you."

"The family doesn't know me."

Racer's response fell somewhere between a smirk and a simper. "Apparently they do."

"I don't know any Hamiltons. Not one."

"It was another name." Racer punched the intercom switch again, told Fiona to get the AC on the line. "This woman—friend of the AC—had a nephew, or the dead woman did—hell, I can't remember all the details—that was murdered somewhere around Philadelphia. The States." Racer was searching around his desk, looking under the blotter. "Where the hell are those tickets? I left them right here. And where are my color chips? They were here, too."

"I don't get this. What does a killing in the States have to do with us?"

"Victim was born here."

"So?"

Racer stopped his search for the color chips, flipped the switch, and asked Fiona if she had the assistant commissioner on the line. "And this woman's a *friend*." (Is this the way you treat your friends, Jury?)

"Look, I'm supposed to be on leave. I'm sure whatever cops caught the squeal over there, they can handle it. I'm sure they *prefer* to handle it." Infuriated, Jury stood up. Usually, he had more patience. Not lately, though.

"You don't have to get so damned shirty about it. No one's telling you you have to do anything. Just go along and see this woman and mollify her. That's all."

The AC wasn't there. "His temp sec"—Fiona always loved it when someone higher up had temporary help—"wants to know, didn't you get the fax?"

"Well, *did* I, Miss Clingmore? How the fucking hell should *I* know, if I've been out of the office?" Racer was peering at the facsimile machine. "And where in hell are my air tickets, Miss Clingmore? I left them right here tucked into the blotter!"

Racer's hols, naturally, took precedence over anything else.

Jury thought he heard a series of cracks of Fiona's gum, like tiny pistol shots. "You're the one wants that fax machine in his office. Maybe it fell on the floor."

"I've *looked* on the floor."

"Well, she says she sent it, that's all I know."

"Stop wasting my time arguing, and call her back. Bloody hell!" Racer flipped off the intercom. "I don't know how this goddamned place operates with these civilians who can't even count their toes. That effing cat would make a better typist."

The fax machine burped and then stuttered out its message. Racer ripped it out, read it, said, "SW3, Jury. Warminster Road. Belgravia. Her name's Cray."

5

She opened the double doors of the elegant sitting room with both hands, one on each of the brass doorknobs, making an entrance that would have seemed theatrical if it had been any woman other than Lady Cray.

And she looked, thought Jury, exactly as she had the last time he'd seen her in the Lake District. That had been at the inquest. Her well-tailored suit might have been the same one, a silvery-blue-grayish material of wool silk that exactly matched her eyes, eyes that were precisely the tint of crystal, that elusive gray called "Waterford blue." The January afternoon was in league with Lady Cray. Slants of silvery light lay in decorous oblongs along the pale blue Chinese rugs and sparked the Waterford bowl on a little rosewood table. The sun, unusually clear for this time of year, striped the twin sofas and upholstered side chairs, all of them done in a shimmering crystalline-finished material the shade of Lady Cray's suit.

"Superintendent, I am overjoyed you have come!" She looked brightly from Jury to Sergeant Wiggins.

If any miserable case could be said to have in it a pleasant turn of events, Lady Cray was just such a turn. He took her hand and accepted her offer of tea or champagne or both.

After she had settled them into chairs of cloudlike comfort, she said, "I know you haven't called to talk about old times, but my God, those were the days, weren't they?!"

No, thought Jury, they weren't. Jane Holdsworth appeared to him, not as he had last seen her but as he first had, standing there in Camden Passage in a white macintosh, inspecting something from one of the rain-wet antiques stalls. The piece of clothing she was holding up, an amber-colored shift or something, exactly matched the color of her hair. A shift —or something? He remembered, of course, very precisely that it had been a negligee, taken from a rack of vintage clothing. And there had been a brooch she had held to the coat, testing its color and shape. That had been amber, too. This scene of a lifetime ago unrolled in his mind with a torturous slowness, as if warning him that, having remembered at all, he would have to look at every glint of light in the brooch, every wavering shadow that fell across the cloth, the folds becoming more palpable, as if each little fold were statue drapery set in marble. He felt this in a moment of blinding acuity. And this was a mercy, really: that he had remembered the first time he saw her and not the last. But Lady Cray had not known Jane Holdsworth, though she had known the family, finally. Jane was there at the beginning, Lady Cray at the very end.

He was only partly conscious of asking her about the Holdsworths, but he supposed he must have, as he looked away, through the french windows to the cold garden beyond.

"Of course I've seen them! Did you think I wouldn't? Alex and Millie . . ."

Jury was only half listening as she talked on about Alex Holdsworth and the little girl, Millie. The smile frozen on his face must have looked natural enough, for she didn't seem to notice anything absent in his responses.

"They live there now, you know, with Adam. He still goes to Castle Howe occasionally, just to drive them all crazy. We have an absolutely *wonderful* time, Alex and Millie and I. We go to violent films together— terminators, aliens, and so forth—and I get a few of my unsuspecting friends together and we all play poker. Alex does, rather. And we spend a good bit of time at Cheltenham races."

"Winning?"

She raised her eyebrows. "Well, of *course,* winning. We'd hardly go to lose, would we?"

His smile now was genuine enough; it was hard not to smile, thinking of Alex and poker and the ponies.

A maid entered with a silver tray and ice bucket, managing to set down silver tea service and Dom Pérignon with practiced movements. Wiggins rose to help with tray and bucket and was rewarded with a timid smile; the deployment of the champagne in the ice bucket and the tall, fluted glasses was done in a dither of cast-down glances, as if she wondered if she had the right to be in the drawing room. To Wiggins's kind murmurings, she made no reply.

Said Lady Cray when the maid had made her exit, "Afraid of her own shadow, I sometimes think. Don't take a blind bit of notice, Sergeant Wiggins. Sugar?"

Wiggins had opted for tea, and when Lady Cray held the silver bowl aloft, he told her three, please. "But she seems quite good at her job," he said, his glance having followed the little maid all the way out of the door.

Jury took his cup, and their hostess poured herself a glass of champagne.

"She's certainly a superior cook. She's clever, too, surprisingly enough. I always think it's too bad to combine superb cooking with social awkwardness, but there you are. I put up with the speechlessness to get the cooking. Fanny was very fond of her, though." Lady Cray sighed. Here she leaned forward and picked up an unusual bit of sculpture, a block of turquoise banded with silver and adorned with a little silver figure playing a flute. "I shall truly miss Fanny Hamilton, Superintendent. It's her nephew I talked to the commissioner about. But may I first tell you something about Fanny?" She replaced the turquoise piece and sat back.

"Of course."

"She moved in here with me about a year ago, after I came back from Castle Howe. . . ." She paused and gave Jury a look. "Incidentally, I'm not sure what might have happened had it not been for that whiz of a barrister."

Pete Apted, Q.C. Jury smiled. He was the legendary barrister who had taken on the defense in that instance. "Yes. Mr. Apted doesn't take hostages, does he?"

She went on. "Fanny was, in many ways, a silly woman. Well, perhaps I am too. But we weren't very much alike, and I might not have had her here to live had it not been for the great friendship of our respective husbands. Bobby and Dickie—Dickie was Lord Cray, incidentally—were just the best of friends imaginable. Both of them were pretty silly, too; but they were lovable. And when it comes to the 'male bonding' thing, well, Bobby and Dickie could have given lessons." Here she held up crossed fingers to testify to this close friendship, causing an enormous diamond to spark into life. "They lived together, and died together."

"Died together?" asked Wiggins, his pencil poised over his notebook.

"Yes, Sergeant. On the cricket ground."

"What?" said Wiggins, astounded.

There was too much opportunity for a risible response here, and Jury bit his lip and refused to look at Wiggins, although the sergeant's capacity for comic reactions was not notable.

"Bobby was batsman, you see, and he had a tricky heart. Fanny was constantly after him to give up his damned sports—the cricket, the polo, the hunt, even—but Bobby wouldn't hear of it. Trying to keep up with my husband, who was absolutely expert at sport."

"So how . . . ?"

"Bobby had a bad heart, and so, giving one furious bat, he simply keeled over. Then *my* husband, seeing him go down, dropped the ball and dashed to his rescue. And he tripped." Lady Cray took a long swallow of champagne. "Ran straight into the wicket! Can you imagine such a freak accident? He fell and hit his head. I was always telling those boys that they'd do better to choose sports that weren't so damned dangerous. I can tell you, both of us—Fanny and I—were heartbroken. Fanny was deathly ill herself; I wondered then if she had a heart condition." Her eyes glittered, and she took another long drink from her glass. "But to tell the truth, it might have been just as well they died that way. Dickie would have had a very hard time of it without Bobby. It was funny, really, to watch Bobby try and keep up with my husband. Dickie was Master of Foxhounds, and Bobby could hardly ride." She sighed. "Accident prone, both of them. There were accidents at polo, at billiards, at the Chichester boat race. Fanny and I knew they'd come to it in the end."

The way she rendered the antic histories of the two husbands was to pace before the fireplace, backlit by the jumping flames, brandishing her tulip champagne glass like a dagger so that "come to't in the end" was absolutely Jacobean. Then Lady Cray heaved a sigh and said, "And of course, with both of them pegging out right there at the match, well, we'd certainly got something in common. We did get along quite well, in spite of her unabashed envy of my title. The Hamiltons had a great deal of money, much more than I, but she loved the British aristocracy. I think she was always in search of her pedigree, corresponding with professors at Oxford and Cambridge and one, even, in America. I don't know why; it wasn't the DAR that interested Fanny, it was *Burke's Peerage.* I tried to console her by saying the title wasn't, after all, anything I'd ever *earned*— I mean, it isn't exactly the Victoria Cross, is it? We hardly ever *earn* them, do we? It's all an accident of birth or marriage, unless you're in the theater, or something like that. Like Olivier or Peggy Ashcroft—I expect they did earn theirs. Americans love nothing so much as a title, wouldn't you agree?"

Thinking of Melrose Plant's aunt, Jury had to.

"It was certainly so in Fanny's case. Oh, Bobby didn't care for a title; it was cricket he loved." She hooted. "But there it is again. Cricket! The aristocracy and cricket. Well, it doesn't even have to be a peerage—any lowly baronetcy will do. As long as it isn't Irish, of course!"

Jury laughed.

"The British peerage! Sometimes I believe Americans think that's England in a nutshell. I remember when I first met them, it was at Lord's during the second innings. Fanny was a friend of one of the people I was with; we'd taken a hamper along—you know, cold chicken and white wine—and were having a lovely picnic in the mound stand. She was fascinated that I was 'Lady' Cray and almost immediately confided in me that she'd love nothing so much as a title. If only her husband had been born to the purple, she said. I laughed at that. They all think it's terribly royal, don't they? Americans are so romantic. Ermine and scarlet and all of us living in places like Woburn Abbey. 'I do want a title,' she said, 'though Bobby doesn't'—as if they were arguing over duck for dinner!"

Lady Cray topped up her glass and poured Sergeant Wiggins more tea. Jury declined.

"Tell me about her nephew's death." He knew she'd been avoiding this painful subject with all her chatter about titles and cricket.

"His name was Philip. He was killed—murdered."

"I'm sorry. This was in Philadelphia?"

"Not in Philadelphia. That's where he worked. Upper Pennsylvania somewhere. He had a little cabin in the woods, very isolated, and someone just walked in"—she shrugged her shoulders—"and shot him. It happened two months ago." She shook her head, anticipating Jury's question. "The police think it must have been robbery. Why, I don't know. Philip had nothing of value. He'd gone to the cabin for one of his weekends—a friend of his told the police all this—and he might not have been found for some time if this same friend hadn't got worried when he didn't come back on the Sunday evening. They had some sort of date."

Wiggins looked up from his notebook. "A lady friend, was it?"

"Yes. Helen, or Heather . . . well, I don't quite remember. Philip had talked about her once or twice. Fanny flew over, of course. She talked to some sheriff or other in Pennsylvania, where it happened. Sinclair, his name was, I believe. Then she stayed on for a while, went to Texas, or . . ." She paused with a frown of attempted remembrance. "Somewhere out there. Abilene? She brought me this." Here she retrieved the piece of turquoise from the table and held it up. "Beautiful, isn't it?"

Jury agreed. "What about the rest of Philip's family?"

"Fanny was his only relative. I should explain that the Calverts— Philip's father and mother—were both killed when he was a little boy. Plane crash. Fanny wasn't related by blood, but I can tell you she simply adored him. I'm convinced people really can die of a broken heart. Anyway, she's dead."

Lady Cray looked away, through the window, where a chill breeze scattered and rattled old leaves like copper. "I met Philip; he was here two years ago. And he got on famously with my own nephew, my great-nephew, Andrew." Lady Cray stopped to handle the turquoise block again, regarding him with her wonderful silvery eyes, whose expression was now full of sadness. "The thing is, Superintendent, I feel I could at least do this for her: carry on with trying to find out what really happened to Philip. She was absolutely devastated by his death. You can't imagine."

Oh, yes I can, thought Jury. He stared at the silver flautist embedded in the turquoise. For something to do, to be able to turn his back on the room, he got up and walked to the tall window that overlooked the cold garden, dripping as if last night's rain were still trapped here, the trees still raining. He had been sitting on that bench in the Tate where Fanny Hamilton had sat; the portrait of Chatterton swam before his eyes. White skin, red hair. Lying on his narrow bed. He shut his eyes. Some composure returned, he turned with a half-smile to Lady Cray. "And you thought perhaps I . . . ?" He left it as a question.

"Please. I know it's asking a lot; I know you're on holiday. But that also means you aren't tied up. . . ."

"Lady Cray, there's protocol. This killing happened in the United States. Scotland Yard can't go messing around in the affairs of American sheriffs."

"How bloody pompous," she said, matter-of-factly.

He smiled. "It's not really pomposity. I don't mean to be difficult."

"Well, you *are* being. A few days' holiday in Philadelphia would make a change, wouldn't it? Naturally, I'd pay your expenses. First class. Or take Concorde if you like."

"That's not really the point."

"Oh, ho-*hum*, Superintendent." She patted her mouth with the tips of her fingers, simulating a smile. "You know, when Alex plays poker he uses an expression I like. 'Calling in markers.'" Her smile was bewitching, turning the face of this elderly woman into that of a much younger one.

"Uh-huh. You getting this, Wiggins? Bribing a police officer?"

"Pardon, sir?"

"Considering all the *work* I did for you at Castle Howe . . . well." She smoked, regarding him. "With a great deal of help from Mr. Plant. How is he? Such a clever man."

Jury smiled. "Yes. He is. And so I take it, Lady Cray, you're calling—"

"Calling in my markers."

6

Staring through the plate glass window of the Starrdust, Wiggins was munching on some vegetarian melange he had bought over at Cranks in Covent Garden, and trying to muscle his way closer to the window and in between a little boy with spiky hair and a small girl wearing big glasses that dwarfed her face.

"Would you just look at that, sir?"

The Starrdust Twins, Joy and Meg, had outdone themselves with this window dressing. It was a replica of Covent Garden Market—not the new one that lay just over the street, with its collection of boutiques, health food restaurants, and space-age neon places, but the nineteenth-century marketplace. Jury felt a wave of nostalgia as he looked at the fruit and vegetable stalls, spilling over with tiny cabbages; at the floral hall and the flower sellers; at the miniature figures of porters balancing baskets on their heads or pushing carts. He could almost feel the bustle, smell the fish and game—two acres of it.

The Starrdust's owner was an astrologer and antiquarian; given that the shop dealt only in celestial, astrological, or otherwise otherworldly matters (not the least of which were the fortunes told by Carole-anne Palutski in her silken tent), Jury wondered at this backwards look into London's history. And while he was wondering, the scene changed from light to dark as the scrim, all but invisible until now, rose on a night scene of little dark streets, a square with a horse-drawn carriage, and gaslights.

All the children gasped and applauded. This included Wiggins.

To enter the Starrdust was to step not back in time but out of it, much as if one were walking through a doorway open on nothing else but sheer blue sky and brilliant white clouds in a surrealistic painting. Light flowed and winked from the ceiling-sky, across which spilled a backlit Milky Way and planets which lit up and faded as the hidden lights brightened and dimmed. The shop was long and narrow, and the farther end was in total darkness except for the blue neon sign which spelled out "HorrorScope." This must be a new sign, one Andrew Starr had made for the Wendy-house-like structure at the rear of the shop, which was the children's favorite part of the Starrdust. Starr was a man in his late thirties chronologically, but one who seemed never to have grown out of childhood. Perhaps this was why he was the only shopkeeper Jury knew who never tossed unaccompanied kiddies out the door.

"Super!"

Out of the darkness walked Carole-anne Palutski, carrying a plate with a huge slice of coconut cake that she forked up as she advanced. "Want some?" She held out a forkful.

"No thanks, Madame Zostra. You look gorgeous, as always."

Madame Zostra, teller of dubious fortunes, lately taken to reading palms when she got bored with the tarot, was in her Pre-Raphaelite phase. The harem days of bare midriffs, gauze trousers, chiffon veils, and tinkling ankle bells had given way to the Spanish influence of mantillas and bejeweled combs; that in turn was dropped in favor of the Arthurian phase and the Guinevere look.

But now it was Rossetti and Burne-Jones stuff: long, floating gowns, shapeless except for the shape that Carole-anne lent them, which was plenty. After gazing at a few pictures of long-haired ladies reclining on fainting couches and chaise longues—doped up, Jury imagined, with laudanum—she again had changed her look. She had even invested in "scrunching" at Vidal Sassoon (something that she'd also put poor Mrs. Wassermann through, until Jury put a stop to it: he didn't care for Mrs. Wassermann scrunched). Now she wore her red-gold hair in a waterfall of crinkly waves. No fancy combs, no coronets, thank goodness.

"So, Super, what're you doing here?" Her mouth was full of cake, shreds of coconut dusting the air when she spoke. It was a wonder, with the stuff she ate, she kept her figure, but keep it she did.

"To have my fortune told, of course."

"I told it once."

In Carole-anne's galaxy, Jury's stars seldom shone and never moved. Despite all evidence to the contrary, she saw no relationships with women (except herself and Mrs. Wassermann), no moves or promotions, no trips, no travails. Whenever Jury did venture beyond the limits of Greater London, she told him he was tempting the Fates. And all of the lines in Jury's hand appeared to be parallel ones, never meeting, never converging, just going back and forth uneventfully, like underground tracks.

"Things change," said Jury.

Casually, she lifted his left hand, dropped it, and said, "Not for you." She mashed the prongs of her fork down on cake crumbs.

"That's my *left* hand. You said the left was just 'what you came in with.' I believe that was your way of putting it." He held out his right hand.

She barely tossed the hand a glance. "What you came in with is what you go out with."

"I thought maybe this time you might see the trip before I return from it."

She frowned. "What trip? You just got back from Yorkshire."

By now Wiggins appeared to be next in line for the HorrorScope. Probably shown the kids his warrant card, thought Jury. As Vaughn Monroe's smooth rendition of "Racing with the Moon" was being scratched to death by a needle in need of changing, Carole-anne grumpily invited Jury into the tent where there were a small table and two big cushions. On one of these sat a huge stuffed Wild Thing animal that Jury had brought back from Long Piddleton. It was understood (at least by Carole-anne) that trips meant presents.

She moved the stuffed animal and set the cake plate near her crystal ball, used more for checking makeup than calling up her familiar. "How long you going to be gone this time?"

He smiled. "Can't you tell?"

She drew his right hand towards her (having already given the left the cursory glance his birthright deserved) and said, "Well, trips don't show up in hands, really. Where're you going?"

"Northants. Long Piddleton."

"Oh, *there*." She dropped his hand, obviously relieved. Northamptonshire, by virtue of being the home of Jury's faithful old friend Melrose Plant, did not qualify as a trip at all. Since there was obviously nothing (given all the times he'd been there in the past) in Long Piddleton to inflame Jury's mind, there was consequently nothing to disturb Carole-anne's.

Stratford-upon-Avon, now, he'd best keep quiet about. This was uncharted territory in the Carole-anne galaxy.

Jenny Kennington lived in Stratford-upon-Avon.

There had been, several months ago, a bit of an episode in his flat. When he'd come in, Carole-anne had been lounging (and dressed for it, too, in her new pajamas) on his sofa, leafing through a fashion magazine.

"Who's JK?" she'd asked.

"Beg your pardon?"

"JK." She'd taken a tiny wad of pink paper from the pocket of her cerise lounging pajamas and unfolded it, then refolded it into a small pink square, as she seemed to be considering its message. It was one of those "While You Were Out" sheets from his telephone message pad.

"Did the lady leave anything but her initials?"

"Janey? Something like that."

"Jenny." He snapped his fingers. "Hand it over."

All of Jury's lady friends were referred to by Carole-anne by initials only. She had managed to oust SB-slash-H from the lives of the Islington house (which was just as well, Jury had later realized); JH she had been truly remorseful about; JK was an unknown quantity.

He said now to Carole-anne, "I just thought I'd call in and say goodbye." That had really been Jury's purpose, hoping the Starrdust's ambience and Vaughn Monroe would cushion what small blow there was. "And what happened to the nice couple who came to see the first-floor flat?" Jury uncoiled himself from the cushion.

"Those two?" Her frown was horrible. "You couldn't have stood those ones overhead, Super." She leaned closer to her crystal ball and wiped a bit of coconut from the corner of her mouth. "He walked with a walker and she needed two sticks. They'd've been clumping back and forth, back and forth all night. Said they never went to bed before one or two. Well, you'd've gone stark staring mad, wouldn't you?"

"Thanks for watching out for me, love."

"No problem, Super."

7

Sam Lasko had the same secretary, and age hadn't mellowed her. She ran by fits and starts, like her typewriter. Lasko wasn't a nervous type, but his office appeared to be. Lasko wasn't there; he was out on a case. And his secretary's tone implied that Jury should be, too, not mooning around here like the last time. Probably she had forgotten: "the last time" Lasko had dropped a case in Jury's lap. Or maybe that was it; maybe she was afraid other cases might get dropped and Jury would become a permanent fixture in Stratford-upon-Avon. Perhaps she feared change. God knows, he could certainly understand that.

So she kept on typing, her back stern, her disapproving expression set like cement, until he commented on the color of her cardigan, how pretty it was, how it went with her coloring. The typewriter stopped clicking; her face softened a little. The cardigan was new; he had seen the price tag sticking up over the top of the collar.

The girl who answered the door was probably no more than eight or nine and wore a large apron. Jury's heart sank. Jenny was always moving; he always seemed to be saying hello and goodbye to her in rooms full of packing crates and boxes. Now he was afraid the girl would tell him, Oh, she's gone.

She did.

"But she'll be back. She's only gone to the top of the road, to get an aubergine."

He loved the way she said it. But she seemed uncertain as to how to deal with him.

"I'm an old friend," he said. He handed her his card and watched her trying not to be impressed by its origins.

Finally, she said, "Well, I expect it'll be all right."

She had been accompanied, in her visit to the front door, by a rough-looking black cat that was not impressed at all. Jury frowned over the cat: Didn't he know it? Hadn't he seen it before?

The little house was in the old section of Stratford-upon-Avon, off the road that wound around the Royal Shakespeare Theatre and the church-yard. He had been here a few years before, that time he was working on Lasko's case. It had been just before she let the house in order to take an ocean voyage with an aging relation. The woman had since died.

Downstairs was a long sitting room that reached to the patio door at the rear and that, in turn, opened onto a little garden. This was the only room down here, except for the kitchen, from which must be coming that heady mixture of cooking smells that Jury couldn't identify.

"I'm Elsie. I've come to help cook."

"Well, Elsie, if my nose is any judge, you're doing a great job of it." Jury closed his eyes and sniffed. The mingled scents were absolutely voluptuous. For the last two or three weeks, he'd had no appetite to speak of; now he was starving hungry.

Said Elsie, importantly: "We're doing a venison and beef casserole. It takes a lot of cooking—two or three hours. She—we—put a lot of red wine in it. And, let's see, there's some trout mousse for starters, and some soup that's been cooking *forever.*" Here she put her hands on her aproned hips and sighed hugely, as if there never had been such a belea-guered cook as Elsie. "And for the sweet there's pudding. It's Guinness pudding—" she paused to give him a chance to show surprise; he did— "that takes over five hours steaming. So you're smelling a lot of things."

"With a menu like that, you must be having a dinner party. I expect I've come at a bad time," Jury added, unhappily.

Quickly she said no, and told him to sit down. Having judged him to be a very appreciative audience, she was now anxious for more applause. "Oh, there'll be quite a few people here, I expect. Though I haven't laid the table with her best silver yet. I do that, you see." Her feet, which barely reached the floor from the high wing-backed chair, were crossed, and she pulled the apron down over her knees in a gesture she'd no doubt seen many young ladies use. Elsie was herself trying hard to be a young lady, proper and aubergine-worldly. The persona slipped as a pot in the kitchen started to clatter and she jumped up and ran. Then back she came, complaining that the old gas cooker wouldn't simmer properly and was really messy and she was trying to talk Lady Kennington into getting halogen. The pronunciation of that word went the way of "aubergine."

"Does she entertain often, then?"

"All the time. She has ever so many friends. She goes to the theater a lot and knows all the actors. She knows Daryl Jackbee"—Jury thought that one over: Derek Jacobi, he decided—"and she goes to London a lot. She likes to shop. She has cupboards full of clothes."

This did not sound like the Jenny Jury knew. He smiled. "A busy lady."

"Well, she is, you know. A Lady, I mean. She has a title."

Jury watched the black cat sway in from the kitchen and thought—could it be Tom? The cat they'd once taken to the vet? Oh, but that was years ago. "I don't even like that cat," Jenny had said, sitting in his car with the injured bundle of cat, a stray she'd found roaming around the house at Stonington, her old estate in Hertford. And here he was, still looking as imperious as a cat with mangy tail and a chewed ear could look. Stonington. Jury smiled a little and then felt saddened by the passing of those years. Something, he felt, had been wasted. He reached his hand out towards the cat, who was sitting on the hearth like a bucket of coal, and who ignored the hand and started washing.

At the sound of the door opening, Elsie jumped up and went out into the hall, and Jury overheard a brief exchange. Then Jenny Kennington was in the sitting room, smiling.

He had felt, until this moment, uncertain and even stupid, coming here unannounced. But when she spoke his name and smiled at him as if his appearance were the most wonderful surprise she could imagine, he no longer felt stupid.

"Hello, Jenny." He glanced, smiling himself, at what she was wearing. For a woman with a cupboard of clothes, she certainly stuck to one favored sweater.

She noticed his expression, looked down at the sweater, and said, "Oh, lord! Same old sweater. I know you think it's all I have to wear."

It was black, shot through with some metallic thread, with too-big sleeves that she kept pushing up on her arms. She'd been wearing it when they first met. And the nervous mannerism still went with it. "According to Elsie, you've plenty of clothes. Always doing the London shops. Selfridge's, Liberty's."

Elsie had shot off towards the kitchen immediately after Jenny had come in, and was now putting the silver on the table.

Jenny whispered: "It's because I'm 'Lady' Kennington. She invents all sorts of romantic and expensive pastimes for me."

"Like tonight's dinner party?"

"No dinner party. Did she tell you the entire cast of *Henry IV, Part II* was coming?"

"Only Daryl Jackbee. If it's no party, what's that incredible menu for? Unless Elsie was exaggerating and it's really cabbage and mash cooking?"

"For me. Now us. You will stay, won't you? There's also some excellent Sancerre and Stilton with apricots that no one knows about except me.

And I can rummage around and find a bottle of Châteauneuf-du-Pape that we can drink with the casserole."

"I'll think about it."

Elsie had been paid her "salary" and had flown off—almost literally, the way she danced, with that little skipping step, out the door.

The dinner lived up to its romantic preview. It was wonderful.

They had between them settled a number of things over the soup and the venison casserole: that Jenny hadn't made any plans to leave Stratford; that she had made plans to buy a new outfit following their last meeting in London; that the cat was Tom—*the* Tom.

"The cat you can't stand."

"I couldn't just leave him there, at Stonington." Pushing up her sweater sleeves, she looked nervously at Tom, as if he might think his fate still in abeyance. Tom walked away, towards the source of the trout mousse.

"That cat doesn't appreciate you."

"I know. That's one reason I can't stand him."

They ate their pudding in silence for a few moments. Then Jury said, "I never called you to apologize or to thank you."

"Apologize for what?"

"The way I just walked out of the Salisbury that afternoon and left you sitting there. To say nothing of the insults I hurled at you about your sweater."

She laughed. "You couldn't hurl an insult if someone put a gun to your head. You told me black didn't suit me, that's all. And you were just nervous or upset about—" Jury heard the pause, though she picked up on it quickly enough—"a case, I expect."

He just watched her calmly pouring from a decanter of port. If she wanted to be delicate, he would let her. He smiled. "I expect." For he knew she knew about the whole business; anyone who read the papers would have done. And Jenny had also done something about it, without ever telling him. "It wouldn't have worked out, in any event," he said, elliptically.

"I'm very sorry."

Beside one of the white marble candlesticks was the little alabaster figure of a woman that she had bought that day in St. Martin's Lane, in the same shop where he had got the ring. Jury picked it up, turned it round in his hand. He thought of the marble figure in the inner courtyard of Stonington, the figure that could be seen from every room, at different angles. The first time he had ever seen Jenny Kennington had been with the black cat, Tom, on the steps of Stonington and, later, in those big, empty rooms from which she was moving. Some of the pieces here in this cottage had come from there: the marquetry secretaire, the ivory-inlaid writing desk, the delicate-looking but sturdy neoclassical chairs on which they now sat.

"You were thinking of going back the last time I saw you, to Stonington."

"It's been let since then," she said sadly, the small glass of port raised to her lips. "I'm thinking of opening a restaurant."

"*What?*"

She looked round the table. "It wasn't that good?"

"The meal? It was superb. It's just a long way from superb cooking to a restaurant."

"Oh? Why?"

He laughed at her genuine surprise. He supposed the confidence pleased him. Jenny was shy but by no means shrinking. "No reason, I expect."

"What I'm doing is practicing. I cook up these elaborate dinners for myself; sometimes I invite one or two people, and sometimes just Elsie. She really is learning to help out."

He pictured it: Elsie and Jenny, sitting opposite each other across this festive little table, talking about food and the Royal Shakespeare Company. It stabbed him a little, this picture of poignance. "It's a wonderful idea, Jenny. Is there somewhere around here you're thinking of?"

"Outside of town there's a pub that needs a new manager. They could do thirty, maybe forty covers."

"You've really looked into this. I can see you as a landlady."

"No, you can't." She smiled and changed the subject. "You said something about 'thanking' me. For what?"

"For Pete Apted. Pete Apted, Q.C. The man does not come cheap. It took me a long time to work that out, who had retained Pete Apted."

"You of all people should remember that I had a little money. And also that if it hadn't been for you, I wouldn't have."

That was a massive exaggeration. She was talking about the emerald necklace, but her husband had not died a poor man. And she had also inherited money from that relation of hers she'd travelled with.

She said, "It was something good to do with the money I got from that necklace. Something really worthwhile, after all the hell it caused. And Pete Apted's fee wasn't that high. I think he made concessions; I think he liked you. And he didn't have to go to court."

"No, thank God. But he'd have won. You just have that feeling about him. I don't think Pete Apted, Q.C., ever loses. He helped out a friend of mine. Three friends, actually." Jury smiled. The smile faded. It was also that whiz of a barrister, Pete Apted, who had worked out just what was going on. And had made Jury face it. For a few moments in his office a year ago, he had hated Pete Apted as he had seldom hated anyone. Did Apted have to be so damned clever?

"Something wrong? You look furious."

"What? Oh, no. No."

A pleasant silence drew out while Jenny sat there turning the stem of her glass. She asked: "Did you come to Stratford just to see me, then?"

"Yes."

"No, you didn't."

He laughed. "In addition to you, I wanted to see Sam Lasko. Warwickshire constabulary. I'm job hunting."

She gasped. "What?"

"I'm tired of London. And for God's sake don't quote Dr. Johnson, will you?"

"Are you sure?"

"Sure of what?"

"That it's London you're tired of?"

"You mean, am I tired of something else?"

She looked away. "Memories, perhaps."

"Like Jane, you mean?" There was no need, really, to avoid the subject.

"If that was her name." Her voice was bleak.

He looked at her for a moment. "I think I always knew it wouldn't work out with Jane. I knew something was wrong; I only wish Pete Apted hadn't told me what, exactly," he said dryly. She did not ask what, and he was a little disappointed that she did not. "I expect I'll never be sure just how she felt, now." He paused, smiled. "Anyway, I thought, hell, it might be nice, for a change, just to get a bicycle, mooch around, drop in every day at the pub for a good old natter with my mates."

"Sounds bucolic."

"You don't think it's a good idea." When she didn't comment, he felt, again, disappointed. He had been depending on her enthusiasm for his making a change, especially if it were here he were to change to. He picked up the alabaster figure with the broken arm and stared at it in the candlelight. "You might be right." When she smiled slightly, he realized he'd assumed she had said what he himself was thinking. "Perhaps it's not being 'tired' of something at all." He kept his eyes fixed on the little figure, not wanting to meet Jenny's eyes, afraid of what he might find in them. With the thought of that notion possibly gone, the notion of release from his present malaise or lethargy or accidie—whatever it was he'd been feeling over the last couple of years—another feeling crept over Jury. It was the old sense of desolation, similar to this so-called accidie, or perhaps disguised by it. But it was also different, and devastating, and inescapable.

Dressed in that dark sleeve, Jenny's arm lay languidly across the table, her hand briefly touching his own and then turning over, palm upward, as her finger touched the tip of one of the brilliants that dripped from the marble candleholder. Jane had been dressed in black the last time he'd seen her. But beneath that image was what might have been an even sharper one. More painful, if that were possible. The memory was always with him of the bombed-out house on the Fulham Road, and he wondered if it wasn't waiting just below the surface of any event, any meeting, any touch, any kiss to engulf him again. His mother's body beneath the plaster ceiling rubble—buried in it, except for that arm flung out in its black sleeve, fingers curled in that beckoning gesture.

"What is it? What's wrong?" Her tone was anxious.

"It's nothing." He got up with his glass of port.

"Nothing." Her smile was very slight, a mere glimmer.

He left the table and walked over to the window facing towards the stone wall that edged the pavement beside the church. He remembered, years ago, walking over there in the park between the church and the theater. It was night, and he'd been walking along thinking about his lack of tranquility in the midst of such a tranquil scene. Even in the dark one sensed the sunlit riverbank, the gliding swans, the ducks sawing to shore for their bread crumbs. He was tired then, and he was tired now, of slogging through London's sulphurous atmosphere.

"I was thinking of the war." He told Jenny about the air raid, when he was six, and his mother.

After he finished, Jury shook himself loose from those inchoate images, and there was a long silence. He kept looking out the window, thinking, and then wondered how long he had been standing here, dreaming away, and turned and saw that Jenny was still sitting at the table, looking not at him but straight ahead, her gaze fixed on another window, the front one. Jenny had thoughts of her own. That made him smile. A calm settled over him at the idea of this shared silence. He moved over to the armchair in which he had sat before, sat down, looked at her. Her attention was still fixed elsewhere, probably inward.

This experience he found unusual, and very pleasant, this ability to coexist in perfect privacy, thinking one's own thoughts, and not having to be filling up gaps and silences or straining to engage, to connect.

She said, into the surrounding stillness, "That's horrible; that's awful."

The context was her own, in her own mind. Jury assumed she was still thinking about what he'd told her.

"How often have you done it since?" she asked.

"Done what?"

"Pulled women from burning buildings."

8

I

"It's the Stendhal syndrome," said Diane Demorney, holding her glass aloft as a signal to Dick Scroggs to run and fill it.

They were sitting, the four of them—six, if one counted Lavinia Vine and Alice Broadstairs at a distant table—in the Jack and Hammer. The pub, its mechanical Jack freshened up once again with a coat of turquoise paint to his trousers, sat on the High Street next to Trueblood's Antiques. The group sat at their favorite table, the one in the half-circle of casemented windows through which shone light, almost misty, a light suitable for a late-January afternoon. The Jack and Hammer had been open now for less than an hour, but the settled state of its custom made it appear that a substantial inroad had been made into the working day.

Or nonworking one, since those who took up the two tables could not be said actually to work, if by "work" was meant some regular occupation of reporting somewhere in the morning and leaving at some time in the afternoon. Before Diane Demorney had dragged in her arcane topic, hoping for an audience, "work" had been the topic of discussion. Joanna Lewes denied that any work at all was involved in writing her books (in reading them, yes, plenty). Marshall Trueblood, on the other hand, being a shopkeeper, should have been able to lay claim to "work"; he, however, spent his time loafing about amidst his king's ransom in antiques next door, his flexible hours allowing him to use the Jack and Hammer as his anteroom. (No one knew precisely what his background was; he made vague references to London, but Melrose Plant insisted he'd been found in a Chinese urn.)

The subject of "work" having been raised and quickly dropped (none of them being, as Plant said, in any way expert in this area), the visit of Richard Jury was the next topic for speculation. Where was he, and *when* was he coming to Long Piddleton?

Melrose Plant, having known Richard Jury for more than a dozen years, was again put in charge of Jury's whereabouts. Melrose had no idea where Jury was or when he was coming, beyond a vague promise from Jury of "in a few days." That had been a few days ago, so it could be any time now.

What Melrose Plant said was: "He's taken the 9:10 from Paddington." He was glancing at one of the books in the pile near his pint of Old Peculier. "And he should arrive in Glasgow early this afternoon."

They were uniformly surprised. "Glasgow? What the devil's he doing in Glasgow?" asked Trueblood.

"A triple murder." Actually, *The 9:10 from Paddington* was the title of Polly Praed's latest thriller and a blatant theft of one of Agatha Christie's titles. "In a prominent Glaswegian family."

"Really?"

No, thought Melrose, not really, but now they wouldn't hound him hourly for an update on Jury's movements.

Joanna Lewes lit a cigarette, frowning. "Thought he was working on that business at the Tate."

And it was just then that Diane Demorney, who'd been sitting in the fading limelight, dragged attention to herself with her comment "It's the Stendhal syndrome."

The only thing that kept Diane Demorney from being a pathological liar (a role she would have relished), was that she didn't need to be, since her particular cachet was marshalling esoteric and arcane bits of knowledge, just enough to make her look as though she really knew something. Which she didn't.

Ordinarily, Melrose Plant refused to rise to Diane's bait, but now he couldn't help himself. He squinted at her. "The *what*?"

"The Stendhal syndrome." She played her eyes round the table, resting her look upon the three of them in turn. She toyed with her ten-to-one dry martini and said, "Well, I assume you've heard of Stendhal? *The Red and the Black, The Charnelhouse of Parma*?"

Joanna rolled her eyes heavenward; Melrose choked on his Old Peculier. Trueblood said, "So what's this 'syndrome'? You're dying to tell us."

Diane sipped her martini, making them wait. "Stendhal, you see, was a passionate lover of art. He'd stand about for simply *hours* looking at it. But it had a strange effect on him. He was always fainting. In Florence, especially. Well, *you* know what the art there is like." This was directed to Joanna. "It was too much for the poor man."

"No, I've never been to Florence," said Joanna.

"But one of your *books* was set there," said Diane, smoke from her cigarette pluming delicately upwards.

"So? You don't think I actually have time to *visit* those places, do you? Are you telling us Stendhal collapsed whenever he looked at paintings?"

Diane was pleased as punch that she'd bested them, one and all, yet again. "If he looked too long."

"Fainting in Florence and pegging out at the Tate don't strike me as especially like," said Melrose, adjusting himself on the window seat.

"It's looking at art that does it, whether it's in Italy or London or wherever. Stendhal was such a *marvellous* writer, wasn't he?—"

As if Diane had ever read him, thought Melrose.

"—that it makes me almost *green* I can't do it, too. Doesn't it *you*, Joanna?"

Completely ignoring the taunt, Joanna said, "Any idiot can write a book. Not like Stendhal, of course, but a book. I should know."

"Yes, you should," said Diane, sweetly agreeing.

"You're always selling yourself short," said Melrose. "But it's encouraging, what you say." He shifted uncomfortably.

Marshall Trueblood plucked a thread from his wool silk jacket sleeve. "Good heavens, dear Maddy, that's too much self-denigration."

"Maddy" was Trueblood's fond diminutive for Joanna Lewes, who was known as Joanna the Mad, a nickname that had nothing to do with her mental state, but with the coincidence of her dead husband having been named Philip. Joanna had found it rather jolly that King Philip I of Spain had driven his wife, Joanna, round the twist, and the benighted queen had come to be known as Joanna the Mad.

Joanna Lewes had just been belittling her own writing ("romantic tripe"), which nonetheless enjoyed an enormous commercial success. This seemed to embarrass her. "Believe me, Marshall, if people will buy *Petersburg Passion*, they'll buy any damned thing." Joanna used place names as titles: *London Love, Mexico Magic, Florentine Fancy, Rome Romance*. Her latest place was St. Petersburg, and when asked about the setting, she said, "Russia, Florida—who cares?" Long ago she had discovered that all roads that lead to Rome (and Petersburg) lead farther and farther away from the Inland Revenue. Joanna never seemed to take advantage of travel tax deductions, though. She was too busy writing about foreign love-affairs to visit the places. Authentic background was never one of her strong points.

"You two are collaborating or something? I thought I saw you writing."

"No—oh, no," said Melrose.

Trueblood sucked in his lower lip. "It's just . . . my accounting book. You know, for the shop. Melrose was helping me with the entries."

"Cooking the VAT intakes, I hope." Joanna sniggered.

Since they did not want its existence bruited about, Melrose had immediately whisked the black notebook off the table and sat on it when they saw Joanna approaching. It was this little book that was causing him discomfort. He shifted his weight and rearranged the others in the stack; ordinarily he could sit in the Jack and Hammer for hours and read.

It was these books that Joanna pulled over to inspect. She looked at the dust jackets, smiled kindly over Polly Praed's latest effort, but seemed genuinely enthusiastic about the one called *Windows*. "This," she said, tapping it with her fingers, "is fascinating. A good example of a minimalist novel."

Windows was Ellen Taylor's new book—new in England, that is, for it had been published in the United States two years before. It was by no means that Brontëesque extravaganza Melrose had feared would come out of Ellen's acquaintanceship with the North York moors; nor was it like her earlier *Sauvage Savant*, which had threatened to be the first in a quintet about the New York boroughs. *Windows* was entirely different. It was also entirely opaque—to Melrose, at least.

"Minimalist?" said Melrose.

"Minimalist?" repeated Marshall Trueblood, who was anything but, at least in dress. Beneath the Armani jacket was a shocking-pink shirt with an iridescent shell-pink stripe and a tie that looked as if it had wiped a painter's easel clean.

"You know." Joanna's attention was caught by the two women in the back of the pub, Lavinia Vine and Alice Broadstairs.

Actually, Melrose didn't. He could not make head or tale out of Ellen's story, and he hadn't been able to think of a single intelligent thing to say about it when he'd talked to her only that very afternoon, an hour or two ago.

Lavinia and Alice were waving at their table. They were Long Piddleton's avid gardeners, who got together only for their pub port and biscuits. Otherwise, they were generally warring. Always, they were the first to purchase "the latest Lewes," and Lavinia was now holding up *Petersburg Passion*, waving it like a hand. They wanted it signed.

"I'm not surprised," said Joanna, speaking of Ellen Taylor's book, "that it won that literary prize."

The nice thing about Joanna Lewes was not only her realistic assessment of her own talent but her utter lack of professional jealousy. She was the sort who would cast blurbs upon the water, encouraging for first-time-around novelists. She would read tattered manuscripts, answer letters, and so forth.

Such generosity of spirit could not be claimed for the next person who came through the Jack and Hammer's door, Melrose's aunt.

Whenever she saw Joanna Lewes, she bridled. And never failed to mention that she, too, had a book in the works. "The world is full, Miss Lewes, of unsung writers."

"Yes, and too damned many sung ones, too. Pardon me." Joanna left to join her book-buying fans, a subspecies to which Lady Ardry had never belonged, finding her nephew's library sufficient, if she ever got round to actually reading a book.

"Conceited," murmured Agatha, with a sniff. "That's the trouble with all this celebrity. What are you two doing? Ah, here's Theo," she added with evident displeasure.

Actually, Theo Wrenn Browne was only winning by default with Agatha. He disliked the same people she did, with the exception of Diane, over whom he fawned. Theo owned the village's only bookshop and had refused until just lately to stock the novels of Joanna Lewes.

Diane Demorney, hardly a charitable person, looked like Mother Teresa when put side-by-side with Theo Wrenn Browne. She had stopped by the bar to instruct Dick Scroggs as to the precise ration of vodka to vermouth in her martini. She supplied him with her own brand of vodka —some unpronounceable mouthful of consonants, "Wybrvka" or "Zrbrikov," that she swore by, and that nobody stocked. She said it was buffalo grass vodka, and it did indeed have a long plume of stuff stuck in it. Trueblood claimed she made it in her bathtub and pulled up weeds from her back garden.

Theo Wrenn Browne glanced at *Windows,* dismissed it as pretentious, and shoved it aside. If there was anything Theo Wrenn Browne hated more than a writer's commercial success, it was a writer's literary prize. Owner of the Wrenn's Nest bookshop, he was in constant danger of apoplexy, since he was surrounded on all sides by evidence of both—and in the case of writers such as Updike, Brookner, Byatt, Ishiguro, of both *together.* The dilemma was that he had to sell the stuff; it was his livelihood. Thus he could only solace himself with the fates of benighted writers who during their own lifetimes had found neither—the Melvilles, the Hart Cranes, the Chattertons. Theo had himself written one astonishingly bad book years before, called *The Last Race,* about guerrilla warfare at Doncaster (which made his disdain of Ellen Taylor as "experimental," "avant garde," "minimalist," or anything else just a little hypocritical). He had tried to get Joanna the Mad to send this to her own editor and she had refused. With his own book unpublished, he had aligned himself with the unappreciated, maligned, betrayed, and even suicidal. Theo Wrenn Browne was a connoisseur of failure.

Naturally, he despised Joanna Lewes. But although he had refused to carry her last several novels, he was now forced to bow to the pressure exerted by her local fans to stock "the new Lewes." And having failed to expunge the blot of its success from his shop, he had turned to far easier game: Miss Ada Crisp, whose secondhand furniture shop was just one door away from the Wrenn's Nest. Inspired by Lady Ardry's legal battle with Jurvis, the butcher, he had hired a Sidbury solicitor. It was Theo's notes, his documentation of the hazards Miss Crisp (and her Jack Russell dog) held for the village, that he now dropped into Melrose's hands.

Melrose dropped them back. "Are you kidding?"

Theo Wrenn Browne was hardly pleased with this assessment of his case against Ada Crisp. "I don't see why. Her shop is a danger to the community. All of that rubbish out on the pavements, and that rat terrier of hers grabbing at anything that moves!" He ran his finger round his high starched collar and sat there envying Trueblood's expensively turned-out nonchalance.

"Oh, come on, old sweat," said Trueblood. "Ada's shop's been just that for forty years, and no one's fallen into one of the chamber pots."

They were interrupted by the appearance of Vivian Rivington, wearing her rose wool and her woebegone look. She plunked down her sherry and herself and sighed and said she'd been packing. Vivian was always packing, either in England or in Italy. She'd been back now for just three months and was being kept here by the wiliness of Marshall Trueblood and the cunning of Melrose Plant and her own unconscious—or even conscious—inclination. They were certain she did not want to marry the odious Italian count, but after all of these years of engagement, they supposed she couldn't think of an honorable way of ending it.

"Vivian," said Diane, her smile as dry as her martini, "you should know about all that drop-dead art, having spent so much time in Venice and Florence."

Melrose and Trueblood exchanged a glance. Diane would lose no opportunity to remind Vivian of the fiancé lurking in Venice, not having slipped and drowned as yet during *acqua alta*. Vivian was scheduled to return to Venice next month.

"I don't know what you mean. And I don't spend all that much time— not *that* much," said Vivian, as if the expenditure of time were somehow a reflection of the strength of the attachment.

Diane hated it. She hated that Vivian would be a countess, and also lost no opportunity to decry it as an all-too-ordinary little title. "Aren't counts rather thick on the ground in Italy?" she said ruminatively.

Said Marshall Trueblood, "Thick under it, Vivian's sort."

"Oh, shut up!" Vivian's shell-like complexion turned the color of her rose wool frock.

"Titles—how do they signify, anyway?" offered Agatha, making Melrose look up in astonishment.

Getting no mileage out of his proposed suit against poor Ada Crisp, Theo Wrenn Browne went back to opining the total lack of merit of Ellen Taylor's book, while Diane took to opining the lack of merit of Ellen Taylor's face. That face was on the back of the dust jacket, and Diane was scrutinizing it as closely as if the cops had asked her to pick one out of a lineup.

"She looks," said Diane, "as if she's just got squashed in a revolving door."

Melrose looked at the picture. Ellen's face did have a bit of the Silly Putty look to it, true, together with the wide-open, astonished eyes. "Well, she doesn't look like that. She's quite pretty."

"She is; I remember," said Trueblood.

Diane tapped the little biographical paragraph. "She's from Baltimore." She paused a bit dramatically. "E. A. Poe and Johnny U."

Everyone turned to stare at her, which was what she wanted. She was as pleased over this coupling as ever she had been over herself and any of her lovers.

"What are you talking about?"

She raised a feathery black eyebrow. Diane was quite beautiful, with her perfect skin, marble white against the satiny black fall of her hair. But despite the inclinations of Nature, nothing seemed to have rushed in to fill the vacuum: Diane's mind was hermetically sealed. That was why it was always mildly astonishing when she came up with some esoteric fact that no one else knew. That, of course, was the idea. She was a gatherer of esoteric facts. Trivial Pursuits had been invented for the likes of Diane Demorney. "I assume you've heard of Edgar Allan Poe."

"Oh, don't be daft, Diane," said Trueblood irritably. "We're talking about Johnny whoever."

"Good lord." She heaved a sigh and lifted her giant martini glass. "Johnny Unitas. You've never heard of the Baltimore Colts? God! I assumed *everyone* had heard of them."

"Melrose has been rattling on about going to Baltimore," said Agatha.

II

The rattle had taken place at Ardry End accompanied by the dire rhythm of Lou Reed strong-arming his guitar. Melrose loved Lou Reed. Lou Reed ("the Maniac") drove Agatha crazy, but, unfortunately, not away.

At the time he got Ellen's call, this eschewer of titles was sitting upon his hearth (metaphorically speaking) pawing over Debrett's in search of one. She had been zipping through the pages with the speed of a centipede for the last hour, trying to track down her heritage. Spurious heritage, Melrose imagined. It had been pointed out to her in a letter from one of her Wisconsin relations that her paternal great-uncle (or great-great-) had been a certain Baron Fust—Fust being Agatha's maiden name before she had married Melrose's uncle. That entitlement might actually be something that ran in her veins (well, in the veins of the male descendants) and not something to be caught on the fly ("Lady" Ardry indeed!) had her slavering even more than did the jam-laden scone in her hand. Titles before tea, Melrose supposed.

"Baron Fust! Imagine!"

"Everyone will be a baron for fifteen minutes," said Melrose.

At that moment Ruthven brought in the telephone extension. "Long distance, sir, from America."

"Ellen!" Melrose straightened suddenly and came out of the somnolent state the presence of his aunt usually induced. "Where the hell are you? . . . Baltimore?"

Agatha relaxed her ear a bit. Whoever Ellen was, she was far enough away to present no immediate problem.

"Your book? Yes, yes, I did. Thank you." Pained, Melrose's eye strayed to the end table where Ellen's book had been lying, unfinished. "I know it won that award, yes, I know. That's wonder— . . . like it?" Since he hadn't read all of it, his answer would be qualified a bit. "Naturally. Yes . . . Oh, quite, well, *different.*"

The book in question was now in Agatha's hands. *Hand*—in the other was a brandy snap. Ellen's book had been stacked atop Polly Praed's newest which she had sent to Melrose in the form of galleys. Perhaps he should become an editor?

"Come to *Baltimore*?" Oh, Christ, why had he said it aloud? Agatha was staring over the top of the book. She had even stopped chewing. "I'll see. . . . Well, yes, I know I said I would . . ."

What Ellen told him next was rather surprising, and he only barely missed echoing it when he saw Agatha's eyes riveted on him. So he registered no emotion, no interest, just kept saying "umm" and "ohmm" like a mantra, as Ellen related her little tale.

It was so difficult for him to make a trip, to bestir himself, to drag himself away from hearth and home and the Jack and Hammer. He sighed. He would like to see Ellen, though. "Policeman? . . . Are you talking about Richard Jury?" Pretending not to remember his name! "He's going to be visiting me, as a matter of fact. . . . Yes, but, Ellen, Scotland Yard CID men cannot simply throw up everything and go racing off to the States." Actually, Jury could drop anything he damn pleased, given he was on leave. ". . . In another day or two. Yes." That was when Jury was supposed to come. He wanted to see Pratt in Northampton, for some reason.

Agatha was all ears. She was even forgetting to eat her brandy snap. He really should have taken this call out of Agatha's earshot—if there was such a place. Saddam Hussein's bunker, perhaps. Melrose sipped his sherry, said, "I absolutely promise, Ellen. . . . Yes. I'll call. . . . Yes. . . . No. . . . Yes. . . . Yes. . . . No. . . . No. . . . Goodbye."

"I know that name—I'm sure of it. Ellen, Ellen. Haven't I met this person?" Actually, she had. At Victoria Station when Vivian had been leaving that time for Italy.

"No."

"You're not considering going to the States, my dear Plant?"

"No." Yes, he was. Not only was he very fond of Ellen, but he knew she would have slashed her wrists before calling him if she hadn't been in dire straits. He frowned. He had no doubt about the "dire," but he wondered if the "straits" were what she'd said they were.

"I should think not. However, if you *do,* let me know, of course, and I'll go along, as I haven't seen the Fusts in years and I would like to have a chat with them over Debrett's. Now here's a Life Baroness. 'Dixie Bellows . . .' "

Dream on, thought Melrose.

III

". . . a mere count," Agatha was saying now in the Jack and Hammer, relegating Count Franco Giopinno to the title scrap heap. "Now the Fusts—"

"Were merer barons," said Melrose.

Diane Demorney, still pushing her bit of arcana about like a stale canapé on the cocktail platter, cut across the Fust family's baronetcy, saying, "If you're going to Baltimore, Melrose, you'd better read up on baseball and football. The 1969 game between the Jets and the Colts, for instance." She directed her seductive curl of a smile towards Melrose as she drew the vodka-pickled olive from her glass. It was her own thin-stemmed, broad-brimmed glass, and she had brought it to use in the pub. Melrose calculated the circumference of its bowl; frozen over, it would have accommodated the skaters at Rockefeller Center. That brought America back to mind, and he looked again at the picture of Ellen on the back of the dust jacket. He smiled. That affrighted look, as if the photographer had been holding a gun on her instead of a camera, made him want to laugh.

"Victoria!" Agatha banged her fist on the table, jumping her glass of sherry. "That's where I saw her!" Agatha's eyes were riveted on the picture. "You saw her, too, Vivian."

"Saw who?"

"This Taylor woman. Strange-looking person. When we were at Victoria Station seeing you off. You remember."

Vivian looked as if she'd prefer not to. "No." Vivian did not want to travel backward in time to Victoria any more than she wanted to travel forward in time to Venice.

Diane was clearly annoyed that the spotlight, something she was sure God had given into her own white hands for safekeeping, was capriciously moving around the table. She snatched it back with her next obscure reference:

"Nickel City."

They all looked at her again.

"Well, that's what they used to call Baltimore. Nickel City."

"Why?"

"They made nickels there." She went on: "The Colts and the Jets . . . Joe Namath. One of the most famous games ever played—Supper Bowl III."

IV

" 'Supper Bowl.' Do you *believe* that?" said Melrose Plant to Marshall Trueblood after the others had finally cleared out of the Jack and Hammer and he was able to retrieve the notebook.

"Anyone who'd call Kuwait 'Kumquat' can make me believe that, yes. Now, I'll dictate, you write."

"*I'll* dictate, *you* write. I wrote earlier."

Trueblood sounded exasperated. "I was right in the middle of a thought, old sweat, when everybody trooped in."

"Your thoughts have no middles. Beginnings, endings, no middles." Melrose uncapped his pen and smoothed down the page.

"Now: she'd been put in the crypt. The crypt . . . hmm."

" 'Dank vault,' " quoted Melrose.

Trueblood pursed his lips, said, " *'The poor monk, Franciscus, standing at the opening of the dank vault with his stick and bowl—'* "

"Who's Franciscus?"

"The *monk.*"

"There was never any monk." Melrose was thumbing back through the pages to see if he'd missed the monk.

"He's new. Believe me, the monk is necessary for the poor girl's spiritual comfort."

"What the hell for? She's dead, isn't she?"

"Just write, will you?"

Melrose shrugged. "Okay."

Trueblood repeated: " *'Franciscus, standing there with his bowl and stick'*—no, 'his stick and bowl.' That's rather poetic—*'standing there with his stick and bowl.'* "

Melrose mouthed the words slowly: "Standing—there—with—his—stick—and—sup-per—bowl—"

"Not *'supper* bowl,' damn it!"

V

When Richard Jury, directed to the Jack and Hammer by Ruthven, was passing the pub's casement window, he saw Ruthven's master, head bent over a book or a notebook, seated just inside the window tête-à-tête with Marshall Trueblood. They were sitting, backs to the window, at the table that looked out over the High Street. Trueblood's voice wafted out to him:

" *'O God! My sufferings are . . .'* "

The voice faded. The casement window was open the barest crack, and Jury reached out and opened it another half-inch. Trueblood's voice again:

" *'My sufferings are not complete! If she but knew it, my own death is nothing—'* no, say 'is *as* nothing.' "

" 'Is *as*'?" (said Melrose). "Sounds rather stilted, doesn't it? Anyway, we don't want crossings out."

"Oh, all right. *'Myowndeathisnothing,'* then." Trueblood was impatient.

Outside, and in spite of himself, Jury was fascinated by this mawkish prose. What were they doing? Collaborating on a novel? A play? He doubted it. That would have been too much of a strain for Marshall Trueblood's five-minute-max attention span. Jury kept his back against the outside wall of the pub, his face tickled by dry ivy that had claimed most of the Jack and Hammer's facade. Its tendrils dug in, clung, obscured the rims of the windows, which was one reason he couldn't be seen.

" '. . . *that dank vault, that icy trickle of water, that mould—'* "

"Sounds like your basement."

" *'—that high peal of bells—'* "

"Wait, wait a minute. How'd he get her from his—" Melrose's voice diminished, then grew fuller—"to the crypt and then still have time to—" dimmed—"the sleeping draught in her wine—" rose, fell—"and the bells—"

"It doesn't have to be coherent, for lord's sake. He's crazy!"

"Well, but—"

Jury's attention was drawn by a little white dog that barked at him from the far curb. This was Miss Ada Crisp's Jack Russell, and out came Miss Ada to remonstrate with the dog and wave at Jury.

He felt ridiculous, hanging there around the ivy.

Nor did the dog give a tinker's damn about the remonstrance. It danced about like a trained circus dog and then hurled itself across the street towards Jury. It went down on its front legs and raised its rump in the air and snarled and growled. Jury toed its belly to try and get it away, but the little dog merely thought he was playing dog games, and grabbed his trouser leg and shook and shook.

Hearing a raised voice inside, and seeing the casement window suddenly open, Jury shrank back against the wall. The bit of golden hair he could see (Melrose Plant's head) was thrust out, quickly withdrawn, and he heard Melrose say, "Just Ada's Jack Russell."

Bored, the dog finally relented, released the cuff of Jury's trousers and trotted on up the street to find more willing playmates. The window, however, was wider open now, and Jury could hear more clearly.

There was still some disagreement about the prose not making sense. "*He* might be crazy, but that doesn't mean—" Melrose's voice trailed off, and strain as he would toward the sound, Jury could not make out the name—"is, does it? She's got too much sense."

"No, she hasn't. Come on, come on. Let's get on with it. Now: *'From the cellar came those screams that tear my heart and lacerate my soul.'*"

"Hang about, you're going too fast. I got 'tear my heart and—'?"

" *'And lac-er-ate my soul.'*"

Silence. "Got it. Go on."

From the shadowed ivy, Jury glanced over to the other side of the street again and saw someone else. This was Jurvis, the butcher, standing there staring at him, his hands warming under his big white apron. He removed one of them when Jury looked over and waved.

Jury waved back.

Jurvis still stood, rocking on his heels. He liked Jury; the policeman had done his best to help the butcher in his altercation with Lady Ardry. The plaster pig was still doing its dogsbody work, holding up the little sign advertising that week's specials. The pig and Jurvis were of the same height and girth, just about. They made a pretty pair there on the sidewalk.

" '. . . *made me sick with fright. O my soul!*'"

Jury had taken out his cigarettes and was lighting one, hoping to give the appearance that he'd sheltered there among the ivy in order to keep the match flame from the wind. He pursed his lips, checked his watch—waved again at Jurvis—held it against his ear and looked this way and that along the street.

In another moment or two, Jurvis turned back to his shop, arms round the pig as if they'd jig off down the road together, and then they went in. Early closing, Jury imagined. He checked his watch. After two.

The coast was clear again.

". . . battering—no, 'creaking'—'*The creaking of the coffin lid assaulted my senses and I quickly rose from bed, only to . . . only to . . .*' Oh, hell—'only to' *what*? You're not contributing much."

"Me? I'm writing. I can't write and think at the same time."

"I've got it—'*only to feel the icy fingers upon my cheek.*' "

"Well, ain't this"—Jury jumped at the voice and the clutch of the wiry fingers upon his arm—"somethin'. Ain't it Mr. Scotland Yard hisself, then, come to Long Pidd t' eavesdrop." The cackling of Dick Scrogg's char brought on a rheumy cough.

"Hullo, Mrs. Withersby," said Jury, his face burning. "I was just about to go in and have a pint."

She was chomping down on the remains of a cigarette butt and hauling along her pail, which she had brought out of the pub's side door. She now dumped the dirty water in the gutter. "Drain's broke back there. 'Bout t'ave a pint?" She wiped her hand across her mouth. "Ah, well, there's some a us got to wark fer a livin'."

When Jury at last entered the Jack and Hammer, he was heartily welcomed by Dick Scroggs but had to wait a few moments for the hearty welcomes of Melrose Plant and Marshall Trueblood, as they were busily engaged in secreting some object from his view.

When he got to their table, the envelope he had seen was being whisked away, but not before he noticed the stamps on it were foreign. Not British, certainly. He had a trained eye. As for the black book, it was nowhere in sight. Probably, he thought, Trueblood was sitting on it, since Trueblood had not risen to extend his hand. He had simply held it out from a sitting position.

Mrs. Withersby was clanging about the table with bucket and broom, and making a desultory swipe at one of the grimier of the casement windowpanes, and rattling on nineteen-to-the-dozen about "them as hadn't to *wark* fer a livin'," a monologue in which Jury had heard her indulge before when Melrose Plant was around and when she wanted a drink. Now, she was pulling Mansion polish from the pail of cleaning things and spraying the table, not being too nice about avoiding Trueblood's fingers.

"Withers, for God's sake, the place is nearly empty," said Marshall Trueblood. "Spray elsewhere."

Jury wondered if the book could be under the cushion.

"I got me schedule, ain't I? Just like junk dealers!" She lifted his pint and swiped the damp circle beneath. "Ah, but this here's thirsty wark. Thirsty and thankless both."

"They don't appreciate us, do they, Mrs. Withersby?" Jury offered her his packet of cigarettes at the same time as he scanned the floor beneath the table. Trueblood must be sitting on it; it was too big to be slipped in a jacket pocket without showing.

"Ya got that right." She took four cigarettes, jamming three in her apron pocket, and leaning across the table for Plant to light the fourth, upsetting his pint in the process. "Ah, looka there, Lord Ardry. Pity." She tsk-tsked and ran her oily cloth over the spill.

"Oh, get El Withersby a gin, Melrose," said Trueblood, not about to rise himself.

"I'd prefer one of Dick's brews," said Jury.

"If you're drinking that stuff, you must be back on the job," said Melrose, smiling.

"Halfway, partway," said Jury, and then, as Melrose went off the bar, he said to Trueblood, "Oughtn't you be seeing to your customers?"

In the act of lighting up a jade-green Sobranie, Trueblood raised his painted brows. "Customers? What customers?"

"There was a lot of commotion in the shop as I walked by."

"What? Couldn't be . . ."

"Stuff might be going out the back door, then."

Mrs. Withersby cackled and leaned on her broom. "Mebbe 'twas the van I seen down the back alley."

Trueblood was up and off in a flash. Jury looked at the seat. No, nothing there. As Mrs. Withersby rambled on about the new Long Pidd constable being blind as a bat and how the Withersby clan was not one to depend on police for protection, Jury casually ran his hand under the cushion of the bench beneath the window. Where was the damned thing, anyway?

". . . an' drug in little Eddie fer nickin' the . . . I took umbrage, I did. . . ." She kicked at the pail, dislodging the Mansion polish rag.

Jury looked down at the pail. There it was. "Mr. Plant's signalling you, Mrs. Withersby."

She turned toward the bar, and Jury quickly extracted the black leather book, shoved it down in his raincoat's big pocket, and was smiling as Melrose Plant returned with one gin and one strong brew in which the sediment was still settling.

"Cheers!" said Jury, raising his glass.

Mrs. Withersby rejoined them and drank off her tot of gin, collected her broom and bucket, and set off towards the nether regions.

It had been a safe enough repository. Mrs. Withersby couldn't read and rarely worked. She was probably only plying that pail and rag today to see what it would get her by way of strong drink.

"Where's Vivian?" asked Jury.

"Probably packing." Melrose cast an agonized glance toward the retreating bucket.

VI

"I'm very fond of him," said Vivian Rivington, her tone a bit defensive, as she clamped the lid back on the tin of cheese puffs.

"Really? I seem to remember you saying exactly that about another man, years ago, right here in this room." Jury sipped his coffee. "Remember?"

Vivian looked at him speculatively. "I remember."

"Then why don't you stop all this nonsense and break it off?"

She sat back, *fell* back, in her chair, holding the cheese puff aloft and seeming to address it, not Jury. "How high-handed. As if you had some superior knowledge."

He smiled. "I do. You as much as told me."

"Nothing. I told you nothing."

He drank his coffee, Vivian crunched at her cheese puff, and they were silent.

"Anyway, he's too busy playing games with Marshall."

" 'He'?" asked Jury innocently.

"Oh, stop being ridiculous."

"I don't know why you can't see the truth."

"I do not see what is not there."

"Knowing how much Plant hates to leave Ardry End—I don't think he'd leave even if someone shouted 'Fire!'—how about that trip to Italy they took? You think he doesn't care what happens to you?"

"Hates to travel? Well, he's certainly putting on a damned good imitation of a man who's about to embark for the States." Vivian's glowing complexion glowed more ardently. "Some American girl, that I'm supposed to have met or seen, called him up. Did he tell you?"

Jury was surprised. "No. Who?"

"I don't know, do I? Agatha said I saw her at Victoria. All I saw at Victoria was Marshall Trueblood pasting a cutout of Dracula to my trunk." She started to laugh, bit it off. Serious again. "So all *I* can say,

Richard dear, is some American floozy rings him up and he's off so fast you could play cards on his coattail."

"Ellen? Ellen Taylor?" Seeing Vivian's expression, he was sorry he'd named her, thereby showing he too knew her. "Just some kid with a Bronx accent. For God's sake, he's probably bored, what with *you* going off again to Venice. Vivian, come on! Toss the guy overboard, into the canal, or something. Hell, marry *me.*"

She stopped munching the biscuit, even stopped being irritated with him. "Is that a proposal?"

Jury studied his coffee cup. He smiled. "Of course."

" 'Of course.' " She laughed. "You know, I honestly think you would. Marry me, that is. Just to keep me out of the clutches of the blood-drinking count."

"I'm very fond of you."

"Well, I think we've finally got something sorted out here."

"Thing is, you don't love me."

"Oh, stop being stupid." Her smile at him was nonetheless loving.

"And I *still* say, you don't place enough importance on that trip they made to Venice."

Vivian leaned forward, saying very deliberately, " 'They.' The operative word is they. It's all a game. Playing silly buggers." She tapped her foot impatiently against the beautiful cabriole leg of her coffee table. Vivian's house was filled with antiques that made Trueblood salivate. "Thank goodness you at least are serious."

There was a silence. Jury glanced at the chair in the hall where his raincoat was lying.

"And what is that silly smile for?"

Quickly, Jury wiped the silly smile from his face.

"At times I think you're as bad as they are."

Jury smiled again.

VII

"So we can go together," said Jury, fairly collapsed in the comfortable armchair by the fireplace. The dinner that Plant's cook had just served up rivalled Jenny Kennington's. Jury was thinking about the previous evening.

Melrose was thinking about flying. They were sitting, whiskies in hand, before a blazing fireplace, in front of which slept his dog of uncertain breed. "It requires so much *effort.*"

"You liked her, as I remember."

"*Liked* her? Of course I liked her. I like Mindy here, too." The dog, hearing its name, let out a slumbery *woof.*

"And Vivian?"

Melrose frowned over at him. "Vivian? Well, naturally. One of my favorite people."

"Yet, she's going off to Venice yet again. Why the hell don't you stop her?"

"Stop her? My God, we've been stopping her for years. One way or another." He grinned. He chuckled.

Jury sighed. "Then I think you should go to America. Both of us can go."

"You mean you really are?" Melrose considered this.

"To Philadelphia. How far's Philadelphia from Baltimore?"

"I don't know. Several thousand miles, probably. The damned country is so big."

Jury shook his head. "They're not that far apart—one, two hundred is my guess. Don't you have a map of the States around here?"

"Oh, there's an atlas somewhere." Melrose motioned vaguely with his hand at nowhere in particular. He yawned. "What airport?"

"Don't know. Kennedy? LAX?"

"That's *L.A.,* for God's sake."

Jury shrugged. He had told Plant about his conversation with Lady Cray. "I feel I owe her something, so I'm going to look into the death of Frances Hamilton's nephew. It'll make a change, what the hell? I'm taking Wiggins. Make a change for his allergies, too."

"She was wonderful, Lady Cray!" Melrose thought of her fondly. "She was clever. If she thinks something's wrong, something probably is."

"Perhaps."

Melrose went on. "But I can't stay away long. How long is it going to be?"

"Not more than a few days, certainly. I doubt I'll find anything. Tell me more about this student of Ellen's, Beverly—"

"Beverly Brown. According to Ellen she was murdered in—a churchyard, I think. Happened just a day or two ago. January nineteenth, she said. It had something to do with Edgar Allan Poe's birthday. Peculiar. Anyway, she was rather incoherent, and I wasn't paying all that much attention, anyway. Too busy trying to work out how to make an intelligent comment on her book without having read it."

Jury was thoughtful. "How about Sunday? We could leave on Sunday."

Melrose hesitated, frowning. "Trueblood and I have a sort of project going."

"Oh? Well, you did seem rather busy at the Jack and Hammer. Writing something, were you? I thought I saw you with a notebook."

"Writing? Oh, that's just Trueblood's account—no, his *inventory* book." Melrose looked rather pleased with himself. "Yes, I'm helping him with his inventory."

"Trueblood? Taking inventory? I thought the only thing he ever inventoried was his wardrobe. His shop has been growing steadily more stuffed since I met him. It'll take you years to inventory that lot."

"I expect so. But I promised."

There was a silence while they both got rather dozy, and then Melrose muttered something about Lady Cray again. "I get the unpleasant feeling wheels are coming full circle. Did you know there's a rumor the Man with a Load of Mischief has been bought up? Or leased? By some London people."

Jury poured himself another whisky from the decanter. Thoughtfully, he said, "That was a long time ago, wasn't it?"

Melrose sighed and nodded and ran his long fingers through his hair, which looked, in the firelight, like a gold froth. "Maybe I *should* get the hell out. I'm beginning to feel this is where I came in."

VIII

Happily full of both food and drink and friendship, Jury lay in bed, reading.

He tented the black leather book over his chest and stared up at the ceiling. What the hell did they think they were writing . . . ? He yawned. Sunday. That was just the day after tomorrow. He supposed he could wait until he got back to see Pratt in Northampton. Tomorrow evening they could go up to London, then.

Again, he opened the book. What were they up to?

He fell asleep with the question unanswered.

Interlude

In the soft black hat and black overcoat, Wiggins looked as if he were palely loitering there beside the check-in counter at Heathrow. He was clutching his holdall to his chest like a breviary.

"What've you got in your carry-on?" Jury knew the question was superfluous. He still wanted to hear the answer.

Wiggins unzipped the small black bag. The original shaving kit was now doing duty as a portable medicine cabinet: the old shaving tackle had been removed and the plastic containers (such as the soap dish) pressed into service to hold throat lozenges, black biscuits, and some green liquid with which Jury wasn't familiar. In addition, Wiggins had cleverly sewn in a strip of Velcro and pressed a companion piece into loops against it to hold half a dozen brown vials. A few of these were prescription medicine (the heavy artillery), but the others had been assembled from the Wiggins pharmacopoeia. Jury recognized the tobaccoey-looking herb as rue. At least Wiggins didn't have it up his nose.

"What's that stuff, Wiggins?" Jury, fascinated notwithstanding years of watching Wiggins at his desk with tubes and teacups mixing up concoctions like a chemist, pointed to a plastic bottle filled with something that looked like sludge.

Apparently it was. "That? Oh, that's purely topical, sir. I've been bothered by a rash on my elbows. This is a mud pack mixed with herbs. It's quite effective."

Only Wiggins would have a rash on his elbows, thought Jury. "Got any Dramamine? I don't see any."

"For travel sickness, you mean? No. The best thing for that is to lean over and grab your heels with the opposite hands. I don't believe a person should take more medication than absolutely necessary."

A number of replies occurred to Jury, but he settled for silence. Wiggins looked painfully serious. "Here's Plant," Jury said, raising his arm so that Melrose Plant, threading his way through the swirl of passengers, could see where they were.

Melrose distributed reading material: *"Punch, Private Eye,* and a cou-

ple of paperbacks—in case you want to read the newest by Polly Praed."
He held up an incandescent cover. The gold foil glittered.

"Excellent," said Jury. "It's been years since I've read one of Polly's
books. What're the others?"

"Remember Heather Quick?"

"Joanna Lewes's heroine? The one who seemed to be spending a lot
of time slogging across the fens? Of course." Jury fingered this equally
garish cover. "What's yours?"

"A new Onions. In case I have trouble sleeping."

Sitting in the lounge waiting to be called to their flight was a woman
with a mass of hair, chewing gum and rereading a romance novel. She
had her little family with her: a baby in a carry cot and two tots. Melrose
had entered into a staring contest with the moon-faced tots, a boy and a
girl with eyes hard as pebbles. The girl stuck out her tongue, finally. The
mother saw this and gave the girl a swift smack.

"That lot will be sitting in front of us, just wait."

"Umm," muttered Jury, turning a page of the book by Joanna Lewes.

Nor could he get a response from Wiggins, who was ministering to
himself with nose drops. He snuffled and dropped his head forward.
Melrose sighed.

One of the airline personnel was at last calling the first-class passengers to their comfortable seats and champagne, and Jury asked, "Why
are you flying coach, anyway? It wouldn't be out of consideration for
your penniless comrades, would it?" Lady Cray had told him to be sure
to get first-class seats; Jury had gone out and booked coach.

"No. I don't like the film they're showing in first. I always make my air
travel plans according to the films. It's one of the few chances I get to go
to the cinema."

Now they were up and moving toward the gate. "What 'always'?"
asked Jury. "You never fly anywhere."

"I beg your pardon? Who was it went all the way to Venice?"

"What's the film, then?"

"Wait and be surprised." Melrose didn't know.

"I'm not sitting in the middle," said Wiggins.

"I'm not sitting in the middle," said Melrose.

"Stop haggling," said Jury, as they displayed their boarding passes.

Wiggins and Plant both turned and smiled at Jury.

"Forget it," said Jury.

They moved past the barrier.

* * *

Now they were seated, amid the convivial hum of voices and laughter one hears from passengers eager to embark, who will probably be at one another's throats before the dinner tray is served. Melrose watched the flight attendant. He felt a little sorry for her, flogging her orange life jacket and pretending the oxygen mask was dropping from above, and pressing instructions for their use on her inattentive audience. At least Wiggins was watching the young woman carefully, thereby letting her know her training had not been wasted. Wiggins was even following along with her, reading the printed instructions for bail-out and oxygen loss. He had carefully mustered all three of the paper bags for safekeeping.

Jury had the window seat, Melrose the aisle, and Wiggins was sitting in the middle, having been talked into it by Melrose, who recited mind-numbing statistics from a report that proved that the person most likely to escape injury in the event of an accident was the passenger sitting in the middle on the left side. The one least likely to survive was the one in the window seat. Both of them turned to look at Jury, who was reading his book and paying no attention. Wiggins told Plant that was very interesting; he hadn't known that, and why was the left side safer than the right? Melrose thought for a moment and answered that it had something to do with wind velocity.

As the plane lifted off and gained altitude, Melrose began to realize the fix he was in: My God, he thought, gripping the arms of the seat, this huge craft with its load of innocent victims was about to test the laws of gravity. None of his neighbors appeared to realize this: the sweet-faced old woman across the aisle was clicking her knitting needles, slowly increasing the length of some white garment—a shroud probably; a leather-jacketed couple a few seats away were already sleepily entwined, the fellow with his mouth open in an O, snoring softly. How in heaven's name could anyone sleep? And beside him, even Wiggins had his eyes closed, his hands linked in his lap, head bent in some form of meditation. Suddenly the plane broke through cloud cover into startling brightness and levelled off.

He opened his eyes to the clatter of the flight attendant shoving the drinks trolley down the aisle. Thank the lord. Jury had a beer, Wiggins a Diet Coke, and Melrose two miniature bottles of whisky and a can of soda.

Armed with his whisky and soda, he opened the Onions. The venue was a shop that sold baby birds. Inauspicious, he thought, and thumbed forward to see if the milieu changed. Yes, to the Caribbean. Someone was carrying a caged bird into a hotel there. He wondered, turning back, how long he'd have to hang around this bird shop in London EC1 before he could get to Antigua. He was absolutely certain by the time he'd reached page fifteen that *The Parrot and Pickle* was one of the books the monkeys had cast aside on their way to writing *Hamlet*. God, why were mystery writers so awful? Even Polly Praed, who could run rings round the Onions woman, could be pretty bloody awful.

He replaced the Onions in his holdall and took out Ellen's book and resettled himself. Ellen was no Onions, thank God. And if *Windows* was somewhat baffling, that did not obscure its quality. But he still found it incredibly enigmatic, despite or perhaps because of the style, which was simplicity itself. "Simple" was not the word, though, he would use to describe some of its other qualities: The name of the protagonist, the odd displacements in time, the relationship—if you could call it that—between the two characters (there seemed to be only two). He sighed and replaced it and looked once again at the Onions. Horrid cover. What were publishers thinking of, anyway? If Onions could get published, Joanna was right—*anybody* could, including him. He drew a composition book from his small bag. He had told no one he had taken up mystery writing, and he held it so that neither of his companions could see what he was writing. Wiggins was crawling over him for the third or fourth time with another vial of pills. He made his way to the water dispenser.

Melrose turned to the last entry, where Smithson and Nora were hurtling along a narrow road on their way to Bury St. Edmunds. He frowned. Why? He could not remember any scene he'd planned in Bury St. Edmunds.

"What're you writing?" asked Jury.

Melrose sighed. Wasn't this *always* the way? A person could be sending out frantic SOS's, or holding up huge signs fairly *yelling* "Save Me from This Ax Murderer," and no one would notice; but just let a person try to get away with writing something in *secret* and everybody was all eyes. "Nothing much."

Jury plucked the paperback from the webbed holder in front of Melrose. *"The Parrot and Pickle?* What a strange title."

"I wouldn't recommend it." Melrose chewed his pencil but couldn't for the life of him remember anything happening in Bury St. Edmunds. "One of the characters is poisoned by eating a pickle laced with cyanide. How Ms. Onions is going to solve the problem of that particular pickle landing in that person's mouth, I don't know."

"Ghastly cover." A brightly plumed bird was hovering over a jar of gherkins. "Is it a pub name or something? Sounds like one of the Bruce's Brewery lot."

"No. At least that would make some sort of weird sense. No, it's a literal parrot and a literal pickle. That cover's not the most seductive marketing approach, I agree. Here, read Ellen's book."

Wiggins was back and crawling in. He looked whiter than usual. "You all right?" Jury asked.

"A bit nauseous, sir."

"Something you ate?"

Said Melrose, "Given the looks of that meal trolley that just rolled by, I'd say it will very *soon* be something he ate."

Wiggins was searching through his flight bag. "I wouldn't wonder if I've got fear of flying. Claustrophobic." He looked at Jury. "Have you ever known me to be?"

Jury was looked upon as the repository for Wiggins's medical history. Am I allergic to aubergines? Does rue make me break out in a rash? "No," said Jury, opening Ellen's book. "And you're not going to find a cure for claustrophobia in that bag, anyway."

"Best cure for that, Sergeant, is walking round the plane," Melrose said. "But you've got to do it . . . well, ritualistically." Wiggins loved ritual. "You've got to make a circuit—down, over, up the other aisle, through the seats and back. Do that twice. Or three times. Works every time. I used to be violently claustrophobic."

"Really, sir?" Wiggins was already getting up again.

Melrose nodded, still puzzling over the Bury St. Edmunds trip. Had he been writing in his sleep?

And that reminded him. He'd forgotten to ask Marshall Trueblood if he'd rescued their notebook from Mrs. Withersby's bucket. Melrose started biting the flesh round his thumb. Surely, Trueblood had. If the Withersby person found it, though, she'd ransom it off. Oh, well, nothing to be done from up here.

Had they been, perhaps, a bit too theatrical?

Part 2

 NICKEL CITY

9

Ellen Taylor hadn't changed by a day, by an hour. She might even have been wearing the same clothes: jeans and a black leather jacket; her chain mail jewelry; a white T-shirt sporting a cartoon child with a square head topped with a spiky blond haircut, saying, "Yo Dude." The leather jacket was tucked under one arm; in her mingled nervousness and excitement, she kept switching it from one arm to the other as the three of them approached.

For she was excited, that was clear; she was also trying to disguise it by assuming an abstracted air, looking far and wide round the terminal, as if Melrose, Jury, and Wiggins were only three of many she'd come here to meet.

As Melrose dragged his calfskin case from the carousel, she said, "Well, at least you didn't come loaded down with luggage."

At least? Of what breach of traveller's etiquette *had* he been guilty, then?

She seemed pleased as punch to have Sergeant Wiggins, whom she'd never met, and Richard Jury, whom she had, but briefly, to lavish a bit of attention on, so as not to appear ungrateful for or unmindful of the trouble others were putting themselves to for her sake. Melrose was a different kettle of fish altogether. *He* (she appeared to like to pretend) was an old friend like an old sock, to be pulled on or cast aside till the next wash came around.

Thus, she was all the more flustered when Melrose set down his case and swiftly put his arms around her and gave her a big, warm hug and a kiss he let linger on her cheek before he stepped back to watch the color wash across her face. To avoid his eyes she looked down at their suitcases and asked if this wine-colored calfskin and the dark blue canvas one were theirs in much the same way airport security had scrutinized them at Heathrow.

"They have not been out of our sight; we packed them ourselves; no one's passed us any parcels to take out of the country," said Melrose.

Jury laughed. "More or less."

"Say again?" Ellen's face was still blotchy with receding blushes. She wore no makeup except for several shades of eye shadow running from dark brown through khaki to champagne. None of this eye art did a thing to enhance the large brown eyes beneath the lids, though. Melrose had always liked Ellen's face, its triangular shape, pert chin, clear skin. Her hair was oat-colored and long enough to half-cover the shoulder-length metal earrings that swayed and clicked when she moved her head.

"Are we riding on your motorcycle?"

She did not appear to see the joke in this. "It's in the shop. We're taking a cab."

"Oh, I'll do that, miss," said Wiggins, seeing her about to shoulder his backpack.

"That's okay; I like to carry things."

Melrose doubted this, and put her wrestling her shoulders into the backpack down to the same nervous excitement. Anything for a distraction.

As they made their way towards the exit, she asked them about their flight, and Wiggins obliged by telling her the details. He told her all the way across the lakelike lobby, down the ramp, and out the door into the cold wind of a Maryland afternoon.

Jury sat in front beside the driver, the other three in back. Ellen sat between Plant and Wiggins, paying far more attention to Wiggins than to Melrose, which he took to mean that she needed him more than she cared to show and was unnerved by this fact. She had stuck a book in his hands as a rather grudging welcome-to-Baltimore gift, saying he might need it for getting around.

As she chatted nineteen-to-the-dozen with Wiggins, pointing out nothing of interest that Melrose could see in the flying landscape, he perused his book. It was a narrow but thickish volume bearing the title *Strangers' Guide to Baltimore*. Each corner of the patent-shiny red cover was adorned with a little drawing of one of Baltimore's historic sites. Trails of tiny black footprints wandered from one of these corners to another, looping from corner to corner as on a children's game board.

Melrose was suspicious. He glanced over at Ellen, but she was busy plying Wiggins with crystal mints and pointing out the window at God only knew what, since there was nothing much to see in this typical airport-to-center-city trip, which could have been in London, Baltimore, New York, or anywhere except possibly Calcutta. A huge hoarding advertising Black Label beer that looked overambitiously frothy; another shouting the pleasures of Johnnie Walker Red; another of a huge bucket of chicken. Dirt shoulders, concrete pilings, building equipment. Could have been anywhere serviced by an airport.

His suspicions about Ellen's gift were confirmed when he looked inside the red book. A family of four, the "Stranger" family, were about to set off on a junket ("junket" being the word chosen by the Bessie sisters, guide writers Lizzie and Lucie) to the Inner Harbor, a place of bright lights, little shops, and eating establishments—a place of glory to the Stranger children, apparently, given their exaggerated smiles. The trail looping around had a definite yellow-brick-road-ish tint to it. Thus the reader was to be treated to a footstep-by-footstep ramble with the Strangers, past monuments and stadiums, through parks and gridlocked streets, quite often taking time out for various treats, such as ice-cream cones and cappuccino or lunches and dinners involving a lot of ocean-catch food. Here was what looked like a platter of starfish. He looked closer at the illustration; no, they were not starfish—tiny crabs, maybe. Then came illustrations of oysters or clams with happy faces, dancing about a big serving platter; here was a rockfish frisking and grinning on a fisherman's line and dangling above a creel; then there were lobsters merrily waving their claws above huge pots. Maryland seafood had a decided we-who-are-about-to-die-salute-you attitude. Probably why they won the Revolutionary War, thought Melrose. He'd never known Dover soles or kippers to act so cavalierly before the firing line.

"What are you *doing*?" asked Ellen, as if she herself hadn't been the instrument of his present occupation.

"Reading, obviously." Melrose turned a page. Washington Monument? He thought that was in Washington, D.C.

Ellen mumbled something about not reading guidebooks, and answered Jury's question about the structure on their right.

"Camden Yards, the Orioles' stadium. It's brand new. The Orioles played their opener there."

Melrose closed the *Strangers' Guide* and drummed his fingers on it. He could just picture Ellen in the children's section of some bookshop, leafing through this book and chortling. He refused to react and stared straight ahead as the mute cab driver delivered them into the city of Baltimore. "Deliverance" it could very well be for Sergeant Wiggins.

For the tallest building in the cluster that had come into view before they turned right on Pratt Street was a Florentine clock tower around the face of which was spelled out the words "Bromo-Seltzer."

The cab pulled to the curb in front of a handsome brick structure in Fells Point called the Admiral Fell Inn. The Admiral Fell had not been ignored by the Bessie sisters; the *Strangers' Guide* pointed out that it had once been a vinegar factory. "And a lodging house for seamen," added Melrose, looking studiously at the book.

"It's a hotel, but it's like a bed-and-breakfast. I thought you'd like that. I thought it would make you feel at home."

"Ardry End isn't a bed-and-breakfast," said Melrose.

"It's fine," said Jury.

"I'll get it," said Ellen, yanking bills from a worn wallet. "Until you learn to count," she added, extinguishing the spark of generosity. This was, naturally, directed at Melrose alone, Jury and Wiggins being credited with enough intelligence to sort out another country's decimal system without a lot of practice. Ellen reached in with the money to pay the driver.

As they walked up the steps of the inn, she asked (again of Melrose alone, it seemed), "Well, what do you want to do? Take a nap?"

Melrose ignored this. "What I want to do is find out what the hell's going on so that I can get back to Ardry End."

Wiggins was concentrating on a large dog that lay beside the desk. It began to get to its feet, apparently thought the better of that move, and returned its head to its paws, looking up at them out of baleful eyes.

"Grumpy, aren't you?" said Jury, smiling at Melrose. "I have to make some phone calls."

"I have to teach a class," said Ellen. "It'll just be an hour, an hour and a half. Maybe we can meet around five?"

"Fine. Where?"

"We can go to the Horse. It's just down the street. Thames Street." She pointed out the window.

"What's the Horse?"

"A local dive. I always go there. But you probably won't like the beer. They do have Bass, though."

"Okay by me," said Jury. To Melrose he said, "Are you going to have that nap?"

Oh, ha, thought Melrose. "I'm taking a walk."

10

Fells Point (Ellen had told him, as he'd set off with his *Strangers' Guide*) was the oldest part of Baltimore, was indeed what Baltimore had really grown out of, and was probably the last working waterfront left in the country.

Despite the obvious quaintness in danger of sliding into chic, Fells Point was a genuine period piece. Left to itself for over two hundred years, it was evidently becoming trendy, but it still kept the appearance of its eighteenth-century origins. It had about it a pleasant sort of scruffiness that the galleries and shops hadn't managed to glamorize or suppress. Narrow row houses faced narrow strips of sidewalk on narrow streets. Slate roofs crowned them and sally ports divided them, walkways with painted iron gates that Melrose assumed had once been used for the passage of livestock.

Melrose walked around the streets and along the waterfront for an hour before turning back, once again passing the Admiral Fell Inn in search of the pub where they were to meet and found it within perhaps a hundred feet of the inn.

The flaking white paint on the sign made the swayback horse look even more like an old nag pressed into servitude by a bunch of Irish tinkers. Its expression was rather stupidly pleased, as if glad it had finally been put out to pasture. The sign of The Horse You Came In On hung above a door that probably hadn't been painted in this century. It was a door one would pause at before opening if he didn't know what lay behind it. It looked sly, that door.

Melrose liked both the sign and the street. It was called Thames Street, and with its warehouses facing the water, its Belgian block, and its brick pavements, its cobbles, it reminded him a little of Whitechapel and Docklands. It was black night along the London river now, he knew, and even here a late-afternoon darkness seemed to be settling in. It had started to drizzle as he was walking, and out across the Patapsco River fog was rolling in, and the smaller craft that were moored along here would soon be enveloped in it.

It was a low-key, no-frills little pub, narrow, with a bar along the left wall and tables and chairs along the right. He could barely see the ceiling for the substructure of smoke that clung to it, effluvium of cigarettes and cigars; and the humidity level must have risen thirty percent from the flow of beer—pitchers, bottles, cans. Still, it was a relief after the plummy Victorian accents of London's West End. The place was packed with people, many of whom were in a state of frenzy, standing two and three deep at the bar, all of them watching the screen of a big television. A swell of voice had hit him when he'd opened the door, and he felt himself awash in a sea of color. Melrose wedged his way in and joined the telly viewers, whose eyes were riveted on the football pile-up now in progress.

American football was as far beyond his ken as a moon landing. Melrose knew nothing about competitive diversions except for snooker, and he liked that because it was slow and silent—in other words, civilized. Pool was too easy and billiards too stuffy. Snooker was perfect. One heard nothing other than the occasional click and rattle of balls and the odd rousing ripple of applause, unsustained. He despised cricket, polo, and tennis. Once he had gone to Wimbledon, but got no enjoyment out of watching a couple of Slavs thrashing about with rackets, expending more energy in one backhand shot than Melrose used up in a week of sitting around in the Jack and Hammer.

He took over a cramped stool between a burly man in a paint-smeared blue shirt and white painter's cap turned backward and a tall black in leather and dreadlocks. "POUND IT INTO THE FUCKING END ZONE!" yelled the painter, standing up at his stool like a jockey in stirrups. The woman coming down the bar (whom Melrose assumed to be the bartender) gave him a playful punch on the shoulder and called him "Elroy." A heavyset man and woman (man and wife, surely) dressed head to foot in football togs (red and gold), even to the woman's earrings (miniature ball-carriers), were trying to grab her attention, but she ignored them.

"WHAT'LL IT BE?" she asked Melrose—or, rather, yelled at him, cranking up the pitch to make herself heard.

He thought he should forgo his Old Peculier (which they probably didn't have, anyway) and order something American. Glancing at the row of bottles on the shelves behind her, he said, "How about an Amstel Light?"

"WHAT?"

He raised himself slightly and leaned over the counter. "AMSTEL LIGHT."

"YOU WANT A GLASS WITH THAT?"

"DOESN'T IT COME IN A GLASS?"

She thought he was trying to be funny and cut him a look.

He noticed that the painter was drinking from a bottle and the black from a silver can. "BOTTLE," he said.

"YOU GOT IT."

His accent had, of course, attracted the attention of the men on either side of him, and he smiled at them, and nodded towards the television. "Who's playing—Baltimore?"

The two exchanged a glance over his head. "Baltimore ain't got no team, my man," said the black before his attention was pulled to the screen, as a cry went up from both stadium and room. "Skins and Eagles, man. Where you from?" The tone of the question (to which Melrose made a mumbled and forgettable reply) implied it surely couldn't be this planet.

And now, looking around, Melrose couldn't say he blamed the man. Although he knew he'd wandered into a wave of burgundy and old gold and green, the emblematic words printed on the jerseys and knitted caps and satiny jackets hadn't registered. REDSKINS and EAGLES.

"Sorry," said Melrose, a break that he supposed was a time-out allowing him to speak in a fairly normal tone. "I don't know much about American football." He knew enough, though, to tell the woman behind the counter to set his friends up with refills.

The improvement in Anglo-American relations underway, the tall black said, "It's a playoff game between Washington and Philly."

"*Play*off?" It had looked pretty damned serious to Melrose.

"Super Bowl, dude," said the painter, smiling broadly and displaying a mouthful of rather chipped teeth.

The Supper Bowl.

He cursed himself for forgetting Diane Demorney's morsel of information about the Colts. Before he left, he had called upon Diane to see if in her mental stockpile of arcana she could come up with anything newsy about Baltimore. Although no one had ever been deceived into thinking Diane Demorney wise, a great number of people thought her knowledgeable. Actually, Diane didn't really know anything; her bits of information—and to give Diane her due, they were admittedly legion—floated around in a contextless sea. Most of her acquaintance had no idea that the tip of Diane's iceberg was floating free.

"The Orioles," she said when Melrose asked her about Baltimore. He was seated in her stark white living room, drinking a martini. Using a long glass wand filled with stars dropping through purple-colored oil, Diane was stirring her pitcherful of vodka barely kissed by vermouth. The price of her help had been his acceptance of her invitation to stay for a drink. "A great team," she added, tapping the glass wand on the pitcher. "Baltimore is full of rabid baseball fans." She handed Melrose one of her sunshade-sized glasses and sat herself down on her white sofa next to her nasty white cat, which had been glaring at Melrose ever since he'd sunk into the shapeless, bottomless white leather chair. "There's Orel Hershiser, if you're interested."

"He's an Orioles player?" Melrose was keeping his eye on the cat.

"No, no. Los Angeles Dodgers. He's one of the reasons they won the Series in '88."

"I thought it was the *Brooklyn* Dodgers." The cat was struggling with itself, waving its rump in the way cats do before they charge.

"It used to be, but they sold the team to L.A. The name goes with them. Same thing happened with the Colts. The Baltimore Colts, it used to be."

He asked her more, but she'd clearly exhausted her baseball-football fund of knowledge. She moved right along to Edgar Allan Poe, who (Melrose was certain) she had never read, but about whom she knew what she considered the salacious detail that he'd "married his cousin and she was only fourteen at the time."

Melrose undercut this bit of gossip by telling her that marrying one's cousin was not, in the mid-nineteenth century, at all unusual; and also that girls in their teens, even thirteen and fourteen, often married.

And although Diane knew even less about politics than she did about literature, she moved smoothly to the Clinton administration. After she informed Melrose that the only Democrat who should have beaten George Bush was Perry Como, he drained his glass, gave the white cat a wide berth, and left.

A black player intercepted a pass and Elroy stood up again, yelling "Go, Art!"

"You ain't from around here's my guess," said the black man during the next time-out. His name, he said, was Conrad; his handshake was knuckle-bashing; Melrose felt to see if the small bones were still intact. He had to confess that no, he wasn't, and a brief exchange followed about the rather boring subjects of heads of states and politics and what Melrose thought of Baltimore and whether he was going to Murder City.

"I beg your pardon?"

Conrad chortled. "D.C., dude. Crack Capital."

Elroy, whose eyes didn't even leave the television screen during the commercial, said, "Philly's worse."

They argued, their argument intermittently punctuated by epithets and jeers aimed at the television, occasionally interrupted by a shout of approval.

"It's a shame Baltimore doesn't have a team. Didn't the Colts—"

There was a troubling moment when they both turned to glower at him, but that passed quickly enough, and Elroy said, "Well, maybe we will again."

"Not a Chinaman's fucking chance," said Conrad ("Connie" to the young woman behind the bar). "Shit, Elroy, we're sittin' here pinned between the Skins and the Eagles."

Sounded uncomfortable, thought Melrose, matching their sour head-shakes with one of his own as he tried to look clever. He was glad the others weren't here so he didn't have to look clever in front of them.

Play had resumed, and a chant was swelling the upper reaches of the bar—"D-D-D-D-D-D-D"—accompanied by bottles and glasses pounding on the bar in a sort of jungle-drum rhythm.

One of the most enthusiastic of this group was a youngish, light-haired man who stood out not only for his focused chanting but for the absence of colorful garments. No Redskins scarf, no Eagles sweatshirt. No burgundy, no green—nothing. Nothing except for what Melrose could see were very expensive clothes, no matter that they were casual. He recognized quality because he wore it himself. The fellow looked like renegade management here amongst the shop stewards, the sort of role Peter Sellers might have played in one of those labor-union-oriented comedies popular thirty years ago. He looked *rich,* that's all; Melrose could sense it, being rich himself. And he also looked *happy,* swaying there to the tune of "D-D-D-D" and rising with the others to yell.

One of the players had intercepted a pass. Elroy banged his bottle on the bar. *"Shee-it!"* he yelled as a voice announced a flag on the play. He slapped his cap down.

Melrose squinted upwards at the screen, searching for a flag.

"Whose penalty? Whose? Holding? Holding, God-*damn!*"

If only Melrose could figure out where the ball was—ah, there! My God, but that chap could throw! The quarterback had moved back, taken aim, and put the ball in the running back's hands as smoothly as if a wire had connected them. The receiver clasped the ball to his chest like a newborn infant. Melrose ordered his fourth beer and the same for his companions as the running back peeled yardage before he was brought down by two defensive players big as lorries.

He was just getting into the game when he felt a tug at his elbow that he tried to shake off. Ellen was yanking at him.

"Throw it to the posse!" yelled Elroy, up in the stirrups again.

"Who's playing?"

Another cheer went up around the bar, more chanting from the other end, this time "RYP—RYP—RYP—RYP—RYP."

Jury, Wiggins, and Ellen were standing behind Melrose. Ellen craned her neck to look at the screen. "It's a playoff, right?" Then to Melrose she said, "Too noisy for you?"

With massive irritation, Melrose turned with his bottle of Amstel Light. He was tired of being Old Man Melrose, taker of naps and hater of noise. "Skins and Eagles, for God's sake." He tipped his bottle into his mouth and recrossed his arms along the bar.

"No kidding? You know anything about it?"

"Do I *know* anything about it? Ha!" Then, "What are you drinking?" he asked.

"Whatever you aren't. You sound pretty smashed."

"Amstel Light." He held up the bottle.

"Bass," said Ellen. "Or we could get a pitcher. Or do you want bottled?" she asked Jury and Wiggins.

Wiggins, naturally, wanted a cup of tea, which he couldn't get, and so was left standing there trying to settle on something else after the others had taken their pitcher and found a table.

Ellen waved to the fellow at the end of the bar whom Melrose had noticed. Now he also noticed the chap was rather handsome, decidedly so when he smiled.

"That's Pat. Patrick Muldare. He was a friend of Beverly Brown. Some say a very, you know, *good* friend."

Jury studied Patrick Muldare for a few moments, then said, "This woman was a student of yours?"

She nodded.

"What happened?"

"The night of January nineteenth is Poe's birthday."

They all looked at her. Jury asked, "Poe's birthday? What's that got to do with it?"

"A lot. Poe was buried in the churchyard of Westminster Church. Every year, the night of his birthday, someone—no one knows who, except it's a man—brings cognac and flowers, roses, to his grave. It's a tradition that's been going on for years. Some years, a few people have gathered there in hopes of discovering who the person is. No one ever has. Anyway, Beverly is—was—a real Poe fancier. She loved his writing, and he was to be the subject of her doctoral thesis. Just for fun, she'd go to this little birthday party. She did; she was murdered. Strangled. It must have happened, the cops say, just after the crowd—well, not a crowd, really—had dispersed, because no one saw anything."

"But why wouldn't the Brown woman have left with the others?"

Ellen shrugged. "I have no idea. Unless she thought the man who came wasn't the real one. See, it was the habit of the curator of the Poe museum, or one of his people, to come in advance of the flower giver, pretend he was him in order to get rid of the little crowd that would collect there. Now, she might have thought the person who'd appeared was a fake, that it was a ruse. She was right. So she hung around. And she got killed."

Sergeant Wiggins was making his way back to the table with a glass of fizz. He sat down. Ellen went on:

"Beverly took a couple of courses from me. Three, to be exact." Ellen frowned. "I guess she liked me—I don't know. She was awfully critical of her instructors. One thing I can definitely say about her is that she was very smart. She was clever and she had a lot of imagination. And she was a superior researcher—she had an eye and a mind for detail. She was assistant to Owen Lamb, and he's pretty demanding.

"Beverly asked me if she could use these newspaper reports as the subject of a paper I'd assigned." Ellen dug around in her bag and brought out some clippings. "I said yes, of course. It sounded interesting. I really think she was going to try and—well, not solve, but do some sort of 'Marie Roget' thing—you know that story by Poe called 'The Mystery of Marie Roget'?" They nodded, all except for Wiggins, who frowned and continued stirring his fizz with his finger. "So I saw a lot of her notes, because she'd check in with me every once in a while to see what I thought." Ellen pulled some more papers from her MPTV bag. "Beverly had just been in to see me the day she was killed. And she left all of this stuff with me." Ellen lined up two of the clippings. "I don't know exactly what she saw in the newspaper accounts, but she must have thought there was some sort of connection between these two murders."

"Which two murders?"

Ellen pointed to an item, or a paragraph no more than an item, from the *Baltimore Sun.* "An old guy, a street person called John-Joy. He was found in Cider Alley; that's a narrow little street off Lexington, near the Market. He was found by another street person, another old guy he used to hang around with. The man who found him was named Milos. No one seems to know his last name, either. Milos hangs out all the time—you know, panhandling—in front of a store run by Patrick Muldare's brother. Or half-brother, stepbrother—I don't know which. Milos is blind and deaf. But he's not dumb. He can speak perfectly plainly. Or yell perfectly plainly, I should say. Like a lot of deaf people, he raises his voice.

"The other murder that Beverly seemed to think is related—I can only guess about this because of these notes she left—is going to surprise you." She was speaking now directly to Jury as she shoved the other clipping towards him.

Jury looked from it to her. "Philip Calvert? The *same* Calvert?"

"Well, I guess there wouldn't be two, would there? In Philly?"

This one was a longer piece than the other and was clipped from the *Philadelphia Inquirer.* Jury scanned it, passed it to Wiggins.

Ellen went on. "And there was this piece of paper stuck in with the notes and things—just doodling, really, but there're these three sets of initials on it. See? Her finger drew a line through the set of initials: P.C.: J.-J.: P.M. "And 'Barnes Found.' written here." She pointed to the slanted handwriting. "That must be the Barnes Foundation, outside of Philadelphia. But the P.C., P.M., and J.-J.—see?"

Jury, with Wiggins looking over his shoulder, gazed down at the notebook page.

"I suppose I wouldn't have thought much about it if that 'J.-J.' weren't hyphenated. I don't see what it can refer to but John-Joy. And the Barnes Foundation connects up with Philip Calvert."

"But who," asked Melrose, "is P.M.?"

"Ellen thinks it's supposed to be me."

The voice at Plant's and Jury's backs belonged to the handsome, youngish-looking man Ellen had waved to at the end of the bar.

"Hullo, Ellen."

"Patrick Muldare," said Ellen, and made the introductions. "He teaches with me at Hopkins."

Muldare laughed. "I'd hardly say *that.*"

His age was difficult to guess, for Patrick Muldare had one of those perennially boyish faces, all the more so because of the flyaway, unruly hair that he had to keep scraping back. He dropped a hand on Ellen's shoulder and smiled around the table. Equally automatic was Ellen's hand dropped on his, patting it a little. Both gestures, Jury thought, were all but unconscious; nothing seemed to pass between them. But Plant, Jury saw, was watching this exchange narrowly.

Ellen invited Muldare to join them. With a nicety of feeling that Jury found unusual, Muldare refused; he seemed to realize that they were newly arrived and probably didn't need a stranger at their reunion. And he might have picked up on Plant's reaction. He stood there, drinking from his pint of beer.

"We were talking about Beverly," said Ellen.

"Do you think they're my initials? God only knows why they would be." He shook his head, returned the scrap of paper to the clippings.

Jury smiled at him. "The question is, do *you* think this set of initials is yours?"

Muldare shrugged his shoulders. "No. Sure as hell hope not." He looked around the table. "Seeing what happened to the other two sets." Despite the comment, he flashed them a smile of supreme unconcern.

Ellen looked up at him, started to say something, paused and said, "I don't know why she gave me all of this . . ."

"Trusted you, I guess. One would." Muldare smiled again around the table and went back to the bar.

"He's a teacher?" asked Jury.

Ellen laughed. "Only one course, just for fun. He's one of the richest men in Baltimore. Rolling in it. Old money. *Very* old money. And the old money's begotten a lot of new money. Construction, mainly. He's supposed to be really brilliant at business, but then he comes from a long line of brilliance at making money—real estate, the usual stuff. And he's not much more than thirty. Thirty-two, I think. But he lives in Fells Point, over on Shakespeare Street. He's very unassuming, really. You'd never know he had money, except for the football thing."

" 'Football thing?' " asked Melrose, feeling perhaps now they were into his territory.

Ellen didn't seem to agree and ignored him.

Jury was silent for a moment, thinking and studying his sergeant's glass of bubbling liquid. He frowned both at his thoughts and at the glass. "And you think Beverly Brown was murdered because of this information she'd gathered, or something she knew?"

"Not necessarily." Like a magician with a bag of tricks, Ellen drew from her bag this time some typed pages and one page between plastic covers. "She could have been murdered for this."

11

Jury fingered the page that looked, beneath its protective plastic cover, parchment-brown, stained with ink and blurred with age. His and Ellen's eyes met over the top of the page. Jury looked down, looked up at her, said nothing, and read:

Violette

By Edgar A. Poe

Madam

I cannot tell you with certainty when I first made the acquaintance of the gentleman you refer to as "William Quartermain", for I knew him only as M. Hilaire P—, and met him only once, in a large, decaying and gloomy house near the Seine. The circumstances of our meeting and our acquaintanceship were most extraordinary.

M. P— first appeared before me — an appearance so sudden and unearthly, it was as if a wraith or spirit had suddenly formed itself from the drifting ground mist and shaped itself into a living man.

As he was stumbling over the manuscript, made difficult by the ravagements of age, Ellen pushed some more pages in front of him, these of ordinary typescript. "She typed it over. Beverly, I mean."

Melrose and Wiggins looked down at the page Jury put aside, and Jury started again to read:

Madam

I cannot tell you with certainty when I first made the acquaintance of the gentleman you refer to as "William Quartermain," for I knew him only as M. Hilaire P——, and met him only once, in a large, decaying and gloomy house near the Seine. The circumstances of our meeting and our acquaintanceship were most extraordinary.

M. P—— first appeared before me—an appearance so odd and unearthly, it was as if a wraith or spirit had suddenly formed itself from the drifting ground mist and shaped itself into a living man. This meeting took place on an evening in November, an evening of near-impenetrable fog and rain, in the Tuileries. The gentleman appeared to be in some distress; I could not tell whether this was owing to some physical malady or to the malaise that so often overtakes us when the weather is dreary almost beyond bearing, as this evening rain certainly was.

"He's mad," said Melrose.
"What?" said Ellen. "Don't interrupt."
"Well, just listen to the way he's talking."
Ellen nudged Jury. "Go on."

. . . as this evening rain certainly was. In any event, he stumbled and only managed to prevent himself falling by sinking down onto a bench.

I was about to pass by, but in the lineaments of his face and posture were that which prevented me. I asked him if I could be of assistance— Was he unwell?—and attempting, however I could, to put myself at his disposal.

He raised eyes to me that burned in their intensity; he smiled; he made light of the faint into which he had nearly fallen. He rose, but I was loath to leave him in this condition. Finally, after we had talked for a few moments, and as the rain dissipated and the fog dispersed, he suggested that perhaps I would care to accompany him to his rooms in the Rue ——— and join him in a glass of wine.

I was happy to do so; I had found, even in the few moments I had been in his company, a strong inclination to keep by his side, so magnetic was his presence.

But I was ill-prepared for the richness, I might almost say the voluptuousness of M. P——'s surroundings. The delicate lace of the curtains, the lavishness of the wall hangings, the volutes of the draperies, the burnished wood of the heavy chairs whose feet and arms were carved in shapes resembling the wretched faces of the agonized religious, the walls so crowded with paintings framed in gold and umber that the blood red walls themselves were scarcely visible between. And through all of the room wafted mingled scents from a strange glass globe containing an oil constituted of rare herbs.

We sat in these extraordinary surroundings as the wind coming off the river lifted the curtains and drew the pungent fragrance of the oil across the room, he, perfectly silent with the head slightly downturned, in one of the phantasmagorical chairs.

"The oils soothe me," he said, "for I feel at every moment that I am being torn apart."

His voice reached a new depth of melancholy and I murmured some fatuous words of hope and comfort of the sort that often serve only to deepen the feelings of oppression in the sufferer, showing as they do that the respondent understands nothing of his pain.

I remember a shudder passing through my body at the sight of such an excess of woe on the countenance of one who, judging from the luxury of his chamber, was in want of nothing. As he closed his eyes and breathed in the fragrance of the oil, I observed the tall window at his back. Through this window, which opened onto a small iron balcony, I could observe, across the courtyard, another window belonging to the opposite house, another window of almost precisely the same proportions as this one; and through that window, on the opposite side of what appeared to be a very large room, yet another window. So it was that my view through the window at M. P——'s back seemed framed in an ever-diminishing perspective impossible to achieve merely by looking upon some distant low horizon where the only measure is the earth below and the sky above.

And I have come to believe, in the days and weeks succeeding my visit to M. P——'s apartments, in this PERSPECTIVE, the diminishing view as given by and through that strange series of windows, a view as in a world's collapsing, that it is Perspective that constitutes what we know of reality and not what generally presents itself in our diurnal round of walks and drives—trees, strangers, gardens, houses—these but the shadowy fancies of the mind—

For it is that portal, facing on that portal, and again on that and all

of its contiguously floating images that stretch endlessly—this alone
allows us what we know of reality, this dissolving view of the world.

Jury stopped, looked beneath the page in his hand as if another might
appear underneath, like one of those windows.

"That's all, sir?" asked Wiggins, his glass of now-flat foam half-raised
and held in midair.

In the brief silence that hung over the table there came the sounds of
tribal chanting from the bar, and Jury had to shake himself free of his
sense of dislocation, the fleeting notion that he had wandered into an
outpost of the earth. He looked towards the television screen; the fans
were cheering on one or other of the teams.

"It's rather fascinating," said Melrose, lighting up a little cigar. "There
are four stories going on simultaneously—or very nearly. There's the
narrator and his relationship with Monsieur P. There's the tale that
Monsieur P. is telling. There are the letters pointing to a relationship
between Monsieur P. and the woman. Then there's the narrator's relationship to the woman."

"Is there more?" asked Wiggins of Ellen. He obviously enjoyed being
read to.

"Yes. But I keep it locked up in my filing cabinet. In my office. It
makes me uncomfortable carrying the original around. I mean, what if it
were . . . ?"

"Written by Poe himself?" Jury asked. "Has somebody read this who's
capable of judging its authenticity?"

"Well, there's Professor Irwin; he's a Poe authority. There's Vlasic,
who *thinks* he is. But then he thinks he's all things to all students. And
then there's the one I mentioned, Owen Lamb, the professor Beverly was
assistant to. He's a genealogist, an historian, a specialist in old documents, that sort of thing."

"And?" Jury urged her. "What did they say?"

"They disagree, somewhat. For the most part they think it's a fake.
Vlasic, naturally, won't commit himself. He doesn't want to be wrong.
Lamb doesn't think it's genuine, but he admits his reasoning is based on
things other than textual evidence, since he doesn't seem to think the
actual *content* of a questionable manuscript is decisive. And Poe didn't
secrete manuscripts."

"But if it is one of Poe's stories—in the last hundred years or so, any
number of things could have happened to account for its turning up.
How did she find it? *Where* did she say she found it?"

"Beverly said she was going through an old trunk at an antique shop
near here. That's where."

"A trunk, for God's sake." Melrose laughed.

"A shop in Aliceanna Street. Back there." Ellen nodded in a direction behind her.

"And what about the handwriting?"

"That's something else again. A document expert is going over that."

Jury shook his head. "It's the sheer magnitude of such a forgery I find staggering. Good lord, even to copy a signature requires a lot of talent. To write an entire story in the hand of another person strikes me as an almost insurmountable task. Was this girl capable of such an undertaking?"

Ellen thought for a moment as she fingered the plastic sleeve of the original page. "Yes." She sat back with a sigh. "Beverly was ambitious. She was determined to get what she wanted. What she wanted, after she got her Ph.D., was to teach at Harvard. Not just an Ivy League school, but Harvard. *Harvard,* period. That was the thing about her: she was never vague about what she wanted."

"I imagine jobs at Harvard aren't too thick on the ground," said Wiggins.

"Unless," said Melrose, "the subject of your doctoral dissertation is the dissection of a freshly discovered manuscript purporting to be the work of none other than Edgar Allan Poe. *That* ought to land you a job anywhere. I take it she was a good student."

"Oh, yes."

Wiggins had put down his glass, empty now but for a dusty white sediment. "Thing is, though, doesn't it usually take a very long time to write a doctoral thesis? It wouldn't do if someone came along and pre-empted your conclusions, would it? Somebody else might prove it was a fake before you'd got your thesis finished."

Melrose said, "You'd just shift gears and incorporate those findings. It wouldn't be so dramatic as if you'd reached the conclusions by yourself, but look at all the notoriety you'd've got by then. And, anyway, at the outset, before you'd started you'd know whether someone was going to come along and knock your position to bits because, after all, the manuscript had undergone the scrutiny of experts.

"So she would have had a chance of finishing her thesis before there was any further serious dispute. And, of course, she could simply have refused to let anyone else see it, couldn't she? It belonged to her, after all. Now, this would be very clever: for her purposes, it makes no difference, aside from the *intrinsic* value of an authentic manuscript, if it *is* genuine since she's attempting to demonstrate this point in her dissertation. Very clever. You invent a fake manuscript precisely in order to show it's a fake."

"Yes, but if that's the case," said Wiggins, "why would anyone murder somebody in order to get their hands on a manuscript that's not genuine?"

"True." Jury thought for a moment. "If there's a question about its legitimacy . . . Why the church?"

"Because people knew she'd be going there. January nineteenth is Poe's birthday. Of course, I thought it was a peculiar spot to choose; it would be rather public, wouldn't it?"

Jury was looking down the bar; Patrick Muldare had left. "What about Patrick Muldare? This third set of initials. Why do you think she meant him?"

Ellen shrugged. "I don't know why. They were very good friends. Well, I think maybe lovers. And she worked at the shop his brother manages."

Wiggins had his pocket notebook out now. "Where would that be, miss?"

"It's sort of an offbeat antique shop . . . well, not really antiques, I guess. It's called Nouveau Pauvre. It's over on Howard, with all of those antique shops. It's gotten to be kind of trendy. There's a cafe now attached to it—the Hard Knocks, it's called. Beverly worked there part-time. I don't know if she worked in the shop or the cafe. Then there's the professor I mentioned. She was Lamb's assistant. I don't know anything about her other friends."

Jury thought for a moment as he reread the *Inquirer* piece. "Philip Calvert." He looked at Ellen. "Did she ever mention Philip Calvert to you?"

"Not directly, no. But you see there that he worked for the Barnes Foundation in Philadelphia. Last semester Beverly was taking a course in art appreciation; the Barnes Foundation offers a number of courses. So it would be quite a coincidence if there wasn't any connection."

"No one—the police, I expect I mean—has indicated in any way that the murders are connected." Melrose had spread the articles out and was going from one to the other. He looked up at Ellen. "What information did Beverly Brown have the police didn't?"

"I don't know."

Jury was still studying the torn page. "She's certainly linked the names. Assuming, of course, the initials stand for those three names."

"They must. I mean," said Ellen, "it's not just the newspaper clipping; but what other JJ could she mean with that hyphen between the *J*'s? John-Joy."

Jury leaned back. "I'm going to this little town in northern Pennsylvania tomorrow. Blaine, Pennsylvania. Perhaps I can manage to talk to the friend of Calvert's at this Barnes Foundation on the way."

Wiggins asked, "Will you be needing me to go along, sir?" His tone suggested he clearly didn't want to.

"No. This is a holiday for you, Wiggins."

"I really would like to see the sights. Johns Hopkins, for instance."

"Go with me," said Ellen. "I have to teach tomorrow morning."

"I was thinking more of the hospital." Wiggins drank off the dregs of the white stuff.

"What the hell *is* that?"

"Bromo-Seltzer, sir. Quite tasty, it is."

Jury rolled his eyes and shook his head; then he said to Melrose, "Perhaps you could call in at this antiques place where Beverly Brown found that trunk. Where was it again?" he asked Ellen.

"Aliceanna Street. A couple of blocks over from here. And I'm through teaching at two, so afterwards you can meet me at Hopkins. Gilman Hall."

Some quiz show had now replaced the game, and the regulars at the bar were staring up at the television in that slightly slack-mouthed way of viewers who aren't really interested but, having nothing else to watch, watch whatever's available. The flickering bluish shadows gave their faces a slightly cyanotic appearance. At the rear of the room, a young guitarist was setting up a couple of portable amps and a mike.

Jury looked at his watch. "It's after one a.m. London time and we haven't had any dinner yet. I'm starving. How about the rest of you?" He drank off his beer and started up. Ellen pulled him back down.

"Not yet." She was rooting through another bag now, this one full of books. "Before I eat, I've got to go and feed my cat."

Melrose glanced at the pouchlike bag. "It's in there?"

She shot a look at him. "Don't be stupid. I'm looking for something." She brought out a colorfully jacketed book and what appeared to be some more manuscript pages.

"My book," she said, indicating the manuscript.

"Which one? The sausage one?"

Ellen glared at him. "*Sauvage Savant* was *not* about sausages!"

"You said it was a delicatessen. A deli somewhere in Brooklyn, you said."

"In Queens. Never mind about that. This is *Doors*."

"Doors?"

"That's the name of it. It's the second one in the trilogy. After *Windows*," she added.

Jury picked up the gaudy-looking book, which appeared to be by some Italian, and asked, "What's this all about, Ellen?"

"She's trying to steal Sweetie."

12

Sweetie.

"Is that your cat, miss?" asked Wiggins, who'd been about to go to the bar for another Bromo-Seltzer.

"*No.* It's my pro-*tag*-o-nist, Sergeant Wiggins." Ellen all but hissed at him; her face flamed up and then saddened again.

Unembarrassed by his error, Wiggins still looked sorrowful in the face of her distress. He went off to get another round of drinks.

Melrose had never seen anyone look quite so woebegone as Ellen did at that moment, as she drew a worn copy of *Windows* from the bookbag. It probably wasn't the best time for him to mention that a protagonist named "Sweetie" was causing him problems. He plucked up a few pages of manuscript, gave them a cursory reading, decided this book wouldn't be any easier to understand than the first, and hoped he wouldn't be expected to say anything intelligent.

Apparently, Melrose's intelligence was not in question—whether he had any, whether he didn't. Ellen, the mind reader, said, as she fingered the copy of *Windows* fondly, "Some people have a hard time warming up to a character named Sweetie, which is understandable. Did you?"

"Me? Well, I did wonder about . . ."

"Not at all," said Jury. "I think it's a great name. I think it's a great book, Ellen."

When did he . . . ? Melrose stared at Jury. On the plane! Jury'd read the whole book—well, it wasn't very long—coming over here. No wonder Richard Jury was so successful with women and witnesses alike.

"Well, but just look at this!" She held up the other book, which was wrapped in a glaring multicolored jacket with a Picasso-like fractured torso. *Lovey* was its title. That, thought Melrose, boded ill.

"Listen." Ellen began to read from *Windows:*

Sweetie picked the white envelope from the carpet. It was damp from the humid morning. Sweetie felt her throat close as she pulled out the square of thick paper and saw the familiar handwriting. She read:

"Lily: You must be careful."

Mid-morning, but Sweetie went upstairs to her bedroom and lay down while the morning turned into evening and that into night and that into another morning. All this time she lay there watching her ceiling. Sweetie had painted stars and a moon above her. The ceiling drifted above her with its silver stars and ghostly moon.

"Now," said Ellen, "listen to this." She picked up the other book and opened it to a page marked with a paper clip.

Lovey opened the door and looked up and down the street for whoever had rung. Heat, like a warm hand, seemed to push her back, blossomed in her face. She saw no one. She walked out on the porch and nearly tripped over the wooden bench when she saw the package. It was the fifth one, addressed to her own fictional character, Baby. Lovey was afraid to touch it.

Ellen slammed the book down on the table, shuddering the glasses there and causing several people at adjoining tables to stare. "She's trying to turn Sweetie into Lovey and Lily into Baby. My God! 'Her own fictional character, Baby'—she doesn't have the remotest clue as to what's going on in *Windows*!"

"But that's terrible, Ellen." Melrose was truly incensed. "And this got *published*? How can someone get away with such a blatant case of literary theft?"

"It happens all the time. If it's not word-for-word, it's nearly impossible to prove."

Melrose looked at the cover again. "Vittoria Della Salvina—she's Italian?"

"She's from Queens. Her name is really Vicki Salva. God! What a nonentity she was." Ellen was grabbing at her hair, pulling at the roots. "A total zero. I should have known."

Jury was riffling through the pages. Probably have the whole thing read and indexed by the time Wiggins got back with the drinks. Melrose sighed. Why hadn't *he* paid more attention? Well, he'd certainly read assiduously from here on in.

"You mean you know this woman?" asked Jury.

Her hands still on the sides of her head, Ellen nodded, as if the hands were moving the head, puppet-wise. "Oh, yes. *Oh,* yes. Two years ago I taught at the New School. You know, in Manhattan. I taught writing. It was just after *Windows* was published. This Vicki Salva sat right in the front row, sucking up to me like you wouldn't believe. She'd hang around before class and after class—talk, talk, talk, about *Windows* and how marvellous it was. Talk, talk about my style, about Sweetie, about the theme. The point is, it was pretty obvious she'd *read* it; in other words, she certainly had what the law likes to call 'access,' usually the hardest thing to prove. But even with proof of that I can't get at her. I've been to two lawyers. You have no *idea* how hard it is to prove something like this."

"But, my lord," said Melrose, "it's so damned obvious. You win this prestigious award and this—*person* . . . Hell's bells, it hardly bears thinking about." He added, "Poe, at least, is dead. He doesn't have to suffer plagiarizing vampires."

"Not only that, but her writing's terrible," said Jury. " 'Heat blossomed'? The thing is, she's such a rotten writer and you're such a good one—that's probably one reason people aren't noticing."

"It sucks. The whole thing absolutely sucks." Ellen laid her head down on her outstretched arm.

This, thought Melrose, was really what she'd called about and why she'd wanted him to come to the States. "Never mind. Nobody will pay any attention to this tripe. She's got this book published on the strength of yours. There's an end to it."

"Oh, but it isn't. She'll do it again. I'm writing a trilogy with Sweetie in it." She pointed to the manuscript of *Doors*.

"Oh, surely she wouldn't try it on again, miss," said Wiggins, downing half of his drink.

"Why not? She got away with it once, didn't she?"

Melrose looked at Jury. "What are you going to do about it?"

Jury smiled. "I'm afraid it isn't a case for the CID."

"When her second book comes out, it will be," said Ellen.

13

The door of the shop on Aliceanna Street was flanked by cinder blocks doing service as planters for some frostbitten poinsettias probably left over from the Christmas rush. Although a rush at the shop on Aliceanna Street would have been a surprise, given the crowded assortment of objects in the window, in which hung a blue neon half-moon, throbbing off and on, along with a cabalistic design underneath it. Together, they gave the impression of a fortune-teller's premises rather than an antique dealer's. In front of this window clutter stood a girl, her face squashed against the glass and framed with both hands, peering in. When she found Melrose standing next to her, she looked around impatiently, and he saw she was quite young, her eyes like currants in a doughy face and with a very unpleasant expression. Interrupted in her survey of the window's contents, she cast him a nasty look and walked off down the pavement.

A bell jangled over the door as Melrose walked into a well of cool shadows. No one was about, although something had stirred the curtain over the door at the back of the shop and set the metal curtain rings clicking. He thought he heard the clatter of crockery from somewhere beyond that drapery, and in the dimness he could distinguish a large bird cage, from which came a sound like claws on sandpaper.

It was not a large room, and it was stuffed—stuffed with small pieces of dark and undistinguished furniture, more secondhand than antique, he would have thought; glassy-looking necklaces and cameo brooches arranged in black velvet trays; racks of vintage clothing; carnival glass and a rather cheap-looking set of willow-patterned china; books, stacks of magazines. From a spill of books on a large oak bookshelf that helped to prop up the old velvets and organdies, Melrose took out one bound in leather the color of winter moss and thick with a gold edging. The pages crackled as he leafed through them. Dark, necromantic symbols and sinister designs of demonlike figures stared back at him. He put that book back and tried another, equally depressing, a story in woodcuts that depicted some poor wretch's progress up a rocky promontory with a sack on his back.

The walls, from which portraits of two censorious women (sisters, surely) looked down, hugging their prayerbooks to their chests and wearing lace mittens, dripped curses and benedictions: nasty looking African masks hung between old prints of pale saints, their heads ringed in milky aureoles. A plaster Virgin Mary in faded blue seemed unaware of the fat cherubs playfully dragging at her gown and apparently trying to call her from her matins.

On a mahogany desk lit by a green glass-globed floor lamp were a stereopticon, some slides, and a small pamphlet, ribbon-tied. This was a souvenir booklet—or so it announced itself—of the St. James Hotel, on Charles Street. There was a picture of that hotel on the front.

Melrose read the introduction, written by the St. James's then-manager, a Mr. Adams, who had taken some care to detail the many pleasant hours that awaited the visitor to the St. James Hotel. Mr. Adams's prose was languid, almost British in its wordiness, as though he were in no special hurry to survey the many advantages of staying in his hotel.

To help the guests in their visit to Baltimore, Mr. Adams had thoughtfully included photos of points of interest in the city. One could stroll through the booklet's text and pictures, stopping here at Druid Hill Park, there at Monument Square, in strangely untrafficked places, when one thought of the vast crowds now to be seen in Harborplace. A tiny ensemble of people against the snowbank of Monument Square and a child with a hoop on the corner.

There were pictures of the lobby and of the dining room, where one could obtain dinner with wine for one dollar. And a room for a dollar and a half.

Melrose took some change from his pocket. He looked at the several quarters, dimes, and nickels. Imagine! For this one could stay at the St. James Hotel. One could have a complete meal with wine!

He picked up the stereopticon and wiped it and the dusty brown pictures with his handkerchief. Then he inserted one in front of the shovel-like lens. A railway station, the old Baltimore and Ohio station, sprang into three-dimensional relief. A little group of four—no, five—people had either just got off the train or were about to board it.

He slotted in another picture and saw a hansom cab carrying several people—it might even have been the same group—along the cobbled street, the station now in the far distance.

Next there was a shot of a wide lobby, potted palms against pillars and another little band of people, who might easily have been guests at the

St. James, he thought; they might have come, pleasantly full, from their one-dollar table d'hôte dinner.

Had these old pictures been arranged to tell a sort of tale? Or was the story purely accidental, the order supplied by himself? The point, he thought, was an important one, although he didn't know why.

Yet he wanted to join the little group, to pick up his bag, climb into the cab, feel the wheels' rackety progress over the cobbles, and find himself, together with the others, disgorged from the cab into this well of sunshine that lay across the pavement in front of the St. James. The six of them would walk through its cool lobby up to the desk, where Mr. Adams would greet them cordially and hand each a ribbon-tied souvenir.

Then down to the dining room. Half the tables would be full, and all would be white-clothed. There would be a broth to start, followed by a roast. He enjoyed his new companions' conversation, though he could not hear what he or they said to one another. In the silence, curtains billowed, lips moved, waitresses darted—

He came out of this fugue to see that although he still held the stereopticon, he had not replaced the last picture, so that he was looking through the shovellike holder at the face of a girl who seemed to have sprung up in all of her dimensions in the same way as the station, the horse and cab, the people. Her face was caught in the latticework of shadows created by the effect of a lighted wall sconce.

"Oh. Hullo," he said to her, embarrassed he'd been caught dreaming.

"I put those that way," she said.

What was she talking about? Ah, the photographs. So the question was answered; the arrangement hadn't been random.

She was standing at his side, fingering the pictures. "The ones who got off the train look like the ones in the hotel. She's wearing this hat." The girl slotted a picture into the wire holder and held it up for Melrose's inspection.

Melrose frowned. Was he to validate this child's fantasy? To appease her, he sighed and looked through the stereopticon. "Well, but how can you be sure they got *off* the train? Maybe they're *waiting* for one." Oh, good lord, why was he arguing?

"Because," she said patiently, "their suitcases are already on the cart."

Annoyed with himself for not noticing this clue, he refused to verify it as he looked into the three-dimensional past. She was under twenty-one, which put her in the child category, that group from which one could exact intelligence only after gummy bears had changed hands. Reluctantly, he abandoned the stereopticon, and with it the past, to set about getting his information. No one else was about, so it would have to be this child.

She must have been left in charge, for she asked him if he was looking for something particular.

"Yes—books," he said. "First editions."

She walked over to a bookcase and stood before it. "Here are some old ones." Her face was peaked, her expression sad, perhaps from cohabitation with grim reminders of hellfire and the almost equally unattractive prospect of heaven, given the pallid look of the saint in the tarnished frame above the bookcase, who certainly didn't appear to be looking forward to the place beyond the ceiling toward which his eyes were raised.

"These look a bit newer than what I want," said Melrose, fingering the cracked bindings. "Actually, I deal in old manuscripts. I don't expect you have any?"

"Are you English?"

"Yes. How did you guess?"

"From the way you talk."

"It's a dead giveaway, isn't it?"

"Yes."

He wished she'd stop answering his rhetorical questions. She must be awfully literal. He opened a copy of an Arthur Rackham–illustrated version of *Peter Pan*. The cover was shabby and the endpapers spattered, but the pictures were lovely: fairies flitting about in the faded blue and pearl-gray dawn or dusk of Kensington Gardens.

"That's my favorite book."

"It's very nice. I'm more interested in American writers, though."

"I was in England once . . . I think," she added meditatively.

"You mean you're not sure?" He wished she'd stick to the subject.

She positioned herself where she could see the open book in his hands. "This looks familiar."

"That's a statue of Peter Pan."

"Maybe I dreamed it."

The macaw chose this moment to squawk. It sounded like "Eh-more."

"Be quiet," she said to it, quite sharply.

"You mean it's alive? I could have sworn it was stuffed."

The damned bird, awakened now to the fact of its own life, decided to celebrate itself with a squawking iteration of "Eh-more," which was apparently the sum and substance of its vocabulary. It preened, flapped its wings, danced along its perch to the sound of "Eh-moreehmoremoreehor." Did it think that would excite someone into giving it a biscuit? Not even the cat was interested. It slumbered away on its camouflage of rags and pillows, only mildly disturbed when the girl pulled a large square of material out from under it and set about draping the blood-red shawl part-way over the cage. "If I don't do this, he'll just keep it up. It's supposed to be saying 'Nevermore,' but all it can get out is the 'more' part. One of my aunt's friends tried to teach it. I wish he'd just left it alone."

Melrose decided that the girl was, after all, quite sensible, if that was her verdict on the silly business of teaching birds to talk. "Is this your aunt's shop, then?"

"Yes, but she's gone to the store." She turned to a rack of old jackets and gowns and outmoded frocks and wedding clothes. There was a stiff, white wedding dress, folds creaking with age. These, he supposed, were euphemistically termed "vintage clothing." She took a dark green velvet gown from a hanger and held it up to her small frame, inspecting herself in the mirror.

"And when will she return, do you know?"

"Not for hours. It's her shopping day. I'm in charge." She had turned to look at the sweep of the skirt. "Does this look like Scarlett O'Hara?"

"Not particularly. Look, have you any old manuscripts?"

In her *Gone with the Wind* mood, she wasn't interested in old manuscripts. Perhaps, he thought, seeing her slight scowl, he should have told her yes, she bore a strong resemblance to Scarlett O'Hara. Actually, observing her closely, as if he were again gazing through the stereopticon, there *was* a resemblance, for she had very dark hair and a slightly tilted nose. Her eyes were an unusual shade of brown, something like the color of the Russian amber necklace he had seen on the jewelry tray. He picked up a dark green bonnet and stuck it on her head. "Now you do. Look like Scarlett, I mean. If you tie that ribbon under your chin."

The hat was much too big and nearly engulfed her face, but she seemed to think this was a grand idea and tied the velvet ribbon in a bow.

The several long-casement clocks started chiming, each coming in a split second after the other, and she said, "It's time for tea. We always have tea mid-morning. I guess you want some because you're English. I'll be back after I put the kettle on, in a minute."

He took the minute to inspect the inside of the lid of the trunk she had opened. But lightning doesn't strike twice.

In a very short while she was back, still wearing the bonnet, rooting through another of the several trunks stationed around the shop. Over the top of the raised lid were draped various garments of white—or what had once been white—linen and lace. She picked out a blouse and tried it on over her T-shirt.

Why, he wondered, was he bothering to be so circumspect in his questions? It wasn't as if she had any reason to be on guard. As she was putting a green jacket on over her jumper, he said to her, "Someone told me that a very important manuscript was found in a trunk here. By accident, by one of your customers."

She became suddenly very still, as she turned away from him, buttoning up the green jacket.

"Very valuable," he repeated. He thought, seeing her reflection in the mirror, that her face looked white and drained.

She shrugged her apparent indifference to the turn this conversation had taken.

He did not think she was indifferent. "Did you happen to see this trunk?"

"Yes." A larger silence drew out, and then she said, "She's dead."

A kettle screamed. Melrose started.

"I'll get the tea," she called back as she rushed from the room.

The macaw, which had been in a flurry of excitement when the kettle whistled away, had jostled the shawl part-way from the cage. Now, seeing there was only Melrose left to entertain him, it dozed on its perch. A dish of little white biscuits sat on a plant stand beside the cage, and Melrose pinched one up and through the open cage door. The bird ignored the proffered biscuit and the door to freedom. If the only thing on the other side of a cage was Melrose Plant, it might as well stick to its perch.

"Suit yourself," said Melrose and turned to the cat, who shivered himself awake, arching his back and yawning widely. He sniffed at the biscuit and recoiled himself on the cushions.

Once more she was returning, this time balancing two mugs and a teapot on a tray; a bowl of sugar and a jug of milk sat beside them. There was also a plate with lemon slices, cakes, and stacked-up biscuits. The cakes were round and thick with icing and coconut; the biscuits were chocolate with creamy centers.

"What," Melrose asked, conversationally, "is your name?"

She answered, "Jip," in a flat tone, as if she'd rather not have answered him at all. They were silent for a moment as she offered the sugar, which he spooned out, and the lemon, which he refused, pouring out a bit of milk instead.

"Well. Mine's Melrose. How do you do?"

Unhappily, he thought, she drank her tea, her deep golden-brown eyes regarding him over the rim of the cup. "Jip. That's an interesting name. What's it a nickname for?" For he assumed that it was.

"Nothing. It's just Jip."

Her expressive face was now solemn, as if she too knew it did not sound like a real name, like a name one would be likely to find on any birth certificate. Was it possible, he wondered, that she did not know her real name? Her face, under the fold of the ridiculous wings of her bonnet, was woeful. She replaced the biscuit and yanked off the hat. Play-time was over. Or something was over.

"It's probably a patronym," said Melrose, taking a seat in a very low old chair with a cushion through which you could see the shape of the springs.

In the process of licking the icing from another biscuit, she stopped. She frowned. "A what?"

"Oh, you know," he said breezily, "the Russian thing. You find it in the Russian novels. Patronyms. They have this affectionate way of referring to people. I have one. A patronym, I mean." Oh, why was he saying this? He hadn't any name at all except Melrose. His parents hadn't even given him a middle name. He became unreasonably irritated by this. Why couldn't they have named him Melrose Fyodorovitch? A middle name—several middle names—might have come in handy in the circumstances.

"What is it?"

"Melrovitch." He cleared his throat. "You see it's rather like, say, Petrovitch for Peter; or Anna Petrovna, say." He smiled and consulted the biscuit-plate. "And then there's the diminutive. In my case it's Mel-shi. What are these?"

But she didn't for a second seem to hear him. She was holding the two halves of her biscuit aloft, one piece in each hand, staring at him. "Mel-shi," she said. Then she answered his question: "Oreos and Snowballs."

"Did you make them?"

"No. They're store-bought."

Melrose selected one of the round, white cakes, thickly covered with gluey white frosting and shreds of coconut. One bite was enough. He set it down on the rim of a plate holding a selection of antique coins.

"Go on. About the names," she said.

He scratched his head. "Of course, you're probably not Russian—are you? There are many people who aren't but who have these patronyms and diminutives. Although, as I said, you do find most of them in Tolstoy. Or Dostoyevsky."

She watched him closely as she licked the icing from her Oreo.

Melrose had decided long ago that if you were in deep, the only thing to do was go deeper. "I once knew—well, he was my very best friend really—a Russian named Alexei. But the diminutive was Alyosha." Jip was leaning back against the rack of old clothes. The stiff white gown rustled. "I was at his wedding. He was quite wealthy; it was a huge wedding. I got a piece of white cake in a small white satin box—"

"I thought it was only ladies got that."

"Not in Russia. In Russia it's the men. In Russia, the men need the luck more."

She nodded and divided another biscuit.

Absently, Melrose was turning the plate full of foreign coins beside his mug of tea. "But when I opened this box I found not a piece of wedding cake but a ruble and a note all folded up. It was a note telling me . . . no, *warning* me, to leave, uh, Leningrad right away and go to—" His eye fell on a stack of old postcards; one was of the Rockettes kicking out lustily, old babies in satin diapers, and he thought of the graceful Georgian dancers. "—to Georgia. Yes, I was to leave Leningrad and go to Georgia." He tried to think of some reason for the ruble's being in the box but couldn't.

"Atlanta?"

"What?"

"Were you supposed to go to Atlanta or where?"

"No, no. I mean Georgia. The *Russian* Georgia."

She nodded and set down the now-denuded biscuit beside the first one, also icing-less, and picked up another. He looked at the Snowball and continued: "It was winter." The rack of clothes swayed behind Jip as she nestled into it. There was a ratty old fur coat behind the white gown. "I was provided with warm clothes and a sleigh. I seem to remember the coat I was given was Russian sable." Looking into her Russian amber eyes, he wondered, should there be a woman in this sleigh?

"Who gave you the sleigh and stuff? Was it Alyosha?"

"Yes." Ah, good! She was providing the background herself. "He was wealthy."

"You told me." She pressed the two halves of the licked biscuit together and replaced it on the glass plate. She took another from the stack. "Go on."

"You have no idea how deep the snow was. Great mounds of it everywhere." Melrose could almost feel the heavy, wet, fat flakes on his face. "It fell in . . . droves. We travelled for three days and three nights." Things always happened in threes in stories.

"We?"

He had forgotten to add The Woman.

"A friend of Alyosha. A woman."

"You met her at the wedding, I guess. Do you want more tea?"

"Yes, thanks." She was an excellent audience. As the fresh teabag plopped into his cup and she added water from the pot, tepid by now, he went on. "She was Alyosha's sister."

"What was her name?"

"Julie." Where had that come from? "Julie" didn't sound Russian. This was pointed out to him. "She doesn't sound very Russian."

"Her mother was British."

"But she's Alyosha's *sister*. So she must be Russian, too."

"His half-sister," said Melrose briskly. "But she's—I mean, she *had* been living in Russia her entire life. Is it important? She was stunningly beautiful. Her hair was very dark, and her eyes were like . . . the color of sand at sunset. In Arabia." His mind drifted off to smooth and endless golden dunes, the red sun sinking behind them. . . .

She prompted him. "You and this Julie—then what happened?"

Both to stall for time and to ease his back, Melrose rose from the broken-springed chair and moved to some shelves containing bits and bobs of clothing—scarves, gloves, squashed-looking women's hats.

"Well? Go on."

Melrose poked his hand into a white fake-fur muff and thought of Julie. Julie Christie! That was where the name had popped up from! Driving through the snow with that heavily mustached actor in *Dr. Zhivago*. "Julie was wearing a cape with a hood outlined in ermine. She had a muff. There was a gun concealed in it." He looked out of the corner of his eye to see how this news was being received.

Fairly well, for she had stopped eating and wore an expression of mild alarm.

"You see, Julie was running away from the KGB. Or what had been the KGB. Things have improved now," he added vaguely.

"What did Julie do? Why were they chasing her?"

"They claimed she'd killed—your telephone's ringing."

She looked over her shoulder. "It's just for my aunt." As if she were pursuing a line of thought apart from Melrose's, she added, "She's not my real aunt."

"Oh? Then how did you come to acquire her?"

Enough of real life. "Who did Julie kill?"

"The husband of a woman very high up in the government. Madame Vronsky. That's who she was accused of killing, at least. No one was sure. Except she trusted me enough to tell me the truth. Naturally, it was a dark secret. But she knew she could trust me." He looked down to see his hands were still in the muff. He was glad no one had come into the shop.

"So did they catch her?"

"No. But you're getting ahead of my story," he added, rather too impatiently, considering he himself was so far *behind* he had no idea what these Russians were up to.

"You still haven't said why Alyosha told you you had to get out of— where was it?"

Where? Oh, yes. "Leningrad. That was only clear to me much later. Don't jump ahead so much." Melrose rubbed his forehead. In his mind's eye he could picture it: the great frozen wastes; a line of black trees, the beginning of a wood, across the horizon; the purple shadows. Was it dawn or dusk? A band of pale pink hung like a scarf above the distant trees. And he saw himself (and Julie) gliding along in the sleigh over the silent snow, as the sun slowly rose. And then, looking at the pavonine splashes of light thrown by the green and blue insets in the shop windows, he thought, But this is wonderful! And he thought of Joanna the Mad, sitting there in the Jack and Hammer and talking of the job of writing as completely mechanical. Ah, surely she was wrong. It had nothing to do with the hard, greasy machinery of life. Oh, it was work, yes, but the work of gathering dews in a teacup or riveting stars to the moon.

"Well, *that's* glory for you!" he exclaimed.

"Huh?"

Melrose had forgotten momentarily where he was. "Sorry. Just a little Alice in Wonderland. I got carried away."

He got up to stretch and visit a small cupboard of what appeared to be brightly colored and carved little animals. He picked up one painted as brilliantly as the macaw with a long snout and shingled tail. Armadillo? Iguana?

"We drove in the sleigh for what seemed days, but of course was only a few hours. Suddenly, the horses whinnied and stopped. Something had slithered across their path. I just caught a glimpse of something very small, running. It had a tail."

"A rat? Baltimore gets a lot of rats."

"No," said Melrose. "This is Georgia in Russia we're talking about."

"I guess there are rats in Russia."

"Look, I said it *wasn't* a rat."

She nodded.

He replaced the armadillo or iguana. "Julie grabbed my arm and said we might have just seen one of the fabled *trotskitoskis* of the Russian steppes. They are a sort of animal, something like a small fox, said to bring luck to anyone whose path they cross. 'Trots' for short."

"Did the trot bring you luck?"

Melrose was pleased with himself for having thought up the trot. "Wait and see."

"I have to wait and see about everything."

He had to admit, his story was laden with detail. But wasn't that what it was all about? He frowned. He wasn't sure. Ellen's story had practically *no* details except a few pieces of furniture and this Sweetie person waiting for a letter to slip through the door. He stood idly fingering the old lace and satin and tulle gowns, heavy with pearl insets and tiny, iciclelike beads and wondered if his story was too heavily embroidered, too weighty with ornament.

"Anyone at the ball could have been the dreadful Madame Vronsky."

Her eyes opened wide. "*What* ball?"

"The fancy dress ball."

"You didn't say there was a fancy dress ball."

In his mind, he had seen the sleigh pull up at a huge stone mansion from which music floated. Balalaikas. Clear as crystal. "Sorry. Well, it was going on when our sleigh pulled up at the house. A big house."

"Have you got to Georgia by now?" She seemed very forgiving of his springing this ball on her, especially as it followed on the heels of the trot.

"No. We were near the steppes."

"Of the house?"

"No, no. The Russian steppes. You know." Of course she didn't; neither did he. That was Siberia, anyway, wasn't it?

"This house was very grand. It had its own stables, even its own chapel. Julie slipped away from the ball, evading Rudolf—he was one of the sons of this wealthy family, and she was having a bad time of it with him. He was actually a *count* and she was engaged to him. But she didn't want to marry him. Anyway, she told me she had slipped away from him and that she had to meet someone outside by the chapel. I stood on the terrace watching as her white cloak disappeared around the little path that circled the chapel." Melrose heard the dozen long-case clocks chime. It was eleven o'clock! He'd been here well over an hour. "And that's when I heard the shot."

Jip jumped slightly. "What shot? What happened?"

"Rudolf had followed her. He shot Julie."

"*No!*" In her distress she upset the plate of Oreos. Her tone was full of bitter disappointment when she said, "That's not *fair.*"

"Life," said Melrose sententiously, "isn't fair. That's just in books." But her face had paled so much and her amber eyes were full of such distress, he added quickly, "She didn't *die*, for heaven's sake."

Jip turned her head and the colors of the Tiffany shade washed over her hair. She put the hat back on, as if she wanted the big brim to hide her. Then she lowered her head, pleated her skirt with her fingers. Her voice, when she spoke, sounded strained. "I thought it was like that girl in the churchyard."

The mood had changed considerably. Perhaps it was simply the fact of the unseen dangers that one had to face that upset her. "The girl in the churchyard." He sat down again and asked for another cup of tea. "I understand someone visits the grave of Edgar Allan Poe every year. And takes brandy or champagne and some flowers."

She nodded. The big hat seemed too heavy now for her head. "My aunt thinks he's crazy. I don't think he is. I think it's very nice to visit somebody's grave and drink champagne. It means you're not forgotten." Her tone and glance suggested she herself might have been.

"It certainly does," said Melrose. "It certainly does. Though Poe would not be forgotten, anyway, would he? Because of his writing."

"It's not the same." She picked up her cup, didn't drink, set it down. "What happened to Julie?"

"She married a corsair. They live in Minsk. This trunk that the young woman purchased—did you ever look inside the trunk after Beverly Brown bought it?"

"But she was shot!"

"Not fatally. Did you look inside the trunk?"

She chewed her lip, debating her answer. "Will you tell anyone?" She had risen to lift the shawl from the bird cage. *Squawk.*

"Tell? No. I can keep a secret." Melrose was sure that she knew something.

"No, you can't."

"What?"

She resat herself and inspected the small pillar of ruined Oreo biscuits. "You weren't supposed to tell anyone Julie's secret."

Julie's secret? What was—oh, drat! He searched for an explanation for his betrayal of Julie. "Not while she was *alive,* I wasn't."

"She is. She married somebody and lives in Minsk."

Melrose racked his brain. Then he smiled. "Not she, *Julie*—she, Madame *Vronsky.* Whose husband Julie killed accidentally. Probably Julie worried that Madame Vronsky might seek revenge." How he could pull chestnuts out of the fire!

Jip appeared to be chewing this bit of information over with one of the discarded chocolate biscuits.

And Melrose returned to the secret he had sworn himself to keep. "Tell me about this trunk."

Suspicion of his methods seemed to fight with regard for this romantic stranger. "I wasn't supposed to look in it, but I did. It was full of old clothes like petticoats and blouses that were stained, and a lot of them torn. Why would anyone want them, I wonder? There were just a lot of old clothes and some sheets and stuff and a few books."

"Did you see this so-called Poe story in it?"

She frowned. "I don't remember. There were pages of writing, and old books that looked like the sort we keep records in—" here she looked back towards the counter—"but I don't remember anything else." She shrugged.

Jip didn't seem to feel there was anything odd in his asking all these questions about Beverly Brown and the suspect manuscript. "And she took the trunk and all of its contents?"

She nodded. "What I wonder is, why didn't she just take all the stuff out of the trunk if the trunk was what she wanted. It took her and the cab driver and me to carry it out to her car, it was so heavy. Why did she leave all the old clothes in it? A lot of people have bought trunks and they just ask to take the stuff out. It's the trunk they want."

"That's an excellent point." Unless you didn't know what story you were going to tell about exactly where this manuscript was located. Melrose got up from his bench. "I must go, Jip. I shall be late for my appointment."

As she herself rose, she asked, "But what about Julie? You never finished."

"Ah, yes. Well, don't worry. I'll return and finish the story."

"Tomorrow?"

"I'll try, yes."

"You're forgetting your book!" she called after him.

That old thing. He went back to the counter, collected the volume she'd wrapped, and as the little bell jangled when he opened the door, he heard the cry behind him: "Eh-more."

He wondered what would have happened to poor Poe's career if he'd chosen a macaw instead of a raven.

14

Melrose returned to his room at the Admiral Fell Inn to collect his *Strangers' Guide* and his copy of *Windows* and then went in search of a cab. He was not to meet Ellen at Hopkins until around two, and he thought he might as well do a little sightseeing. Jury was in Philadelphia, and Wiggins was roaming around at the Johns Hopkins Medical Center, probably getting inoculated.

No cabs passed. Finally, he came upon a black one sitting at the corner, the cabbie reading a newspaper and smoking a cigarette. Melrose tapped on the windowpane with his walking stick and the cabbie rolled down the window and squinted out at him.

"Yo."

"Are you off duty?"

"Just reading the sports. Where you want to go?"

"Actually, I have an hour or more and I'd like to see Baltimore. I thought perhaps I could do it by cab. Do you have a spare hour or two?" Melrose checked his watch. "I don't have to be at my destination until one-thirty or two. Johns Hopkins. That would be my last stop."

"Okay by me. I just flip on the old meter and away we go."

Melrose asked, as he positioned himself in the rear seat, "You're familiar with Baltimore, I expect?"

The cabbie snorted and pulled away from the curb. "Been hacking for thirty years, buddy. If I ain't now, I never will be." He wrenched his neck around to regard Melrose over his outflung arm. "You ain't from around here. I can tell by the accent."

"British."

"Thought so. I never been to England. Always wanted to go. I got a cousin lives over there. In Cornwall. You been to Cornwall?"

"Oh, yes. It's beautiful." Melrose pulled out Ellen's book and sat back. His plan to continue with *Windows* as they drove along was very soon nipped in the bud by the cabbie, who started talking about himself and told Melrose his name was Hugh, "but everybody calls me Hughie."

Hughie was a square, squat man with a round, rather shiny face partly hidden by a cap of black and green plaid with ear flaps. His quilted shirt was of a similar material. Melrose was very soon apprised of Hughie's hacking history, the number in Hughie's large family, and their whereabouts across the United States from the Dakotas to Wilmington, Delaware. There was even a cousin who lived in England. The tour was turning out to be a voyage around Hughie.

"Lives in some little place called Mousehole. It's on the water."

"I've heard it's charming."

"I seen pictures. Always wanted to go. Which part you from?"

"Northamptonshire. About a hundred miles northwest of London."

"Guess I never heard of that. No, I lived in Baltimore, man and boy, fifty-nine years."

Melrose smiled at the pronunciation. But it was all part of the same thing, wasn't it? Constant usage had worn the sharp edges from the syllables, eliding "Bal-ti-more" to "Bawlmer" and "Mousehole" to "Mowsel."

"You couldn't do better than me. Been hacking for a good thirty of them fifty-nine years." He proceeded to bring Melrose up to date on most of those fifty-nine years. His wife was dead; his daughter lived in Towson.

"What's that monument, there?" They were driving along Pratt Street, and Melrose craned his neck, watching it go past his window.

"That? Naw, you don't want to see that. There's lots better along Fayette Street."

"Perhaps, but we aren't on Fayette Street," said Melrose, quickly flicking through his *Strangers' Guide.* He could not find whatever they had just passed.

"You got your Aquarium, you got your Harborplace, you got your H. L. Mencken house, your Babe Ruth birthplace—I guess everybody's heard of the Babe. He's the only player in baseball history ever got an intentional walk with the bases loaded. Then there's Lexington Market. And you got to see the new ballpark at Camden Yards. Man, what a stadium! One hundred million bucks that cost, that's what I heard. Orioles play there. There'll be a new football stadium, too, if we ever get the fucking franchise. Excuse the French. We oughta be in line for it. Hey, there's your Aquarium! You gotta go in there. We could stop, you want to."

Melrose said no, not today, and Hughie shrugged. Then he pointed out the ship docked on the far side. "Now, that's your USF *Constitution.* First ship ever in the U.S. Navy, and fought in the Revolutionary War. You ought to go on board it sometime."

As they turned up Charles Street, Melrose leafed quickly through his guide in earnest. The tranquil ship they had just passed wasn't the *Constitution* but the *Constellation*. And it wasn't the Revolutionary War but the Civil War in which it had seen action. He started to say something, but Hughie was now on the subject of the last presidential election.

At the top of Charles Street, Hughie pulled over and parked in the square, where one of the monuments he considered worth seeing sat. Monument Square, Hughie told him it was called. It was a pretty, well-kept little square and the monument to George Washington sat in the center of it. "First monument to George in the U.S. of A. This was before the one in D.C." General Washington stood atop a beautiful marble shaft. "Over two hundred steps, but a great view of the city. You want to go up? I'll wait."

Melrose declined; he was too busy checking out Hughie's information. It was correct—so far. They both stood looking upwards at the statue, where the sculptor had depicted Washington in the act of signing or handing over something.

Hughie said in a rather reverential tone, "Signing the Declaration of Independence." He stamped his foot hard, several times, on the ground. "There's a couple hundred Civil War soldiers buried right here in this quarter-acre."

Melrose was riffling the pages. "Wait a minute. You're confusing Washington and Jefferson, aren't you? And are you sure you don't mean the *Revolutionary* War?"

Hughie mumbled something about hair-splitting, and they both climbed back into the cab.

"But the monument," said Melrose, determined to explode this mine of misinformation, "is to General *Washington.*"

"You got it," said Hughie cheerfully as he slammed down on the gear shift. "Where to now?"

"Westminster Church." Melrose sighed.

As they drove on towards the church, Hughie started talking about Napoleon's brother. "Married a Baltimore gal, no kidding."

Napoleon's brother. Melrose's finger itched for a gun.

"Got his button caught in her lace dress. I wonder—" Hughie was driving with his arm slung across the back of the seat, and now he turned his head and added "—where the button was." He laughed hysterically, just managing to veer out of the way of a huge semi.

The driver of the big truck, a black man about the size of the Redskins' wide receiver, leaned on his horn, which only prompted Hughie to roll down his window and yell, "Get a life, asshole!"—which further incited the truck driver to mouth, from behind his own window, "FUCK YOU."

Now, having improved road and race relations, Hughie aimed to run a yellow light like a charging bull as it turned red.

He grumbled about the drivers, about the glutted Baltimore streets, about hacking in general. "Aw, it's a job," he exclaimed with disgust, with a wave towards Melrose in the back, as if Melrose had been arguing with him. "So what do *you* do?" he asked.

" 'Do'?"

"Yeah. For a living. You don't mind my saying it, you sure don't look like you're hurting." He was half turned in his seat as the cab idled at the next light, giving Melrose's cashmere coat, his silk scarf, his Egyptian cotton shirt the once-over.

"I'm one of the idle rich."

Hughie laughed. "Hey, lucky you, right? You got one of them stately homes my cousin says she's always touring through?"

"Yes." He turned the page of his *Strangers' Guide*, following the little family in their walk round Monument Square. They hadn't been much help.

"You a lord or a duke or one of them? You got a title?"

"Well, 'lord' isn't really a title; it's more of a form of address. But I am one, yes. Or used to be." Ordinarily, Melrose avoided this subject of his orphaned titles, but he thought Hughie would get a kick out of it.

"Naaaaaw! You're pulling my leg."

"No. Earl of Caverness, that's me. And Viscount Ardry, and other things to boot. But I gave them up, the titles." He snapped shut his book, watched the panoply of crowded little shops going by.

"No kidding?" There was a brief silence while Hughie mulled this over. "So how come you gave them up?"

"Oh. Didn't want a title, I expect." Melrose was sorry he'd brought it up.

Hughie chortled. "You afraid your relatives will ice you?"

"I beg your pardon?"

"See, I'm kind of a student of history. These Delawares, what happened was, the nephew murdered one of his uncles to get the title, and it turns out the asshole, pardon my French, kills the *wrong uncle*. Can you beat that?" Hughie laughed uproariously. "Well, I guess that kind of thing happens all the time over there."

"I don't think so. Where is Westminster Church, anyway?"

"Not far. Listen, you know what happened there—I mean, near Poe's grave?" Melrose said he didn't. "Girl was murdered a week ago. Christ. Can you feature it?"

"I believe I read about it."

"Black kid, Hopkins student. Probably raped, but the cops, they don't tell you much."

Melrose wondered if he might actually know something helpful. "What *did* they—?"

But Hughie, never topic-less, was on to another. He said, again over his shoulder, "I just remembered: you seen *Diner*?"

"Seen what?"

"It's a movie. *Diner.* You want to know about Baltimore, you should see it. This guy, this director, he's from Baltimore, and he's made these movies all about it. *Tin Men* is the second one. *Diner*'s got Mickey Rourke in it. Danny DeVito, he's in *Tin Men.* It's all about aluminum-siding guys—you know, how they sell it and all."

"Sounds exciting," said Melrose, turning a page of *Windows.*

"It's a trilogy. What's the third one?" Hughie hit his palm against the wheel in an effort of remembrance. "The hell's that last one? Anyway, this director's got a real thing about Baltimore. What's his name?" Hughie was mumbling to himself.

Melrose sighed. Another trilogy. Life was taking on a definite tri-ad-ish look.

Westminster Church was a not-very-attractive pile of brown bricks located on a corner near the vast Lexington Market. Its little graveyard lacked that sense of the past to be found in English churchyards. Here there were no listing gravestones bound with vines or trailing ivy, no mounds fattened with spongy mosses.

Although there was a handsome monument to Edgar Allan Poe near the front of the churchyard, the actual gravesite was located down the path and near the back. It was here that Melrose and Hughie stood looking down at the slightly sunken ground and the grave bedecked with a bouquet of plastic pink flowers. Where, Melrose wondered, were the roses? He thought it a bit sad.

"Avalon!" said Hughie suddenly, snapping his fingers.

"What?"

"That movie. You know, the one I was trying to think of. The third movie by that director that I can't remember his name. *Avalon* is his third one. See, it was all about this family of immigrants—I guess that was the director's family, maybe his granddad and so forth."

"Avalon was the island limbo of King Arthur," said Melrose.

"That what it is over there? Well, over here it's a movie."

As Hughie filled him in on the history of the immigrant family, Melrose studied the poet's grave and wondered about Beverly Brown. He turned and walked slowly back down the path that led around the church and to Poe's monument. Hughie followed, talking all the while. Finished with his movie-trilogy commentary, he would now treat Melrose to a helping of his forensic genius. "That kid that got killed must've been lying here," said Hughie, spreading his arms to measure off a segment of pavement near the white marble monument. "See that gutter there? That's where they found the body." He encased his thick neck in his two hands to simulate the act of strangulation.

"Why here?" asked Melrose, more of himself than of Hughie.

"Maybe she wanted a peek at the oddball that brings the flowers and champagne. Every year, on the guy's birthday." He nodded toward the monument, indicating Poe. "January nineteenth. Who knows? Maybe it was the oddball offed her." The hands went around the throat again.

"That's unlikely. What motive would he have?"

"Yeah." Hughie scratched his neck. "You want to see Lexington Market? Biggest market in the East."

"Another time, perhaps." It was still early, not yet one o'clock, but Melrose had had enough touring for one day. "I have to meet someone at Johns Hopkins."

Outside Gilman Hall, Melrose tipped Hughie generously. "I enjoyed that more than I can say."

"Hey, no problem. Any place you want to go while you're here, just give me a jingle." Hughie jotted his number on a scrap of paper. "I'll be hanging out in Fells Point, anyway, same place."

"If I want a guide, I'll know where to find one."

"Right. And you can toss that thing away." Hughie nodded towards Melrose's guide book.

"Absolutely." Melrose saw a dustbin a few feet away and threw it in.

"Yo. See you around." Hughie manhandled the steering wheel, reversed, and spat up a bucket of gravel. Arm out the window, he called back a farewell and started down the drive. Two students jumped and dropped their books.

Melrose waved and moved over to the rubbish bin. A girl in a sort of Indian wrap stood and watched him as he rooted through the debris for his *Strangers' Guide.* "I dropped this," he said, smiling.

The look that followed him from under her dark, Groucho Marx–ish eyebrows was unbelieving and disdainful. Tramps on campus.

15

"Philip?"

The young woman's eyes widened behind glasses unsuitably large for her delicate, triangular face. Backlit by the light of the wall sconces, her hair was like transparent gold.

He'd been lucky. She was the first person he'd come across in the Barnes Foundation, apart from the guard at the end of the driveway and the lady in the cubicle at the entrance taking tickets and seeming to wish that she weren't so engaged.

She shifted her stack of books from one arm to the other and repeated the name: "Philip?"

Jury was also lucky that the girl standing now before him appeared friendly; his impression thus far was that the Barnes Foundation had opened its doors to the public only under extreme duress and would be perfectly happy to slam them shut again, even in the face of Scotland Yard. The hours (he'd noticed) were very rigid, as were the rules. No Spiked Heels Permitted! He had mused over this.

"Philip." The third time it was not a question but a statement, a sad one, the way she said it; she said it slowly, as if she were tasting the name, straining after a memory, an exact place and time to fit it to. Or was he simply being overimaginative? Could one invest a name with all of that meaning? It might have been her expression, then—more wistful, even, than her voice.

"Philip Calvert worked here, I understand," said Jury.

She dropped her eyes to the several heavy books. "He did, yes. Once."

There was such a woeful note of finality in her "once" that Jury hesitated to question her further. He was used enough to having to confront friends and family of the deceased; this girl had that sort of effect on him, and he wondered if she did on others as well—and if people didn't tend to shy away from such a person, one who could make them feel helpless. Yes, he was lucky to have hit, straight off, on someone who knew Philip Calvert, but unlucky she had known him that well, or been that fond of him.

"You wouldn't be Heather, would you?"

That surprised her. "I'm Hester. But how do you know me?"

"From a Lady Cray. Lady Cray lived with Philip's aunt, Mrs. Hamilton. Frances Hamilton."

"Philip used to talk about her—about both of them, yes. But I didn't know them."

"They knew you. *Of* you. Philip talked about you, you see." Jury smiled, hoping this would be good news.

It was. The pale face brightened with mild hints of color—cheeks rosier, eyes a less vapid blue-gray, deepening. "We were good friends." Even the lips, as she smiled, seemed fuller.

"Hester, would you like to have coffee with me? Or is it too near your lunchtime?" Jury checked his watch; it was barely eleven. "Or is it too early for you?"

She shook her head. "I bring sandwiches. I have two today; do you want one?"

Her offer of a sandwich struck him as so unabashedly generous—she didn't know who he was; she hadn't even asked—that his throat constricted. Jury turned away to look up at the wall behind her, which soared upwards, crowded with paintings, as if the person who had acquired them was so intoxicated with each one that he had hung them all feverishly, and with no concern for convention. The effect was overwhelming. Jury was used to the more sober march of carefully spaced, eye-level works, arranged according to artist or period and collected similarly in different rooms. But this wall, shooting twenty feet up, made no distinctions. Goya nearly leaned into van Gogh; Renoir all but stepped on Cézanne; impressionists fought like children for attention. The four walls were awash with paintings. Pulling his eyes away from the riot of colors before him, he said, "Would your sandwiches keep? I'd really like to talk to you about Philip Calvert. I'm from Scotland Yard. A policeman."

"Really?" Her eyes widened. And then she looked hurt. "Oh, I *hope* you'll find out what really happened."

"I intend to." She was the sort of girl you made promises to and then hoped like hell you could keep them.

She returned wearing a bit of lipstick and a coat that looked too lightweight for January. The small, round collar added to the illusion of youth. Jury wondered now whether her relationship with Philip Calvert were a romantic or a sexual one, for she seemed so unsophisticated and artless.

The cafe she took him to was one of those depressingly white ones full of hanging baskets of ferns and spider plants that looked as though they'd drown in one's soup. They both had coffee, and Hester had a Danish pastry.

"When his parents died, he went to England to live with his aunt—Mrs. Hamilton. I think he said she was his only relative. He went to Cambridge and majored—you call it 'reading,' don't you?—he read art history. He had to lie about Cambridge for this job. Experts are barred here. For ten years Phil lived in the U.K., and then he came back to Philadelphia."

"Why did he come back?"

"He didn't want to live in England. His aunt did, though. She loves England."

Jury realized then that Hester wouldn't know the aunt had died. He told her.

She didn't speak for a long time, just kept turning her fork over and over. "I wonder if she died of a broken heart."

Jury was taken aback. Hester sounded as if it wouldn't be difficult.

She told Jury what she knew of Fanny Hamilton. "She kind of planned her life around him. Pinned her hopes on him. I wonder if she was disappointed because he didn't become a great artist or something. She had a lot of money and told him she'd be glad to finance a year in Paris. Do people still think that way? That you have to go to Paris to be an artist?" She sighed. "Phil didn't care about money, though—only art. He *breathed* art."

Jury smiled. "He seems to have found the right place for it, then. I've never seen such an art gallery. Was Barnes rather eccentric about painting?"

She laughed. "About everything, probably. But especially about art. It wasn't until recently you could even get in to see it; I think it's probably the greatest private collection in the world. You mustn't call it a 'museum,' either. It's the Barnes *Foundation.* He wouldn't let in the art experts. He hated them; he hated them telling people how they were supposed to experience art. And in his will, he set down that none of the paintings could be moved—each had to stay just as he put it. He wouldn't let them out on loan or for exhibitions. It's only just recently, after a lot of infighting about the estate, that there's to be an exhibition in Washington. For the Barnes Foundation to permit this—" She shrugged. "It's a real art-world event." Hester sighed. "I think it's nice, really. His collection's so *personal.* No one could tell him what to do. I think it's good to be the type who can just say 'fuck off.' "

She bit into her pastry, and Jury was slightly taken aback to hear the words in Hester's mouth, uttered so matter-of-factly. "Yes, it is good. Wish I could."

"Oh, you probably do, but in a different way."

Jury laughed. He asked about Philip. "Did he paint, then?"

She shook her head in that stern, quick way children often do, so that her hair lifted and swung about her shoulders. It was a darkish blond that would have been an indifferent shade had it not had such a high gloss. It looked polished. "He was happy just to look. I think he knew every single painting in the collection and everything about it. He'd straighten them. If one was the barest millimeter out of alignment, he'd straighten it. Do you know, when I see him in my mind's eye, it's not his face I usually see, it's his back, and he'll have a finger raised to a frame. Barnes would have loved him." Her smile was distant, not meant for Jury. She lifted her fork and set it down again, as if eating caused her uncertainty. "I think he was lucky."

"Lucky?"

"He was just what he wanted to be—I mean, doing what he wanted to do."

"That would be lucky. Not many people do."

"Do you?" she asked.

He was thrown, again, off guard. It was disconcerting. Hester was like one's alter ego. "I don't know. You can get so wrapped up in your work you don't stop to wonder."

"You're really good at it, though." She put down the small wedge of pastry she'd been holding, as if she'd found it wanting.

Jury laughed. "Well, thanks. How can you tell?"

"Look at all the talking I've been doing."

"I appreciate it. Would you tell me what you know about his death?" He hoped the question wasn't too harsh.

But she was very matter-of-fact. "He has a cabin up north. It isn't much, just a big room with a kitchen and a bed and a wood-burning stove. But he never did need very much. Just the basics, as they say. I hate the phrase, but it fit Phil."

Jury thought it probably fit Hester, too.

"Maybe that's why he liked me," she said, musing with unselfconscious candor. "We used to drive up there weekends in his Jeep. I wasn't with him that last time, of course. I can't tell you what happened. I only know what the police told me. That he was shot. That it might have been an attempted robbery."

"You look as if you don't agree."

She studied the tendril of a spider plant and answered, "Well, you'd sort of have to see the place to know. Have you seen it?"

Jury shook his head.

"You know it's mine, now?"

Jury was surprised. "No. He left it to you?"

She nodded, pleased. "See, there was only his aunt. At first, I was surprised that Phil had made a will. I mean, he was only twenty-seven. But he was a very tidy person, no loose ends. He was—composed. And he was very thoughtful, always."

"I'd like to see it, the cabin. I have to see the sheriff up there, anyway."

Her response was to search in her shoulder bag and produce a key. It was tagged "Phil's." "I can tell you how to get there."

"I thought you might come with me."

Her eyes opened wide and her expression was wondering. "Oh!" She stretched her arms out, as if here were an idea worth an embrace. "When?"

"Well, what's wrong with right now?"

This *was* an exotic notion. "But I have to work!"

"Oh, but I expect the Foundation could let you off for an afternoon." He pulled out his ID, held it up between index and third finger, moved it back and forth. "For police business. Hell, how many requests do they get from Scotland Yard?"

As if it were hypnotic, something dangled there to put her in a trance, the warrant card held her gaze.

"When was the last time you went skiving?"

" 'Skiving'?"

"Fooling around?"

She raised her finger to the drooping plant and touched it as if it might have been one of those picture frames Philip was always righting. "Not since Phil died. I guess that's what we did. We went skiving." She smiled at Jury. "Skiving." She was bemused by the word, just as she was by Philip's name.

Bud Sinclair looked at Jury and chewed the end of his cigar. He sat behind his desk wearing a neon-bright vest that Jury assumed was for hunting, and warmed his hands in his armpits. "We got something international going here? I was kind of surprised."

Jury smiled. "Well, I was, too. I'm just doing a favor for a friend, really. It's not my case; it's yours."

Bud Sinclair smiled broadly. "Aw, you can have it, Superintendent. I sure as hell ain't having any luck. And it's a cold, cold trail by now. That must be some friend, you'd come all this way for."

"She is. His aunt—but you would have talked with her: Frances Hamilton?—died a short while ago in London. It's *her* friend I'm trying to get some information for." Jury told him what Lady Cray had said.

"Aw, that sure is a shame. Nice lady, that Mrs. Hamilton. Kind of excitable, though."

Jury wished he could say the same for Bud Sinclair. Right now his attention was drifting to the magazine on his desk, *Guns and Ammo*, which Jury had interrupted the reading of. Jury himself was looking down at the police photographs that Sinclair had spread across the desk for him to view. "You said the place was taken apart?"

"Huh? Oh, yeah, all tore up. Well, hell, you can see—there, and there." Sinclair pointed to two of the photos. "We thought this Calvert must've surprised someone, maybe in the course of a B and E—break and entry," he explained.

"We have those in London, too."

"Yeah." Sinclair's eyes were riveted on his magazine. His fingers seemed to itch to turn the page.

"What do you think, Sheriff?"

The sheriff clasped his hands over his pot belly, assumed a serious and meditative pose. "Well, like I said, all's we could come up with was robbery. We sent the forensics stuff to Philly." He shrugged. "No prints, no latents; some fibers, but what's to match with?"

He had a deep voice with a raspy edge to it. Too many cigarettes, perhaps. He also had a direct gaze, when he could lift his eyes from the tantalizing picture of a twelve-point buck, and piercingly blue eyes. "What I mean to say is, for all we ran a check on Calvert, we came up with jackshit." He shrugged. "If it wasn't a thief, well, then what? But, hell, that little old cabin away out there in the woods? Nothing in it of any value anyone knew about. Well, it just made me wonder."

"Wonder?"

"Still do. Never got past the wondering stage." He picked up a small wooden stick with a clawlike end and ran it down his back, up and down. "Trouble is, I got no one to wonder *with*." He flashed Jury a thin smile as he scrubbed at his back. "Until you."

The air was redolent with the scent of pines, crisp and cool. There was no proper road to the cabin; what had been the road here tapered off to hard, rutted earth and a worn few square feet where Philip must have parked his Jeep. Jury saw a number of crisscrossed tire tracks. He and Hester got out, still a distance from the cabin of perhaps fifty feet.

It was a log house with a chimney on one side and a small porch in front. The cabin reminded him of a child's drawing—square and sturdy, a window low on each side of the front door and one on each side of the house. The only thing missing from the drawing was smoke rising from the chimney.

There were trees, a lot of them, mostly pine interspersed with oak and walnut. The trees were clumped around the house and behind it, stretching on for some distance through parched brown fields. The ground sloped upward, on and on, and Jury was surprised how distant the woods and how far the horizon looked. It was a lonely place.

Hester had either not wanted to go in yet or not wanted to go in without him. She was standing some feet away, her hands shoved down in her coat pockets and her back to him. Leaves drifted down. There were rustles—small animals, he guessed, but no birds sang. It was too late in the day for that, he supposed. Then a V of dark birds, swallows or perhaps wrens, flew above them across the milky sky. From somewhere came the throaty honking of geese.

He walked toward Hester; his feet made soft sucking sounds in the needles and fallen leaves. Pinecones plopped at his feet.

She was standing looking down at a stream where the barest trickle of water showed there had been no rain for some time. He put his hand on her shoulder and she turned and they went toward the cabin.

It was very simply furnished, probably with secondhand stuff he might have picked up from one of the barn-cum-antique-stores they had passed on the way. There was, as she had said, a potbellied stove. Against one wall was a big horsehair sofa, its worn cover hidden by a couple of bright Indian rugs. Two more rugs were tacked up on the walls. A platform rocker sat beside the sofa, and near the kitchen were a large wooden table and a swivel chair. This was probably an all-purpose table, for it held books and papers and a gooseneck lamp. At the rear of the single room was a bunk bed covered with more of the Indian blankets. Bookcases lined the back wall. It was all very cozy.

Hester was inspecting some records that were stacked beside an old phonograph. Jury picked up what must have been a paperweight from the table and saw that it was a small music box. "It plays that music from *Dr. Zhivago,*" said Hester, returning a record to its sleeve.

The top of the box was a large, round glass bubble inside of which was a winter scene amid drifts of snow. Jury shook it and watched the snow fall. He smiled. He heard a clock ticking, looked towards the shadows at the rear and saw a grandfather clock. He looked at Hester.

She gave a little shrug. "I wound it when I was here last week. I didn't see the harm in it, though it isn't officially mine yet." Then she sat down, wearily, in the rocker, placed her hands on the arms, and started rocking.

Jury still stood looking around the room, feeling its sentience. His work had found him in many rooms like this, all different, but similar in their air of expectancy, or so he felt it, the sense that the person would return. It was in the small things—the cup and saucer on the kitchen counter, the dishtowel and washing-up liquid, the book splayed on the shelf, the music box that rested on some papers. Nothing had been put away; they all seemed still to bear the weight of the fingers that had lifted them. He was so young, thought Jury. He was too young never to come back and read the book or wash the cup and saucer.

There was some coal in a black scuttle; he made a fire, and Hester moved her chair closer. And then he started an inspection of the cabin. Useless, of course, after all these weeks. Nevertheless. He opened the bureau drawers, riffled the pages of the books in the bookcase, checked the windows, the door.

"I hate to go home."

"What?" Her voice brought him out of his musings about Philip Calvert.

"I hate to go home now. Before, there was always the thought that maybe Phil would call and we could talk on the phone. Or maybe meet at the coffee shop. Sometimes we went to movies. Now I go back to my apartment—it's only an efficiency—and I can't stay in it. I go out and sometimes get some ice cream or a cup of coffee. I walk a lot. I'm just waiting for a reasonable hour to go to bed. You can't go too early; it makes you feel old. So I walk or sit in a coffee shop until it's all right to go back and go to bed."

He sat down in the chair at the table, looking at her, and thought of the text of that Holman Hunt painting in the Tate. To sing songs to someone with a broken heart is like taking away a coat in cold weather. Something like that. Words of supposed comfort that offer no comfort at all to the sufferer but that let the comforter off the hook. He said nothing.

Neither of them had removed their coats, and both of them fell silent until Jury put a question to her about Ellen's student. "No. Phil never mentioned anyone named Beverly. Who is she?"

Jury told her. "A friend of Beverly Brown thought she might have met him when she was taking some sort of course sponsored by the Foundation. Did he teach?"

"No. But I think he might have attended—wait a minute. A black girl? Really good-looking? I saw him talking to a black student a couple of times. He never mentioned her to me, though; I don't think he knew her well."

They were silent for a moment, she rocking, Jury turning the paperweight over and up. "He didn't have any enemies you know of?"

She sighed. " 'Enemies.' It all sounds so melodramatic."

"Yes. I know. Did anyone, any other of his friends beside you, come up here for a visit?"

She shook her head. "No. That's the same question that detective asked. I honestly don't think so, or Phil would have mentioned it."

"Not, perhaps, if it were a woman."

Hester threw him an impatient glance. "Yes, he would. We were friends. I told you. If he was seeing someone or in love or having sex— yes, he'd have told me. He wasn't secretive."

"I assume that people knew he had this cabin and came up here regularly." She nodded, and he went on. "So that anyone could have come up here while he was here." Again she nodded. "Well, I agree that robbery seems very unlikely. Why would anyone come upon this deserted little cabin by accident? Maybe it was him, Philip, after all, Hester. Maybe somebody wanted him out of the way."

"Of *what*? I told you he didn't have any enemies—not Phil."

"I know what you told me. Yet here's a cabin miles from nowhere that no one could come upon by accident."

"Somebody could have followed him not even knowing who he was, but just followed him to see where he was going."

"Someone could have done; I think someone did. But I also think it was someone who knew him or knew who he was. I think he was killed for a reason that had nothing to do with the cabin here. If it was a thief, why didn't he wait until Philip left the premises?"

"I know." She sighed. "But *what*? Why?"

Jury shook his head. He turned the paperweight, shook it, and watched snow fall on the snowman, the skaters, the horse and carriage, and then resettle in little drifts. He turned the keys on the bottom and watched again as the scratchy tune, the theme song from *Dr. Zhivago,* played, while the skaters slid in one direction across the mirror pond, and the horse and carriage bobbed off in the opposite direction. Jury dropped his chin on his folded hands and contemplated the tiny tin skaters in their jittery glide along the improvised lake. In the carriage, two tin women rode with hands raised, waving. Beneath his chin he raised a finger, let it fall.

Then he sat up, noticing the quiet. "It's very hushed here, isn't it?"

Hester had been humming along to the music, eyes closed, rocking. She said, "Very. The silence is like thin ice. Even a bird chirping cracks it. It's peaceful."

They shared the quiet.

She looked from his face to the cluttered table. "You can look through Phil's stuff—I don't think he'd mind. Anyway, that sheriff—" She seemed to be searching for a name.

"Sinclair."

"Yes. He came up here. I called the local police when Phil didn't come back. He asked me some questions afterwards; I didn't hear from him again."

Jury pulled a small stack of papers towards him and leafed through them. Bills, a couple of letters.

I hate to go home now. He looked at Hester, again deep in some reverie, and thought of her words and her sadness and said, "It's nice that you got this place, Hester." He leaned back. "Seems right, your getting it."

"Thanks." Her voice was weak. She drew a handkerchief out from the cuff of her sweater, touched it, in an old-fashioned gesture, to the corner of her eyes, and then blew her nose very loudly.

"Hardly anyone that young ever thinks about wills—"

Or graves, or epitaphs, he didn't add.

"—and what to leave to his friends or family."

Jury couldn't somehow get the boy Chatterton out of his mind. "I expect at that age we think we'll live forever. You know, one of the things that strikes me most about Philip Calvert is how sensible he was. When you're twenty-seven, you might be charming; you're seldom sensible."

She rocked, resting her fine, fair head on the chair's back. "He is. He was." She turned her face away from the potbellied stove. He did not know if it was heat or unhappiness that had brought the color up. She said, "He helped me a lot because he was calm. I tend to be excitable and impulsive."

Jury stopped his shaking of the paperweight; he had to hide a smile as he said, "Yes, you are. You came up here with me."

But she did not hear his mild joking. "So it was good to have someone —you know—steady."

He watched the snow fall over the still scene. Then, after a few more moments of this shared silence, he rose. "I expect we'd better be getting back."

She gathered her coat about her and stood up. The chair kept on rocking.

It was late afternoon, and on the way back they stopped at a diner that Hester liked, one that she and Philip had often eaten at.

"I love diners," she said when they were settled in a booth with green Naugahyde benches, Jury's mended with gray electrical tape. "If the benches aren't fixed with tape, it doesn't count as a diner."

"Any other rules?"

"A lot of them. The menus have to be splotchy and the specials written in, preferably in pencil and misspelled. If nothing's misspelled, you know you've been taken. Let's see, do you have roast beef sandwiches with mashed potatoes and gravy in England?" Jury shook his head. "With cole slaw on the side?"

The waitress came back, took their order, and served it all up with what Jury considered near-breathtaking speed. They ate their roast beef sandwiches in appreciative silence.

Hester pulled over the menu again: "Pie, preferably à la mode, preferably apple—here it really is good."

"I can't." Jury groaned.

"Oh, for heaven's sake—what a sissy!" Hester ordered her pie. The waitress returned with it, a scoop of vanilla ice cream oozing across the top of the thick wedge. The crust, crisp and golden brown around its thumb-depressed edge, had risen high from the filling, so that Jury could see the slices of apple. Steam still rose from the plate. No wonder this was the great American dessert.

Hester watched him with a smile on her face.

Jury signed the waitress that he'd have some too.

They forked into their pieces.

Sweet, tart; hot, cold; smooth, sharp—the taste was sensational.

"Hester, we were meant for this."

16

With his copy of the French Romantics, his *Strangers' Guide,* and Ellen's book, he made his way across the campus, his mind moving between the twin puzzles of Beverly Brown and her Poe manuscript and Sweetie and Maxim. He thought of the window in Monsieur P.'s room looking into the building across the courtyard, and there another window looking across the expanse of that room to yet another window. Maxim's rooms were huge, the floors luxurious in their Oriental carpeting, but Spartan in their furnishings. One room was empty save for a grand piano draped with a blue shawl. Melrose remembered these details; the description was striking. And in the dining room, Maxim sat in the single chair at the bottom of the table. . . .

Melrose stopped, sat down on a bench outside an imposing white building, and read:

> Sweetie saw Maxim through what seemed a colonnade of door-ways, each one opening onto the room beyond, at the end of which was the dining room where Maxim sat at breakfast at the long mahogany table.
>
> She walked through the doors and into the room. She stopped and looked from the table to the bank of high windows to the wide lawns. The fountain was dry; the bronze boy rode the fish through dark-stained cement.

What was going on? It made no sense at all. A dozen pages ago, the gardens beyond the windows had been choked with flowers, absolutely fecund in the warm spring day. The pool had been full of water.

And now Maxim was lying on the dining room floor in a pool of blood. What was going on? Irritated at himself for being caught up in this weird story, he snapped *Windows* shut. But unable to help himself, he reached into his satchel and drew out the chapters Ellen had given him, and started to read:

In the kitchen Sweetie stood with the spatula in her hand poaching an egg and trying to imagine her own death. She watched the transparent white of the egg turn opaque as the envelopes lying beneath the slot. In another pan, sausage fried, spitting up grease. She lifted the egg and drained it and laid it carefully on a piece of toast.

She sat at the table taking small bites of sausage and wondering as she chewed what it felt like to die or to go mad. How did one "go mad"? What could it possibly feel like? Would there be something like a mental eclipse? Her kitchen was in the English basement and through the bars of the window that opened on pavement level sunlight filtered and lay in bands on the white linoleum. Sweetie thought she should go out, go out and walk, get some air, banish these thoughts from her mind but—could she? Would the sunlight dazzle her and herd her back inside?

What other explanation could there be for these letters to Lily except that she was going mad? And yet she felt in the same relationship to the things of this world as she had before. She looked at the little face of her wristwatch and saw that the second hand was proceeding around it with the same stuttering sweep, that the minute hand was bisecting time in as orderly a fashion as always. But how else to explain what was happening? As she spooned sugar from the flowered china bowl she felt comfortable with the familiar belongings of the kitchen. Sugar bowl, white milk jug, teacup. She could name them as easily and familiarly as ever. But what if she forgot? In madness, did one forget the names of ordinary objects?

Carefully, she tore a corner from her napkin, took a pencil from the jelly jar and wrote the word down S U G A R and put the piece of napkin in the bowl. She looked at that and smiled a little and wrote S A L T on another bit of paper and put that under the salt cellar. With her tongue she wet another bit just to dampen it— G L A S S—and this one she pressed to her glass of milk.

The telephone rang.

Sweetie sat perfectly still. She was sure if she picked up the receiver there would be nothing on the line but silence. Or if there was a voice it would say "Hello, hello, hello? Lily?"

On the ninth ring she thought, But it might be for me, it might simply be Bill or Jane or anyone. She went on eating her poached egg, wiping the last corner of toast around in the yolk and listening to the ringing. Thirteen rings. When it stopped she thought it had probably been for her, and if it rang again she would answer it.

It rang again. She didn't.

Here, she said to herself, is what you could do: you can sit in the sidechair opposite the door and watch the mail slot and when another envelope slides through, open the door quickly. And she did so; she was unaware of the passage of time.

Ultimately, though, she knew this was useless; whoever it was was braced for that and would disappear before she saw him. Him or her. The person would vanish before she could confront him.

There is something else you can do, she told herself then. She pulled an envelope from the paper band, folded a sheet of stationery and slipped it in. She licked the flap and pressed it shut. Then she turned it over and printed on it

MAXIM

Sweetie went to the front door and shoved the envelope through the letter slot. Dark had fallen. After she put her dishes in the sink she went upstairs to bed.

Melrose was slumped down on the bench, the manuscript pages still in hand, thinking these thoughts. Students were coming out of buildings, released for a while from their classes. They all seemed very jolly, flowing back and forth on the path beyond his feet.

"He's dead. He must be dead." He looked up to see two students staring at him. Probably, they thought he was crazy, babbling away here on a campus bench. The two students smiled uncertainly and gave the bench a wide berth.

17

I

Sweetie.

She looked at the name, hoping there was a magnetic field around it that would draw other words into its circle. She retyped it in caps: S W E E T I E. Behind her closed eyelids the name pulsed slowly on and off like a neon sign over a diner: EAT—EAT—EAT.

Thinking about a diner was a mistake; it made her hungry. If it hadn't been for the chain, she would have been out of her office in a flash, gone-zo up the third floor to sit with a cup of coffee and a sugar doughnut. Even better, to the cafeteria for a cup of coffee in a china cup and a cinnamon pull-apart. But it wasn't time yet; she surely had another good forty-five minutes of writing to do. She looked up at the clock on the wall; that told her nothing, because her scarf hid the face. She always threw something over it; otherwise she'd spend a lot of time looking up there to see how much more tortured time remained. There was the alarm clock, of course; it was inside the filing cabinet, the ticking muted, but the alarm itself was loud enough to shatter glass. It was set for two o'clock.

Jesus Christ, if anyone who read her books could see her now! She formed a mental image of the Writer, or at least what she supposed a reader would think of a writer writing (if readers ever thought of them). What she saw was herself in a book-encrusted den with mahogany wain-scoting, random-width pine floors layered with Oriental rugs, windows overlooking misty fields (writers being always up at dawn), ink across a calfskin notebook, forming words from a Mont Blanc pen with the flour-ish of a calligrapher. To write in longhand with an inkpen (Ellen mused over why pens were called "inkpens") was breathing the true, rarefied air of the writer; it was getting down to the very bone of writing. It was much more difficult than typing; far, far more difficult than word processing. Word processing was precisely what it sounded like: churning words like butter into some oleaginous mass. The words came out smoothly, having nothing to do with art, and with that magical quality of letters just popping up almost out of nowhere onto the computer monitor. They looked as if they'd arrived on the screen by way of an extra-human agency.

So Ellen gritted her teeth and wrote with her ballpoint Bic:

SWEet i e
> *Sweetie had been sitting with the box of candy on her lap long enough for dusk to turn to dark.*

Ellen got up and dragged herself over to the window, wondering: who was trying to kill Sweetie? *Was* someone trying to kill her? For it was Lily, not Sweetie, to whom the messages were addressed. It was a mystery. Sometimes an answer would dust Ellen's mind with a mothlike flutter.

The chain pulled at her ankle. In her concern about Sweetie she had wandered from the window to the filing cabinet, and her fingers were feeling across its smooth surface for the key. It had happened before, this all-but-unconscious trek to the cabinet; thus, she had had to put the key to the bicycle chain up on top and out of reach. (The alarm clock was in the bottom drawer, which she could reach, just. She had made the mistake of putting *that* also out of reach, and once, in the ensuing blast, several of the faculty had run out of Gilman crying "Fire!") At first she had positioned the key at a place on the top of the cabinet that she could still reach if she really stretched and strained. That was no good; she'd made a lunge for it one day and banged her chin on the metal handle. So she would first put it up there out of reach before she shoved the lock through the chain.

It was embarrassing to have to flag someone down at the end of her two-to-three-hour writing stint, and she marvelled that anyone believed that she had "somehow got her foot caught up in the damned bike chain," or was in the process of playing some wacky game or winning a bet with a colleague.

In a funk she sat back down heavily, wondered if the swivel chair might just be too comfortable for her, might be molded a little too much to the contour of her back. She recalled reading a comment by some writer, probably a sportswriter or someone else who had a column and a deadline: if somebody held a gun to your head, you'd write. Ellen closed her eyes and imagined someone was holding a gun to her head, but it didn't help. Of course, it had to be a real gun, that was all.

She slid down in the chair and pulled up her heavy Aran sweater, arranged it around her head, and sat thinking about the Man in the Iron Mask. If he had been a writer, what would the conditions have been? What would the poor booby have done if he'd been a nail biter, like she was? In this guise she rose and made her way blindly over to the window, arms outstretched against obstacles in her path, felt the cold panes beneath her fingers, stood there. Could anyone see her, down there on the walk? She sighed and pulled down the sweater and chewed at the hangnail on her thumb. Then with her back flush up against the wall she pretended she was Fortunato. If Fortunato had been a writer, imagine the sort of arrangement Montresor would try to negotiate with him! *Not a paragraph, Fortunato? What? A sentence, surely! No?* Ellen raised her arm and pulled it back: *thwack!* Another brick splatters home.

She dragged herself back to the chair, sat down in a slouch, and picked up the pen. Put it down again. She was so hungry.

She had tried locking the chain to her ankle in her apartment, but it didn't work because nothing she could find to wrap it around was heavy enough to work as a restraining force. She reminded herself of someone intent on suicide looking for a stout beam or heavy hook to toss the belt or rope across. And she had wound up several times dragging furniture by her foot—the heavy wing chair, even a dark Jacobean chest that she'd been sure would have stopped a mule team in its tracks—to get at the key so she could leave and go to the Horse or the Pizza Palace. Even after she had anchored the chain to the stove, there had been enough play in it to reach the telephone, and she'd got the pizza delivered. And it just barely reached to the door. The delivery kid was fascinated. She'd told him she had the lead in *Les Mis.* He'd believed it.

It wasn't that she couldn't write because she didn't like Sweetie. She loved Sweetie. She liked her plain dresses, her pleated skirts and pastel cardigans, her simple hairdo, her clean face.

Why would anyone want to drive her mad? But Ellen wasn't sure that anyone *did* want to. She bent her head back over the chair, wondering how far she could lean back before she fell.

She stared up at the fluorescent lighting fixture, the shadowy carcasses of dead moths caught within it. Then she leaned forward and wrote:

Sweetie's head was bent over the white candy box.

The trouble was: it was in this second story, the one she was writing now, that *Lily* was receiving letters from someone she didn't know and had even, yesterday, got a box of candy. Ellen closed her eyes. Forget Lily for the moment.

Sweetie didn't know what kind of candy it was.
She was afraid to open the box.

Ellen stopped and leaned back. There was something ominous about the box of candy. She put her head in her hand, rubbed at her temples in a benighted-old-woman gesture that she disliked. No, she decided. The box of candy is just that. What is ominous is the way in which Sweetie sees it.

Poor Sweetie. Ellen bit her lip, put the heels of her palms against her eyes, pressing them into the sockets. Something awful was going to happen, something truly awful. *Had* happened. And was now working itself out. It had happened at the end of *Windows,* but Sweetie did not know what her role was to be. *That* was the source of the dread.

> The box was covered in a satiny white paper and tied with purple velvet, a wide, generous band of cloth, not some stingy length of narrow ribbon. Sweetie pulled at the end. The big bow unraveled, almost voluptuously.

Ellen's thumb and forefinger rubbed together, felt air, felt the width of velvet. Red, it should be. Not purple, red. Why? Red, because purple seemed too weighted with meaning and the ribbon means nothing but itself.

She watched as Sweetie removed the lid. Inside were two layers of little fluted cups arranged in neat rows. There was no candy. Sweetie picked up one of the cups and inspected it carefully. Ellen wrote:

> There never had been.

> She returned the fluted cup to its position and looked at the neat rows, empty of chocolates. Sweetie closed the box and remembered Maxim saying: "They left notes on my plate, by my glass, in the bowl on the table. The notes said: cheese, wine, fruit. It was because I'm a writer and I should have been able to dine on empty air and drink the memory of wine. They thought it was a laugh. They did not know it, but they might well have been right. The material world falls away. Listen: what if what happens is precisely what doesn't happen? For instance: you cut the paper doll from the surrounding paper and there is the empty space, the doll-outline. It is a perfect match—perfect. Then which is which and which is real?"
> "Oh, but that's sophistry. I hate talk like that."
> "No. They are not separate. The outline belongs to the doll. The doll only appears to be wrenched from its place. Dress the paper doll in its paper clothes. It makes no difference. It only mimics its

true self; a shabby imitation; a mutilation, a static echo. Do you see?"

Ellen put down her pen and stared at the wall. She thought about the dreadful Vicks Salve. The mutilation of Sweetie. The *murder* of Sweetie. No. According to Maxim, it was impossible. Impossible.

Then she thought of Beverly Brown's Poe story. Maxim would say this too is impossible. Only Poe could write a Poe story. Anyone attempting to copy him would leave fingerprints—*mental* fingerprints all over the pages. It couldn't be avoided. To write Poe you had to *be* Poe.

II

A face behind the frosted glass of the office door.

Before she could get at the key, the door was opening and the shadow on the glass turned into Melrose Plant.

"Well, well," he said, taking in the chain around her ankle.

Coolly, she asked him, "Would you mind handing me that key?" She nodded toward the filing cabinet. "On top there."

He looked from her to the filing cabinet and looked back. They looked at one another for a few seconds, locking eyes.

"Please. The key." Her tone was full of condescension, as if she'd been waiting for ages for her page, her messenger, her locksmith, her lackey Melrose, to appear.

He found the key, handed it to her, waited for an explanation. Finally, bent down to the lock at her ankle, she said, "I had to see how it felt, didn't I?"

" 'It'?"

"Felt for the character in my book. He was once on a chain gang. In Louisiana." The chain came off. She sat back, staring at air. "He was one of David Duke's guys. Neo-Nazi." She looked up at the ceiling. "He murdered . . . someone," she mused.

"Why is there a chain wrapped around your foot?"

"I just *told* you."

"No, you didn't."

She tried to untangle the end of the chain. "Instead of the Q and A I could use a little help."

Melrose was enjoying himself. He didn't move. "A Louisiana chain gang somehow doesn't strike me as a proper mise-en-scène for Sweetie and Maxim."

"It can't be two o'clock yet." With this convenient change of subject, Ellen finally unwound the chain and plunked it by the typewriter.

"According to my watch, it is almost precisely that. There is, however, no way to verify that by university time, as the clock on the wall is covered." He did not wait for the answer he knew he was not going to get anyway.

"Then I'm through!" she said happily. "Writing, I mean."

"Oh! That's what you were—what the *hell*?"

The sound was deafening. Melrose dropped his books; Ellen lunged for the cabinet, yanked open the drawer, and fumbled out an old double-belled alarm clock. She smashed the plunger in and tossed the clock back in the drawer. Then she picked up her jacket. "It's two o'clock."

"Why . . . ? Oh, never mind." He helped her on with her leather jacket and asked, "How is Sweetie?"

"Good as can be expected, I guess." She gathered up her old leather bag and hooked it over her shoulder. "Given her situation." She slid her door keys from the desk.

"I hope it's no worse than Maxim's."

On the way to the cafeteria, Ellen did not answer any of his questions about either *Windows* or her manuscript, regarding the answers as superfluous outside the scope of the book. She asked, "You see what I mean about Vicks Salve's book? You see the similarity?"

"Painfully obvious. Clearly, she plagiarized."

Ellen pulled at his sleeve, eager. "Did you figure out a way to whack her yet?"

Melrose smiled. "I have an idea. It's excellent."

"What?"

"I haven't thought it through yet."

She walked backwards, gazing at him beseechingly. Given all of her problems, Melrose thought, she had a wonderfully untroubled expression —pristine and childlike. A few students were lounging on benches and even on the grass, enjoying the sunshine in spite of the cold.

"Let me mull it over a bit." He held up *Windows*. "Won't you please answer one question? Who murdered Maxim? It wasn't Sweetie, was it?"

"What makes you think he's dead?" They passed through the double doors of the cafeteria. "I hope they're not out of pull-aparts."

"What makes me think he's *dead*? Oh, I expect because he's lying crumpled on the floor with blood oozing out of his body and a knife nearby. That aroused my suspicions." He followed her over to the counter, through the tables and a scattering of late lunchers.

Ellen didn't comment; her chin was nearly resting on the top of the glass display case as she looked at the rows of doughnuts, buns, and pastries. "I don't see any pull-aparts. I'll have a cheese Danish." Sitting on top of the case were several small boxes of candy; they were for sale. She frowned.

The black woman behind the counter scooped a large pastry onto a white plate and looked at Melrose.

"Just coffee for me."

"Don't you want a cherry Danish? They have good ones here." Ellen indicated the cherry Danish, and the woman put that one on a plate also and slid it across to Melrose.

As cups were clattered into saucers, he said, "Are you telling me Maxim isn't dead?"

Ellen hugged the bun to her chest as her eyes ranged over the room for a table. "Not exactly. Oh, hell, there's Vlasic. Ignore him."

"That should be easy, since I don't know who you're talking about."

He followed her, wedging between pushed-out chairs and rucksack-laden tables, wondering how someone could be lying in a pool of blood and "not exactly" dead. Well, it was useless. Clearly, *Windows* was not the sort of mystery served up by Elizabeth Onions.

Ellen was nodding her head in the direction of a middle-aged man with sparse hair, a sharp nose, and a thin, sinewy dancer's body. "He's an ass."

"A successful ass? Your department reeks of success."

"To hear him tell it. And he's not in the same department. He teaches English; I'm in the seminars program. I think he's published a couple of pamphlets, maybe a book, nothing spectacular. Obscure poetry."

"What's his name, did you say?"

"Vlasic. Alejandro, he wants people to believe. I call him Alex. He hates that."

Vlasic did not look as if he were too eager to share any of the writing limelight, certainly not with a colleague who had proven herself infinitely more successful than he, but he braved it out by smiling widely and booming out her name. Melrose was surprised at the operatic quality of his voice. He would have expected something reedier.

"Hullo, Alex."

Vlasic flinched slightly as Ellen went on to introduce Melrose as an authority on the French Romantics, which he modestly denied, and Ellen contradicted the denial.

The two girls sitting at Vlasic's table turned their heads in concert. They were wearing peasant skirts and shapeless blouses. One was wearing hoop earrings the size of tires; the other had a long scarf coiled around her hair. They were dark and looked like gypsies.

"How's the new book coming?" Vlasic's smile was about as insincere as a smile could get.

Ellen's jaw tightened, but she didn't blink. "Okay." She cut her Danish into symmetrical little wedges.

"Smoothly, hmm?"

There was something annoyingly sleek about the man. Melrose thought at any moment he might curl up and purr.

"No problems."

"We've just been discussing the creative process."

"The what?" Her expression was bland.

One of the gypsies leaned toward Ellen and said, as if she were uttering prophecies, "What worries me is not so much that I don't have the *talent,* but that I don't know if I want to make the sacrifice." Here she made a pretty gesture of putting the beringed fingers of one hand to the tag end of her scarf, pulling it across her cheek. "I don't know if I have the *nerve,* to be truthful, to lay myself bare." Her thin, high laugh was flutelike. "I don't know if I'd be able to make the kind of commitment it takes. It really worries me."

"It'd worry me too." Ellen chewed on a wedge of cheese Danish, pulled over an empty chair, and plunked her feet on it.

The gypsy looked uncertainly at Vlasic and tried a new tack. "It must be deeply satisfying to achieve recognition for something you've worked on so long and so hard. It must be wonderful to have molded, sculpted your feelings so that others can share them, to have crystallized some part of the psyche and projected it."

"Oh, I dunno. Any fool can write," said Ellen.

Melrose loved it; he was thinking how well Ellen and Joanna the Mad would get on.

"Ha!" bellowed Vlasic theatrically. He brought his hand down on the table and rattled the cups in their saucers. "Ha!"

Ellen regarded him without expression. "It's true. Even he could do it if he tried." She jerked her thumb in Melrose's direction.

Relegated to the company of writing idiots, and feeling no comment was necessary, Melrose merely inclined his head. No one, however, seemed interested in the scribblings of this particular idiot; their eyes did not gather him into the company.

The first gypsy was obviously unhappy in the thought that her sights might be set on something any fool could do. "You're too modest." Her voice was much deeper than her friend's, throatier. When Ellen didn't help her by denying or affirming this assessment, she continued. "I've read *Windows.*" There was an infinitesimal pause as she waited to be congratulated for her trouble. Again, Ellen didn't respond, so she plowed on. "It's incredible how there could be such narrative thrust in a piece of writing where such a reductive use is made of symbolism, where prose has been stripped to the bare bones."

Ellen merely lit a cigarette.

Now the one pulling at her scarf took over with her tremulous uncertainties. "It's being motivated that worries me. Motivated to get up every morning and face the blank page . . ."

"You could always sleep in."

The girl discounted this with a little laugh. "It's being able to stick to it, to commit yourself to a piece of writing that may never speak to anyone else, to—" she paused, perplexed over what further sacrifice might be necessary— "work for years and be able to write nothing but commercial fiction. What reward could keep me going through all of that?"

"Money." Ellen considered the crust of Melrose's cherry Danish. She dropped it back on the plate.

Again, Vlasic let out a snort of laughter. "You know the percentage of writers who can live on their earnings?" No one answered, so he told them. "Less than two percent."

Melrose considered abandoning his writing career.

Outside again, Melrose said, "How could you stand listening to that nonsense?" They walked against the flow of students escaping from classrooms into the more aromatic and filling environs of the cafeteria.

"Vlasic's students all talk that way. They can't help it. They're all little Vlasics."

They walked on for a few moments in silence, and then Ellen stopped and said, "You know what Maxim just told Sweetie?"

"What? No, I don't. The last time I saw Maxim he was lying in a pool of blood. So how could he *just* have told Sweetie *anything*?"

"Maxim told Sweetie that if you cut out a paper doll—this is a metaphor, understand?—if you cut out a paper doll, to what does the empty space, the outline, then belong? And does the doll then exist without its outline?"

"That's metaphysical s—"

Ellen interrupted, nodding. "Sophistry. That's just what Sweetie said."

"Metaphysical *shit* is what it is. And would you stop talking about Maxim and Sweetie as if they were back there in the cafeteria having coffee?"

"Oh, don't be simple."

Ellen was pouting, as if he'd just insulted her very best friends. Very possibly, he thought, they were. He held his tongue. It wasn't easy.

"I'm thinking about literary theft."

"The redoubtable Vicks Salve?"

"I was at first, yes. Then after what Maxim said—"

Melrose heaved a huge sigh, hoping it would register, but Ellen ignored it.

"—I started in thinking about this Poe manuscript. A person can't copy style; it would be like trying to paint the real colors of a rainbow, and there are too many incomparables of atmosphere and air that go to producing a rainbow. It's like that with style. The whole thing's going to have a strange, stuttering quality. Beverly Brown would leave her mental fingerprints all over the pages."

Melrose considered this. "It's a good point. But one would have to know Miss Brown's mind to bring up the prints, in a manner of speaking."

"Maybe it's not so subtle as the permutations or colors of her mind. Maybe the fingerprints are in the details of the story. Details that only *Beverly* could have put in and that Poe simply couldn't've." Ellen shifted her book bag from one shoulder to the other. "For instance: Sweetie was opening a white candy box a while ago, and it wasn't until we were getting our coffee that I realized a white candy box has been sitting on the counter by the cashier *for days.* It registered on my unconscious, and I guess when I was trolling through it, I pulled up the white candy box." Ellen stopped and looked up at the slate-blue sky. "Well, what if that sort of thing is almost unavoidable? What if there're things in Beverly's story like that?"

"Difficult to determine, isn't it?"

"It might be *impossible.* But then again, what if there's a ginger jar in her rooms? That's just an example. What if there were something she looked at every day, perhaps without realizing it, and it crept into the story?" Melrose held the door of Gilman Hall open for her, and a little flood of students rushed out like lemmings. "I wonder if we could get into her apartment," Ellen mused. Then she added, with a sigh, "Of course, the authenticity of this manuscript isn't going to help find her killer."

Melrose was thoughtful. "It might. It might suggest something more about motive. Incidentally, we've been so busy getting you unchained and then talking about reductive symbolism, I forgot to tell you: I met the little girl, Jip—you know, the little girl in the antique shop. She was there when Beverly Brown bought the trunk. The trunk stayed in the shop for a day after she purchased it. Jip looked in it." Melrose stopped, frowning. Was this one of those secrets he couldn't keep? He felt unpleasantly ashamed of himself.

"Really? Well?"

"She couldn't remember clearly. But it's my impression that she *knows* something, I'm sure of it." Melrose frowned again and shook his head. "Anyway, we had a long talk."

"About what?"

Melrose paused and changed the subject. "What about the rest of that so-called Poe manuscript? Are we going to see it?"

"I'll bring it along this evening."

"I believe Richard Jury is supposed to be seeing Professor Lamb when he comes back from Philadelphia. Incidentally, how *is* your book coming along?"

She winced. She hated that question. "Pretty bad."

They were walking down the corridor toward her classroom, and Melrose said, "What I can't understand"—among many other things, he didn't add—"is why Sweetie's writing him a letter *after* she'd just seen him lying in a pool of blood at the end of *Windows*."

"Who says it's blood?" Ellen stopped outside her classroom, nodded to a few students who appeared to be straying in rather than going in intentionally.

It was clearly hopeless, getting Ellen to tell him anything. "What's the title of this one?" That might offer up a clue.

"I told you. *Doors.*"

That was no help. "What about the third one? Have you got a title for it?"

"No."

"Hallways? Porches?"

Ellen turned to give him an evil look.

Still intent on investigating Maxim's debatable end, he said casually, "I expect you begin *Doors* with what happened to Maxim?"

"Why? Everyone knows what happened to Maxim." Ellen sailed into the classroom.

18

The sound of convulsive sobbing came from behind one door; through another, obviously a lab, three technicians moved between their equipment and blood-stained clothing spread out on a table. Jury walked down the corridor, paint fading from its walls, lino chipped along its floor, past a couple of secretaries stamping numbers on empty binders. The numbers were running into five or six figures. Unsettling to Jury that the binders were empty; it was as if Fate were about to step in out there on the streets, interrupting some simple errand of a man, woman, child—a trip to the mall or the market—and deliver that person up to another empty binder that would start filling up with police reports and morgue shots.

He passed a big plate-glass window, behind which sat a selection of witnesses (at least, Jury assumed they were), some hard-faced women on a vinyl couch, sending out a few bales of smoke between them from their cigarettes; sending out signals, too, to whoever was available to pick them up. A couple of black kids with fade haircuts looking by turns very pleased with themselves or very scared, depending on which witness a detective picked to escort out; a half-dozen more blacks in high-tops rapping coolly over to one side, as if they'd just been cornered on the basketball court; an elderly man tossing his arms about and demanding his rights; a few others contributing to the squall of noise. A pretty young woman came out accompanied by a police officer; a less pretty one, also with an officer, went in. Back and forth the witnesses moved, none looking happy about it. Their escorts looked even less happy. Bad food, eaten at bad times, in bad company, at bad hours, could do that to a person. Washed-out lighting, weary detectives, snarling witnesses—all familiar. Familiar, too, was the sound of a raised voice coming from one of the officers off somewhere that he couldn't see, shouting (probably to one of the inmates of the fishbowl Jury had just passed), "Stop BULLSHIT-TING me, lady!" This line had variants, at least six of them—different emphasis on words, different arrangement of epithets—but the shouter was making his point. The interrogation room production, thought Jury, smiling slightly: a performance sometimes as lavishly staged as a West End musical, with its entrances and exits, the detectives playing their roles, knowing their lines, the witness-suspect playing too, only without a script.

Then out of one of the doors behind Jury burst a tallish, wiry detective who moved past him like a case of whiplash and was now shouting back to "CHARGE her ASS with first-degree," hastening along, turning again, shouting back, "NUKE her if she don't talk!," and who then cut directly in front of Jury and walked through the door Jury had been about to open, the one with PRYCE stencilled on it.

"Jack Pryce?"

The detective turned, said, "Oh—hi," in such a marvellously pleasant tone Jury wanted to laugh; he would have thought Pryce never had to toss threats at zipper-lipped witnesses. "You're the Scotland Yard detective? Come on in."

Jury, who was expecting to get a little nuking himself, was relieved he wasn't going to have to deal, apparently, with some egocentric bastard who wouldn't want to share a single photo or bit of forensic evidence.

"You're working on a case in Philly, right?" Jack Pryce picked up some teletypes, scanned them, muttered something about fucking Florida, a couple more homicides in Florida and the perp last seen in D.C. "Is this D.C.?" he asked Jury, rhetorically.

Pryce put the papers aside and picked up a pencil. He chewed along the length of the pencil like a man eating a cob of corn. Pryce's office was awash in maps, morgue shots, aerial photos tacked up on a bulletin board and spread across his desk and a couple of tables. Black-and-white shots of a dead girl's face. Not Beverly Brown—that case would not be recent enough to be spread around the office. These photos were of a girl little more than a child.

"Not *in*, precisely." Jury told him about the death of Philip Calvert, about his conversations with both Hester and the sheriff. To Pryce's question about the connection, Jury could only shake his head. "I don't know." He told him about the notes, the list of initials Ellen Taylor had found in Beverly Brown's papers.

"Yeah, we talked to her. Teaches at Hopkins?" He dragged several binders out from the mess on his desk, flicked through some office reports, found what he wanted. "Bunch of people at Hopkins I talked to, but none of them seemed to be really intimate friends. Except for a couple of guys, I got the impression she didn't really have 'intimate friends.'" Pryce made a note. "I'll check with Sinclair."

"What guys?"

Pryce chewed his pencil, tossed it down, picked up another. "Well, there's one here that everyone seems to think needs special handling—he's rich, he's got influence." Pryce shrugged away the special handling. "He was sleeping with her. Since he's a part-time teacher and she was a student, I don't know how well that went down with the powers that be, but hey, big deal, right? His name's Patrick Muldare. Then there's this Hopkins professor—Owen Lamb—that she worked with, or was assistant to; then a jerk named Vlasic—Alejandro Vlasic—who was directing her thesis; he's another professor. Then there's this weirdo shop on Howard where she worked that's run by Muldare's half-brother . . . no, step-brother. Alan Loser." Pryce bit the yellow pencil and stared thoughtfully at the ceiling. "There is a connection."

"What?"

"There's this homeless guy—we used to call them 'bums,' but no more—hangs out around this shop; it's sort of his permanent spot. Name of Milos—first? last? who knows? This guy claims he found the body of the Cider Alley victim. . . ." He paused, looked down at the binder.

"John-Joy?"

"Yeah. Anyway, he's deaf and blind. Great witness, right? One of these days we're gonna get ordered to Mirandize in braille. This Milos isn't dumb, though. I mean, he can talk. Christ, could he ever *yell*! So he says he's hanging around there, Cider Alley, when the cops came. But he wasn't. *No one* was around there when those two blues stumbled on the body. We canvassed the block, but who's to question? It's not residential around there."

"Strange. How're you getting information from this Milos, anyway, if he's blind and deaf?"

Pryce's brief laugh was more of a grunt. "That's the whole point. It takes forever, because you got to write on his fucking *hand*. He's pretty practiced at it, I'll give him that, but Christ! Now, what he said was that someone wrote in his hand that he—the someone—was the police. Well, obviously, it wasn't. The guys who found the body sure as hell didn't. This Milos wasn't even around. We found him a couple days later because he kept telling people he'd found this body. So we questioned him. More or less."

"You mean the murderer wrote on his palm?"

"Uh-huh. What I figure is, Milos must've caught him in the act, or come on him before he had a chance to make off. Started yelling for the cops. Why the killer didn't just run I don't know. Must've had nerves of steel." Pryce shrugged. "But go figure. If it wasn't a cop and this bum's not lying, then who else?"

"Yes, who else?" Jury thought for a moment and then asked, "Is it all right with you if I talk to some of these people? I don't want to mess with your case if you don't want—"

Jack Pryce said, "Listen, you can make this case go down, be my guest. We've come up with zilch on Beverly Brown. I had witnesses couldn't identify their own faces in the mirror." He pushed one of the binders towards Jury.

It was full of color photos stapled to pages. Jury looked down at the dead face of Beverly Brown. She was beautiful. *Had been* beautiful. The ligature mark circled her neck, crisscrossing just below the base of the skull.

"Nothing. No fingernail scrapings even for DNA or blood typing. Was there a struggle? Can't tell. A few hairs, Caucasoid, found on her coat. Trace evidence—but the integrity of the trace evidence is questionable. Look." His tone became slightly defensive, as if perhaps Scotland Yard could do better about keeping evidence sterile. "Autopsy surroundings could be better, right? Things are crowded. We got bodies stacked from here to Sunday. Some of that trace 'evidence' could've come from the ME's investigators, from the paramedics—hell . . .'"

"We've got that problem, too. What about the man in Cider Alley?"

"The ME says probably a lead pipe to the skull. Cuts, abrasions, contusions. Lots of bruising."

"Different MO."

"Yeah. But that doesn't mean a different perp, necessarily."

"Why was Beverly Brown in this churchyard?"

"The thought on that is, she probably went along like a few others to the churchyard on Poe's birthday to keep a watch out for the messenger with the flowers. You heard about that?"

Jury nodded. "Strange place for a murder. So public. And with several people there for the express purpose of keeping watch. . . ."

"Go figure." Pryce shrugged again. "I think this is someone absolutely relishes putting it over on the next guy. He or she had a clever little plan. In a way, the fact it was public, I think that's an advantage. It's got the benefit of being totally unexpected, and the environment, unless you screw up with prints and so forth, is foreign to you. Smoke someone in your home or his and you got all sorts of things that can go wrong. And he didn't have to make an appointment, did he? Knew she'd be there. Him or her, I mean. Could've been a woman."

"No motive?"

"Muldare might have had one, maybe. Jealous lover, that kind of thing. Of course this fancy-pants stepbrother of his might have had the same motive. Nothing else, nothing suggested."

"What about this alleged Poe manuscript?"

Pryce rocked his hand back and forth. "Very iffy. Valuable if it was real; but was it?"

Wiggins's point.

"And she didn't have it, so . . ."

"No, but . . . who might benefit from the scholarship?"

"Vlasic. Alejandro. Alejandro, for shit's sake—what a name. My guess. Or maybe anyone at Hopkins. He was supposed to be the thesis advisor, that's all."

"This derelict, John-Joy?"

"Nothing there. That's even harder, because it's like a vacuum. He had buddies in the alley, but . . . Cider Alley—" Pryce grimaced—"that's too close to Harborplace for my money. You don't want to smoke someone at Harborplace."

"Why's that?"

"Mayor don't like it." Pryce flashed a grin and chewed his pencil.

Jury rose. "Thanks. I appreciate your help."

"My help? Let me tell you something: the homicide rate in this city is something like between two, three hundred a year. The clearance rate in my squad on homicides is one-third, thirty-three percent." Pryce flicked the edges of a stack of files. "Seventy-two cases. Fifty-five open files. Bad."

He looked so bleak, Jury said, "Lies—damn lies and statistics, Detective. What *kind* of homicides? Drugs? Domestics? It makes one hell of a difference."

"Drugs, mainly. Fucking right it makes a difference. Domestic, you know who the shooter or the guy with the knife is—he's sitting right there having his dinner. But like I said—statistics, lies or not, are what gets your ass in a sling. If there's a conviction, the death's down, correct? Makes no difference the perpetrator walks a week later; it's still down." Pryce sighed and tossed the chewed pencil on the table. "Christ, I should complain. At least it's not D.C. That place is unbe*liev*able. We get detailed over there sometimes. But we're catching up; Baltimore's getting almost as bad. Jamaican drug wars. Southeast and Northeast D.C.'s a war zone, believe me. If the devil stepped through that door and gave me a choice between a detail in D.C. or a detail in hell—"

"You'd take hell."

"You better believe it."

19

The shop was called Nouveau Pauvre.

The name was painted in an unravelling web of spidery black cursive on a white oblong sign screwed into the red brick. Beneath the wrought iron steps that formed a canopy above him sat a bearded man of uncertain age, bundled into a heavy coat fastened around the middle by a rope. His hands buried in his sleeves, he appeared to be dozing. Above him another sign was hand-lettered: "MILO'S GRATE. DON'T EVEN *THINK* ABOUT IT."

"About what, I wonder?" asked Wiggins.

A dog, also of uncertain breed and also apparently dozing, lay with its head on its paws beside a white plastic Hardee's cup with some token change in it. The dog had the baleful face and long ears of a basset.

When Jury and Wiggins stopped there on the pavement, both man and dog sprang awake, the dog whining and thumping its tail, the man holding out the cup beside him in a blind side-to-side movement of his hand. "Quarter! Got any change? Quarter!" It was more of a demand than a request. It was certainly yelled rather than spoken.

"You're Milos?" asked Jury.

No answer.

The man's barked request had momentarily made Jury forget Milos was deaf.

Milos shot out his hand and commanded, "Write it!" He pointed to his palm, then drew his forefinger along it in a simulation of script.

Jury sketched "MILOS"—with a question mark.

"No. Madonna." With a look of absolute disgust, he lifted the hand with the cup and indicated the sign behind him.

Jury took the hand again, tried to work out some simple way of identifying himself, could think of nothing. He traced his name; Milos frowned. He traced the word "COP."

Milos snatched back his hand. Then he retreated into his Buddha-like doze, hands snuggled back into frayed coat-cuffs, head inclined.

Even the dog snarled, as if it wanted to know if they made fun of hound dogs, too. Then it tucked its snout into its paws.

Frustrated, Jury touched his arm.

"Fuck off."

"They could do," said Wiggins, as he and Jury climbed the staircase, "with a bit of smartening up."

The youngish man who had tented the book he was reading on the counter was in no need of smartening up. He bore a strong sartorial resemblance to Marshall Trueblood, though dressed in colors far less ripe and blinding. His oyster-colored trousers ballooned slightly at the hips, and the cuffs were both turned up and nipped in at the ankle; his creamy-rose cotton jacket was deconstructed enough for Trueblood and Armani; and also, like Trueblood, he wore a silk scarf, but neatly tucked into the open neck of his shirt, and of a pale, pale yellow.

At first Jury thought the shop dealt in art deco stuff, given the prevalence of blue glass, prism-cut mirrors inset with blue and black triangles, and nubile pewter maidens on tiptoe holding white globes for lamplight. But then he decided this was simply the shop's decor, not its speciality.

The speciality, if the cardboard cutout of Donald Trump was any indication, was a rather eclectic representation of hard times and bad luck. In the bushelful of apples that constituted the "Trump Dump" was a sign telling the customer to "Watch Out for Worms." Wiggins sniggered.

Indeed, it was a Wiggins-ish place, definitely the sergeant's milieu, an atmosphere he could embrace: Wiggins was always on the side of the disenfranchised. For the sergeant, the cup was half-empty, the cloud lead-lined; and if tomorrow was another day, he assumed it would be just as germ-laden as this one.

Nouveau Pauvre appeared to be a celebration of ruin, a paean to poverty, a chorus of swan songs. Little signs graced the glaringly white walls:

DOWN-AND-OUT?
DOWN AT HEEL?
DOWN ON YOUR LUCK?
DOWN-IN-THE-MOUTH?

they asked, suggesting the condition might be alleviated and sorrows drowned if the customer would buy one thing or another from the stock of Nouveau Pauvre.

As the youngish man drifted toward them like a big petal, Jury studied a lovely rosewood dining table in the center of the room. It was covered with a cloth of Irish linen and set with gold-rimmed china. On china and stemware were tiny crowns, a hotel logo; and the napkins were embroidered and emblazoned with intertwined initials.

"Helmsley Palace," the beautiful fellow informed them. "But these are the old ones, I should tell you. The napkins they use now are pink and plain." When Wiggins looked puzzled, he added, "You know, the Helmsley Palace—Leona's place, poor thing. She went inside April fifteen a year ago."

"Inside?" asked Wiggins. "Inside where?"

"Ah, you're British. Not up on local gossip? They did her for tax evasion. Inside whatever upholstered pink prison they reserve for millionaires. Looking for something special?" He wore a tiny gold ring in his ear and hair shoulder-length sixties-style, but very well tended. "Gift for a friend? Lost his job? Stocks fell?" He smiled, as if such circumstances needed only a bottle of champagne to make them complete.

"No, not exactly. We're looking for Alan Loser."

"I'm your man. Actually, the name's pronounced 'Low-zher.' But I've given up correcting people; and it goes with the business."

Jury's eyes swept over the room, snagging on a blow-up of Maggie Thatcher exiting from 10 Downing Street, suitcase in hand. "You're certainly in an unhappy one, Mr. Loser."

"Call me Alan," he twinkled, and looked from Jury's ID to Wiggins's and gasped with evident delight. "Scotland Yard? Why on earth? I don't understand."

"We're interested in one of your former employees. Beverly Brown."

"Beverly. Oh, God." His sigh was deep; he looked away and indeed seemed stricken. "Horrible. But I've talked to one of the city detectives—"

"I know. He told us we could question a few people who might know something."

"Let's sit." He pulled out the chairs around the rosewood table and the three of them sat down. Wiggins took out his notebook.

"We won't keep you long." Jury looked around the room. "You know, I'd imagine you'd have to have money to take a chance on something like this, original as it might be."

"Marketing of bad luck, you mean? Grubbing around for the leavings of somebody else's bankruptcy?" When Jury nodded, Loser simply laughed. "You'd be surprised at how popular it is. Actually, I've come to believe nothing is more saleable than somebody else's misery. My favorite saw is that comment of Gore Vidal: 'It is not enough that I succeed, but that you fail.' He's probably right; it's one of humankind's nastier traits. Wouldn't you like a Ross Perot mug to take back to England?"

Alan flashed a smile as he held up the white mug by its big ear-handles. "One of the sad leavings of last November."

"Beverly Brown worked here, is that right?"

"She did, but only a few hours a week. Over in the Hard Knocks." When Jury raised his eyebrows in question, Alan said, "That's our cafe. Nouveau did so well that when the row house next door became available, Patrick decided to buy it and turn it into a restaurant. Only open until five o'clock—that's an hour before the shop closes. Lunches and teas. We close off the lunch service at two-thirty and set up for the teas at three-thirty. The teas are especially popular. I thought of Hard Knocks because of the fame of the Hard Rock Cafe; it's all the rage in London. Perhaps you'd like some tea."

Jury said "No, thanks" to the tea, ignoring Wiggins's look, which strongly resembled that of the hound. "When was the last day Miss Brown worked here?"

"I told the police that. It was January nineteenth. She finished up in the cafe about five-thirty, stuck her head in the door"—he nodded toward a door on his left, above which was a sign, "Hard Knocks Cafe"—"and said goodnight. Seemed just the same as always." Loser shrugged.

"Did you know her well? I mean, more than in a business way?"

"Oh, yes. Although Patrick knew her better than I."

"Patrick?"

"My stepbrother and business partner. My idea, his money. For him, though, it's a hobby."

"How much better, then, did he know her?"

Alan Loser appeared to be reflecting on his answer. Then he shrugged. "Well, I don't think it was any secret that they were sleeping together. But it wouldn't have been popular on the Hopkins campus." Then he picked an aluminum cup with an odd handle from a table. "Popular item: the Power Cup. Handle's a portable phone, so when the guy who's out of a job is out on the street, he can keep in touch." Alan smiled. "Milos has one."

Wiggins frowned. "But he's *deaf,* sir."

"He can always phone *out.* Does, too."

"What do you think Beverly Brown was doing in the churchyard that night?" asked Jury.

He shrugged. "I'd guess it's the Poe birthday syndrome. That's why I remember the date, the nineteenth. People go to Westminster Church to get a look at the fellow who takes the flowers to the grave. Beverly was a lit grad and she wanted to do her thesis on Poe."

"And this manuscript she claims to have found—did she mention that?"

"Yes, she was incredibly excited about it. Mentioned it to everyone, if you ask me." He rearranged the Helmsley Palace place setting, moving the spoon a bit to the right. "I understand she let one of her professors keep the original. Her name's Ellen Taylor—she teaches in the writing seminars program."

"You know Ellen Taylor, then?"

"Oh, yes. Ellen comes in now and again. She was here just the other day, wanted a little gift for a friend. Swell person, fine writer—though I'm no judge of fine writing," he said, with a self-deprecation that Jury thought he didn't really feel.

"It would be," said Jury, "a very valuable document, that manuscript. Assuming, of course, it's genuine. Do you think it's genuine?"

"Well, I simply have no way of knowing."

"Was she honest?"

Loser opened his mouth in a soundless laugh. "Do you mean that in a Hamlet sort of way? If you do, no, I certainly wouldn't think so—not Beverly, no."

Wiggins looked up from his notebook.

Jury smiled. "I expect I meant it in a literal sort of way."

Alan Loser shrugged. "Not especially. But then, with her looks and brains, I imagine it's too much to expect her to be virtuous, too."

"Would her looks or lack of virtue get her killed?"

"Hell, I certainly wouldn't be surprised. Patrick—" He stopped.

"You mean Patrick Muldare?"

Alan Loser nodded.

"Where is he, then?"

"Could be at Hopkins, I suppose. Teaches the occasional seminar there. Could be a number of places. Patrick's got a lot of pots and a lot of fingers. Patrick's filthy rich."

Jury detected a hard note underlying the breeziness of this statement. "How did he get that way? Filthy rich, I mean?" Jury smiled.

"Family, mostly. He comes from a long, long line of entrepreneurs. Father, grandfather, great- and great-greats. They all had the Midas touch and the temperaments to match. Well, I guess you don't get far in business without being testy, do you? The great-great-great got so angry with the relatives he not only changed his will, he changed his name. Just to let them know where he stood."

"Mr. Muldare is temperamental?"

"Well, ye-*ess,* you could say that. He's certainly *obsessive* about things. Some things. Like football. It's almost childish, in a way, this flea he's got in his ear about the football franchise. You wouldn't know about that, not if you're not from Baltimore or one of the other cities that's angling for it. The NFL is handing out franchises this year or next. Patrick really can work himself up into a fine passion— Hey, wait a minute." Loser smiled, but somewhat uncomfortably. "I don't mean to imply . . ." He hesitated.

"Imply what?" asked Jury mildly.

"Nothing."

Jury looked at him.

"Patrick might have been in love with her, that's all."

"And how do you think she felt about him?"

"Oh, I imagine she saw him as a stepping stone to something else. Money, power, reputation." He smiled, but there was an edge to the voice, an altered and somewhat pugilistic posture as he leaned forward to take one of Jury's cigarettes. Jury struck a match. "Patrick has them all."

Something in the tone tempted Jury to add "And you don't," but he was silent.

20

Jury's experience of quads and spires was limited, but he could still appreciate the difference between this wide, expansive American campus up whose long drive their car moved and the dreamy and rather secretive enclosures of the ancient British universities. When he thought of Oxford and Cambridge, Jury saw beautiful old buildings rising high above windy squares where black-robed students and tutors hurried.

Here at Hopkins, the students seemed to saunter a bit more, to amble along pavements crisscrossing the snow-covered grass and joining the mixture of white-columned and more modern glass-and-steel buildings. With their book bags and in their jeans and down jackets, they dispersed amongst classrooms and car parks. *Acres* of cars, Jury noted, surprised that penurious students (or so he imagined them) would have so many cars. And not enough parking spaces, either, he realized. Wiggins drove the rented car around and around and finally opted for a slot clearly marked for a dean. Without even blinking, Wiggins took out a police identification tag and slapped it on the windscreen.

Students were coming out of the building on their left holding styrofoam cups, sandwiches, slices of pizza. This building must be the source of these comestibles, Wiggins decided, and he asked if they could just slip in for a cuppa, reminding Jury that he'd refused Mr. Loser's offer of tea in the cafe. "I'm really parched."

Jury told him to go ahead. "I'll talk to Vlasic and Muldare if he's around and come back and collect you before I go to Professor Lamb's office. That should give you plenty of time. Sit at a table near the door."

Wiggins was ever so grateful and took himself off.

II

Alejandro Vlasic, despite his name, looked neither Central American nor Central European. He was pure American, and one who had gone to some trouble to lay on a veneer of Britese, both in looks and in voice. Standing at the door to Vlasic's office, Jury could easily hear the voice as it addressed students both entering and leaving. Vlasic smoked a pipe (rather obviously, Jury thought), wore green corduroy with elbow patches, and kept his hair just long enough to make him look careless of the attentions of barbers and slightly Bohemian.

Jury finally had to intrude upon his conversation with a student who looked as though he probably had a motorcycle, if not a whole gang, waiting outside.

Professor Vlasic was not at all put out by the visit; indeed, he even appeared to enjoy the attention of a Scotland Yard CID man. Like Ellen, he taught creative writing and American literature. Unlike Ellen, who was a successful novelist with two commercially viable books and one literary prize-winner, Vlasic was a poet with only one thin volume to his credit. *Unleavened Crises* was its name. Jury knew this because he assumed that with three copies rather artfully arranged on different surfaces around the room (desk, bookshelf, coffee table), it could only be Vlasic's. The book had a brown cover, gold title to simulate leather tooling, rough-cut paper, gold edging—pretty, and pretty pretentious, Jury thought. Beneath the desk, he saw, there were a couple of boxes filled with small brown books; by turning his head slightly sideways, Jury made out that they were more of the same.

Vlasic's office was like Vlasic: studied. A length of walnut shelving completely covered one long wall and made its way round to the other, where it finally had to give way to the couch, the cretonne-covered easy chair, the coffee table. It was a smallish room, stuffed with furniture, masses of flowers in slender vases, and curtains at the window. No beat-up pine; no government-issue gray metal filing cabinets, either. No, everything here seemed home-away-from-homish and top-of-the-line.

Before Jury could state his business, Vlasic—thesis director, poet, and self-styled Poe expert—started dropping names: Edward Albee, John ("Jack") Barth, Doris Grumbach, among others. The "others," however, included no poets, although Jury was quite sure Johns Hopkins had poets whose fame was equal to that of its novelists and dramatists. The name dropping posed a problem, though: on the one hand, this professor would like to think of himself as one with this high-profile literary scene; on the other, his name was pretty low down on the list.

In the middle of this star-studded Milky Way of names, Jury dropped Beverly Brown's.

"Very sad," said Professor Vlasic. "Tragic. She was a brilliant girl." He sighed and turned his head so that the light from the window struck his high forehead and hawklike nose. Jury assumed that his right profile was the one he preferred. With the chin tilted that bare fraction of an inch, Vlasic might have been striking a Byronic pose. Too bad he didn't have Byron's face to strike it with.

"You were Beverly Brown's thesis advisor?"

"Yes. She was a superior student. I had sometimes to restrain her imagination, though; my own notion of Poe's—"

Jury didn't want him off on his own notions. "Any idea why someone would kill her, Professor Vlasic?"

"Absolutely none. It's unthinkable."

"Somebody thought of it."

Vlasic winced, as if the comment had been in poor taste.

"You liked her yourself, didn't you?"

"Why, of course. Why wouldn't I?" Vlasic bridled.

"Going back to her doctoral thesis—what did you think of this Poe story?"

"*Suspect* story, Superintendent. *Suspect.*"

"You think it's a forgery?"

Vlasic decided to fence-sit. "Well, a good deal about it might be thought authentic. The Poe vocabulary was there."

"I don't understand."

"Poe tends to repeat words and phrases over and over in his work. It's like an actor having stock monologues to entertain his audience with, you know. If you sift through his work, you find much of the same language—'impenetrable gloom,' that sort of thing."

"She wanted to use the story as the basis for her Ph.D. dissertation, I understand."

"We hadn't agreed upon that."

"Why would you hesitate?" Jury smiled. "I'd think that it would make a *sensational* thesis."

"But that's the point, isn't it? We want scholarship, don't we, not sensationalism."

"I wasn't meaning the word to be pejorative."

But Vlasic was listening to himself, not to Jury. "And the question of authenticity . . ." He buried his chin in his chest, chewed on the stem end of his pipe. "She wouldn't give over the whole of what she had for inspection. Just a fragment. That in itself is suspicious."

"Maybe she was afraid someone would nick it."

"Yet she gave it over to one of her other professors for safekeeping."

It was the "other" that bothered Vlasic, Jury imagined. Patrick Muldare's words came back to him. "Perhaps she trusted Ellen Taylor."

Vlasic was surprised. "You know her?"

Jury nodded.

"Just had a cup of coffee with Ellen this afternoon. A few of my students were there. You know, it's quite impossible to engage Ellen in any sort of scholarly discourse. I don't like to speak ill of my colleagues—"

Um-hmm, thought Jury.

"—but Ellen Taylor isn't the most responsible one amongst them, either in her teaching or in her scholarship." Vlasic knocked out ash and settled in. "Ellen and I both teach writing, as you know, but our methods are different as night and day." Now he had out a pipe cleaner. "I spend half of the semester on methodology. Two weeks of *straight lectures* on structure *alone;* another two on the deconstruction of the poetic symbol—"

Jury raised his eyebrows.

"You'll pardon me if I don't try to explain that concept?" Here, Vlasic actually looked him up and down, as if he were deciding whether to give Jury a nickel. "I refuse, *refuse,* to let them put one word on paper for eight weeks. Not *one word.* That's an ironclad rule of my teaching."

"They might be doing it in secret."

Vlasic waved this suggestion away. "Now, Ellen Taylor doesn't believe in anything but a pencil and a piece of paper. Ellen does not *teach;* Ellen had them writing from day one. Ellen has—"

"Ellen has done rather well for herself."

"I don't know what you know about semiotics, Superintendent—"

"Precious little." Jury had plucked the brown book from the desk.

"Ellen's trouble is, she believes in *words*—"

"Given her job, I'm not surprised."

"—and the trouble with readers is just that: they try to find the matrix, the clues to meaning. Deconstruction is the only viable—"

"This yours?" Jury interrupted by flagging Vlasic down with *Unleavened Crises.*

Vlasic looked extremely pleased. "You know what they say: 'The novelist bows when the poet passes.' " He stuffed the pipe back in his mouth and aimed a flame-throwing lighter at it.

"Yes," said Jury, noncommittally. "Tell me, do you know a man named Patrick Muldare? He teaches here, doesn't he?"

"Ha! A dilettante if ever there was one. The only reason he's permitted to teach here is because he's given the university a considerable amount of money." Vlasic pulled a catalog from his row of books, flipped through it, and handed it to Jury. "Can you imagine? A course in *football?*"

Jury took the catalog, read the title, smiled. "Entertaining. Where can I get one of these?" He held up the catalog.

"Keep it, keep it."

His eye on the two cartons of books under the desk, Jury asked,

"Would it be too much of an imposition to ask for one of *your* books, Dr. Vlasic?"

"No, no—delighted." He pulled one from a box.

"Autographed?"

Vlasic signed the flyleaf with a huge flourish, as if his arm were unwinding: "VLASIC."

"I'm ever so grateful, thank you," said Jury humbly. "You know, whether that Poe manuscript is genuine or not isn't precisely the point in terms of its value to Beverly Brown. Or anyone in a similar position," he added.

"I don't follow you."

"Well, it would be valuable to any *scholar*. Even if it's not the real thing, a dissertation could be written taking it apart, breaking it down, and so forth. Disproving it would be nearly as much of a plum as proving it." Jury picked up *Unleavened Crises* again, leafed through it. "I mean, say, for someone who might want to write a book exposing the fraud. Be a leg up for a career, wouldn't it?"

Vlasic made no comment.

21

"Beverly, Beverly, Bever—ummmm."

Owen Lamb talked like that. Proper names seemed to call up magical incantations, soughing off into mantra.

He sat in his office at Johns Hopkins, surrounded by tiers of books, shelved and unshelved, some on his desk, most on the floor, engulfing his small frame. Professor Lamb had a short torso, and his red suspenders made it appear even shorter, as if they were yanking his waist up to mid-chest. His skin was fine and white, almost translucent, like old rice paper, and delicately webbed.

"An awful thing—yes, awful." He shook his head, scratched at his earlobe absently. "Have they found out anything yet?"

"Detective Pryce is still investigating the death. Did you know her very well?"

Lamb seemed to find this amusing. "I don't know *anyone* very well. I keep pretty much to the books. Beverly did some work for me. She was a pleasant girl, extremely bright. Extremely." He frowned, turning this assessment over. Then he leaned back and stared up at the ceiling. "As far as this alleged Poe manuscript is concerned, though, I consider it highly unlikely she could have written it."

"You think it's genuine?"

"I didn't say that. Hell, no, I don't think it's genuine. Whole thing smacks of forgery, doesn't it? Hard enough to forge his signature, much less an entire story."

Jury frowned. "But you're contradicting yourself, Professor Lamb."

"Hmph! I am, I suppose. I simply mean, it seems utterly impossible."

"I'm not that familiar with the works of Poe, but it does have a kind of Poe-esque ring to it."

"Oh, but he'd be fairly simple to imitate in substance, wouldn't he? I mean, as writers go? Let me tell you something about forgery, gentle-men: it's not the substance, no, it's the style. Difference between a forged and genuine document is nearly always with the form. Beginning with the handwriting."

"What about that?"

"Inconclusive. But I'll tell you something." He stopped, he smiled, as if taking pleasure in a rather good trick. "Whoever wrote that script has awareness of an important concept: that writing has a certain rhythm, and the rhythm is nearly always destroyed by an amateur because an amateur depends upon visual input. That way, you get the kind of hesitating script that breaks the wave formation."

Wiggins looked confused. "Could you explain that a bit, sir?"

"Sure, but first let me say, I'm not really that expert when it comes to handwriting. The reason I know anything at all is because, being a genealogist, I get a lot of documents in here to study, and I've seen quite a few forgeries. To really be conversant with handwriting, you have to understand anatomy: bone structure, complex of small bones of the hand and wrist. You have to know about ball-and-socket joints, about wrist pivot, that sort of thing. But going back to the wave formation thing—line movement, line quality, is very important. What you see almost all of the time is the natural, meaning smooth, uninterrupted flow of curves. Now, the more slowly the pen moves, the more disturbance you get in line quality. Try it yourself; just slow down your handwriting and you get the tremor, the hesitancy, the slight stutter. Letters are not discretely formed, see. That's the way we formed them when we were small and just learning how to write. But now that we can write, our writing sets up a definite rhythm. The rhythm results in wave formation. Then there's 'monitoring'—something you can see in a forged document or signature. You can easily write your name with your eyes closed, correct? Not, though, if you're forging a signature. You 'monitor' the letters—you look back and forth, back and forth." Owen Lamb gave a self-deprecating little shrug. "However, someone a hell of a lot more knowledgeable than I will have to pass judgment on that document. As I said, my field of expertise extends more to documents trumped up by some charlatan selling aristocratic pedigree to some damned fool who wants to be related to Napoleon. Signatures, I suppose I'm pretty good on, but—" he stopped and shrugged—"occasionally, I get some bona fides that aren't totally out in orbit." He stopped again, frowning slightly. "I did a while ago, actually, from your country."

"There was a signature on that manuscript," said Wiggins.

"I must admit, it passed my cursory tests. That Poe signature appeared more as a pattern than as a string of letters, and it's the string of letters you see in a forged signature. I didn't detect the usual pauses, pen lifts, that sort of thing. But it won't pass an expert's scrutiny, I'm sure." He laughed. "You don't think a bunch of crusty old experts are going to let her get away with such an outlandish attempt? A mere *schoolgirl* putting it over on the academic community!"

"Chatterton did." Jury saw himself in the Tate once more. The mental image saddened him. "Or would have done."

"You're right there. And just look at Walpole's reaction when he discovered he'd been had."

"And she was hardly a 'schoolgirl,' Professor Lamb. Twenty-eight and working on her Ph.D." He did not think Beverly Brown should be dismissed so summarily. "And if the document passed your examination, why are you so sure it's a forgery?"

"Oh, I'm not. I'm merely prejudiced against its being genuine. It seems so unlikely. According to Dr. Vlasic, who brought it to my attention, Beverly Brown found it in a *trunk*. Really, now." He shook his head.

Jury smiled. It was the same thing Melrose Plant had said.

"What about paper, ink, that sort of thing? Wouldn't it be difficult to find paper made at that time?"

"Oh, yes. But not impossible. Forgers sometimes use flyleaves from old volumes."

"But here we're talking about more than a single page. That would take a number of volumes, all with the same sort of paper."

Owen Lamb thought for a moment. "It's possible she might have come across stock from a paper mill operating at that time. Perhaps one in Britain. The ink she used—I'm assuming *she* wrote the manuscript, now, understand—doesn't look to me like an example of the really old stuff. The ink on those pages has that brackish, purplish tinge you see on forged documents. And ink before about the middle of the last century would show evidence of corrosion because of the iron in it. This alleged Poe manuscript doesn't. But with someone as resourceful as Beverly Brown—" here he smiled a little—"she probably would have gone to a great deal of trouble to find the right equipment. Who knows?" He shrugged. "Maybe she found a batch of antique paper and got ideas."

"Did she ever talk to you about her friends?"

"Oh, possibly. But I didn't listen." Behind his thick spectacles, his eyes swam and darted. He wiped his hand down over his face, readjusting the gogglelike glasses.

"What sort of work did Beverly Brown do for you, Professor Lamb?"

His chair creaked forward and gently disturbed a stack of books by one of the legs. Dust rose and settled again. "She was helping me with the index for my book," he explained, pinching the bridge of his nose and again resetting his glasses. He waved his arm toward the shelf to his right. "Indexes are boring. She's probably the only person around who's dipped into the infrastructure of one of these centuries-old families besides me. History and literature were her subjects." He scratched his balding head and asked Jury: "Who's head of the department these days?"

Jury smiled. "I wouldn't know, Professor. I'm from Scotland Yard."

Owen Lamb began rocking in his swivel chair, spinning his thumbs around each other. "Beverly used to chatter away about E.A. Poe. Some sort of nonsense dealing with the Poe arcana—perhaps it was his family, I don't know. I don't care too much for Poe, do you? All of that Gothic stuff. Beverly seemed to like it, though. Anyway, she wanted me to help her with someone's lineage—you know, the family tree stuff. Chic, nowadays. I told her I was a genealogist, not a family historian. I get a lot of requests from these DAR types wanting to know if their great-great-great-aunties had ever consorted with George Washington."

"Do you remember who the 'someone' was? The person whom Beverly Brown was interested in tracing?"

Lamb waved his hand dismissively. "Beverly spent a good deal of time rummaging through Poe's ancestors. She had a good mind for genealogy —which is unusual for an intellectual. Perhaps she stumbled on one of them whom she thought important—I don't know. One of the Clemms, maybe."

Wiggins turned from the chart on the wall, a complex charting of ancestry. "This is interesting, sir. Mark Twain is a distant relation of the Princess of Wales."

"Everyone's related to the Princess of Wales. Even that bum the police found in Cider Alley is probably related to the Princess of Wales." Owen Lamb looked at the chart. "Thirteenth cousin isn't much of a relationship, is it?"

Wiggins had a way of attaching himself to the working life of witnesses; it was either as if he had always wanted to do what they were doing, or as if they possessed some power and wisdom that would save him from some future debacle. He stood there in front of the chart pinned to the bulletin board, rocking on the balls of his feet, and said, "One of my own ancestors was a genealogist and sociologist, I recall."

"Really?" asked Lamb.

"Yes, sir. Now I think of it, I believe he was titled. Family name was spelled differently. W-I-G-H-A-N, or something like that. He chronicled the plague, too, as I remember. Like Defoe. He was a . . . viscount? No, a baron. That's it. Baron Tweedears. D'ya know, I'd all but forgotten that!" Wiggins smiled broadly, obviously happy he'd remembered it now.

Jury's eyes widened. *Tweedears?* He was always surprised when one of his sergeant's relations popped up, usually out of the blue of conversations such as this one; Wiggins was himself the sort of person one always thought was travelling light, as it were, without benefit of family. Jury knew he had a sister in Manchester, but that was more or less the extent of family. Nor was it surprising that Wiggins would have some distant kinship with the Black Death.

And although it was never Wiggins's intention to exact an answer from a witness by showing interest in his line of work, this was sometimes the happy result. The fact was, people often forgot Wiggins was a policeman because the sergeant seemed to forget it himself.

Owen Lamb was running his finger across a row of shelved books, all with forbidding black bindings. "Tweedears, Tweedears." No expert, not even one as modest and unpretentious as Owen Lamb appeared to be, wants to admit ignorance in his field or be bested by an amateur. He pulled down a musty volume, wet his finger, and riffled the pages, damply. "Ah! Here we are!"

" 'Tweedears,

" 'Sir Eustace Wickens of Ranesley, County Mayo, son of Avery D., by Mary, da.—' " Wiggins looked a question at Owen Lamb.

"Daughter," said Lamb.

" '. . . daughter of Fitz-Hugh of Aintree, nephew and h.—' H?"

"Heir," said Lamb. "Here, let me.

" 'Nephew and heir male of Eustace Lord Leith, born about 1545, sole heir to said uncle in family estates, 9 April 1570, was created a baronet, county Banff, and subsequently, 21 May 1579, was created Baron Tweedears—' et cetera, et cetera—let's get to something inter—ah! 'In 1580 joined in conspiracy to place the Queen of Scots on English and Irish throne and was—outlawed—' "

Wiggins took an involuntary step backwards.

" '—and his title forfeited.' His brothers apparently took part in this rebellion. They were attainted, too. Then we get a lot of barons de jure— third baron, de jure; fourth baron, de jure; fifth, sixth, seventh, eighth. . . . There we get 'James Arundel Wickens, Gentleman of Bedchamber, died after casual encounter with prostitute—' not the happiest marriage of events, hey?—'on whose death lands regranted by patent 1 October 1790;' then Aubrey, 'title and land regranted by letters patent, 1790, died 1804 following casual encounter with prostitute, and consequent duel.' Well! Title attainted once again, good grief, just for a casual encounter and duel? Seems rather hard on the fellow. 'Succeeded by son—' this is your guy, isn't it?—'Elphinstone Fitz-Hugh Wickens, spelling changed to Wiggens, distinguished genealogist and writer on heraldic subjects, ninth baron de jure'!" Then Owen Lamb snapped the book shut. "How about that, Sergeant?"

Wiggins was speechless. "Pardon me, but does that mean . . . ?"

"You're Baron Tweedears? Possibly de jure. We've only just got through the ninth baron and you don't know but what the title might be in abeyance, dormant, forfeited again between the ninth and whatever the last baron—you? I'll have to check my Cockayne. Haven't you ever looked in *Burke's Peerage,* Mr. Wiggins?"

Wiggins was looking nowhere but at the copier over in the corner beneath a window. "I was wondering, sir—could I just make a copy of that page?"

"Be my guest. But what about your father, Sergeant?"

"What about him?"

Lamb blew air through his nostrils, dragon-wise. "That's what I asked *you,* isn't it? Didn't he ever say anything about this lineage?"

"No, sir. He didn't. Never knew, I expect." The light flashed in the Xerox machine, scanning the page.

"Give the book here when you're through."

Wiggins handed it to him, and Lamb flipped through the pages again. He smiled. "I forgot your coat of arms. Here it is:

'Argent a bear rampant and lion displayed gules. Crest: Burning bush proper. Supports: Dexter, a swan; sinister, a fish, scaled.' "

Wiggins beamed.

Jury sighed. Alfred Edward Wiggins, Baron Tweedears. God.

A title to kill for.

22

"It's ridiculous, of course," said Wiggins, but the rather elaborate way in which he touched his tie and raised his glass, as if he were toasting his ancestors, suggested he thought it was anything but.

The four of them had enjoyed an excellent meal, consisting largely of mussels ("with sand," said Melrose), at Bertha's, and they were now gathered in the Horse You Came In On at the same table they had occupied the evening before.

"A peer of the realm! Imagine!" said Melrose.

"It'd be a turnup for the book as far as Chief Superintendent Racer is concerned, wouldn't it, sir?" Wiggins said to Jury. "Go spare, he will, I shouldn't be surprised."

"He'll go spare, all right," said Jury, thinking that if there were any going spare to be done, he, Jury, might be the first one to do it. Baron Tweedears—good God! "Your guvnor'll likely put a gun to his head. We might finally get rid of him." Jury was carefully arranging the manuscript pages Ellen had handed him.

Melrose had complained that it was his turn to read; Ellen said no, it wasn't, the superintendent hadn't finished what he'd started yesterday; Melrose said this was a fresh batch of pages; Wiggins questioned Melrose about the Ardry-Plant coat of arms; and so on and so forth.

Jury let them quarrel for a few moments and then hushed them with a look and a rustle of pages and said, "Another letter."

Madam,
   I was not long in the company of M. P—— on that evening before I was made aware of his acute distress of mind, as he recounted to me his strange story. I, lost in my contemplation of this odd Perspective induced (or so surely I thought it must be) by the aromatic oils, bade him continue.
   "This affliction—for I cannot call it an illness—"

Wiggins interrupted. "I wonder if this is what we call 'essential oils' this 'Hilaire P.' has got going."

Jury cut him off from speculating on a fresh cure for something—
anything. "*I* don't call it anything, Wiggins. Just listen."

"This affliction—for I cannot call it an illness—was a faintness, a
shortness of breath, but was so disabling that I took at once to my bed
until it might give over its hold on me. And so I lay in a fitful doze off
and on and into the early morning—awakening at last to the sharp
sound of a cry from below. It appeared to come from some point
beneath my window. Still drowsy from the effects of the cordial I had
taken to allay the dizziness that had so swiftly overtaken me and that I
had hoped would assist my slumbers, I rose to investigate the source of
the disturbance.

"Looking down into the courtyard, I beheld two figures, in dark
cloaks, who, from their rapid movements, appeared engaged in a duel. I
could hear the clip of metal striking metal, the scrape of what I took to
be swords or rapiers.

"Who they were, how they came to be there, what was the cause of
their quarrel—to these questions I had no answers.

"Furthermore, as you yourself can judge—"

Here he directed me to the window and I hastened to oblige him by
going to it—

"—the courtyard is enclosed."

And this was certainly so: the two dwellings—M. P——'s and the one
opposite—were separated by the cobbled yard and also joined left and
right by high walls. Entrance could be gained only by means of the
doors to each of these dwellings or by way of a high fretted gate,
padlocked and, he said, never used. Once the gate might have opened
for the conveyance of carriages, but no more. Holding back the velvet
curtain beneath its black volutes, upwards I looked from courtyard to
window which seemed but a mirror-image of this one and thought I saw
a mirror-hand holding back a mirror curtain and drew in from a night
that seemed itself drenched in black perfume.

But the manner of these duellists coming hence was not the chief of
the mysteries that surrounded this peculiar affair, for even assuming
they had entered the closed yard by one or another door, the question
remained: why had they done so?

This was the observation of M. P.——. I myself had immediately put
the strange story down to the combined effect upon him on that night of
wine, the fever he appeared to have contracted, and the essence of the
oils constantly emitted into his sitting room and most possibly his
bedroom. For I myself was feeling the effect of the room's atmosphere,

an atmosphere further enhanced by the light from the flames that crimsoned over the remarkable statuary, and a pearly light thrown down by the chandelier—and I wondered momentarily if these oils were indeed the harmless effluvium of flowers and herbs that he had led me to believe, or rather an opiate released into the air from the curious little circles of glass.

I felt—I must admit it—entranced, <u>enthralled,</u> by the voice of my host and by his lustrous eyes. I had drunk liberally of the light wine which he served and the intoxication that might have allayed my feelings of morbid anxiety served only to augment those feelings. I regarded my host, who sat, quite still and with his high forehead resting on the palm of an elegant hand. Had I been duped? Had I been lured here for some reason I could in no way ascertain? He continued his story:

"And then there came a shout, a flash of a sword as if one of the duellists had struck from the person of the other, some object and sent it flying. It flew into the air and then descended—something small, silver or white, like a fork of lightning or a slice of the moon. And then came a word, also thrown up as if it too had been a sliver of silver—a name— 'Violette!'—fairly <u>hurled</u> at my window." He paused. "And then— nothing! Nothing! The mist that had swirled through the courtyard and around their feet rose until it shrouded the whole. My eye could not penetrate this white gloom, nor my ear pierce the heavy silence that fell in the wake of that single, uttered word: Violette!

"You may wonder," my host continued, "why I did not descend immediately to the courtyard below to investigate; but I thought surely, this must be the result of the fever or whatever plagued me and sleep would dispel these strange sights and sounds from my mind.

"And in the morning when I awoke and threw open the casement and could smell the verdant green of the grass and the flowerbed below and see the clear blue of the sky above, I could but commit that vision of the night before to its proper place—it had been what else but a dream?"

"Yes," I answered him, "that could be the only explanation . . . yet . . . ?"

"Ah. Yet." His countenance as he smiled at me grew not livelier but more despairing. "On that second night the fever had left me and I slept more soundly. And yet, the same scene—the duellists, the sharp cry, the white object flying through the air, the shouting of the name <u>Violette!</u> All was the same, all enacted below my chamber window."

As a violent shudder rent his form, I started up. "Dreams often repeat themselves—" But he waved me back to my chair.

"The next morning I <u>did</u> descend to the courtyard. No trace did I see of the scene I had witnessed and returned here to this room. I put the whole affair down to an overtired and overactive imagination. And that night, the third night—" He stopped, shook his head. "You must wonder why I did not immediately go down at the first cry. I can only say that I felt mesmerized, forced to watch the pantomime and to hear the name that by now seemed to echo from the cold stones of the yard—<u>'Violette, Violette, Violette—'</u> "

Melrose gave his head a violent shake. What was that?

Chanting from the bar: "D-D-D-D-D . . ."

Jury's narration had stopped, and Melrose blinked several times at the flickering images of the big television, where light like blue fire reflected on the faces of the football fans and across the tables.

"Go on!" commanded Wiggins.

"Oh, what the hell are we doing?" Jury rose, piqued that he was being drawn into this story, collected the glasses, and headed into the tumult of the bar.

Wiggins called to Jury's departing back, "But that's not all, is it, sir? Who is this—" Jury out of reach, he turned his question on Ellen— "Violette person? Don't we find out?"

"No," said Melrose, who had taken advantage of Jury's leaving and attention drawn elsewhere to pull over the page and check the ending. He felt, like Jury, unaccountably annoyed that they had all been sucked in—*suckered* in—by this highly dubious story. Not only that, but was he to be obsessed now not only by Maxim and Sweetie but by Monsieur P. and Violette? How extremely tiring. Surreptitiously, he pulled the small pile of manuscript pages towards him. Perhaps—

"Put those back," said Ellen.

Jury was back with their glasses. "If this manuscript is a forgery or if it's genuine won't get us much further, will it?"

"It can't hurt, sir," said Wiggins. "We might as well finish it."

"It's not all here," said Melrose irritably. "This is only another install-ment."

"I told you. I don't want to carry more than a few pages at a time. Unless you want to see me zonked out in the churchyard, too."

"Why would she be attacked for the manuscript if she didn't have it with her?" asked Jury.

"Read the rest," said Ellen, resting her chin on her cupped hands in a listening pose.

Jury read:

He seemed unable to look elsewhere in the room save at that casement, his eye fastening on the billowing velvet curtain there, as if he expected momentarily to hear the name thrown up from below.

"After that third occurrence, again I returned to the courtyard, again found no sign of the duel, and, turning in at my door, I saw—"

"The handkerchief," said Melrose.

Ellen snapped at him. "What? How do you know?"

"I saw the movie—*ouch!*" He rubbed his shin.

Jury's mouth twitched, but he managed not to laugh.

Said Wiggins, his tone plaintive: "Mr. Plant, you're ruining it for the rest of us."

"Sorry, but surely that was pretty obvious? What the hell else could he find in the courtyard? Probably got her name on it, too." He stuffed another handful of popcorn into his mouth. He looked over at Jury, who was looking down at the page of manuscript and asked (smilingly), "I'm right. Right?"

Jury continued to read:

"—I saw, caught in the thicket surrounding the fountain—this!"
From the silver reliquary he drew a small white square of linen or silk and held it out to me. I was loath to touch it, knowing what it must be: that which was flung from the tip of a sword into the dark and was now palpable proof of the recurrence of these strange events. And in the corner of the handkerchief was worked in stitches so tiny as to be hardly discernible to the naked eye—

As another cheer went up from the bar, Melrose said, "V?"

"Oh, be quiet," said Ellen.

—HP, the initials of M. P——.

Ellen and Wiggins looked at Melrose balefully. He ate popcorn and kept his eyes on the television screen. "Wrong again."

I regret, madam, that my spirits are too low to enable me to continue this letter.

"A night at the Horse would revive him. Yes! *Yes!*" Melrose rose to his feet, punched his fist in the air, joining the fans at the bar in cheering on the team.

Ellen yanked at his jacket. "Sit down!"

He fell back into his chair. "Is that all?"

Ellen didn't, or wouldn't, answer. She turned around in her chair, back to Melrose.

"What's the matter with her?" Melrose asked of the other two.

Jury laughed. Very carefully, he was returning the pages of manuscript to their plastic sleeves.

Wiggins said, "Probably because you spoiled the story."

"Oh, for heaven's sake. I'm going to sit at the bar."

"I'm going to bed," said Jury, returning the last of the pages to its cover. He turned it over.

No, thought Melrose, regarding the back of Ellen's obdurate head. No, it's not the *Poe* story—it's Sweetie, that's what's wrong with her. He put his hand on her shoulder, but she shrugged it away. "Well, Tweedears, you leaving too?"

Wiggins, recalled to his title, did not answer directly but said, "It's unfortunate, sir, but the title is tainted. Some bad business."

" 'Tainted'? Sounds unlikely. Let me see that."

Wiggins pushed the Xeroxed copy over.

" '*At*—tainted,' Sergeant Wiggins. That simply means . . . uh, cancelled, or taken away. It's done by an act of Parliament. See here—" Melrose pointed to this parliamentary axing of the Tweedearses' title in the sixteenth century and later. "Clearly, if Eustace and his bros—"

Ellen retched.

"—and his *bros,*" Melrose repeated, "were going to run around rebelling and putting Mary Queen of Scots on the throne, Elizabeth would take a dim view, wouldn't she? But attainders can be reversed. As did indeed happen in the *eighteenth* century."

"But forfeited again," said Wiggins, sighing.

"Well, but it's probably not *extinct,* Sergeant Wiggins. Take heart. And you're in good company. The Duke of Monmouth, the Earl of Westmoreland—those titles are under attainder, don't forget."

Wiggins had certainly not forgotten; he looked wisely at Melrose, raising one slick eyebrow.

"Plantagenet, Sydney, Beaufort—those titles are all extinct. Just imagine the glory *they* once attested to. Extinct now, uncrowned in the urns of mortality . . ."

Ellen depressed her tongue with her finger and made her mock retching sounds as she leaned her head over her knees.

Melrose went on: "And just consider the Tudors! The third son of Henry VII—and we know who his *bro* was, right, Wiggins?"

Ellen was writhing, nearly under the table now.

"Henry the *Eighth*! Anyway, his brother Edmund was created Duke of

Somerset, and died before he was five years old, and that dukedom became extinct."

"Tweedears might be merely, uh, de jure?"

"Hell, it might still be alive and well!" Melrose slapped him across the back. "Let's see your coat of arms, Sergeant. Is that here?"

Wiggins showed him. "Professor Lamb explained it. I didn't quite understand all of the argent-gules business. I'm new at this." He looked horribly self-satisfied.

"Never mind. Ah, I like the motto."

Wiggins read it. "*Sans* what?"

" '*Sans Malaise.*' "

What else? thought Jury.

23

"Aquarium? No. Why should I go to the Aquarium?" asked Melrose of Hughie as he got into the cab the following morning. "The Poe House. Edgar Allan Poe, his house."

Sighing in the boredom of it all, Hughie switched on the engine, let it idle. "You just got to see the Aquarium before you leave. Or what about the new stadium—what about that?"

"Amity Street. The Poe House. I expect you've never been there, have you?"

As the cab pulled away—*lurched* away would be a better description of the galvanic movement that tossed Melrose back against the rear seat—Hughie said, "He was a writer, right? So what's interesting? It ain't like he kept giant sting rays." Hughie thought this marvellously funny and slapped his hand on the steering wheel as he barrelled up Broadway. "At the Aquarium they got this big bunch of rays—biggest in North America, somebody told me."

"How do you find time to visit these museums? Don't you have to work? Don't you have to hack all over Baltimore?"

Hughie sought Melrose's eyes in the rearview mirror. He looked pained. "Listen, I been doing that long enough. I told you—thirty-plus years of it. I don't deserve some time off?"

Melrose didn't answer; time off appeared to be Hughie's forte.

As they drove up Lombard Street, Melrose saw the tiny sign: "Cider Alley." He watched it go past from the rear window, and decided he would get Hughie to drop him off there on the way back. He asked, "Do you get many homeless people murdered in Baltimore?"

"Hell, I guess. Seems sort of stupid, don't it? I mean, you could hardly rob one of them. It's crack wars, cocaine, you know. Christ, no one knows what the hell's going down anymore. We're getting to be like D.C. I'll say this for D.C., though—they got the Skins. They got Art Monk—man, do I love Art Monk. I told you Baltimore's hoping for an expansion team. I tell you that?" Hughie squirmed around, turned his neck so he could eyeball Melrose on this important matter.

"You mentioned it, yes—and you're running into a lorry."

"Yo, man!" Hughie gripped the wheel and sliced the car off to one side and gave a loud and angry squall from the horn that sounded like a flock of Canadian geese.

"Anyway, did I tell you Barry—Barry—hell, what's his name?—*Levinson!* That's it, Barry Levinson! Anyway, he made those Baltimore movies I was telling you about. He's in one of the consortiums. Now what I say is, if Barry could drag in all that studio money, then maybe the NFL would sit up and take more notice. He made *Bugsy,* right? It has Warren Beatty in it. And his wife in it, too. Annette Bening—you know her?"

Hughie stopped for a light but not for an answer, then accelerated again, car and voice. "Then there's this out-of-town bunch, these big-time real estate and business people that don't strike me as too damned savory, that want the franchise. It's like in that Danny DeVito movie about the guy that does takeovers. You see that? Well, he tried to take over Gregory Peck's company, but he didn't. There's such a thing as the American way, though you'd never think it to watch Japan." Hughie thought this very funny and gave his hacking laugh. "I mean, there's so many want to get in on this franchise. The chicken guy, what's his name, the one with the squeaky little voice? Perdue, that's it. People said he was going to be one of the backers, but that didn't happen. I still say the bunch Barry Levinson is in is the best bet, but I don't think he's the big gun in that group, which is too bad. But those NFL owners, wouldn't they love to rub elbows with that guy, or maybe Tom Clancy?"

"Absolutely," said Melrose, who was only half paying attention to what Hughie was talking about. He'd tripped up over Annette Bening, whom he was still trying to place, while at the same time perusing his city guide. The Strangers didn't appear to be going to the Poe House. He turned a page as Hughie made a left.

"The one about the aluminum-siding guys was called *Tin Men*—"

"You told me." Melrose studied the map grid.

"—and Danny DeVito—he's a scream—he was in it. And Richard Dreyfuss. Yeah, this Levinson's from Baltimore, and that's who should own this football club, right? A Baltimorean. Or Baltimoron, as some people like to say. Hell, we can take a joke, can't we?" To demonstrate how good Baltimoreans were about taking jokes, he did his thigh-slapping hawking-laugh act.

As they passed the intersection of Howard and Baltimore streets, Hughie told him that a long time ago, end of the last century, there was some kind of centennial thing, and there was this big arch painted and decorated and put there. "That's what Barry Levinson put in *Avalon,*" said Hughie, "with a lot of fireworks. You got to see that. And *Diner.* You got to see *Diner.*"

"With Mickey Rourke." Melrose turned another page.

"Yeah, Mickey Rourke."

Melrose felt he was touring not Baltimore but Beverly Hills.

Hughie, movie maven, told Melrose he'd just drive around for a while and pick him up later. That or he could wait in the car, read the paper. No problem.

Amity Street was in a somewhat shabby section of northwest Baltimore, but Melrose warmed immediately to the humble prospect of this little house, with nothing but the narrow street before it and the tiniest of gardens behind.

The house was very modest both inside and out, offering no clue that its former occupant, for the years that he had lived here, was a person of intense imaginative grasp and dreamlike meanderings. A house of more Gothic proportions—a gable here, a tower there, and set among untamed trees and tangled vines—would have been more appropriate as a home for Poe. Poe, Melrose thought with a start, should have lived at Ardry End, although Ardry End wasn't (except for his aunt) exactly "untamed." Still, it had in part a sort of creepy ambience, and windows that, in the rear of one of the wings, looked out over a view of broken branches and storm-felled trees. And that pool with the lead fish could have passed, in wintertime, for a dark tarn.

The curator was a tall man with a pleasant manner who let him in and had to go off and speak to the workmen, the painter and carpenter, he said. The room in which Melrose stood, a room which must have been used as a front parlor, was very small and made smaller by its present disarray, for they were (the curator had told him over the telephone) in the process of repainting and repairing. They did this every year. The house was closed to the public now. He had made an exception for Melrose.

Furniture was covered against the threat of paint splatter; some chairs had been upended on a large table; portraits had been removed from walls and propped against another table. The naked squares in which they had hung looked to Melrose like pale reproaches, as if secrets were being unmasked.

It was this transient aspect of the room, this look of things on the move, that filled Melrose with an odd poignance. The older he got, the more he guarded against change. Any change to him boded a flaking away, a crumbling of the existing order, and he strongly resisted it: he even got annoyed when Dick Scroggs started slathering his aquamarine paint on the Jack and Hammer's wood trim.

He looked at the famous portrait of Poe, the face saved from fragility by the dark mustache, the expression of the eyes (those eyes!) called back to earth by the overcast brow. As he was studying it, the curator returned with a mug of coffee and led him away to see the other rooms.

The rooms were all tiny; it was amazing to Melrose that Poe, his wife, Virginia, and Mrs. Clemm could have lived here so amicably. But that attested to their devotion to one another, for devoted they certainly seemed to have been. The curator told him of all of this in a tone of affection for the absent family.

In the little room that housed the glass cases and pictures and prints, the curator stood with his coffee mug hooked between thumb and forefinger, forgetting to sip, instead gesturing with the cup as he talked about Poe's life. An appalling life in most ways. Poverty, *abject* poverty, lay almost permanently across the man's path like his own black shadow. They looked into the case, at the obituaries clipped from old newspapers, and the curator talked about Poe's detractors with a bitterness that Melrose found rather poignant. This Griswold, he said, tapping the glass, managed even to turn Dickens against Poe, to say nothing of hundreds of others. He hated to hear people accuse Poe of drunken debauchery when the man could barely drink at all, he was probably allergic to the stuff; or people excoriate him for marrying his fourteen-year-old cousin, forgetting that the marrying at a very young age and the marrying of cousins was common practice at that time; a bushman (said the curator) would probably think we were uncivilized fools because we couldn't throw a proper boomerang, wouldn't he? Other cultures, other times.

Yes, he said, the police had talked to him at length, of course, as he and "his people" had kept watch the night of Poe's birthday, as they did every year, a ritual, a ritual watch in the churchyard, waiting for the gent to bring his roses and brandy. He had, *they* had, been questioned closely, *uncomfortably* closely. The curator smiled. After all, he shrugged. But it was his view that she, this Brown woman, was aware, was familiar with, the habit of imposture—an imposture carried out by one of "his people" dressing up as the flower bearer in order to fool whatever little crowd would collect on the pavement near the church. After they *thought* they'd seen the man in the cloak with the flowers and the bottle, they'd go away. They did. Why she (the Brown woman) had not left too . . . He shrugged. Don't know.

They stood one on each side of the glass case holding the clipings and letters as the curator brandished his coffee mug and spoke of the absurdity of the claim this girl had made regarding the manuscript. Poe was never coy about his work, didn't secrete it in drawers, didn't hide it in trunks; for God's sake, he needed the *money*. That an entire, a whole, or nearly whole, story would come to light—well, it was too preposterous to consider. He had not seen the manuscript, no. He would not be objective —no hope *there* (he laughed).

He was a nice fellow, a friendly fellow, and he laughed at his own involvement here. But it was obvious that he was disturbed by this manuscript, this so-called "find," this "coup." He took it, Melrose thought, very personally. Poe was, after all, his charge. And the curator said nearly as much: an artist has his detractors and needs, consequently, his protectors. And the nature of genius, and especially fame, is that the detractors become more numerous and the protectors fewer.

Poe, Melrose suggested, would probably have laughed it off.

Laughed it off? No, he wouldn't have laughed it off. And he shouldn't have. Why should a writer have to pay the double price of watching some hack steal his work and then pretend it isn't important? It was bad enough to do such a thing to a living writer, but this girl—well, it's like grave robbing; it's like pulling old delicate patterns of bone, lacelike patterns, from the earth and rearranging them into some clumsy and unwieldy shape. Worse than murder, really. Anyone who would thieve another's work and pass it off as her own wouldn't think twice about murder.

And things took on, as they talked, a proportionately allegorical nature. The Girl, the Public, the Detractors. Proportionate to the curator's anger at this senseless intrusion of a base and vulgar mind into the life given over (in a sense) into his charge. He did not say any of this; Melrose felt it. Melrose also felt that it was proper for the curator to feel this way. It was refreshing to hear an artist so defended.

Poor Poe, poor Ellen. He felt ashamed of having treated her problem so cavalierly, so lightly. At the door now, Melrose turned up the collar of his overcoat, looked up at the sky, whose threat of snow seemed to have vanished and the opaque, oysterish color changed to a milky blue. He pointed this out as the two of them stood there, hands dug down in their pockets. The weather had changed; the sky, said Melrose, was blue.

"Ah, yes," the curator said, looking skyward, " 'the cloud that took the form, when the rest of Heaven was blue, of a demon in my view.' " He smiled ambiguously and shut the door.

24

The office looked like one that might belong to a grammar-school rugby coach. A glass-fronted bookcase containing football memorabilia partially blocked the long, narrow window in the side wall. Other artifacts and football souvenirs lined the shelves of the bookcase and the back of the desk of the tiny office. It was more of a book-lined cupboard: walls of books, left and right, and between them, a desk, a swivel chair, and a couple of side chairs hugging the walls. That was all the furniture. Close beside the desk was a large Chinese vase that strongly resembled in its antique and chipped elegance the one Jury had seen at the doorway between the Pre-Raphaelites and another gallery in the Tate. Into the mouth of this one, though, a football had been stuffed.

Muldare took Jury's explanation of his presence in the office—the connection between the murders of Beverly Brown and a man in Philadelphia—with obvious disbelief. "That sounds pretty far out, if you don't mind my saying it."

"I know. Still, it doesn't hurt to ask a few questions." And Jury went on to ask them.

Patrick Muldare endured the questions and comments with good grace, sitting back with his arms hugging the book he'd been reading to his chest, one foot up on one of the folding chairs. He was a man who would always appear younger than his chronological age, which Jury put in the mid-thirties, the image of youth helped along by his corduroy jacket (expensive, Jury could tell), his loafers, his wheat-colored hair cut untidily long and which he kept scraping away from his forehead. Tinted glasses, metal-framed, could not disguise eyes that seemed to express constant surprise or astonishment, or even childlike wonder.

Jury started with a subject he thought might not be quite so volatile: the manuscript.

"Do I think it's a fake?"

"Do you think it was *her* fake, more particularly?"

"Knowing her, yes, probably. Can I have one of those cigarettes? I'm trying to quit."

Jury handed Muldare the pack. "Sounds as though you didn't much like her."

Muldare struck a match, inhaled deeply and with evident relief. "I didn't. But . . . well . . . you know."

But. Well. Shrug. That was Muldare's explanation of his affair with Beverly Brown. Probably didn't have to like a woman to go to bed with her. Jury thought he was oversimplifying the matter. "Trouble with her?"

"Beverly was trouble for anyone, in a way. She wanted too much."

"Marriage?"

"To me?"

Jury had to smile at Muldare's genuine surprise at this suggestion, the expression of his eyes growing in astonishment, as if he couldn't believe anyone would want to marry him. "Well, Mr. Muldare, pardon the cliché, but you strike me as quite a catch."

"Hmm. Yeah, I'm rich, that's for sure. But I don't know. Beverly had ambitions that didn't include a husband."

"Did she talk to you about this alleged Poe manuscript?"

"Yep; this little morsel was going to make her career. It sure as hell would be a coup. Beverly had a coup mentality, if you know what I mean. In other circumstances, she'd've made one hell of a guerrilla."

His smile was quick, here and gone, darting like a swallow into the sun. His head turned toward the window and its line of light around the bookcase. "Maybe that's too tough an analogy. I sound pretty cold-blooded. It's just that Beverly had a way of going after what she wanted." He plucked the football from the mouth of the Chinese vase and turned it in his fingertips and grew, as he did this, more studious, more serious. "She was damned smart. Ellen can tell you that; she had Bev in a few classes. You know, even if this story isn't authentic, if it's a forgery, well, what a sweet subject for a doctoral thesis, right? Beverly panted to get into an Ivy League school. Our version, I guess, of Oxbridge."

"That's what she wanted? Doesn't strike me as especially exciting for a woman of her apparent ambitions."

Muldare laughed. "Well, you ain't a woman, and you sure as hell ain't a *black* woman. And it's a hell of a lot better if you can sail into a job like that on your *merits* rather than as an ad for affirmative action."

"Do you think it's the real thing?"

"The Poe story? Naw. Just based on the odds, how could it be?"

"I don't know the odds. But what about her finding it?"

"You mean, did she?"

"I mean, did she have the ability to forge such a manuscript?"

"Ability?" Muldare shrugged. "Nerve?" He smiled. "Yeah. Bev was never short on nerve. But something like that takes more than nerve. You'd have to be goddamned *brilliant* to pull something like that off."

"I wonder. You'd have to be clever, yes. But 'brilliant'. . . ?"

Patrick Muldare laughed again. "You sure as hell don't give much credit, do you? I could never have done it."

"You're not a Poe specialist. You're not an ambitious young black student. And I wonder if the sheer audacity of such a forgery wouldn't tend to make us think that simply because it's so audacious and seemingly unthinkable someone could forge an entire story that way—that maybe it's genuine. Assuming it passes a few tests. Stringent tests, I expect. Still . . ."

"You've lost me. What's this got to do with the case Scotland Yard's investigating?"

"Maybe nothing, insofar as the manuscript itself goes. But wasn't she herself making a connection between the murder of this homeless man who was knifed in Baltimore and Philip Calvert in Philadelphia? She thought these people were linked."

Muldare, who seemed to want to be in constant motion, tossed the football up, caught it, snapped it back. "You're talking about those initials. Including, maybe, mine?"

Jury nodded. When Muldare said nothing more and just kept spinning the ball, Jury asked, "Do you think your brother would know anything about her movements on that night? I know he's talked to police, but—"

"Stepbrother. Alan's my stepbrother. I don't know about that night, but he certainly knew her." He turned his head, rubbed at his neck. "His mother married my father. It was—difficult. Hard for Alan, I mean. Everyone else got on like a house afire. Not Alan. He doesn't like me much, see. For one thing, I have the money."

"I see."

"No, you don't. I mean *money* money. Old money. *Very* old money. Well-used money. A lot of—" He sketched a dollar sign in the air. He seemed defensive, slightly guilty.

"Yet, you teach."

"Well, that's because I like it. And I don't do much." He grinned. "Ask my students, they'll tell you." The grin vanished. "There was a trust fund for Alan, but that soon went. And he hasn't got a head for business. He's clever, that's for certain. Nouveau Pauvre was his idea. But he can't seem to channel the cleverness into anything lasting. What he needs is an endless waterfall of money to indulge his fantasies. Trouble is, he hasn't got it, and I have, which doesn't endear me to him."

"What about Beverly Brown?"

"What about her?"

"Did your relationship with her make him jealous?"

"Yes." The syllable was curt. He offered no assistance.

The silence lengthened. Jury waited.

Muldare studied the football, then said, "I can't really say I blame Alan. After all, he saw her first."

Jury laughed; he couldn't help himself—the statement was so reminiscent of arguments he remembered having in his adolescence, maybe earlier, with some other boy, school chum. *Hey! I saw her first!*

Patrick Muldare grinned, as if he, too, remembered, and as if he, too, heard in his own words an echo of adolescence, the teenager still trapped inside the man. And he didn't seem to mind the joke being on him. "Well, you know what I mean."

Jury nodded. "I get the impression the jealousy was rather violent?"

"Not *that* violent, Superintendent," Muldare said, now very serious. "Alan's not the type."

"I don't know if there is or isn't a type."

"You see, the jealousy wouldn't have been just over a woman, a girl. It would have been another loss to me in what Alan must have thought a long line of losses. Even his mother seemed to like me more. He's not a happy person. It's too bad."

There was another long silence. Jury looked at the bookcase. "You like football?"

Patrick Muldare threw back his head and laughed uproariously. "How'd you ever guess? Thought I'd covered my tracks pretty well." The change in his expression was remarkable.

"Ellen Taylor was talking about you. Then I kind of worked it out for myself. I *am* a detective."

"Brilliant." He tossed the ball to Jury, who nearly fumbled it before tossing it back. Muldare grinned. "I like Ellen. She's not full of bullshit, like a few others. Have you read her book?" In an awkward acrobatic motion, rather like a man reaching back to catch a pass, he plucked a book down from a shelf behind him. "*Windows,* it's called." He held up the cover for Jury's inspection, then opened it, grunted, snapped it shut, and held it against his chest, together with the ball, a kid with two teddy bears, as he studied the ceiling. "Weirdly compelling."

"I don't think I understood it, exactly."

"Aah, 'understand' . . . Me either, but I kept on reading it, and that's the whole point, isn't it?" His look at Jury was wide-eyed and innocent. "Don't tell her I didn't understand it, will you?"

How Jury had come to know Ellen, Muldare didn't ask. Indeed, he didn't seem to question much, simply accepted things as they entered his life, as if life were just one long forward pass.

"Hardly," said Jury, smiling. "I didn't tell her *I* didn't understand it. So I'll just say you kept on reading." From his pocket he drew the catalog and opened it to the page he'd marked, reading, " 'The Psycho-socio Impact of the NFL in the Late Twentieth Century.' Speaking of not understanding—what does *that* mean?"

Patrick Muldare looked up at the ceiling and then around the office, lips moving slightly as if he were searching for laymen's language. "Nothing." He flashed Jury another grin.

"Nothing."

"It's supposed to sound academic and at the same time be a turn-off for guys who think I'm just going to talk about football."

"So what *do* you talk about?"

"Football." Now the grin split his face and stretched ear to ear.

"It must be popular, once word gets around."

"Oh, you bet." Happily, he spun the ball on the tip of his index finger, let it fall in his palm. "We're hoping Baltimore's getting the franchise."

"Your stepbrother mentioned that."

"For an expansion team."

Jury nodded toward the glass-fronted case. "You had one—"

Swiftly, Muldare shot his arms in the air, hands fisted. "Yes!" He might have been sitting in the bleachers. "The Colts."

"Then the city's got to go through some kind of red tape to get another one?"

"It's more than red tape. The NFL only awards a certain number of franchises; we've got to prove we deserve one. That we had the Colts helps. But St. Louis had the Cardinals, too. The NFL hasn't expanded since ' 76. Now they appear to be willing to give out two franchises. Only two. *But* they could even call that off any time they want, because they left themselves legal loopholes. Say they do award them, though—in a couple of months, March, there'll be a short list. And that will cite three —" this time it was three fingers in the air—*"three* possibles. In October, they'll let us know the two out of three." He shut his eyes tightly, looking pained, as if already seeing Baltimore in third place. "This expansion team thing has been going on for seven, eight years, ever since Isray—the Colts' owner—tossed the helmets and jerseys in a bunch of moving vans back in '84 and did what I think you guys call a 'moonlight flit.' He was afraid the city would get an injunction to keep the team here. Bastard."

"How good is Baltimore's chance?"

"Very. Not, though, as good as a lot of people want to believe. It's really complicated. A lot of money's involved, and, naturally, the city has to have a stadium."

"You've got a new one."

"Camden Yards is for the Orioles. Just for baseball. Oh, what a stadium that is! I go down there just to sit and look at it. But we've still got Memorial Stadium, so that's no problem. Baltimore will likely be one of the three, but it's the first two that count, and it's my bet Charlotte will head the list. That's in North Carolina," he added helpfully. "And then there are all the wheels within wheels: the various people and groups who want to buy and manage a team and who have to convince the NFL they're the ones that can do it. People and groups with money and clout have been popping up, dropping out, forming, re-forming for years here. Financiers, hoteliers—even authors. Tom Clancy's one of them."

"The writer?" When Muldare nodded, Jury said, "But surely you're talking about millions."

"A *lot* of millions. Clancy has money, but not that kind. What he's got is marquee value. Like Barry Levinson. You know, the movie guy. The director. Trouble there is Levinson doesn't have the controlling interest in his particular group. Then there's me—" in mock self-congratulation, Muldare inclined his head, smiling—"who also paid my one hundred thousand to get my foot in the door."

Ellen had said Muldare was rich. That rich? Jury's surprise showed in his face.

"Well, I've got backers, too. Yeah, I might be able to raise one or two hundred million, but then there's money to buy the players and so forth. What I'm doing right now is trying to buy the name back. The Colts name. If Isray will sell it. I need to do something, oh—" he squinted upwards, still turning, turning the football between his fingers—"glittery, something stagy, something—*Hollywood.* You know?" He let the football drop softly in his lap as he drew a banner-like stripe in the air.

Jury smiled. "Marquee value."

"You bet," said Muldare. "Thing is, if you were an owner, if you were sitting around the table with the other owners, who'd you rather chew the rag with? Clancy, Hollywood, or just some tweedy teacher type—a Colts devotee, sure, but still. . . ?" He shrugged, tossed the ball up, caught it.

And in his mind, ran it, Jury imagined. Marquee value. Jury frowned slightly as he studied the rim of light around the bookcase, then the shelves themselves, crammed with souvenirs of old games—miniature helmets, a couple of scruffy-looking pigskins, pens, ticket stubs, photos.

And he wondered: just how much marquee value would Edgar Allan Poe have?

He wondered this as Muldare's football got him right in the stomach. "Uh!"

"Reflexes—reflexes, Superintendent." Pat Muldare grinned.

25

It took some convincing to get Hughie to disgorge Melrose into Cider Alley, not because its prospect was somewhat dim and more than a little scruffy, but because it was so near the new ballpark. Camden Yards, home to the Baltimore Orioles, was a must-see on Hughie's tour list, second only to the Baltimore Aquarium. That Melrose would be stepping out of his cab within breathing distance of this spanking-new stadium and not into its glorious environs was something that left Hughie speechless —and that was saying a great deal. The cab did speed off, but only with a promise from Melrose that the tour would continue later.

Cider Alley was just what its name suggested, a short and narrow street, little more than a passage, connecting Eutaw and Paca streets. There was nothing here by way of commerce that Melrose could see, except for what appeared to be the rear of what might have been a bar or a club, through the glass doors of which a handful of people came and went. Further along, past several dark doorways, Melrose saw a small band of people, these appearing to be permanent residents of Cider Alley. Three men were smoking and tilting bottles in brown sacks to their lips; a fourth was warming his hands over the low flames of an oil drum. Melrose approached them, thereby igniting a thirst for charitable contributions that matched the thirst for hard drink. One and all they asked for a variety of handouts, ranging from a quarter (that ubiquitous quarter) to, after they had a better chance to inspect his clothes and up the ante, a dollar. Melrose was pleased to oblige and offered even more in return for information. He had often remarked that money could open mouths, eyes, and, occasionally, even hearts.

"Hey, m'*mahn*!" retorted the black man in mirror sunglasses. "You ain't the *po*-lice, is you? We got the fuckin' po-lice up the ass."

"It's been my experience police don't offer money in exchange for information. They just shoot you."

A round of ribald laughter, and a fat man said, "It's about John-Joy, ain't it? They come round here asking questions after John-Joy got his-self smoked."

"Yes. It's a personal, not a police, matter."

"You fambly? Always said he had fambly," said the androgynous mass of rags by the oil drum who Melrose had taken for a man and who turned out to be female, or at least Melrose thought so.

"Did he, then?" Doesn't everyone, more or less?

"John-Joy, he was on and on about his people," said another black man, leaning against the wall. " 'I got the doin's!' John-Joy say. 'I got the doin's!' " And here he slapped at the area of his heart.

Melrose frowned. " 'The doin's'? What did he mean by that, do you think?"

The black shrugged, lifted his pint bottle, and, seeing that the line was dangerously low, shook it just a bit for their visitor's inspection. Melrose said he would be happy to buy him a drink and pressed a note into his hand. "That there," said the man, hooking his thumb over his shoulder, indicating, apparently, a wire basket on wheels that Melrose thought might be the sort one pushes around in the enormous supermarkets of this country, supermarkets like small cities. It was piled high with the detritus of life on the streets.

The black man nodded and said, "Them's the doin's, we reckon." He smiled broadly.

The "doings" consisted of a couple of blankets, a bundle of old clothes, shopping bags full of cast-off items probably garnered from rubbish bins, like the quarter-full green carton of Cascade dishwashing powder. Also books, and Melrose found that a little odd, given the man's position. And papers. "Why didn't the police take possession of these?"

"Dint know about it, mahn. Wouldn'ta cared if they *did*. John-Joy, he a *street* dude, mahn."

"But they did question you, didn't they?" Melrose picked up one of the volumes, stained and fox-marked—an account of the Civil War, it appeared to be. Then there were pamphlets, notebooks, old ledgers, one of which looked like it might have come out of the St. James Hotel with its list of names.

The black man snorted. "They don't pay no attention to us, mahn. Ast us did we see anythin', hear anythin'. I say, 'Yeah, mahn, we see the moon, we hear the rain.' "

Melrose smiled. "Good answer. What's your name, if you don't mind my asking."

"No, I don' mind. Estes. Easy, they call me. I'm Jamaican, mahn."

"Well, *besides* the moon and the rain, did you see anything, Estes? Or any of you?"

"Only me and Carl was here. Twyla was gone." He nodded towards the woman. "So was Bernard." Nod towards the fat man wearing a poncho. Estes shook his head. "Nope."

"Hmm. Where did they find him?" Melrose looked down the alley.

"Other end," said Estes. "You want I show you?"

The others clearly suspected that more money was about to change hands and started arguing with Easy that they knew just as much as he did about John-Joy. They were not to be left out of this scheme and trotted along to the other end.

Estes, with very colorful language, described the scene as he saw it in his mind's eye. John-Joy trundling his cart along, a figure creeping out of the shadows, and then—here Estes crossed his hands in front of his neck and made a pulling motion.

In a voice so irate it was a squeal, the woman objected: "Hell, you don't know that any more'n *I* do. You wasn't here—you just makin' it up." She turned to Melrose with her own superior knowledge. "You ask Milos—Milos, he says he found him."

"*That* is fuckin' *in*sane, Twyla. Milos is *blind* and *deaf*, so how the hell he'd know?"

"Milos?" Melrose feigned ignorance.

"Blind man hangs out over to Howard Street near some shop named . . . New somethin', . . . I can't remember." Estes turned to Twyla and continued: "The *cops* found his body."

Twyla looked disgruntled and mashed her gums around, but she couldn't deny the truth of this.

Melrose dispensed another round of bills and they all moved, as a mass, back up the alley to the oil drum. Melrose wanted that market cart.

He asked, warming his own hands over the drum in a rush of camaraderie, "Who owns the doin's now—everyone?" He looked around at the four faces, the bare or half-mittened hands fixed above the oil drum, the cheeks of the woman actually rosy in the firelight.

Estes looked a question at the others. None of them laid claim to the doin's, which surprised Melrose. He thought they'd fight over the basket. But perhaps their instinct was that this recent swelling of their ranks meant a fair shake, that he had behaved very well towards them and, with his Old World savvy and, of course, his bankroll, might deliver them from their predicament of Who Owns the Doin's.

Melrose enjoyed thinking this, at least. "Would you be willing to sell the cart—" Melrose nodded toward the wire basket—"for, say, a hundred dollars?"

Their mouths dropped open.

Since no one immediately took him up on it, perhaps he should raise the price. After all he hadn't rooted right down to the bottom. Maybe there was a baby in there. "Two hundred?"

But Estes was suspicious. "Hell you want *that* junk for? Some valuables in there?"

"Not that I know of. You're welcome to go through it if you like before I take it. That is, of course, if you're all willing to sell it. But I'll tell you why I want it: only because it might offer up some clue as to why the man was murdered, that's all."

"Two hunnert, huh? Two hunnert?" The fat man was busy with a mental arithmetic that was getting the better of him. He scratched his grizzled hair and pulled at a ragged ear in concentration.

"Fifty apiece," said Melrose, helping him.

The bargain was struck and Melrose peeled off four fifties, to their delight, since that meant no haggling over who'd get the bills changed or hold the money. Each got a fifty.

"Tell me something: did John-Joy have any particular friends—I mean, besides this Milos person and yourselves—in whom he might have confided?"

"Confided *what*? John-Joy went along chantin' all the time, mister. Just went round chantin' worse'n a bunch of Democrats with rubber checks. He kept on sayin' he was to be rich one day, real rich, soon as he got him a lawyer. 'I got the doin's! I got the doin's!' My, that man could be an aggravation."

"Didn't he ever explain what he meant by that?"

Estes said, helpfully, "Tell you what, mahn. He say he got a friend name of Wes over to the shelter, that big shelter called Cloudcover over on Fayette. Mighta had other friends over there, too. John-Joy used to stay there nights when he had the money."

"Well, thanks very much. I might stop back to talk a little more, if you don't mind."

They certainly didn't.

Melrose stopped on the other side of Harborplace and got out his guide. They'd told him it wasn't too far, and he hoped his Cider Alley cohorts weren't like Brits giving directions: Oh, just go to the top of the street, there, love, and then walk along a bit, and after a little while you'll see Acacia Cottage (or wherever you were looking for and would likely never find)—and then you walk to the top of the street and keep on walking (for days and days, it usually seemed), and next thing you're in Edinburgh. . . .

He'd been trundling the cart before him for blocks, sorry now he'd dismissed Hughie, but not wanting to hop in a strange cab with his grocery cart and ask to be taken to a shelter.

For one thing, he wasn't dressed for it.

He looked down at his cashmere topcoat, his Liberty silk scarf, and frowned. On top of the pile of stuff in the cart was a heavy old coat, a sort of salt-and-pepper wool with big black buttons that wouldn't, of course, fit, but that was hardly the point. He removed and folded up his topcoat and put on the black one. The arms were too short and the shoulders drooped off his shoulders and he wondered what gorilla it had originally been tailored for.

He also removed his calfskin gloves and dug around for the dark brown mittens he'd seen in there. There was a cap, too, with ear flaps. He put that on his head. On top of the pile was a plastic cup shaped like Mickey Mouse, the inside of which he inspected. As he looked over the top of the metal rubbish bin on which he was resting his *Strangers' Guide,* he saw two children, tongues sculpting their soft chocolate cones, staring at him. ·

The mother, who had apparently just walked on up the street without them, as if they were leftover children ("I have more at home, you see"), realized her error and rushed back and started carting them off, one hand on each shoulder. Then she saw what they'd been staring at (Melrose Plant), cocked her head, and started rooting in a bag slung over her frontage.

She walked over and put two quarters in his Mickey Mouse cup.

He didn't really see much to choose between the woman and himself, since she looked like a swamp thing in her outsized jungle-green jacket and all sorts of sweaters and thick gloves and mile-long scarf drawn around and around her neck and up over her mouth.

Nevertheless, he thanked her, and the little family moved away, the girl not forgetting to look back over her shoulder and stick out her tongue.

Melrose sighed and consulted the *Strangers' Guide.* He couldn't even find Fells Point. Unfortunately, the Strangers had decided to have lunch in Little Italy, and then to double back to Harborplace, which was no help to him at all.

He crossed over Farragut, walked along with his cart past steaming manhole covers, traceries of mist rising from them and disbursing into the outer air. They made him think of Victorian London, he wasn't sure why—the ground mist and fog, probably. He walked on, wishing he'd purchased a more detailed map when he'd had the opportunity. He turned a corner that looked familiar and went shoving along for four blocks before he realized it wasn't familiar at all. He was terrible about directions; whenever anyone told him to walk east or south they might just as well have said to walk straight up into the sky. The buildings here were a trifle shabby, housing on their corners small businesses such as convenience stores, jewellers behind furious-looking black grates, and PayLess everything: PayLess Shoes; PayLess Appliances; PayLess Drugs, travel, mattresses.

And then he stopped.

Here it was, a huge old building with a little brass plaque: CLOUDCOVER HOUSE.

26

Melrose could not say that he was exactly hailed by the people on the steps, but he was examined and silently greeted with a nod of the head here, a gesture of the hand there. In and out of its doors a number of people—black, white, possibly Puerto Rican (Melrose lived an insular life)—hung about Cloudcover House, hands shoved in trouser pockets, breath pluming the air. As he stood uncertainly with his burden of rags and books, two of them stopped their conversation and gave what he interpreted as a welcoming smile. Hell's bells, why not? He advanced up the steps and, not wanting to appear too uncertain as to how to proceed, simply shoved his wire cart with a great deal of difficulty up several steps, stopping to lift it in front, until one of the two came along to take over the lifting job. Melrose thanked him very much when they got to the top. He shoved open the big door.

Inside was a long hall, at the near end of which was a sort of bullpen-like area, with a counter. A woman with heavy body and heavy features, a down-turned mouth as if she'd seen too many days of catering for the homeless and had grown less charitable withal, looked at him with a show of indifference. Probably a volunteer, probably unpaid or paid very little; but, really, they could have hired someone with a bit more bounce to cheer up such as he. He felt quite wan as he signed the book, and when she asked for the two dollars, he wondered how the devil he was to skim two bills from his weighty money clip. He mumbled something deliberately incomprehensible as he started searching around through his pile of junk. He kept on mumbling and muttering until she lost patience and turned away, back to the working circle inside the hemmed-in area. In this way he was able to whip out a wad of notes and slip off what he hoped were two singles and not two hundreds and then stuff them into one of the pockets of his cashmere topcoat. The money over here was the devil of a problem; all the same size. He smiled as he waited for the woman to turn back to him, thinking of the boy Alex Holdsworth and the trouble he'd had to go to to fleece his poker-playing friends because the trick *required* bills of all one size. He chuckled. There was a kid he hadn't minded knowing. He wondered if he'd run into him again since Lady Cray—

". . . got all day!"

He realized he'd been standing there with a stupid smile on his face. He handed over the two dollars and she directed him to a room, informing him that he wouldn't be able to use it until seven p.m. that night. Melrose started to push his cart along, then stopped and said, "Pardon me, but do you know someone here named Wes?"

"I ain't the Yellow Pages."

"No. Sorry." He pushed off.

There were four beds, each with thin but very clean sheets and a mouse-colored blanket rolled up at the bottom. On one of the beds near the wall sat an elderly, emaciated-looking man, sitting and staring at the wall. His lips moved steadily. Perhaps a prayer, thought Melrose.

A much younger man sat on the near bed, a guitar against his chest. His hair was shoulder-length, very dark and almost burnished like mahogany; he had a thick mustache and rather humorous brown eyes. He nodded towards Melrose and thrummed his guitar, not really playing anything, just making soft noise.

Melrose looked around, wondering what the drill was. He could not, he was sure, leave his cart unattended.

"You can have either one. Just flop. Never mind what they tell you out there about not using the room till night. The name's Jerry." Here he raised two fingers to his forehead in a mock salute.

"Uh. Mel. Glad to meet you." Melrose moved over to Jerry's bed and stretched out his hand. Having noticed the fellow had a pleasant, honeyed drawl, Melrose decided to engage him in conversation by saying, "You're not from around here. You certainly don't sound like Baltimore. Where are you from?"

"Baton Rouge." The black eyes regarded Melrose. "Yourself?"

Melrose puffed out his cheeks. "I'm English, actually." He sounded too stiff, he thought. "Just one of your Brits."

"No kidding." The tone was flat, but the note of mild surprise was pure pretense. Jerry only just barely kept from smiling. "Coulda fooled me, Mel."

"Yes. Yeah. See, things were bad back there—"

"With an accent like that I can believe it."

What? Melrose had always thought his accent quite passable. What did this Jerry mean? He was lying there with an arm draped over his guitar as if it were a baby, blowing smoke in Melrose's face.

"Newcastle, that's where I'm from. North of England." He doubted Jerry was all that well acquainted with the Geordie accent. "It's fierce up there. Worst employment problem in England. They call the job centers 'joke shops.' " Melrose was warming to his subject and was a little annoyed when Jerry interrupted.

"Smoke?" Jerry reached the pack towards him, punching up a couple of Marlboros.

"Ah, thank you." Melrose's own silver cigarette case was at that moment resting in the inside pocket of his cashmere coat, near the money clip. "Much obliged," he added, as roughly as he could.

"Sure." Again, that smile that reached Jerry's eyes and just missed *twinkling.*

Well, for God's sake, why had he expected to get away with this absurd charade? First he'd treated the heavyset woman at the counter as if she were the desk clerk at the Dorchester, and now here he was trying to get this person to believe he came from Tyne and Wear.

Jerry asked him, "You an actor or something?"

Melrose certainly hadn't expected this. "Actor?"

"Yeah. You know, studying your role. Pretending to be a tramp."

Melrose concentrated on the coal of his cigarette and turned over this possibility.

Jerry went on: "What's the flick? *The Happy Homeless?*" But he did not seem to take all of this in other than good spirits. He grinned.

Melrose laughed. "You're pretty damned smart. What gave me away?"

"Oh, *shee*—it . . ." Jerry more or less lost the word in a spatter of saliva and wiped his hand across his mouth. "Tell the truth, Mel, I ain't one bit clever. I am pretty dumb, or I wouldn't be in here. No offense, but why didn't they get a *real* English dude for the role? Michael Caine, like?"

"Caine doesn't have the right accent, to tell the truth. North London, East End, that's Caine."

"Hey, that's *rich*. He don't, but you *do*?"

"I look the part."

"So what's the story? The movie story?"

"Well . . . it's about this English fellow who's trying to solve the murder of a homeless man."

Jerry lay back on his pillow, throwing his arm across his forehead. "Cretinous, man. Truly cretinous. But that's Hollywood."

Melrose gulped up a couple of laughs. "You got it."

"You can drop the accent, old buddy."

"I'd rather not. It's good practice."

"So who's doing it?"

"Doing what?"

"The flick, man—the picture."

Melrose rolled his cigarette in his mouth. "Barry Levinson."

Jerry scratched his chest and studied the ceiling. "Name sounds familiar."

"You've seen *Diner,* haven't you? Mickey Rourke's in it."

Jerry snapped his fingers. "Shit, yes. Great movie. So who's in the one you're doing?"

Melrose picked at a loose black button on the old coat and said, "Annette Bening."

Jerry sat up, suddenly. "No shit! Lucky fucking *you,* right, man? She's gorgeous."

This Annette Bening must be something. In a slightly smirking tone, Melrose said, "In La-La land, everybody's gorgeous."

"Yeah."

"How long have you been here? In Baltimore, I mean."

Jerry shrugged, thrummed his guitar. "Six, seven months."

Melrose didn't think it would be appropriate to ask him if he liked it. But Jerry went on:

"I had me a nice little franchise in Baton Rouge. Muffler place. But things got bad, just like everywhere else. Couldn't find work . . . the wife walked out." He shrugged again. The old story.

"I'm sorry."

Jerry didn't comment. He was sitting on the side of the bed now, looking in the wire cart. "So where'd you get this shit? Is it a prop?"

"It belonged to a homeless man named John-Joy." He waited for perhaps some sign of recognition, but Jerry was frowning over one of the books he'd picked up. Melrose added, "He used to come here a lot, I understand."

" 'Used to'?"

"He's dead."

Jerry looked up from the book, studied the air for a moment. "John-Joy. Yeah, wait a minute—think I heard him around once or twice. Kind of batty."

"He had a friend here called Wes. Do you know any Wes?"

Apparently, there was little enough distraction in the shelter that Jerry didn't think about, or bother with, questioning Melrose on his interest in John-Joy. "Shit, everyone round here knows Wes. He's kind of on the staff now. Come on; I know where he usually is."

"Place used to be some tycoon's home," said Jerry as they walked down the hall, Melrose still pushing the creaking cart. One of its wheels was turned backwards, and he had to keep kicking at it.

"Private home," said Jerry. "Down here used to be a ballroom. Maybe turn of the century. Or maybe there's an account of it in one of them books in the cart." He laughed.

The room at the end of the long hall was enormous, the size, as Jerry had said, of a ballroom. A few men lounged there, leaning against the wall or just standing, watching a tall black man out in the middle of the room. He was dribbling, or attempting to dribble, a much-used basketball over a floor too rough to take it.

"Wes," said Jerry, nodding toward the black man. "Wes used to be pro. Ten, fifteen years ago. Got into drugs—crack cocaine, that shit. I never got into that shit, let me tell you. Wes was a great player. He's still got some of the old razzle-dazzle."

Yes, thought Melrose, he did. From the middle of the room he moved with the ball, back, forth, hands, floor, down to the "basket" at the end— an old wastepaper bin with the bottom cut out, fixed up on a board, itself fixed to the wall. Wes's arm shot up, dunked it; the ball went through, catching momentarily on the ragged underedge, then falling back into the black man's hands. Then back up what should have been the court he came, a couple of the men separating themselves from the shadows to come out and shadow-play with him, presenting shadow obstacles, moving to get the ball away. Wes just dancing around them. He seemed to be playing in a magnetic field, he and the ball, for the ball didn't want to separate itself from his hands. The hand shot out, calling the ball back. Fingertips of a sorcerer.

"Hey, Wes," called Jerry. The black man feinted to the left out of the reach of the other two, bounced the ball over. He wasn't sweating.

"Jer," he said. "Who's your friend? Great hat, man."

"This is Mel. He wanted to talk to you."

"It's about a friend," said Melrose. "John-Joy."

Wes frowned. "Where the shit you from, man?"

Jerry laughed. "The Coast, can't you tell?"

"Don't sound like no fuckin' coast I ever was at."

"I mean, he's a fucking *actor,* Wes."

"Yeah. Sure. An' I'm fuckin' Kevin Costner."

"Fuck you, Wes." Jerry seemed to dislike having his find called into question.

"Fuck you, man. Why's he want to know about fuckin' John-Joy, he ain't a cop?"

"He knows fucking Annette *Bening,* man!"

Melrose waited patiently for this single-word badinage to end so he could get to the point. They threw a few playful punches at one another and then stopped and both turned to Melrose. Well, what did he have to say?

Melrose stood there, looking from one to the other. Finally, he said, "Look, I'm not a cop; I'm not an actor. Sorry," he said to Jerry. "I don't know Miss Bening. I was just playing the part you cast me in because you didn't seem to believe I am who I am. I'm English, as I said."

"*That* accent's *real?*"

Melrose was not sure he cared for the astonished look, but he said, "Yes, real. The real thing. That story I told you, the cretinous one? Over here investigating a murder. Well, it's true. I know if it were a movie, no one would believe it, but a friend of mine is with Scotland Yard. I'm here with him. This story"—Melrose put his hand on his heart—"is bloody fucking true. Really."

"Hee *hee*," said Wes. "You look just like him, like John-Joy." Wes clapped his own hand over his muscular chest and said, "I got the doin's, I got the doin's."

"What did he mean? What was he talking about?"

They were leaving the ballroom, making their way down the hall back to Jerry's room, Wes occasionally dancing backwards, dribbling the ball. He shrugged. "Seemed to think he'd be famous one of these days."

"Famous," said Melrose. No longer having to conceal his goods and chattels, he reached inside the pocket of his buried coat and brought out his chased silver cigarette case, offered it around. "What claim to fame did this John-Joy have, then?"

"Beats me. This his shit? Looks like it. He was always wheeling this shit around." Wes reached in, extracted one of the books. "He just kept talking about this shit. 'I got the doin's, I got the doin's!'"

"But he never explained that?"

"No, never did. Just a lot of stoned talk about his family."

"What was his name? His last name?"

"Dunno. 'Joiner' was one of his names, though. That 'John-Joy,' that was a nickname." Wes was inspecting Melrose's calfskin gloves, turning them over and over. "Why the hell's some cop from Scotland Yard interested in John-Joy?"

"A CID superintendent. But John-Joy's not the reason he's here. He's here on another case. It's just that there's reason to believe John-Joy's murder is related to the other one."

"Which other one?"

"A man in Philadelphia."

"Well, I never did hear him mention Philadelphia. What happened in Philly?"

"Man named Philip Calvert was murdered. Shot. Up north. You might have read about it."

"Don't remember nothing like that." Wes had wrapped the Liberty scarf around his neck and was running his palms over it.

"So why's this dude got Scotland Yard on his case?" asked Jerry, who was doing the same thing with Melrose's cashmere coat.

"The fellow was the nephew of a woman who lived in London. Well, it's a long story. Try that on, why don't you?"

"Don't mind if I do." Jerry swung the coat around, stuffed his arms in it.

Wes tried on the gloves. "You saying someone had some *motive* to kill John-Joy? It ain't just another—as the newspapers say—'senseless waste of life'?"

Melrose shrugged. "There might have been some motive. You both look excellent." He checked his watch, both to see the time and to see if he still had it. "I appreciate your help, but I'll have to be going."

"You want your shit back, I guess," said Wes, heaving a sigh and sliding the scarf from around his neck.

"Oh, that's not my shit. It's John-Joy's. Keep it."

"All *right,* man."

They both high-fived Melrose.

27

The bird with the dusty plumage screeched as Melrose entered the shop on Aliceanna Street. "Eh-more . . . Eh-more," it squawked, substantially diluting the effect of Poe's poem by appearing, really, only to want another cracker.

Quickly, Melrose divested himself of the awful overcoat and unravelled mittens to go in search of something more suitable. In amongst the vintage clothing over there, he thought, he had seen an assortment of men's garments that would at least do to get him back into the Admiral Fell Inn without the management's mistaking him for a vagrant.

While he tried on and discarded a velvet smoking jacket, he studied the parrot for a moment, the bird and its environment, as it hobbled about in its cage. What if he were to install such a bird—one with more brilliant feathers, of course—in Ardry End? Could he teach it to say "Agatha! Agatha!" and drive his aunt crazy—or least away from his hearth? Had he been rash in not bringing her along to go to her relations in Wisconsin? Well, she'd never have stayed in America. Perhaps he could train a bird to scream out "Vampire! Vampire!" for Vivian. Or it might be nice to have one in the Jack and Hammer, quaking "Gin! Gin!" in Mrs. Withersby's ear. Thus did Melrose move the bird around Long Piddleton before he noticed the girl looking in the plate glass window. He had seen her before, caught a glimpse of her yesterday, he thought. She was lumpish, heavy-featured, and was window-shopping, but determinedly staring towards the rear of the shop, as if she were looking for someone.

He was roused from his concentration on this girl, who was probably thirteen or even fourteen, a few years older than Jip, and unpleasantly rough-looking, by a voice coming from the shadows, asking him what he wanted.

This, he thought, must be the aunt, as he picked the darker shadow from the shadows in the corner. A woman dressed in black, or, rather, wound about in some black garment, mummy-wise, and with a black turban round her hair, sat smoking a cigarette. He saw, as he approached, that the only color apparent in her ensemble was the blood-red polish on her nails. Even the lipstick, slathered on with a generous hand, was a brackish dark red. The garment that enfolded her was a sort of huge shawl, wound round her shoulders again and again, fastening her upper arms to her sides. Beneath the black turban, her face was pale as a moonstone. A cheerless companion for a young girl. Again, she asked him what he wanted, a little as if he were intruding on her coffee break.

"Oh, just looking for some old clothes," he said, moving over among the racks that Jip favored so much.

"What in particular?" she asked.

Melrose sighed as he handled a long cloak sort of thing. He hated going into shops, and had his own clothes tailored precisely to avoid the inanity of shop assistants' questions. Once you gave them a toehold by answering the first question, they would only ask another and yet another.

But vacuum, he thought, picking up an opera hat, demanded to be filled. Melrose loathed empty talk, done merely to fill this vacuum. He supposed that made him insufferable, but he frankly didn't give a damn, he thought, swinging the opera cape about his shoulders, if people thought him intolerant. Better that than engage in a lot of verbal bowing and scraping to appease the gods of meaningless intercourse. He observed himself in the pier glass, looking roguish as he tipped the tall hat onto his head. He had pulled on white gloves, plucked an ebony cane from the Chinese jar filled with tattered parasols and twirled it a bit. He looked like a cross between Fred Astaire and Count Dracula. That brought Vivian to mind again, and her trip to Venice. He sighed as he removed top hat and cape.

"That looked elegant," prompted the Black Aunt from the background shadows.

He unhitched a black jacket with shiny lapels from its hanger. What had Jury been talking about with regard to Vivian? He struggled into the jacket and wound a moth-eaten scarf around his neck. Would that do? His thoughts went back to Vivian's fiancé of many years ago, the past proprietor of the Man with a Load of Mischief (which he should have bought himself to keep it from falling into strange hands—worse luck!). Christ, but hadn't the woman *any* sense? With a black bowler on his head and the shiny black jacket too short in the sleeves, he wondered if he didn't resemble Chaplin.

"I don't think that suits."

Oh, shut up, he thought, removing the jacket and picking something else from the rack. Well, naturally, they all knew Vivian didn't want to marry Franco Giopinno, but just didn't know how to disentangle herself gracefully—suddenly, he thought of the notebook again, and wondered about it. Surely Trueblood had rescued it from the bucket? He tapped a riding crop against his leg— apparently, he'd picked it up unaware.

"Do you ride to hounds? There's good riding around here."

He saw in the mirror he'd struggled into a pink coat without half noticing. He removed it and pulled a floor-length brown overcoat from the rack, his thoughts now straying to Polly Praed in Littlebourne. It had been years since he'd seen Polly; Polly of the amethyst eyes. And the cut-glass tongue, he reminded himself. Anyway, Polly had always been enamored of Richard Jury. At least, he thought so. He removed the coat and pulled another garment from the rack. Well, but weren't most women? He frowned slightly, settling something atop his head, thinking that, actually, Ellen Taylor had never shown any weakness in the knees when Jury appeared. She seemed to like him, yes, but she didn't ogle him. That was interesting, he mused, as he wound something round his neck, by this time so lost in thoughts of the women he knew he didn't register his reflection. Why was he taking stock, anyway? It was all Jury's doing; hadn't Jury appeared in Long Piddleton looking awfully pleased with himself?

Melrose frowned. God, Jury wasn't *enamored* of this Lady Kennington, was he? Was he going to get himself into one more romantic mess? Melrose fiddled with a jabot he had hitched on and thought about Ellen. About Ellen, he could not help but feel protective. And he had to admit, she didn't waste words—certainly not in her writing. Was *that* the appeal of the story of Sweetie? That it was so spare? Poor Ellen. Poor? How could a person with a mind such as hers possibly be "poor"? God, but he could be patronizing. He had moved in his weighty garments to the table with the stereopticon, his mind having registered that the voice no longer spoke from the shadows, and he thought he remembered hearing a rustle and a creak and a fragile movement of the beaded curtain, so the Black Aunt had perhaps left the room.

He remembered a passage from *Windows* as he slotted a picture of the St. James Hotel into the holder and, looking at it, wondered if it had been around in Poe's day. He thought, how baroque was the style of the Poe story by comparison with Ellen's style. Violette indeed. And yet . . . incredible as it seemed, and as much as he agreed with the curator, still it was possible, wasn't it? Possible, yes, but highly improbable. Melrose lowered the stereopticon.

He looked around the room, wondering what it was that was tickling at his mind like something was tickling at his chin. He brushed it away. The bird croaked "Eh-more!" and Melrose slid another double picture into the stereopticon. The little gathering at the railroad station. The same

people, in the next picture, climbing down from the horse-drawn cab
. . . and he started wondering, then, what had happened to Edgar Poe
after he'd emerged from a similar cab on that night that he'd died (or
nearly done) that no one could really account for. Here was the lobby of
the St. James, the potted palms, the long runners of Oriental carpeting;
next, the dining room that flooded him with nostalgia. He sighed. "I got
the doin's! I got the doin's!" Melrose pictured Estes clapping his hand to
his heart, in imitation of John-Joy. Had there been something, then, in a
pocket? The breast pocket of a shirt or a jacket?

Melrose turned the wooden handle idly and thought about John-Joy's
coat. What would the police have done with the clothes? Would they
have inspected everything? Would they have looked in all of the pockets?

"You look lovely."

Melrose whirled around. He hadn't heard the door open.

Jury and Wiggins stood there regarding him. He came out of his par-
tial fugue state and realized he was fiddling with a feather boa. Quickly,
he went to the pier glass and saw that he had donned not only the boa
but a Spanish shawl of red silk and a tall jeweled turban made of cloth of
gold. Hell's bells.

"Couple of bars around here that might suit you," said Jury. "But not
the Horse, if you know what I mean."

Tossing off the turban, the shawl, and the boa as quickly as was hu-
manly possible, Melrose said, "I'm buying myself some vintage clothing."
He kept his tone as cold as he could and pulled the evening cape back off
the hanger.

"Definitely you," said Jury.

"All of this was necessary to get some information from the denizens
of Cider Alley, in case you're wondering."

"You were in Cider Alley, were you? Did you get any information?"

"A bit. What are you doing here?"

"I wanted to talk to the little girl."

"Jip? I expect she's in the back. The aunt was out here."

Melrose brought his palm down on the bell on the counter.

"What happened to your own clothes? Or shouldn't I ask?"

"I gave them away. Here's Jip."

Jury looked at the little girl who parted the bead curtain. She was very
pretty, beautiful even, with skin tinted the color of shell, pearlescent in
the reflected light of the Tiffany lamp. Her hair was reddish brown. The
curtain fell behind her with a windchimey tinkle.

"May I help—oh, hello!" She smiled at Melrose. "I didn't recognize
you in that."

"No, well, your aunt thought I looked quite elegant. I think I'll just have this, then. It seems to be—" Melrose squinted at the tag—"seventy-five dollars. I don't know what my friend wants." Melrose walked away, back to the cart that he'd stashed in amongst the clothes and rugs.

"Present," said Jury, smiling down at Jip. "For a friend of mine, a young lady."

Jip said nothing, just nodded.

"Something really colorful. But I don't know what. Clothes? Jewelry?" He bent over the glass case. For a long time he studied the rings and necklaces, the semiprecious stones. He shook his head. "I don't know. Got any ideas?" On a shelf behind her sat a row of dolls, all looking a bit worn and dusty, a rather international set, for each was dressed in elaborate costume. "Those are nice, those dolls."

Jip scratched at her elbow and looked up there with him. She appeared to have had an inspiration. "Does she like dolls?"

"I expect so." The girl looked so eager that he hated to say, No, she's too old.

"The reason I wondered is, I've got a Barbie I'll sell cheap. And that's really American. The reason I'm selling it is I'm saving for a new one."

"Okay, let's see it."

She was back through the curtain and in less than a minute back again at the counter with the doll. The doll had bright copper-colored hair and was dressed in some sort of western outfit— ten-gallon hat, embroidered shirt, even a lasso.

"The new ones do all sorts of things. I'd like either the rock star one or the mermaid. The mermaid's hair turns different colors when you put water on it."

"Incredible. But this one just sort of sits there."

Her saddened expression told him yes, this was unfortunately so. "But she's in mint condition."

Jury smiled. A term learned no doubt from her aunt and the business. "How much do you want for this one?"

"Is five dollars too much?" Her tone was tentative.

"I wouldn't think so. Tell you what, if she's got a change of clothes, I'll make it ten."

Sadly, the light went out in her eyes as she shook her head. Was the deal now scotched?

"Not to worry," said Jury, letting his eye travel over the row of dolls on the shelf behind her. He caught sight of a male doll, probably meant to resemble some Arabian princeling, as it was dressed in balloon pants and a scarlet vest and holding a scimitar. "See that one? Bring him down a moment."

Side by side, the dolls looked approximately the same size. "Think his clothes will fit her?"

Enthusiastically and without embarrassment, Jip stripped Barbie's breasts of their embroidered shirt and exchanged the jeans for the filmy trousers. "Even trade."

They both contemplated the newly fitted-out dolls. Jury rather liked the olive-skinned, mustachioed Arabian dressed in the Wild West outfit. The copper-haired, blue-eyed Barbie was, like Carole-anne, in mint condition. "What she needs now is a headdress." Jury pulled over the box of handkerchiefs, neckerchiefs, headbands, and pulled out a gold lamé collar, probably once the adornment of a dressy frock. "Now if this were just cut up a bit—wait." He moved across the room to where Melrose sat amidst the vintage clothes and surrounded by the contents of the wire basket, inspecting a brown suit jacket with shiny lapels. On the floor lay an old army blanket, another blanket of some Indian pattern, a pair of striped trousers (that didn't match the jacket), some T-shirts, books, shoes missing their heels.

Jury lifted the bejeweled turban from the hat rack and said, "If you've quite finished with this. . . ?"

Ha ha, thought Melrose, pulling a face at Jury's departing back and returning to his inspection of the brown jacket. Nothing in the breast pocket. There'd been nothing in the trouser pockets either, nor the plaid shirt.

Melrose raised the books, one after another, held spine side up and gave each a shake. Nothing fluttered out. He turned over the one in his hands—a largish, thin volume that looked like an old hotel register, dates back in the 1700s. How had the man ever come into possession of this? Not a hotel register; more like an old church register. He put it aside to look at later and opened the next book.

"Like this one," said Jury, looking at the turban on the counter. "I'll be glad to pay you, say, another five dollars to make a turban for her. That's fifteen dollars altogether."

Jip said she was good with a needle and thread and could cut up and sew the turban first thing this evening. "But you can take the Barbie doll with you now." She reached behind the counter for tissue.

"Oh, I'll just wait till you've finished."

Jip looked back at the bead curtain, anxiously. "I think you should take her."

Of course, the exchange of clothes hadn't been blessed by the aunt, and he wondered if he should not just buy both dolls in case there was trouble.

But she assured him it would be all right. If her aunt noticed and said something, well, she had the extra five he'd paid for the clothes. Then she set about with the tissue paper, wrapping the doll. She said, "I used to live in England."

"Did you? You know, you've got a bit of an accent."

She didn't respond, just pasted a square of Scotch tape over the folded end of the tissue.

"How long has it been since you were there?"

Jip thought for a moment. "Five years, I think. I was five. Or maybe six. It might have been six years."

"When I was six, there was a war on. That was a long time ago, of course. But I'll never forget it. Because of the bombs."

She looked up at him, anxious. "Did they fall on you?"

"On all of us in London. A lot of us kids were evacuated, sent to live with people out in the country."

Her hands stopped on the taped package and she kept her eyes down. "It was a bad time."

"Who did you live with?" She asked this carefully.

"A family in Somerset. A long way away."

Her glance kept straying towards the shop windows in front. Jury finally turned to see what she was looking at; there was a heavyset girl out there looking in. Jury frowned. A chum? A school chum, perhaps. But she did not look chummy, not with that expression on her face.

When he looked again at Jip, he saw her eyes were down now, intent upon the package, or seemingly so. Her face was flushed, a scarlet mottling of the clear skin.

"Friend of yours?" he asked.

She shook her head. Then nodded it, slowly. "Her name's Mary Ann. She's in my school." Her voice was unhappy.

Jury considered Mary Ann for a few moments and then said, "When I was in Somerset my mother wasn't with me. Of course, I had to go to school; there was never any getting out of school. And it's even worse in a new place. Being the new kid in school is always hard."

"I hate school." Again the glance flicked towards the front of the shop. Then she relaxed a bit. Jury turned to look out of the window. The girl was standing stock still. "Well, I especially hated this one in Somerset, because there was a bully—"

A voice behind Jury, Melrose Plant's, asked, "What about his clothes? Did that detective you were seeing check out his clothes?"

"John-Joy's? Yes. There was nothing. Why? What should he have been searching for?"

Melrose shook his head. "Not sure. Just the doin's." He stood there with an old pair of trousers draped over his arm.

"The *what*?" Jury called after him. No answer.

Jip regained his attention. "What about the bully?"

Jury couldn't think, not with Plant standing there, the old pair of trousers draped over his arm. He frowned at Plant and waved him away. Then he said, necessarily keeping it vague, "Something happened, and he claimed he was going to tell our third-form teacher . . ."

"What? What happened?"

Jury thought for a moment. "It was strange. Something went missing from one of the tutors' desk. He said I took it, but I didn't."

She had been wrapping the silky ribbon round and round her finger, listening intently. Her expression changed, became a little crestfallen. The cases were not at all similar.

Jury added, "But that wasn't all. I think perhaps *he* might have taken it himself."

Her expression changed again. Back on track, it seemed to say. "And he said he never did it."

"Yes."

"But what if you really *had* done it?"

From the anxious tone, Jury thought it was safe to assume Jip had herself done something. "In that case, it would have been up to me to either tell the headmaster or not. None of his business."

"What if he'd done it too? The bully?"

"You mean, what if the *two* of us were in on something together? And he wanted to blame me?"

She shrugged. "Sort of."

"Well, I expect I couldn't have stopped him, but that doesn't mean I couldn't have told the headmaster myself."

"Would the police do anything to you?"

Jury thought that past and present were confusing themselves in her mind. "To me? No. We hadn't committed any crime." They hadn't, Jury and the "bully," committed any act at all. But confession was so much in the air, the little girl wasn't even realizing that Jury's story, up to now, had had nothing in it at all about crime or police action. It was her *own* story that had that in it.

Melrose had returned and was hanging over the counter pretending not to listen and looking for some excuse so that he could. He moved his attention from the ring tray to the turban and turned it in his hands, his glance sweeping from Jip to Jury, back and forth, as the two continued their discussion—a rather cryptic one, Melrose thought. He sighed. After his baroque tale of Julie and the sleigh, she seemed all too eager to be taken into Jury's, not Melrose's, confidence. On the other hand, she didn't seem to mind his presence here during this exchange.

"But what if the bully tried to make you believe it never happened *at all*? That you never were there and didn't see anything?"

Were *where* and saw, or didn't see, *what*? Melrose wondered, fitting a Masonic ring on his little finger.

"Well, he couldn't make me believe that."

"Why?"

"Because he was always there, behind the tree."

Jip's "Oh?" was still puzzled.

"Don't you see? If it really hadn't happened, he wouldn't need to keep popping out from behind that tree and trying to scare me. Right?"

She saw the truth of this. More of their exchange followed, largely a reflection of what had been said up to now, a working through of the old muddle, the old fear, until she could bring herself to talk about what had happened.

"I was there," she said abruptly. "*We* were, Mary Ann and me, in the churchyard." Before Jury could say anything, she hurried on. "But Mary Ann says I'm crazy; she says nothing happened." Jip's head was down, turned toward the Barbie doll. It was as if the suspected "craziness" were worse to contemplate than the scene in the churchyard. "She said a lot of people went to the churchyard on these nights, to see the man put the flowers on the grave."

Carefully, Jury asked, her, "And did you see him?"

She nodded. "I think so. I'm not sure now what I saw. We were back behind some headstones—not together, but in different parts of the churchyard. Then when we heard—when *I* heard this noise, it sounded like a yell, cut off—Mary Ann must have run. She ran away and left me there by myself. I stayed. There was someone so near along the path there that I knew if I tried to run, he'd see me." She shook her head. "And I felt something rush by me . . . I had my eyes closed; I couldn't stand to look. And finally I got up when I didn't hear anything else, and I ran. I was cut up from the bushes and rocks."

"You didn't see the person?"

Violently, she shook her head. "Only that he was wearing a kind of black cloak." She paused. "If Mary Ann finds out . . ."

"Oh, you don't have to worry about Mary Ann." Jury took out his notebook and asked for her full name. Mary Ann Shea, he wrote. Next, he carefully took down the Shea address. Jury made it sound very official.

"Mary Ann won't be looking through the window anymore, Jip. I guarantee it."

And as if by means of some sort of Scotland Yard alchemy, Mary Ann had indeed disappeared. When next they turned and looked, the window gave out on nothing else but the wintry afternoon.

28

"I called Pryce," said Jury, coming back to the table with a pitcher of beer. The Horse was filling up; a guitarist was competing at the moment with something on the big TV.

"What will happen to her?"

"To Jip? Nothing at all. Pryce will ask her a few questions, but I told him it was unlikely she could identify whoever it was she saw."

"Poor Jip," said Ellen, looking up from the book open before her.

Jury drank his beer, watched Wiggins spoon the white powder into his glass of water. "Headache?"

"What? Oh, this, you mean?" Wiggins watched—Jury thought almost happily watched—the liquid fizz and the opalescent white froth mist across the top of his glass.

The music of the young guitarist was now replaced by some quiz-show noise on the television that seemed to involve whole families competing.

Ellen was underscoring passages in Vicks Salve's novel with a heavy hand.

And heart, Melrose supposed. It was difficult to keep his mind focused while she sat there sighing, softly swearing and moaning.

Wiggins sipped his Bromo-Seltzer and licked his lips. He said, "Well, I think we've got to assume there's a connection. We've nowhere to start, otherwise. Nowhere."

"All right. If there's a connection between John-Joy and Philip Calvert, and if Beverly Brown's notes are right, then there's a connection with Patrick Muldare, again making the assumption that those initials are Muldare's. Alan Loser says that John-Joy would come around to the shop and hang out with Milos. They were by way of being friends. Then again, Muldare says he never heard of Philip Calvert."

"Beverly Brown knew him, you said," said Wiggins.

"According to Hester, yes."

"Listen to this," said Ellen. She read:

Lovey stood in the heat-saturated air, hardly aware of the heady fragrance of the bougainvillea vines, looking down at the long colonnade with its Corinthian columns glowing in the moonlight, framing the door at the end, and smelled the salt air coming off the sea, pulsing with the ebb and flow of the waves. Victor! He was supposed to meet her, where was he? She looked towards the door.

"Victor—let me guess—has met a fate very similar to Maxim's."

Ellen clapped the book shut, stretched her arm out on the table, and dropped her head against it. Inconsolable.

Wiggins offered her a drink of his Bromo-Seltzer, but she refused.

Melrose said, "The curator called literary theft worse than murder." He reached over and put his hand on her hair. She didn't shake it off.

"What do you think, Ellen?" asked Jury.

"What do I think what?" said Ellen, her voice small with a sadness that seemed born of the ebb and flow of the sea she'd just read about.

"About Patrick Muldare. You know him better than we do."

Ellen refused to raise her head and her voice rose muffled from the table. "All he cares about is football. He's actually hoping his group'll get the expansion team."

"So he said."

"He'll have to beat out Barry Levinson," said Melrose, watching the telly, where the chubbier of the two families was jumping up and down, applauding itself. "It's going to be pretty hard to beat the guy who made *Bugsy* and knows Annette Bening."

"Barry Levinson? Annette Bening? What are you talking about?" Ellen turned her head and propped her chin on her forearm.

"Did you bring along more of the Poe manuscript?" Wiggins asked her.

Slowly, she nodded the chin resting on the outstretched arm. She was refusing to absolutely raise her head, and her hand crept over the carry-all, feeling about for its contents like the hand of a blind person.

"Go on, read it to us," said Jury, coaxing her.

Still with her chin resting on her forearm, Ellen asked, plaintively, "You want me to?"

Jury nodded, smiled.

Her head came up, almost perkily, and she brought out the manuscript. Lovey might just as well have dropped dead as stood there pulsing with heat, or whatever she'd been doing. Melrose was annoyed. When they had first met up there on the Yorkshire moors, he had thought Ellen impervious to the Jury charm.

"We just left off where Monsieur P. was talking about having discovered the handkerchief in the courtyard. It's got his initials embroidered in one corner." Wiggins looked round at them, summing up, in case they'd forgotten the plot.

Ellen coughed a little, balling her fist before her mouth, true to the Poe-esque spirit of putrid afflictions. She read:

My dear madam—

That you appear to be insensible to the sufferings of M. Hilaire P—— only is further proof that the gentleman of whom I speak is not the "William Quartermain" of your own acquaintance. Had you but lingered for a moment in the chamber where I spent so many hours, you would understand. You are convinced that M. P—— was merely employing a ruse to keep me there for motives which you (or so you claim) understand but do not reveal to me; pray, allow me to continue my story—

My host held out the handkerchief, and bade me inspect it, which I did. The initial "P" I certainly saw, entwined with the "H" of his Christian name. He then rose and moved to a cupboard from which he took down an ebony box, inlaid with mother of pearl. He opened this and presented it for my inspection. The box held linen, several more of these handkerchiefs. They were of the finest linen, and the initials worked in a similar manner on each. My host spoke—

"Do you believe me now?"

I hastened to assure him that I had not doubted him except insofar as I thought he might have been dreaming, and he smiled and with a languid wave of his hand said,

"It is of no matter. I would ask you, I would _implore_ you to do me a service: to pass the rest of this night in my bedchamber."

My mind filled with the most unspeakable dread.

"There is no danger!" he cried. "None. I would otherwise not ask this of you. It is only a matter of verifying the truth of my experience, and of my sanity. Man! I must _know._"

"My dear M. P——" I said as kindly as I could. "And if I should _not_ be able to put your mind at rest? What of that? If there should be no repetition of this duel, no crying out of the name _Violette?_"

The interval was over and Melrose watched the guitarist resume his seat on the stool. Well, he wasn't too bad; at least he was playing acoustic and not electric guitar. Melrose wondered what Lou Reed would have done with the Violette story. ("Violette said / As she got up off the floor, / This is a bum trip / And I don't love you anymore.")

"Will you stop that humming!" Ellen said irritably.

Wiggins said reproachfully, "I'd like to know what's happened to Violette."

Melrose said, "She's dead." He was sick of this twaddle. "She's under the floorboards, wait and see. Edgar Poe could play better guitar than Beverly Brown could write."

"Oh, be quiet," said Ellen, crackling the brittle paper as she picked up the next page.

Melrose turned to listen to the pleasantly weepy voice of the guitarist going against the grain of his song.

Jury said, "I think it's rather intricately done."

"So is the L.A. freeway," said Melrose.

Ellen read:

"Then if you hear and see nothing, I must accept my own—"
I understood him and in the heavy silence that followed there was in me a great bewilderment and confusion of spirits. But, finally, I agreed, insisting, though, that before I was to occupy that bedchamber, we must descend to the courtyard where I could satisfy myself as to its security.

We descended, and with our lanterns as the only light to penetrate the inky dark, I observed the cobbled yard. It is difficult to describe that courtyard, which was not long in casting over my spirits, like a cloak of jetty black, its impenetrable gloom. Walls surrounded us on three sides, and on the fourth the iron gate, through which no one—if the rusted lock were to be believed—had passed these many years. The dry fountain, the sere trees, the spongy mosses that pressed upwards through the stones—all, all would testify that no one had been within these walls. I was yet not satisfied. For I believed (despite your protestations, madam) that M. —— was as sane a man as I, and that being the case, these surrounding walls and gate must have afforded entry to the companions of his sleepless nights—the swordsmen. From one wall to the next, I moved, my hands against the moist stones, searching out some possible, secret entrance.

And at one point, fanciful though it must sound, I felt the cold stones weeping—

Melrose interrupted. "Not the floorboards, the walls."

Ellen and Wiggins glared at him. Jury was studying the manuscript page Ellen had just read and set aside.

"How bloody tiresome," said Melrose, yawning. "It's just 'The Cask of Amontillado' all over again. He's gone and walled her up."

"Don't pay any attention to him; he's just being mean," said Ellen, carefully returning the page to its plastic sleeve.

Wiggins stared. "But, miss—what happened? Was there a secret passageway, or something like that?"

Ellen shrugged and sighed. "Don't know."

Wiggins looked crestfallen. "You mean that's the *end*?"

"It's all that she gave me. If there's more, I haven't found it."

Said Melrose, "You shouldn't be carrying that around. You should turn the whole works over to the police. Or Owen Lamb. Or somebody."

"Why? Since it's a fake?" said Ellen, with an acerbic sweetness.

"A dangerous fake."

Jury started to laugh.

They all looked at him.

He was laughing harder.

"Well? What?" asked Melrose.

He turned the manuscript page so that they could see it and pointed to the bit about the handkerchief. "It's the bloody initials. 'HP.' Embroidered on the handkerchief."

"Right. And. . . ?"

"Haven't you ever heard of the Helmsley Palace?" Jury leaned back in his chair and laughed even harder.

29

"Nouveau Pauvre, Hughie," said Melrose, putting the cab driver's expert knowledge of the city to the test. He slammed the door of the cab, making the stick-on Bart Simpson doll dance.

Hughie thrummed his fingers on the steering wheel and repeated "Noo-vo Pov, hmm . . . oh, yeah! That place over on Howard that that fag runs—excuse-a *moi*—I mean *gay,* the one the *gay* dude runs."

As they peeled away from the curb in front of the Admiral Fell Inn, Melrose wondered if "gay dude" might not be a contradiction in terms, but he let it go. It was hard enough keeping Hughie away from the fish; lord knows Melrose didn't want to engage him in discussion of activists rights or politics. "Hold the wheel when you drive, will you?"

Hughie had one arm draped across the back of the front seat and was turning a corner with a finger hooked into the steering wheel.

"And don't slow down," said Melrose, with steel in his voice, "when you're passing the Aquarium." He pulled out his *Strangers' Guide* and his glasses.

"Biggest sting rays in the continental U.S." Hughie was trying to engage Melrose's eye in the rearview mirror.

Melrose refused to be engaged. As they drove along, he was looking up landmarks that Hughie had identified and saw that yes, the one far up ahead was indeed the Battle Monument. "Where's Federal Hill?"

"That's over there a couple miles from Fort McHenry. You want to go there?"

"What? No, no, I was just wondering."

"Union troops occupied it in the Civil War. See, Maryland was kind of pro-South, but no one was ever *sure.*"

That sounded rather sloppy, thought Melrose. He returned the guide to his pocket and tried to think around the voice-over of Hughie and his version of Maryland's history. He closed his eyes and called up the image of Cider Alley, of Estes and Twyla and the peeling doorway where the body of John-Joy had been found. Perhaps Milos could fill him in about John-Joy's secret, if secret it was.

". . . McHenry, that's where Francis Scott Key was when he wrote 'Star-Spangled Banner.' Did he write both words *and* music, do you know?"

"Oh, probably not. He probably had a collaborator."

"Like the Gershwins, maybe."

"Um-hmm." Melrose let Hughie rattle on as they drove along a street on each side of which were ranged antique and secondhand-furniture shops. Nouveau Pauvre, Melrose saw, as Hughie slowed the cab, enjoyed a prospect at the top of a sort of stair-step lineup of stoops and roofs. It was a romantic-looking little place, white clapboard and lacings of filigree ironwork trimming steps and porch.

When Hughie showed signs of searching for a parking place so that he could, no doubt, accompany Melrose in his venture, Melrose told him to drive around for an hour or so, or collect another fare, and then return for him. The cab stopped and Melrose climbed out.

The wrought iron trim work, the sort of thing that Melrose had seen in adverts for "bijou" cottages and in pictures of New Orleans, led upwards to a landing that was high enough off the ground for a man easily to stand beneath it.

A man did, and with his dog.

If Melrose hadn't known his name was Milos, he could certainly have told from the sign behind him warning visitors to stay away from his grate. The burly man, his mismatched suit topped off with what looked like an army greatcoat, looked to be permanently planted in the shelter of the shop above him. Melrose thought he had developed some rapport with the homeless by now, as he smilingly peeled a bill from his money clip. The dog appeared to be friendlier than the man; it was a hound of questionable pedigree, and it barked lightly—*wap wap*—and wagged his stub of a tail.

"I beg your pardon. I wondered if I could have a word with you." Melrose crinkled the bills, hoping that the blind man would be aware he was quite willing to pay for information. This particular blind man had the unnerving eye contact that made him appear to be staring straight at you, which had made Melrose forget for the moment that Milos was also deaf.

Melrose noticed a small collection of cigarette butts in a tin ashtray, and pulled out his cigar case. The dog barked appreciatively, a fellow smoker, perhaps. Then he thought of what Jury had said about writing on Milos's hand and reached for it. He slapped the cigar into his palm.

The reaction he'd expected was a fumbling, clutching, grunting acceptance of the object in his hand. Instead, Milos lifted the cigar, ran it under his nose, and made to put it in the breast pocket of his suit coat, underneath the heavy topcoat. He made several aborted stabs at the pocket but couldn't get it in. He tried the other pocket and succeeded. He made no comment, apparently accepting both the money and cigar as his due.

Well, this would not be a conversation in which one could observe the introductory pleasantries, so Melrose simply raised the man's hand again and sketched on the palm:

"John-Joy?"

"Who, me? I ain't John-Joy. Can't you read?" and Milos stabbed his thumb behind him.

"No, no," said Melrose, the verbal protest automatic. He sighed and raised Milos's hand again, carefully wrote:

"What are the do-ings?"

Milos moved his head quickly, left to right, a gesture that would have suggested, in a man blessed with sight, that he was searching for something up or down the street. He yelled, "How the hell would I know what they're doing? I'm blind, asshole, or ain't you noticed!?"

Melrose grabbed his hand again and wrote, in as large letters as the palm would accommodate:

"No"

which he followed with:

"The doings."

"Yeah? Well, there ain't nothin' doin' with you, either, dickhead, so fuck off!"

If Baltimore police got information out of Milos (which they apparently had, some sort of information), they must have more patience than any police force Melrose had ever been acquainted with.

He sighed and gave up and mounted the stairs.

"Hello there. Looking for a gift? Friend gone bankrupt? Broker bolted? Tax audit coming up? All of the above?"

This series of questions came from an agate-eyed, rangy man who shot them off as he walked towards Melrose. And "shot" was a fairly appropriate word, given the way he was dressed: in an embroidered vest, tooled-leather western boots, and a down-to-the-ground, lightweight coat that would have looked good on Clint Eastwood in one of those spaghetti westerns. It was hard to tell whether he was dressing for business or if the business had been chosen to serve as backdrop—another theatrical arrangement.

"Gay dude" was probably just one of those Hughie assumptions. This one would have a lot of appeal to women. Melrose returned the infectious smile. The patter was certainly more interesting than the usual

"Are you being served?" Melrose answered, "None of the above, actually. I'm a visitor and I'm looking for something to take back with me. Something terribly American."

The man smiled. "There's nothing in there that's *not* terribly American." He shoved his hands into the pockets of his stone-washed jeans and looked happily around, as if he never ceased to be delighted by his own ingenuity.

"Are you the owner?"

"I certainly am."

"My name is Melrose Plant." Melrose extracted one of his ancient cards from his calling-card case and handed it over. Titles usually get results.

Alan Loser studied the engraved card. " 'Caverness.' It is *Lord* Caverness?"

"Lord Ardry, actually. Family name. Earl of Caverness. Et cetera."

"I'm impressed enough by the 'earl' part. Can't imagine what the 'et cetera' might be."

Melrose merely smiled. He was examining a shelf of books, none of which he'd ever heard of, and he wondered if they'd been chosen for their obscurity. And then his eye lit on a familiar-looking shiny red cover. Aha! So *this* is where she'd bought it!

"I see you're looking at the books. Does your friend like to read?"

Could Agatha read? He picked up the copy of *Strangers' Guide.* "Menus, perhaps."

Alan Loser chuckled. "Likes to eat, does she? Then how about this?"

The book he handed to Melrose was titled *Okra Outings.* On the cover was a car out of which several spindly-looking okras, all dressed in sunglasses and little hats, were climbing with picnic baskets.

"Gives you ninety-nine ways to cook okra—for picnics, covered-dish suppers, bag lunches, you name it. I don't think you'll find an okra cookbook in England. Not, of course, that you'd want one in England."

"I don't think I could find an *okra* in England. Isn't it that dark green, slimy vegetable that goes in—what's it called?"

"Gumbo. There aren't any gumbo recipes in this, though." He leafed through the book. "She doesn't want to do the obvious."

"It never occurred to me there was anything obvious to do with okra at all."

"I know. She tells you how to cook it to get rid of the slimy coating."

"But if it's slimy in the first place, why cook it at all?"

"As you can imagine, the book wasn't a huge commercial success."

"I don't imagine any of these books were." Melrose looked around. "Mightn't all of this failure actually put off customers?"

"Good God, are you joking? Or do you have a higher opinion of human nature than I do? You seem to be ignoring man's baser inclinations. That's what I thought of naming the shop at first, the Baser Side. But then I liked the variation of 'nouveau riche' much better."

"Here, I think I'll have this." Melrose handed him the copy of *Strangers' Guide.*

"Good choice. Probably the most idiotic guidebook ever written."

Well, Melrose didn't know about that. He felt like defending the Bessie sisters, having spent so much time with their little family. God only knew, had it not been for Lizzie and Lucie Bessie, he'd have been stuck with Hughie's version of everything. "Friend of mine bought me one." He held up his own copy.

Alan Loser laughed. "*You're* the person? Ellen was in here just a few days ago." They had moved to the counter, and Loser was getting out some ribbon and paper. "How do you know Ellen?"

"I met her in England a couple of years ago. She was careening across the North York moors on a BMW."

"Sounds like her."

Melrose watched as Loser deftly wound the ribbon round the package. "She was researching a book, but I don't think she ever wrote it. I mean, not that particular one. Have you read *Windows*?"

Loser nodded. "Couldn't make head nor tail out of it." He added, "Of course, I'm no critic."

But Melrose thought the tacked-on comment was unapologetic.

"She seems to be having trouble with the new one. You know, a student of hers was murdered, she told me. Horrible. Well, I expect murder put her off writing." This was so far from the truth he very nearly blushed.

"You mean Beverly Brown." Loser snipped the end of the ribbon.

"I think that was the name. Did you know her, then?"

"Oh, yes. She worked here several afternoons a week. A graduate student. Cops were all over the place. Not only that, but a couple of your own countrymen were here. CID men." He placed the wrapped parcel on the counter. "Yes, Beverly created quite a stir, you know. Supposedly turned up a manuscript by Edgar Allan Poe. But I suppose Ellen told you."

"Yes. Extraordinary. Do you suppose it's genuine?"

Loser shrugged. "How could anyone have faked something so elaborate? And since it was unfinished, that removes the problem of having to have the imagination of a Poe, doesn't it?" He laughed.

Melrose had moved over to the dining room table and the Helmsley Palace place settings. He fingered one of the napkins; he smiled. They had decided last night, sitting there in the Horse that Ellen had been right; Beverly Brown had left her mental fingerprints on the story she'd manufactured.

"It's like the candy box," Ellen had said. "She must have seen that table setting every time she went to Nouveau Pauvre."

"But why," Wiggins had asked, "would she leave something in the story that could prove it's a fraud?" Wiggins had not been at all happy about the conclusion they'd reached as to the story's authenticity.

Alan Loser's voice broke into Melrose's memory of last night's conversation. "You know about Leona Helmsley over there? The Queen of Mean?"

"Helmsley? Yes, I've heard of her." Melrose fingered a napkin. "Could I buy one of these?"

"Frankly, I'd rather sell the entire set of them."

"All right. I'll take the lot, then."

"All *twelve* of the damned things?" Loser uttered a short, aborted laugh.

When Melrose nodded, he shrugged and started collecting them from the table. They moved over to the counter again and he started searching for a box.

"Everyone else has his theory. Why do you suppose she was murdered?"

"Beverly made enemies fairly easily. I don't imagine Professor Vlasic was too happy with her 'find.' Since he thinks himself an expert on Poe, I'd guess it'd be galling to have one of his own students acquire something as valuable as an original manuscript and then proceed to overshadow him by writing a thesis on it. Knowing Beverly, that could even be the reason to choose him as advisor. Make him eat some crow. Vlasic is the only professor who ever gave Beverly less than an A. I thought she'd kill him." Loser found a shoe box and started folding the napkins into it. "And then there's the professor she worked for as grad assistant. She got into his computer system—the guy's a genealogist—and messed up his records. She was quite a joker."

"Is it likely, anyway, that a person would have seen the connection between those napkins and this handkerchief?" Ellen had gone on to say. "And, anyway, she probably didn't do it on purpose."

Jury: "She probably did. I'm sorry I didn't meet Beverly Brown."

Melrose was too, as he looked up at a little mobile hanging from a wire: a shark chasing after a school of little fish. He touched it with his fingertip and sent them all swimming about. He wanted to work round to the subject of John-Joy and decided it would hardly be giving anything away to be direct.

"Your city isn't short on murders, is it? Ellen said there was a man killed in an alley who knew that chap I saw outside. Milos? Is that his name?"

"That's it, yes. Actually, Milos knew the man. They were by way of being friends, I've gathered. He used to come around here. Can't picture the two of them having much of a conversation, though." Loser laughed again. Misfortune appeared to have that effect on him. "Actually, I pay him. He's by way of being an employee. I think he strikes the right note, don't you?"

If one likes that sort of note, thought Melrose, thinking of Wes and Jerry. Listening to Alan Loser, Melrose was reminded of Theo Wrenn Browne. Except that Theo was totally devoid of charm, and Alan Loser had a good bit of it, their appreciation of other people's hard luck made them unlikely bedfellows.

"Milos claims he found the body in Cider Alley. That he reported it to the police."

"Did he?" asked Melrose.

Alan shrugged. "Communicating with Milos isn't the easiest thing in the world."

It was easy, though, for some people.

Milos and the dog were sitting on a blanket while Milos opened a flat white box.

Pulling away from a parking space that Hughie was now pulling into was a car with a blue and white cube on its roof: DOMINO'S PIZZA—WE DELIVER.

30

"You got time for the Aquarium now?"

"No. Back to Fells Point."

Hughie slumped in his seat, disappointed. They drove in silence down Howard Street, and Hughie asked, "You going out west while you're here? See the Grand Canyon and all?"

"Unfortunately not. We're only here for a few days."

"Too bad. Me, I travel whenever I can. Since the wife died, you know. It's like a hobby with me." He turned to look at Melrose. "Tell you a secret. You know the best way to see a place, to see part of the country you never been to?"

"Catch a cab?"

"Nah. Not all cabbies are like me. Most of them don't know the points of interest like I do. No, what you do is, you get yourself a real estate agent. No one knows an area like your real estate agents do. You drive around with one of them, you know everything about a place in no time."

"But you'd have to look at property."

"Well, sure. You don't like houses? I do. I like seeing how folks live. And you can pick your life-style, too. You like Boca Raton, you cruise around there."

"Where's Boca Raton?"

"Florida. I was there just last year. Did I hire a car? Hell, no. Why pay an arm and a leg? I got me a real estate agent."

"But what if you'd rather lie in the sun than view properties?"

"Well, you don't go around with the guy all day. Couple hours—three, maybe. They do all the driving, the points-of-interest patter, you just sit and rubberneck. Listen, I got this down pat. I read up on where I'm going, call up some agent in Baltimore and say I'm relocating and to get me an agent in wherever. They're nice to travel around with, these agents. They're chatty, enthusiastic. I think real estate agents really like their jobs. And if you wanted, you could even get a free lunch out of it. But I don't do that; I don't take advantage. A lot of the time I take *them* to lunch. And if you get out in the wide open—Wyoming, like, or Montana or Colorado, someplace really scenic—it's great. You drive around and around, check out a house, drive around some more. I saw Aspen, Colorado, and Jackson Hole that way. Something else, let me tell you."

Melrose looked out of the window as they passed Lexington Market and felt oddly sad, thinking about Hughie spending his holidays in Boca Raton and Colorado, driving around with estate agents, looking into homes from which the owners had fled; Hughie poking around in kitchens and cupboards, flower borders, and white sand beaches, catching glimpses of other people's lives.

He thought about all of this as they were passing the glittering buildings of Harborplace, and he said, "I've changed my mind, Hughie. Let's go to the Aquarium."

II

Hughie's milieu was definitely the deep blue sea.

"Right inside's the sting rays," he said, as they entered a shimmering environment of lights and shadows, green water and blue neon.

Both of them peered down over the concrete abutment at the rays slipping through the water like huge pale fans.

"Man, I wouldn't want to meet up with one of these babies! Look at that sucker, would you? That's a roughnose."

The roughnose made directly for Hughie.

"You got any fish?" asked Hughie.

"Fish? No."

"I was thinking of getting a couple. You know, have a tank, couple of tropical fish in it."

Now the ray was sliding soundlessly away, perhaps fearing a change of venue to Hughie's tank.

They moved up the ramp towards the enormous circular structure that housed the sharks and to the second level, where they were treated to the recorded grunts and snorts of jungle cries and the calls of hippos, seals, and penguins. Whole little worlds had been cleverly devised by whatever resident zoologists and ornithologists the Aquarium depended upon. They were standing before one now called "Allegheny Pond," and Hughie was rattling on about acid rain. "You want to see a beautiful place, you should go to western Maryland. Allegheny or Garrett County." He nodded towards the glass, behind which small fish swam, a turtle inched along, and a bullfrog sat on a flat rock. This was a pond made by an artificial waterfall breaking over rocks. "Acid rain. See?" Hughie pointed to the sign. "It's getting half the streams up there. You got that problem in England?" he asked as they moved to the Chesapeake Bay, next door.

"I expect there's acid rain everywhere these days."

"Yeah, I guess."

They stood there ruminating over the Chesapeake Bay's ecosystem. "I got a sister lives in Delaware. She says the water there's really bad. The beaches, you know. I don't go much to Delaware—hey, did I tell you that story about the Delawares?"

"You did indeed." Melrose wanted to forestall a repetition of *Kind Hearts and Coronets.*

Hughie went on: "So if the Queen tosses in the towel, Prince Charles would take over, right?"

"Right. Only now it appears that Charles might not want to."

"No kidding?" Hughie pursed his lips and seemed to be thinking this over. He put his face closer to the glass. "You got your blue crabs, your terrapins in Chesapeake Bay." He nodded towards the marshy enclosure.

They walked on.

"So then who takes over?"

"William."

"Who's he?"

"Charles's son."

Hughie frowned. "Then who's Prince Andrew?"

"That's Charles's brother."

"You mean the brother don't come first? You mean the *kid* inherits? My God." He clucked his tongue, seeing the inherent injustice of this lineup for Great Britain's crown. "No wonder that Delaware kid bumped off his uncle."

Melrose looked at him, shook his head, looked away. "That's not exactly the same thing. The rules of primogeniture are very strict. Only if Charles, his son William, and his other son, Harry, die or abdicate, only then does Andrew come into the picture. And after Andrew, then his two sons, in order of age."

They were standing now in a darkened area, watching the shadowy little shapes of the flashlight fish blink on and off like fireflies.

Up the next escalator was the rain forest; they entered into an enclosure of huge palms, dense fog, warmth, cawing sounds, chirpings. It was really quite a remarkable simulation, thought Melrose.

"Hey, check out the flamingos! I don't remember they had flamingos."

"Those aren't flamingos," said Melrose, annoyed.

"Sure they are. Look at that bright pink and those real skinny legs."

"They're too small for flamingos."

"So what do you say they are?" Hughie challenged him.

"I don't know."

Hughie was silent for a while, looking at the pink birds. "So what about Princess Anne? Doesn't she get a shot at the crown?"

"Way down the line. Anne is at the very end. The brothers and male heirs would all have to be wiped out first."

"All those *kids*? Before the *women*? What a bunch of chauvinists."

"You could say that. But not so much as the lines where only males can inherit a title. When the last male dies, that's it."

"Like the Delawares?"

"Yes, I expect so."

"You got any brothers and sisters?"

"Nary a one." They had walked halfway round the enclosure, and Melrose was bending over one of the small white signs that informed the visitor about the local inhabitants. "Scarlet ibis. That's what they are, the pink birds."

"Look there," said Hughie, pointing to a mottled brown, thin-legged bird that had the stealthy walk of a criminal. "Pheasant."

"I don't think so."

"Sure it is. I do a lot of hunting. Pheasant."

Melrose looked around for a descriptive text, annoyed by Hughie's insistence that this fowl was a pheasant. "Why would they put a pheasant in a rain forest?"

"Go figure."

The warmth, the mist were making Melrose drowsy. "Probably the female ibis." But Hughie had walked away. Melrose searched the undergrowth for the exotic and equatorial life that one sign said he would find hidden there in the rush grasses and plant life if he looked carefully. But all he saw was that damned bird, stalking.

Hughie waved him over to look at a tarantula, and Melrose passed beneath a couple of cawing yellow parrots that made him think of Aliceanna Street, and he was sorry he hadn't brought Jip along, but she was probably at school. She couldn't have too many bright spots in her life, living over that shop.

He stood looking at a blue poison arrow frog, one of many tiny frogs, frogs no bigger than his thumbnail, encased in the green shades of their mock savannah.

Downward, Hughie and he walked, around the shark tanks. Hughie was still talking about titles. "So let me get this straight: your name's not Caverness, right?"

"My name's Plant. Caverness is a place. Like Devon. Prince Andrew is the Duke of York. His name's actually Windsor."

"So how do you go about claiming a title?"

Melrose was watching a school of angelfish, swimming from nowhere to nowhere. Soon they were back again. Well, they looked like the same ones. "You'd have to get in touch with the Crown Office and produce your proof for the consideration of the Clerk of the Crown."

"Man, I'm glad I don't have to keep all that shit straight. I'm glad all I gotta think about is Bill Clinton. As long as I don't have to think about him too long."

"Titles are complicated." Melrose only wished Hughie would shut up about titles, for it simply reminded him of his own, and his father. He felt sad; he felt sadder, though, about his mother.

He tried not to think about it, but he couldn't help it. He remembered talking years ago to Jury about that lad, Tommy Whittaker, a marquess. Tommy wasn't, Melrose had said, "the real thing." He picked it up again, this old debate with himself—no longer a debate, he supposed. He had found it difficult at first to forgive his mother, and then remarkably easy.

A sinister-looking hammerhead shark moved its bulk on past them as Hughie was talking again about the Delaware family.

They were leaving now, passing the sting rays and Atlantic rays again. As they walked past the glass cages to the exit, Hughie said, "Not bad, not bad. I mean the life here. Protected environment—no danger, get your bed and your three squares and don't have to look over your shoulder."

"I don't know. There's no tension, either, though. Don't you think there has to be tension in life to keep it from crumbling?" Well, that had the ring of proper British pomposity to it.

Hughie obviously thought so too. "Tension? Oh, boy, I bet all the bums —excuse me, all the *homeless*—get a real kick out of being all tensed up."

Melrose thought of Cloudcover and its absurdly ironic name. The faces of Wes and Jerry came into his mind. Cider Alley; Milos. Milos standing there with that cigar, trying to plunge it into the pocket of his jacket.

The jacket.

Oh, for God's sake, thought Melrose, as he suddenly remembered those trousers he'd found in John-Joy's cart. "Hughie, let's go."

"What the hell? Where we going?"

"Back to Nouveau Pauvre."

III

"Goat? I don't have a goat? What in the hell are you talking about?"

This time, Melrose was determined. After two more attempts at palm writing and a wad of bills that would have bought Milos a whole flock of goats, Melrose finally got across the words "coat" and "jacket." When Milos still hadn't seemed ready to give up his suit coat, yelling it was too damned cold, Melrose had traced in his palm

"S W A P."

He hated giving up his one remaining decent piece of clothing—his double-breasted blue blazer—but there was nothing for it. They swapped.

The blazer was a bit snug on Milos, but Milos didn't care. He had carefully run his hands over it, apparently felt its unmistakable quality, and had agreed to give up his pin-striped jacket for it. No, he wouldn't *sell* his jacket. Where would he ever get another so fine, if not Melrose's own? He'd been after John-Joy for a long time about that jacket and John-Joy said it was to be his when he died.

"But if you tell the cops where I got that jacket, I'll say you're crazy, which you must be, anyway!"

Melrose denied he had any intention of doing so.

Milos finished rolling up the cuffs of the blazer, shrugged the shoulder seams about, and shouted, "How do I look?"

"Fine!" Melrose yelled back. He yelled it again when Milos barked out "What?" He wasn't about to go through the palm writing again.

Since he no longer had his overcoat and was hardly going to travel about Baltimore in the opera cape, he had no choice now but to wear the pin-striped jacket. He didn't care. He patted the sewn-up breast pocket (which had prevented the cigar's going in) and felt something inside that sounded like paper.

The doin's, he hoped, climbing back into the cab.

31

The red brick and concrete ballpark, open to a sky like a blue backdrop, was almost redolent with newness and resonant with the voices of crowds not come. Expectation hummed in the air. As he descended the high, sweeping steps of the stands, he marvelled at the structure and the sky-line.

The guard had directed him up ramps and down ramps outlined in red brick arches, and all around the huge webbing of stands and boxes to somewhere in the center of this sea of green seats. "He could be any-where," the guard had said; he seemed more impressed by the name Patrick Muldare than by Jury's laminated ID. The guard had been taking a coffee break, tilted back in his chair. He had thumbed Jury off through an arched doorway behind them and gone back to his *Sports Illustrated* ("swimsuit issue," he'd leeringly informed Jury). He was not unfriendly; he was simply not impressed by Scotland Yard.

The guard had told him to check around sections 35 and 36, right below the press box. Jury would still probably have missed Muldare if the man had not stood up and waved his arms around. Having gone to the bottom, Jury would now have to climb back up.

Pat Muldare said without preamble as Jury sat down beside him, "Isn't it great? A great ballpark?"

Jury had to agree. They sat there looking out over the irregular stretch of the outfield, past the giant Sony scoreboard to the view of the Balti-more skyline beyond.

"Do you come here often?" asked Jury.

"Every chance I get. There was a lot of resistance to spending public money to build this. We've got Memorial Stadium, after all. But it was worth it; seeing it, well, I think a lot of people might have changed their mind. Getting season tickets will probably turn out to be as hard as getting them to the old Colts games. You know, at one time the only way to get season tickets to those Colts games over at Memorial was to pray somebody died." He grinned. "But even if somebody *died* they'd will them to a family member. Last game I saw the Colts play was in 1983, just before they took off for Indianapolis. At that point, they couldn't even fill half the stadium; it was sad, really sad. I'm thinking: maybe I could buy back the name. It'd probably help with the owners. Right now, the NFL might be figuring that Baltimore has the Eagles on the one side and the Skins on the other, so we're pretty football-saturated. But if you look at Charlotte, though—that area's football-poor. They need a team and they've got more money. And they'll certainly build a stadium, too. I think they've got a better chance. But we've got a better chance than St. Louis."

"But the others didn't have the Colts."

"If I could *only* find something to tip the scale."

Jury smiled. "Something Hollywood."

"Something goddamned dramatic, you better believe it."

"Doesn't Johnny Unitas live in Baltimore?"

"Yeah. How'd you know that?"

"I'm a detective. Why don't you get him to coach?"

Muldare laughed, happy Jury was getting into the spirit of things. "That would be dramatic, all right. Yep." Muldare smiled out over the diamond as if this whole park had been his own invention. It would have been fond and fatherly, that smile, had it not been so much like a little kid's. Bereft of his office football, Muldare was digging a fist into the palm of his other hand, as if he were winding up for a pitch.

Jury tried to imagine Patrick Muldare in a business venue: out on one of his construction sites in a hard hat; or sitting at the head of a long, polished table as chairman of the board; or doing some multi-million-dollar deal with the Japanese. But he couldn't do it; or at least each of these images—construction site, boardroom—dissolved nearly the instant it took shape. But Jury could easily visualize Pat out there on the pitcher's mound, or stealing a base, or with a catcher's mitt. He could actually see it, and it made him smile. Here was a man who had found his calling, even though he didn't act upon it.

The closest he got to performance was to sit up here in a green, slat-backed chair, hitting his fist into his hand as if he wore the glove and held the ball. Now he looked up, his blue eyes squinting at the blue sky, as if the ball had left his hand, had been hit, and was making its high, sweeping arc to God knew where.

Jury felt almost envious. And he almost hated to wake Muldare from his dream. But he did. "Your stepmother happened to mention something about your family background. He said your great-great-grandfather got in a squabble with other family members and changed his name."

"That's right. Except I think it was great-great-*great.*" Muldare held up three fingers.

"I don't care about the number, only what happened. Whether there's some possible connection between you and the others."

"Well, there's the name, I guess. Used to be Calvert."

"*What?* What exactly are you saying?"

"Muldare was my grandmother's—great-great, or was that three 'greats' too? I don't know—Muldare was *her* maiden name. Irish."

"Your name would have been Calvert?"

"Look, I'm sorry I didn't make it clearer, but why the hell should I think of that?"

"Because the murdered man in Pennsylvania was named Philip Calvert. I would have thought *that* was pretty clear."

"So? There are a zillion Calverts in this part of the country. There's Calvert County, even. It's as common as Howard. And your guy was from PA, not Maryland, and not Baltimore. You've got to remember, Muldare has been the family name for generations. Ever since the middle of the eighteenth century, maybe longer. Look, I'm sorry. But with this NFL decision coming up, well, I've had a lot on my mind."

"Jesus Christ," whispered Jury impatiently. "Your one-*track* mind, if I may say so."

"Yeah, I guess so."

"Is there anything at all this suggests to you, now?" Jury told him what he knew about Philip Calvert and his aunt, Frances Hamilton.

Embarrassed that he hadn't taken Jury's inquiry seriously enough at the outset, Pat Muldare now adopted a studiously grave expression, and he gazed at Jury, while Jury talked, with the absorption and intensity of a man genuinely interested in what is being said, but also with the studied air of a man who well might not be taking in one damned word. His mind was probably out there running the bases. Jury sighed.

"Pat, are you hearing what I'm saying?"

"Of course. You said this Phil Calvert would have been a rich man when the aunt died, except he died too, and the aunt was leaving nothing to anyone else, there really wasn't anyone else, except for some distant cousin or other. I guess you think that's me, I'm the distant cousin, and I went up there and popped him."

Naturally, a baseball term had to get wedged in there. "Congratulations. You heard me. No, I don't think that. What the hell would someone with enough money to buy a football franchise want with Frances Hamilton's money?"

"I could have had *some other* reason, Inspector." He wiggled his eyebrows, teasingly.

"Superintendent. That's right, you could have. So tell me."

"I was only kidding."

"Well, you can stop kidding and tell me about your family."

Pat went back to his pitcher's gesture, rubbing his fist in his hand, and said, "I don't think of my father all that much, really. An angry man is what I remember. My mother, her I think about."

For the first time, Jury was sure Muldare's mind had followed his eyes as he looked away from the playing field and down at the boards beneath his feet. "She was a Howard. There's a Howard County, too, you know. She might have been a descendant of John Eager Howard—he was the philanthropist who gave away so much of his land to the city. She was a lot younger than my father—twenty, twenty-two years, maybe. And still he outlived her." There was in his tone a note almost of resentment that his father had had *such* nerve. "My mom died in a car accident. We were on our way to Cape May—in New Jersey—"

"You were with her?"

"Yes. It was just the two of us, headed for Cape May. Something went wrong with the braking system and we went off the road, over into a gulley. I wasn't hurt except for superficial cuts." He stopped and looked up again, this time at that sky so blue it looked enamelled and permanent. "I was knocked unconscious. When I came to, well, there was my mom."

There was silence. Jury said, "I'm sorry."

"Maybe I'm still trapped back there. I should be married, have kids, I'd like that, but . . ." He shrugged his shoulders. Then he looked at Jury. "I'll tell you something: I never really grew up."

In all his long years of questioning people—suspects, witnesses, innocent, guilty—Jury had never heard a man make such an admission, evaluate himself, if not harshly, in a way most men would consider unmanly.

"Maybe you're lucky, Pat," said Jury, smiling.

"Look, isn't it likely that it's just coincidence, these names?"

"I'd be more willing to put it down to that if it weren't for Beverly Brown's apparently tying them together. She was a very clever woman."

"Bev." Muldare made no effort to hide his lack of enthusiasm for "Bev." "But that would mean that Bev knew my background, and I never told her what I just told you. Unless Alan told her. I imagine family connections might be important to Alan. He'll get a lot of money, if he's still around when I go." He looked at Jury. "Am I going? Since you seem to take those notes of Bev's seriously—the other two are dead."

Jury didn't answer that question directly. He looked out over the playing field and around the stadium that a few men like Patrick Muldare had helped to build. "You're a very rich man, Pat. Is it possible there might be claims on your money you're not even aware of?"

Reasonably, Muldare answered, "Well, if I'm not aware of it, I don't know how I can answer the question."

"No, I expect not. Well . . ." He got up. "You staying?"

"Yeah. Sure."

Jury smiled, said goodbye, and climbed the cliff of steps. He turned at the top and waved to Patrick Muldare, who returned the wave. He looked out over the irregular diamond, the concentric rings of seats, and felt again that surge of power. He wondered if it were true that certain places drew energy to them, collected it like some huge generator and held it there, setting the atmosphere thrumming as if it were laced with high-voltage wires. The ley lines of Oxfordshire and Wiltshire; Stonehenge; or that town in Arizona with its vortexes—all were such places. He thought of the Rollright Stones in North Oxfordshire that had recently been said to drain power from radios and stop watches. When he looked down from the ramp onto the grassy field, he felt almost as if this grand new stadium was one of the ancient places of the earth.

He checked his watch to see if it was still running.

32

Melrose had repaired to the warmth of his fireplace in the Admiral Fell Inn, where he was picking at the threads stitched across the jacket pocket. He wished he had something else to pick with other than his own fingernails. The stitching had been reinforced, and it took some time to work the edging loose. Finally he did, and pulled out a square of paper that crackled when he touched it. Like the stitching gone over so many times, the paper had been folded and refolded—halved and quartered so that it was a thick square. Melrose took great care in unfolding it; the tea-colored paper was old and so worn that seams of light showed through.

It was a birth certificate for one Garrett John Joiner Calvert. Mother, Ann Joiner. Father, Charles Calvert.

Calvert. Melrose stared into the fire.

Calvert . . . Joiner. Wes's voice came back to him: "That John-Joy's just a nickname." Joiner . . . Joy. But the birth certificate couldn't have been John-Joy's; it was dated 13 August 1784. But it established some relationship—or at least John-Joy must have thought it had—to the Calverts. And if so, did that mean to Philip?

Melrose picked up the certificate again. Philip Calvert (Jury had told him) would be a rich man when his aunt died, this Mrs. Hamilton. But that didn't make sense, killing for that inheritance. Whoever murdered Philip Calvert would hardly have expected to claim the fortune of Mrs. Hamilton. Unless, of course, a new will were to be produced, a new relationship discovered. Was a way being paved towards something in the *future* rather than in the *past*?

Melrose tried to remember the name of the professor Beverly Brown had worked for, the one in history. The genealogist. Lamb. Melrose picked up his phone and asked the desk clerk to put him through to Johns Hopkins. After being switched from one extension to another to another, he was finally told that Professor Lamb had left for the day; no, they did not give out home telephone numbers, he was told, and rather testily. Then he tried Ellen. Not there, either. Melrose gave up.

He wondered about Milos. He could return yet again to Nouveau Pauvre, but the thought of striking up a conversation with Milos was simply too daunting. Anyway, it was nearly seven; Milos might have left his post to patrol the city.

He ran his hands down over his face; he scrubbed at his head with his clenched fists. He was trying to dislodge that little bit of conversation in the cab that Hughie had given him, or tried to give him; Melrose hadn't really been paying attention. Now he was sorry. There was something floating around in his mental ether that he couldn't net, couldn't hook, couldn't pull up. . . . He wondered if Hughie was still out in the street, trawling around in his cab—

Good lord, if he didn't stop this nautical line of thinking, he'd turn into a fish himself.

Then he thought: go to Cider Alley. John-Joy's companions might be able to tell him something else about the man. Probably not; he had a feeling that his contributions to their welfare had bought him every morsel of information they had, and then some.

Melrose sighed, thought for a bit, and remembered Hughie pointing out the Enoch Pratt Library. He got out his *Strangers' Guide,* looked in the index, found it on one of the sectional maps. One call that Hughie had made correctly.

He made sure the certificate was secured in his locked bag, tossed the cape about his shoulders and went down the stairs.

No Hughie, so he hailed a cab from which its present fare was exiting and gave the driver his destination. As they drove up Calvert Street, Melrose asked the driver what he knew about the Calverts.

The driver told him they made whisky.

II

Melrose was not sure exactly what he was looking for, but he asked the librarian for books relating to Maryland history, old records, family history, and so forth. The librarian walked him over to one of the reference shelves and asked him what specifically he wanted. He just wanted to browse, he told her, and she said she might have one or two other books —a history of Baltimore, did you say? Baltimore, or Maryland more generally, he told her, especially seventeenth- and eighteenth-century Maryland.

He took three books over to one of the long tables and sat down with them. There were plenty of seats; the library was not crowded. A few readers were spotted here and there at the long, dark tables, quietly turning the pages of books or writing on index cards or in notebooks, or otherwise engaged in fruitful literary pursuits.

Melrose loved libraries, had always thought them oases, sanctuaries in an otherwise tumultuous world. He liked to hear the soft rattle of leaves of paper, the soft tread of shoes, the whispered exchanges. Directly across from him sat an old gray-bearded man in an outsized overcoat surrounded by books and bags, reading by the laborious means of following a running finger from one line to another and mouthing the words. There was a satchel on each side of him, by means of which (Melrose thought) he would transport reading material out the door, and an oily-looking brown bag, into which he dipped and brought out part of a rough-cut sandwich. He munched it happily and in the process looked across the table at Melrose and smiled broadly.

Melrose returned the smile and sat wondering if perhaps he oughtn't to put in for the post coming vacant at the Long Piddleton Library.

Mindful of the task at hand, he started reading through *Maryland Records of the Colonial Revolutionary Church*. Here were census records, records of marriages and deaths. It was full of the sort of arcane facts that Diane Demorney loved. The pleasant-faced, pink-cheeked librarian stole up to his table, placed two books on it, and crept away. She'd have made an excellent cat burglar. One book included facsimiles of Council proceedings for the years 1636 to 1647. He opened it, leafed through it, and came to one of the many documents listed as taken from the House of Lords Journal.

Melrose read:

Lord & Comons for fforraigne Plantacons, Novem: 1645,

. . . as alsoe of the Letters Patents, whereby his Ma(ty) in the eighth yeare of his Raigne, granted the said Prouince to Cecill Caluerte, and of a Certificate from the Judge of the Adm(lty) that Leonard Caluerte late Gouerno(r) there had a Comission from Oxford. . . .

Caluerte. Calvert, surely.

Leonard Calvert had been the first governor of Maryland.

They were not happy with the way Cecil and Leonard were running things, so what had Cecil's role been?

He stopped reading, looked blindly across at his table companion, who was still lip-reading his book. He frowned. Then he rose and went over to the desk behind which the librarian stood stamping books. He asked for

Burke's Peerage. Briskly, she walked him back to the same shelves and took it down for him.

Melrose took it back to his table and looked up the name.

He shut the book and shut his eyes. It was something Owen Lamb could have told him in an instant. He opened his eyes, looked round the room. Here was a bit of history that probably anyone sitting in here could have told him; he was embarrassed by his ignorance. Suddenly, the voice of Hughie came back to him. *"So this jerk, he tries to poison his one uncle when it's really the other uncle that's the successor, not the one the guy tries to ice."*

Melrose opened *Burke's* again and looked up "Delaware." The nephew of Sir Owen West attempted to poison his other uncle, Thomas West, whom the nephew mistakenly thought was heir to the title of Lord Delaware. Melrose felt almost sorry for him, poor devil. It just went to show how confusing the rules of primogeniture were.

Hughie might not know his monuments, but he definitely knew his Delawares. My God, thought Melrose.

Or, in this case, *my lord.*

III

It was nearly eight by the time Melrose emerged from the cab, and the shop on Aliceanna Street was closed. His breath clouded the window he was peering through, searching for some signs of life, Jip or her aunt. No lights in there except for the floor lamp with its green glass shade painting watery shadows on dark wood. That and the blue neon half-moon hanging in the window were the only lights.

Melrose knocked; no one came. He rattled the knob and got no response. But when he turned it the door opened. At the same time as he was relieved to have access to the shop, he wanted to give Jip a good talking to for forgetting to lock the door. He went in.

The bird cage was covered with the red shawl, but this did not appear to interfere with the parrot's nocturnal activities. Issuing from the cage was a lot of sandpapery scratching and *ch-ch-ch-ch-ch*-ing, as if the bird were busy building something in there.

Melrose found the wire basket shoved in amongst the masses of clothing, well hidden by the gowns and skirts. Perhaps Jip hadn't wanted to keep it back in the living quarters; her aunt might become curious. Melrose pulled it out, peeling away hems and sleeves and trouser legs.

Everything appeared to be here. John-Joy's books had sunk to the bottom as a result of Melrose's having pulled out all of the clothes earlier for inspection. One of the books was an old King James Bible, one a

Michener novel with a tattered cover, one what Melrose had thought looked like a hotel ledger. The fourth one was a flattish book, also of the sort used as ledgers, but smaller.

Melrose took these last two books over to the green lamp and sat down on the footstool. The larger of the two was the sort put to use by churches to record marriages before there were registry offices. The dates here were all the late 1700s, running into the 1800s. He ran his finger down the list on each page, searching for a Calvert, and finally found one: the marriage of a Charles Calvert to an Ann Joiner, date, 6 August 1783. Melrose shut the book and calculated from there to the date on the birth certificate.

The binding of the other book had come loose; some of the pages were torn, and some stained. Its general appearance would certainly attest to its having been around for a couple of hundred years. It was a book of accounts, the columns on the right marked at the top "l—s—d" for "pounds," "shillings," and "pence."

			l. — s — d
1785			
Oct. 23	two pair Canvass sheets		0 · 16 · 0
Oct. 27	one bushell of Oatmeal		0 · 5 · 0
Oct. 27	Nails		0 · 0 · 9
Oct. 28	one Munmoth cap		0 · 2 · 0
		Summ.	1 · 3 · 9
Nov. 1	three clothe for baby Garrett		0 · 0 · 10
Nov. 2	Inkle for garters		0 · 0 · 2
Nov. 9	one pinte of Oyle		0 · 0 · 10
Nov. 11	two pints of Vinegar		0 · 0 · 8
Nov. 11	two falling Bands		0 · 1 · 0
		Summ.	0 · 2 · 8
Nov. 12	one Rugg for C har. bed		0 · 4 · 0
Nov. 12	one suite of Frize		0 · 10 · 0
Nov. 16	one peck of Bay salt		0 · 0 · 8
Nov. 17	one bushell of Pease		0 · 4 · 0
Nov. 21	one pair of shooes		0 · 2 · 0
		Summ	0 · 16 · 8

How long he sat there in the eerie shadows cast up by the green shade, he didn't know. He was brought out of his speculation by the bonging of a long-case clock telling him it was eight forty-five.

He got up, a little stiffly, from the low seat and considered the strange implications of what he'd found. It was very strange if it was true, but Melrose couldn't think of anything else that would explain the murders of John-Joy and Philip Calvert. *And* Beverly Brown.

It gave him the creeps. What an odd motive for murder. He thought again of *Kind Hearts and Coronets*. What had happened to John-Joy and Philip, well, it wouldn't be the first time. . . .

He put the books under his arm, preparatory to meeting Jury and the others at the Horse, and made for the door. As he passed the cage, he lifted the covering. The bird fluttered around and croaked "*Eh*-more! *Eh*-more!"

This was one screenplay about Avalon that Barry Levinson definitely hadn't written.

Now, Melrose wondered: What other Calvert was waiting in the wings with his Letters Patent?

33

Less than an hour later, Melrose found out.

When he walked into the Horse, there wasn't much custom and even less activity. With no football game to fill up the big screen, the regulars were stuck with another quiz show. They were watching it without much enthusiasm.

"I have something to tell you," said Melrose, settling the books on the table and himself in a chair.

"And I have something to tell *you,*" said Jury. "About Patrick Muldare. That's not originally the family name. Listen to this: years ago, Muldare's great-great-great-grandfather got into some sort of argument with the family and made his point by actually changing his name. The family name is Calvert. Interesting? It might be coincidence, of course, Calvert being a fairly common name, but I doubt it. That it's coincidence. Beverly Brown apparently doubted it too. What's wrong?"

Plant's hand stopped in the act of pouring out his beer, and he sat there in silence for some moments, staring. "Patrick Muldare is a *Calvert?*"

"Muldare said he wasn't even thinking of it when I mentioned the murder of Philip Calvert. The only thing Patrick seems to care about is the NFL expansion team." Jury smiled. Melrose didn't smile back. "He's holding his breath, waiting to find out, one, if Baltimore gets it; two, if *he* and his backers get it. He doesn't think he's got much of a chance, though. He thinks the owners might not be too impressed by him."

Melrose took a drink and set down his glass. He said: "They might be impressed as hell if Patrick Muldare were Lord Baltimore."

Wiggins's head snapped up from Debrett's. "If he were *who?*"

"Lord Baltimore. Baron. It's an Irish title, actually, so there wouldn't be any claiming of monies or land." Melrose pulled Debrett's away from Wiggins, quickly found the page he wanted, turned the book to face them, tapping his finger at one of the entries there. "George Calvert, first Baron Baltimore. Calvert is the family name." Melrose took the certificate from his pocket and laid it on the books.

"You've got to be *joking*." Jury laughed.

"No, it's right here." Melrose shoved the ledger book and the birth certificate towards Jury.

"What are these?"

"The doin's," said Melrose.

It was Jury's turn to stare. Something unpleasant was shaping in his mind.

Wiggins, however, newly anointed member of the British peerage, was quick to pull over Debrett's, have a look, and make his comments. "George Calvert, first Lord Baltimore—"

Said Melrose, "Proprietary of the territory called Avalon. Later Maryland. *Terra Mariae*, in honor of an aunt of Louis XIV. This first Lord Baltimore—Baron—had two sons, Cecil and Leonard. Leonard was the first governor of Maryland, and he's important because when, finally, the sixth Baron died DSP—"

Wiggins looked up and said, for Jury's uninformed benefit, "That's without children. Actually, sir, I believe in this case it must be DSMP. Without a *male* descendant."

"Yes. You learn quickly, Tweedears."

Wiggins looked smug.

"Now, the problem arises in the male descendants of Leonard. He being the second son, his male heirs would of course take over the title. But about the time of his third or fourth descendant, William, there's no proof, that the next male descendant is indeed just that. Consequently, all of that line become barons de jure instead of what we might call de facto." Here Melrose nodded in Wiggins's direction, the sergeant being all too familiar, by now, with this thorny little problem. "Patrick Muldare is one of the descendants—"

"Are you saying that so are Philip Calvert and John-Joy?" Jury shook his head. "Impossible."

"Not at all. If these records mean anything, Philip Calvert and Pat Muldare are some degree of cousins. And John-Joy, actually John Joiner Calvert, is some sort of uncle. The precise relationship I don't know. Beverly Brown might have." He turned the two books toward Jury, open. "This shows that Anne Joiner married one Charles Calvert. Issue, at least one son, Garrett John Joiner."

"This is much too far back for the son to be John-Joy."

"Yes, of course. But the birth certificate—" He took it from the place where he'd wedged it in the accounts book—"indicates that John-Joy was in the line of male descendants. This is the implication, certainly."

Jury frowned. "But, my God, that would mean John-Joy would have been—" Jury gazed at Melrose; he would have laughed, had the implications of what Plant was saying not been so awful—"would have been *Lord Baltimore?*"

"That's the idea, yes."

Wiggins said, "But John-Joy died DSMP."

Melrose nodded. "Consequently, if there's a relationship between him and Philip Calvert's *father,* the title would pass to him, to Calvert's father, and consequently to Philip Calvert; and again, if a relationship can be shown between Calvert and Muldare, thence to Patrick Muldare. I think Beverly Brown discovered these old records, and possibly more to show that there was another son—that Charles had other issue. And eventually, Calvert, Philip, and Calvert-Muldare, Patrick, were the result. And my guess is that Philip was next in line, after John-Joy."

Jury frowned. "And why is that your guess?"

"Well, that's pretty simple, Superintendent." He paused, and added, "Because they're both *dead.*"

Jury got up. "Excuse me for a minute." He held up the empty pitcher. "I need a drink."

No, thought Jury.

He leaned against the bar, looking blindly up at the TV screen while the guitarist whined nasally about friends and betrayal.

There were many times in his work when he'd been surprised, even one or two times when he'd hated being faced with a particular person's being the guilty one. But this was the first time he found himself adamantly refusing to believe it.

He pictured the two of them, sitting there in Oriole Park, beneath that glazed blue sky. And Jury supposed that darkness fell even there.

I never grew up.

Jury set the fresh pitcher on the table, and said, "Pat Muldare couldn't have killed them. Not the type."

Wiggins's mouth dropped open. "The *type,* sir?"

Jury ignored this. "Beverly Brown was murdered because she came across this information? Is that what you think?"

"Not necessarily."

Jury looked a question.

"Anyone who could execute such an elaborate forgery as an entire—or near-entire—*story* could surely do something as simple as a birth certificate and fiddle an old ledger."

"But *why?*" asked Wiggins.

Jury said, "Given what I've heard about Beverly Brown—for revenge. Or even, God help us, as a joke. What if she convinced poor old John-

Joy he was one of the barons Baltimore and gave him this certificate to prove it?"

"Revenge?"

Jury shook his head. "Patrick Muldare. I think she got dumped, frankly. I don't think a man would dump Beverly without taking a big chance. And knowing he would give his eye teeth for *something,* as he put it, 'glittery, stagy, Hollywood' . . ."

There was a long silence while they thought this over. Minutes passed. Finally Melrose asked, "Where's Ellen?"

"At Hopkins, sir," said Wiggins. "She said you took up so much of her writing time today that she had to go in tonight to make up for it."

"Oh, certainly, *certainly.* I'm to blame for all of her writing problems."

"Pretty much," said Wiggins, smiling broadly. Then he returned to his study of the ledger.

"You found these books in John-Joy's cart, right? And the cart was still there when the cops found the body."

"Apparently, yes."

"Then why didn't the killer take them? In the first place, such stuff would be incriminating, if anyone is clever enough to work it out, like you are. But more than that, he'd need what's in them to help to make his claim. I mean, what the hell do you present to the House of Lords if you're trying to prove your ancestors were the barons of Baltimore?"

Wiggins turned to Melrose Plant. "My question precisely."

"I'm not sure. More than is here, I'd imagine. But the point wasn't to convince the House of Lords, was it? It was to convince Patrick Muldare."

For another minute or two they sat there, each looking in turn at the documents. "Hell," said Jury. "These have got to be forged. It stands to reason . . . But I don't see any internal evidence of it."

"There's one thing, sir," said Wiggins.

"What?"

"This person who totted up these columns couldn't add."

Jury looked down at the accounts book, ran his finger down the columns, mouthing items: " . . . Rug for Charles . . . clothes for baby Garrett . . . uh-huh." Jury did some simple addition. "This column comes to two shillings, eight pence. But that doesn't square with the ten pennies here for so-called baby Garrett. Look." He turned the book toward Melrose. "If you subtract those two items from these two columns, *then* the sum is correct."

Wiggins and Melrose looked down at the page.

"Meaning that someone *else* probably entered the goods for Charles and baby Garrett, together with their names. This account book is sup-posed to prove such people existed. Charles and Garrett must be the links to the present generation of Calverts.

"Except," Jury added, "that there were no such people."

34

How was she ever to get Sweetie out of this predicament? Sweetie sat, as she had left her, staring down into the empty white box. Ellen wrote.

Sweetie clasped the box carefully, holding it as if it were terribly fragile and might shatter. She lifted her eyes to the letter slot.

Ellen lifted her eyes and stared at the blank wall above her desk. She kept it blank—empty of pictures, of notice boards, fixtures, messages— all the mental stuffing which helped one to embrace the illusion that there was a chronological flow to things. "Ellen: lunch Thursday? Cafeteria?" The message wasn't there, of course, up on the wall. The wall was in limbo (the human condition). Thursday was a concept no more reliable than chocolates in a chocolate box. No wonder Sweetie had to label things: sugar, pitcher, plate. In Sweetie's house nothing was dependable. Time was fractured, lurching around like some Frankenstein monster, dragging, stumbling, broken up into body parts.

Sweetie did not know how long she had been holding the box. She did not know whether it was Day or Night.

Ellen turned to look out of the window. Night, all right. Black as pitch. Then she looked behind her at the clock on the wall. *She* certainly knew how long *she'd* been sitting here at this desk: one hour and thirty-seven minutes. Thirty-seven and one-half. The minute hand swept. Thirty-eight. Twenty-two more minutes to sit here. Surely she could last for twenty-two more minutes.

Oh, *God!* Ellen clenched her fists and pounded on the desk. Then she put her head in her hands. Oh, *she* knew what Maxim was up to, but she didn't know *why*. Air. She needed air.

She got up and moved over to the window, the bike chain dragging at her ankle. She opened the window and leaned out. Freezing air knifed her skin and she was glad for it; it might wake up her mind. She looked down and, for lack of any worthier mental occupation, decided to calculate, should she jump, how far the chain would reach and leave her dangling. She looked back at the chain, measured it with her eye. Five feet of play, perhaps. Then she leaned out further and figured she was not all that far from the ground, or at least that bush down there that would break her fall. Probably the chain would stop her about eight or nine feet from the ground before it broke. . . .

Oh, for God's sake! She'd do absolutely anything to keep from writing! Ellen slammed the window down.

Dragging back to the desk, she glanced (guiltily) at the clock and saw that she'd spent a full four minutes at the window. Well, damn it! (she argued with her guilt). Can't a person even stop for a breath of shitty *air*?

Oh, but you weren't doing that, were you? *You* were hanging out the window and measuring off the chain. Weren't you? You should really reset the alarm and add on another five minutes. Ten, to be honest. You spent another five minutes back there filing your na—

Shut up shut up SHUT UP! Then she thought smugly, Well, I *can't* reset it, can I? Because I can't *reach* it, not with this chain around my ankle.

Really? said her Dedicated Self. If you can't reach the alarm—

Ellen clapped her hands over her ears, as if a voice were actually speaking to her. She knew what was coming.

—then you can't reach your *key*, either. The tone was simply unbearably smug and self-satisfied.

Somebody will come along. *They* would. Richard Jury said he would come along and take her home. Ha ha ha.

Feeling extremely pleased she'd outwitted herself, she was about to sit down again when she heard the footsteps coming down the hall.

I told you, didn't I? she said to Dedicated Self. And then felt depressed, for she didn't really like winning these arguments with herself.

Well, he'd just have to sit around and wait.

She looked up at the knock on the door frame (the door having been left open) and the simultaneous greeting.

"Hullo."

Ellen frowned. What was Alan Loser doing up here?

What he was doing, she realized in the next second, was holding a gun in his hand. It appeared to be pointed at her.

"I think you have some papers here that belonged to Beverly Brown." He smiled engagingly as if for all the world he hadn't actually snicked the safety back on that gun.

At least that's what she thought that tiny, alien sound had been. She stared at the gun and at Alan, open-mouthed. Horrified, she froze.

That is, one part of her froze. Dedicated Self whispered, Now, how the hell long is *this* going to take?

Ellen opened her mouth; nothing came out. Finally she said, "What about her? What're you doing?" She backed up and the chain dragged.

Alan hadn't noticed the chain until now. He actually put his head back and laughed. "The writer at work?"

Drawing herself up, still enough herself to be defensive, she said the usual thing. "It's a scene in my book. I'm acting out. I do it a lot. Please put that gun down." And a thought glimmered in her mind. "I'm not going anywhere, *obviously.*" She tried to make it sound snotty, as if he were truly stupid.

He laughed again, lowered the gun. "No, I don't suppose you are. But that's not precisely the point, in the end."

Her momentary relief vanished. In the end? What end? Whose? She swallowed and then asked, trying to sound as argumentative as possible, "What in hell do you want?"

"For starters, I want whatever Beverly Brown gave you."

"The *Poe* manuscript? But it's a—" Should she tell him it was a forgery? "—questionable. No one knows whether it's even authentic yet." She started backing towards the window, checking the time. Jesus.

"The manuscript. Of course it's not authentic. One of Beverly's little jokes."

Some joke! "You *knew* it was a fake?"

"Certainly I knew. Beverly and I were—well, at least before Patrick came along. I want whatever else she gave you."

Three minutes.

Ellen's glance flicked from the clock to the bottom drawer of the filing cabinet. "Down there."

"Bottom drawer?"

"It's locked." She dragged the little key from the rear pocket of her jeans. Tossed it to him.

Alan nodded towards the chain. "It won't reach, will it?" Holding the gun, muzzle towards the ceiling, he walked over to her. He yanked on the chain, measured the length with his eyes and smiled. "Cooperative of you to chain yourself to the desk like this." Then he moved back to the filing cabinet, knelt and put the gun on the floor as he fiddled the key into the lock.

Two minutes ten seconds.

Ellen stared up at the clock.

She had backed nearly to the window. Keeping her tone idiotically conversational, she asked, first clearing her throat to get the words out:

"What are you looking for?" Her eye was on the gun, right there by his foot. Within his reach, not hers.

"Beverly's notes." He looked up and smiled brightly. "And a birth certificate."

One minute fifty seconds.

"Proof you were born?"

He stared. "Gallows humor? I must say, you have more guts than Beverly did."

Than Beverly did? Oh, God . . .

He was bending over a thick folder, sitting cross-legged on the floor, like some damned student reading his manuscript. "Thing is, she thought she could blackmail me. She wasn't stupid. It didn't take too much intelligence to figure out what had happened to Philip Calvert."

"Calvert?"

One minute thirty seconds.

Alan looked up at her, quizzically. "You hadn't figured it out yet?" He went back to the folder. "Never mind—you would've. It was Beverly's idea, actually; her way of getting back at Patrick for dumping her." He looked up, up at the ceiling, and shook his head. "Sometimes I wonder about him; he's hopelessly childish. And yet I'm the one who was always accused of irresponsibility and so forth." He turned a few pages, seemingly engrossed in what he was reading. "Beverly knew he was a Calvert. I told her. When she happened to meet this Philip Calvert, she got the idea. What a stunning idea, really. And anyone who could manufacture an entire—well, nearly entire—story by Poe, even for five minutes, could certainly toss off a false document or two. Scribble some lines in a book . . ." His hand wrote in the air.

"What are you talking about? I don't know what in hell you're *talking about*!"

Alan looked up. He moved the gun fractionally, as if he were arranging a place setting. It still rested by his shoe. "Please, Ellen. You're not stupid."

"Oh, yes I am! I'm very stupid!" Her progress backward towards the window had been taken by mere inches over the last minute and a half. *Forty seconds. Oh, God—go off go off go off go off—*

"All right," he said, as if concurring with her stupidity. "It might not have registered up to now. But as soon as it got bruited about that Patrick was the present Lord Baltimore, I'm sure you'd've realized." He held up a sheet of paper, waved it tantalizingly.

What in *God*'s name was this maniac talking about?

"Bev's notes. This genealogy."

She followed the motion of the paper. *Ten seconds.* "That's just stuff from her work with Owen Lamb. I didn't pay attention to it."

"You would have. Later. Well, it's been nice talking to a captive audience—"

The sudden noise was ear-shattering.

The terrible racket of the alarm sent him reeling, sprawling as he rose, and in this half-crouch, his foot shot out. The pistol slid across the floor and Ellen fell on it, allowing herself one second of ecstasy over this totally unexpected boon before she fired.

Alan Loser yelled and grabbed at his knee, clamped his hands around the blood oozing through his fingers.

"Goddamn bastard!" she screamed, in the sudden release of tension. Then she cocked the gun and sighted.

At the same time, she heard a rush of feet and in another few seconds, Richard Jury and Melrose Plant burst into the room.

"Ellen!"

Jury went to Loser; Plant to Ellen.

She shook off the arm he dropped around her shoulders. "Writing's a bitch."

35

They were sitting in the Horse having a farewell drink when Ellen said, overcasually, "I don't guess those reporters were especially interested in my writing habits, were they? I mean, they wouldn't bother mentioning it in their columns?"

"You mean such as having to chain yourself to your desk in order to write?"

"I *mean* the way I always try and *live* the experiences of my characters." She glared at Melrose.

He poured another beer from the pitcher and said, "Yes, well, that particular scene must be giving you a lot of trouble, since you chain yourself to the desk every day. And night."

"You don't need to *comment*—no one asked you to."

But he did need to. As if puzzled, he thumbed his copy of *Windows*. "You know, I don't remember anything at all about Sweetie—or Maxim, for that matter—going about in chains." He snapped his fingers. "Ah! Is *that* the title, then?"

She narrowed her eyes, suspicious. "What do you mean?"

"Chains. Is *Chains* the title of the last in the trilogy?"

"How hysterical." Ellen bumped her chair around so that her back was to Melrose.

Wiggins was busily making room in his flight bag for several containers of Bromo-Seltzer. "You were very brave, miss. That took a lot of courage, what you did."

Ellen looked smilingly at him. "It did, didn't it? See, what I intended to do was dive out of the window when the alarm went off. I figured he'd be too confused by the noise to fire. But then he kicked the gun. How is the creep?"

Said Jury, "According to Pryce, he'll live."

"Pity."

"Shattered kneecap. That's painful." Jury smiled.

"I just wish I'd killed the son of a bitch. And how did he ever think he'd get away with murdering *me*?" Her tone implied she must surely belong to that rare breed of mortals who must go unmurdered.

"I expect if the police came up with any motive at all, it would be either the jealous ragings of some of your colleagues or someone after that manuscript. You had it, after all."

"Yes, but it's not genuine, we know that."

"We do, but who else? Your friend Vlasic didn't know, for instance," said Jury.

"Vlasic," said Melrose, making a face, "would love to have discovered that manuscript."

"Made him look a bit of a fool," said Wiggins. "One of his own students coming up with a find like that."

"Wait a minute," said Ellen. "Are you saying that detective might have arrested *Vlasic*?" She thought this over. "I'm kind of sorry I butted in."

Jury went on: "And Phil Calvert's and John-Joy's deaths would probably have gone unsolved. As good a detective as Pryce seems to be, what connection could he have made between the two?"

Said Wiggins, "Not as good a detective as Lord Ardry, perhaps."

Melrose sighed. He wished Wiggins wouldn't adopt this new way of addressing him. But then it was Lord Tweedears to Lord Ardry, he supposed. "It was Hughie who put me onto it. It was all of that talking about the Delaware lineage."

"You're too modest," said Jury.

Ellen said, "My God, and the whole idea was to make it look like *Pat* had killed them. And he might have managed to do it, too, with that title as a motive. But what about evidence? How was he going to link Patrick to that cabin in Pennsylvania?"

"As long as Muldare didn't have an ironclad alibi for that time—and I expect Loser would have made sure he hadn't—then, as long as the police assumed a *motive* for Muldare's killing Calvert, that wouldn't have been a problem. Same thing would hold for John-Joy."

"And he had the godawful nerve to actually *write* on Milos's hand. Why didn't he just run, get the hell out?"

"He wanted the doin's," said Melrose.

Wiggins sighed as the tiny white bubbles erupted across the surface of his glass. "We'll never know what happened." Looking at the circle of uncomprehending faces, he added, "The *story*. 'Violette.'"

"Ah!" said Melrose. "Not to worry, Sergeant Wiggins. I've got the denouement right here."

"Where did you come across that?" Wiggins was astonished.

"It was in the file. Beverly Brown's." He turned to Ellen, adding, "The one in your office."

Jury folded another stick of Teaberry gum into his mouth and just looked at Melrose.

"It was *not*!" said Ellen. "I'd've seen it." She made a motion to snatch the page from his hand, but Melrose pushed her away. "He had the papers—Alan Loser, I mean—spread around on the floor. He didn't give a damn for the manuscript, so this page was just mixed up amongst the others."

Jury chewed his gum, rested his chin in his hand and gazed at Melrose. "I'll just read it, shall I?"

Wiggins's "Yes" was eager. Ellen was miffed and kept saying she couldn't understand how she could have missed it. Jury said nothing.

Melrose adjusted his spectacles and opened his mouth to read, but then asked, "What did you consider the most intriguing question in the story?"

"Nothing," said Ellen, returning to her notebook.

Wiggins was somewhat more enthusiastic. "What happened in the courtyard. It's kind of a locked-room puzzle, wouldn't you say?"

"Oh, that?" Melrose was dismissive. "That's rather simple."

"It is? Well, then what about Violette? How did she die?"

Melrose smiled. "Who said she died?"

Said Ellen, her eyes trained on her notebook, "Oh, *stop*. That's your favorite question."

Melrose adjusted his glasses and read:

My dear madam,

The moisture of these cold stones thickens like blood beneath my fingers, and the ink that flows through this pen in a viscous stream seems dark red upon the page.

This must be my last communication to you.

So enraged became M. P—— at my announcement that I had seen nothing, heard nothing in my long sojourn of the previous night in his chamber that he insisted we descend to the courtyard and to the scene (his sad delusion!) of the dreadful assignation that he had witnessed three times in succession.

How I would, had I the means, return to that horrible fancy of his, if return I could! For the actuality is so much more to be feared!

He became, as we stood below in the inky darkness, increasingly more incoherent—a man driven to the limits of his mental resources by a fancy that had totally overtaken him—until, in his frenzy to convince me that all had passed as he so described it, he drew—from some hiding place—two rapiers, holding down one and throwing the other towards me. I still at this moment can hear that icy clang as it struck the stones at my feet.

I was appalled. Yet, I was forced to wield this devilish sword as M. P —— began his thrusts and parries. I begged him to stop—he would not.

And then he laughed. This was not the laughter of a madman or even of a passionate one. Nor was the melancholic gentleman lost in his world of dreams and delusions. The person who now confronted me was a man of deliberation, calculation and cold reason who introduced himself to my astounded ears as "M. William Quartermain." He then told me the story—

"Another one?" asked Jury, unwrapping his stick of Teaberry. He grinned at Melrose, who ignored him.

This was indeed the dwelling place of one M. P——, but he himself was not that gentleman. Mr. P—— lay dead in an antechamber on one of the lower floors of the house. "Murdered—by a jealous husband."

"Prose seems to be falling off just a bit," said Jury.

Wiggins looked at his superintendent reprovingly.

"And we're going to miss our plane if Poe doesn't wrap this up in another ten minutes or so."

Melrose ignored Jury's exaggerated pointings at his watch.

"—jealous husband."

Almost fearing to ask, and fearing, too, that the answer was all too evident, still I said—"And the wife?" "Dead" was his single word by way of answer—

"Are they still fighting?" Ellen's voice came from the small cave of her crossed arms upon which she had lowered her head. "While they're do-ing all this jawing?"

Said Melrose, massively irritated, "I do not go to sleep when you're 'jawing' around about Sweetie and Maxim."

"I'm not asleep," said the blurry voice. "I'm resting. I just got through entertaining a psychotic killer last night, remember?"

Wiggins was clearly distraught with both Jury and Ellen and said to Melrose, "Please go on, sir."

Melrose continued but sped things up a bit:

"It's a bit patchy here; Poe—"

"Beverly Brown, you mean," said Jury.

"Yes, Beverly Brown must have had a bit of a problem. Our narrator was by way of being a 'fall guy' for Quartermain. He wanted somebody to take the blame, is my guess. But let's get to the surprise," said Melrose enthusiastically.

My dear M. S——

"Who's 'S' "? asked Wiggins.
"The narrator."

I had never meant that you should suffer thus and would, were it within my meager power, come to your aid. Alas, I cannot. Who would believe me?

It was before dawn of that morning when my husband approached you in the Tuileries that I made my escape, fleeing from those rooms as if pursued by all the devils in hell. For I knew, I was <u>certain</u>, that, should my husband find me, he would certainly kill me. Oh! You can not begin to imagine the abstracted fits of passion of which he was capable, and now, having murdered my beloved Hilaire, he would give me no peace, except the peace of Death.

"Definitely fallen off," said Jury, yawning.
Melrose glared at him.

—peace of Death. Wretched and afraid, I hurriedly took myself to another part of the house, thinking that he would never suspect I still <u>remained</u> within view. For it was myself, sir, that you saw there at the window across the courtyard. I have since flown, never to return. Having read of your apprehension by the Sûreté, I felt I must write to you this last time.

You may use this letter in whatever way you see fit. Should it be proof of your innocence in this affair, I should rejoice.

With sorrow and gratitude, I remain,
Violette Pontorson

Ellen's head had come up, swiftly. "What? There was no *face* in any fucking *window* across the courtyard."

Melrose pursed his lips. "The curtains shivered, I distinctly remember —'shiver'd apart as if from a ghostly hand.' "

"So *what*? We're supposed to think Violette was over there all the time caught in the curtains? *Blaaah!*" This unattractive noise came from a head that had fallen like a stone back on her crossed arms.

"So it's been *Violette* all along who's been writing the letters?" said Wiggins. "I'll have to agree, that's certainly a surprise."

"With a Mont Blanc," said Jury, rising and adding, "I'm going to get a cab for us."

"Hughie'll take us. What does that mean, 'Mont Blanc'?" Melrose frowned.

"That pen at the beginning that was sweating blood. Or ink. The ink was flowing through it, if I remember. Must be a fountain pen."

Ellen's head snapped up again. "An inkpen." She looked at Melrose. "He's talking about writing with an *inkpen*. In the 1840s?"

Melrose thought for a bit, then clucked his tongue. "Well, Beverly wasn't perfect, after all."

Jury smiled, slung the strap of his flight bag over his shoulder. "*Beverly* would never have made such an egregious error. I'm going for the cab."

Ellen and Wiggins looked at Melrose open-mouthed.

"Is nothing sacred? Plagiarizing a plagiarist? Good God, is *nothing* safe?"

"I thought it was a pretty good solution myself, sir," said Wiggins, recovered from his astonishment.

"Good? But it wasn't the *right* solution," said Ellen.

"Oh, for God's sake, there *is* no right solution. And any hack can write like Poe—any idiot can imitate writing that distinctive."

Ellen glared at him.

"Excepting yours. Babe." Quickly, before she could bump her chair around he leaned over and kissed her.

She pulled her sweater sleeve down over her hand and made a big production of scrubbing at the damp spot on her cheek.

36

I

The subject of hacks being never far from Ellen's mind, she raised the question of the disposition of Vicks Salve on the way to BWI—"disposition" meaning "how to dispose of." Ellen rattled on at some length about this and concluded by saying, "There are four of us. We can just track her down and kill her."

Hughie, who'd been adjusting his fish mobile with one hand, released the steering wheel to its own devices so that he could hold up his other hand, fingers splayed. "Five. Don't forget me."

"Great. You can drive the getaway car."

Jury turned in the front seat. "You're speaking to police officers, remember."

Ellen sank down into her cramped space in the rear seat between Melrose and Wiggins, who sat with his flight bag, now transformed into a cornucopia of anodynes and amulets, securely on his knees. Ellen said to Melrose (somewhat fumily), "You told me you worked out a way to get her."

Melrose looked around from the flying landscape, bulldozers and fluorescent orange cones finally giving way to grassy embankments and evergreens, and said, "I have."

"What? How?"

"I don't think I should tell you right now; it would diminish the plan's effectiveness." Melrose expected bitter railing, but he was surprised. Ellen pursed her lips, was thoughtful, said nothing.

Melrose continued. "You see, what you want here is not a showdown, a slug-fest, a shootout—"

Ellen smiled as she turned over these three alternatives.

"No. What you want is something that goes on and on. Like living well being the best revenge. That sort of thing. So what I'm thinking about seeps in like poison. It's rather like the predicament Sweetie's in—"

"You're going to seek her out and shove letters through her mail slot."

"No, this is more subtle and much more insidious. There's one possible drawback: it's not necessarily public humiliation, such as it would be if you took her to court and won your suit. Vicks Salve will know, and you will know, and possibly a few astute others will know. But in all probability, not many people will get it."

"Will she know I know?"

"Obviously, or it wouldn't be fun."

Ellen sat back in her place with a satisfied smile. "Are you ever going to tell me what it is?"

"Yes. When you come to Northants. Enough time should have elapsed by then."

She screwed up her face as if she were in pain. "I can't wait that long!"

"Ellen, remember something." Melrose put his arm around her, squeezed her shoulder. "You're a writer, and writers are always at risk. More than musicians and painters, because any damned fool out there thinks if he wants to, he can *write*. He may not be able to brush his teeth in the morning, but what the hell, he can pick up a pen and write. That's why I finished off Beverly Brown's story—to demonstrate how easy it is for a hack to copy a real writer. Beverly Brown knew that. This might not sound all that comforting, but what you've got to remember is that this particular hack is an impostor. But you, you're the real thing."

She was silent for a moment, looking out of the window, thinking this over. Then she said, "I don't know *when* I can get to England, though. My writing schedule is absolute hell."

"That, dear Ellen, is clear to us all."

Along I-95, the getaway car sped on.

II

Hughie had popped open the trunk and was stacking their luggage on the curb; the service roads were choked with traffic. People rushing, horns bleating, blaring, blasting.

Suddenly, Melrose remembered Diane Demorney's comment and said, "Hughie, a friend of mine said that Baltimore used to be called 'Nickel City.' True?"

"Yeah." Hughie turned to give the finger to some cabbie who was trying to maneuver past, turned back and repeated, "Yeah, 'Nickel City' —I remember that."

"Why? She said that once they made nickels here."

Hughie thought this uproariously funny. "Made nickels . . . that's rich. No, it's because Baltimore was so cheap; probably still is, you compare it with D.C., New York. Used to be you could get a lot of stuff for just a nickel. Let me tell you, good buddy—" Hughie smiled and slammed down the lid of the trunk—"you'd better be more careful who you listen to."

"I'll certainly remember that, Hughie." Melrose paid him and gave him a huge tip.

Ellen pulled something from her holdall and handed it to Jury. "This is for you. It's from Jip."

Jury looked down at the rather worn snapshot and frowned. "I don't understand."

"Well, she just said maybe you could find it."

"Find it?"

Ellen sighed. "You're supposed to be a detective."

"Uh-huh." Jury smiled. "I just thought she might have added something to those instructions you're not telling me."

"Well, she didn't. Except it's of her, when she was younger, and she said maybe it was taken in London. Or some city in England."

Jury looked at the snap again; it seemed a generic shot, some building or other, Jip sitting on a sort of bench. "All right. Tell her I'll try."

"And she told me to tell you goodbye," said Ellen, looking up into Melrose's face. "Melshi." She did not even crack a smile.

The taxicab behind Hughie honked his horn, moved forward and crashed right into Hughie's bumper, and another cab driver, leaning out of his window, was shouting at Hughie to move.

The four passengers stood on the curb watching the inevitable result of this minor accident where each party was secure in the knowledge that he alone had justice on his side.

Hughie yelled back at the other driver, which of course resulted in a few more hurled insults, and then the two of them were out of their cabs, doors flung open amidst the porters and the bags, the arrivals and departures, the two of them going at it hammer and tongs:

"Fuck you!"

"Fuck you!"

"Well, fuck *you*, man!"

"Fuck *you*, dude!"

. . . and on and on that litany born of the city streets, repeated over and over, *fuckyoufuckyoufuckyou*, accompanied by gestures, two fingers poked into a shoulder, another poked into the air, poke poke poke, in such a way that it was clear no one was really going to fight, but that they were merely engaged in a ritual of insult, a steady rain of invective as necessary and appropriate for this occasion as the telling of beads in church . . .

. . . until they had both returned to their cabs, slammed their doors, and, leaning out of their respective windows, flung one last "Fuck you!"

Then the final salvo, Hughie yelling:

"—and the horse you came in on!"

Interlude

Sergeant Wiggins insisted on having the seat in the middle and stuffed his Bromo-Seltzer–laden bag under the seat in front.

He sat belted and buckled while the plane taxied along for takeoff, shut his eyes when it lifted off the tarmac, and when the seat-belt sign winked off, climbed from his pinched position over Melrose's feet to begin his circuit of the cabin. He wasn't, he said, waiting until the fear-of-flying attack got too much of a grip on him. He was taking action immediately. Better safe than sorry, right?

"Don't forget," said Melrose, whose own bromide was the astonishingly awful prose of Elizabeth Onions, "it's right-right-right and then left-left-left. Three rights, and back again."

Wiggins frowned, standing out in the aisle. "I don't remember actually changing directions on the flight over. Did I?"

"You did, yes."

"Well, it certainly worked. Be back in a tic."

Jury slept, his head against one of the mingy plane pillows. Melrose, whetted by the events of the last week, shoved what was left of *The Parrot and Pickle* in the pocket of the seat in front of him, pulled out the manuscript book he had purchased, and uncapped his pen. As Joanna the Mad had said (and the Onions woman was a perfect example of the dictum), "Any idiot can write a book."

Fuelled by the experience of finishing up the Poe-Brown story the evening before, Melrose had started again on his own mystery. After casting about for titles, and thinking of Wilkie Collins, he had decided on *The Opal*.

His detective, an amiable fellow named Smithson, was a Scotland Yard CID man with strong lashings of American private eye–ism. And since he had discovered that, in America at least, lady sleuths were all the rage, he had decided to have Smithson aided and succored by his brilliant wife, Nora. Smithson drove a battered car and took his cat (named Chloe) along for the ride, as cats were also extremely popular.

Polly Praed would accuse him of knuckling under to the demands of the marketplace. Yet Polly was one of the great knucklers-under of all time. Her heretofore quite ordinary detective had lately fallen victim to alcoholism, manifested in an obsession with California Chardonnay; was hinted to be sexually dysfunctional; was trying to stop smoking; and was undertaking a health regimen which included eating plates of sea kelp. Polly should talk, thought Melrose.

And (he suddenly decided) he would make it an *inverted* mystery, in the Francis Iles vein. *Yes!* He felt he was back there in the Horse with Elroy watching the Super Bowl. *Yes!*

"What the hell are you doing?" Jury blinked at him, roused from sleep.

"Me? Nothing." Melrose bent over his notebook. Hell, there was no reason for *Trueblood* to do all the writing; Melrose's imagination was certainly equal to—

And then once again he suddenly remembered the black notebook.

Where was it?

Part 3

 GIN LANE

37

"If you'd've been here, you'd've met him. Or her." Carole-anne Palutski waved her freshly polished nails around to dry them and started in on her toenails. Her legs were drawn up on Jury's old sofa, a towel beneath her feet, careful of the fabric.

Jury had been back in Islington less than an hour, he'd called up to Carole-anne to come down and have a cup of tea with him, which she had, bringing her painting equipment with her.

"And what is Him or Her like?"

"He or She is highly creative, for one thing."

That certainly boded ill. It made Jury nervous to speculate on Carole-anne's notion of creativity. "Old or young? Or middle-aged?"

"Yes." Her chin was resting on her updrawn knee as she dotted the polish about.

"Yes *what*?"

"He or She is old, young, or middle-aged."

Oh, for God's— "Carole-anne. I live here. I've lived here for many, many years. I have a right to know who's going to be living above me." Jury stabbed his finger towards the floor above.

She did not even flinch at his tone. Carole-anne never paid any attention to Jury's avuncular commands. "As I said—" perfect nose raised slightly in air, mild sniff—"if you'd've *been* here instead of flying all over the place, you'd have met them. Him or Her."

That was it, of course. Jury had had the godawful nerve to take off for the States and leave her here to live her own life entirely without his aid and succor. Mrs. Wassermann could help Carole-anne out in *some* ways: raising a hemline, lowering a neckline, making mysterious phone calls that cast her in the role of Carole-anne's aged aunt, transporting chicken soup upstairs, and so forth. But one had to face it: Mrs. Wassermann was not six-two with changeable gray eyes and a smile that could cause a meltdown. Not only had Jury left, he had left without telling her; without even writing a note; without even bringing back a present from the States. The States, where she had never been in her whole life. (Jury's glance had slid over to the unpacked suitcase, where the Barbie doll lay nestled in tissue, gold turban and all. He refused to give it to her, refused to mollify her.)

He sat there making circles with his thumbs, teacup poised on arm of chair, glowering at her. Then he smiled. "I can narrow it down easily enough."

"I've no idea what you mean."

"I can tell you the sort of person you let the place to."

She wiggled her shoulders and gave him a smarmy smile. "Well, I don't see how."

"I'm a detective. We can eliminate the following: Female, age group sixteen to sixty, good-looking. That takes care of a sizable number. We can also eliminate the up-to-sixteens—unlikely one would be looking for a flat—and the over-sixties, because you wouldn't need another Mrs. Wassermann to do for you.

"Now: *most* likely would be male, age group sixteen to sixty, good-looking. We can eliminate the young ones, same reason as females, and eliminate over-sixty because you sure as hell wouldn't want a man coming along and taking up Mrs. Wassermann's time and attention.

"So the most likely candidates would be one: handsome, youngish man; or two: unattractive female." Jury looked at her from under lowered eyebrows and with a wicked smile. It was impossible for Caroleanne to keep reactions from showing in her face. "But, you see, there is a flaw in your selection process."

"Don't be daft. I naturally rented it to the most dependable person. He or She I made sure is very neat and clean and a nonsmoker."

Given the state of Jury's ashtrays, that was highly unlikely. He scrunched down in his chair, closed his eyes and waited.

"What flaw?"

He pretended to be asleep. Given the jet lag, it wouldn't be hard.

"What *flaw*?" She raised her voice.

"Huh? Oh. Well, if you rented it to a female, she would be your notion of 'unattractive.' "

"I'm sure we agree on what that is."

Jury shook his head. "The only notion of 'attractive' we agree on is you. And lord knows if many more women looked like you, it'd burn another hole in our atmospheric Islington ozone." Jury smiled. She was frowning, trying to work out if that was a compliment.

Then she said, as she screwed the cap back on the stoplight-red nail varnish, "I always thought SB-slash-H was attractive. Just like you."

"Oh, really? Funny, I seem to remember your mentioning a TV antenna when you were talking about her figure." Susan Bredon-Hunt was an old flame.

"I don't recall," said Carole-anne airily. She swung her feet from the sofa, wiggled her toes and leaned back, displaying a body that bore no resemblance to a TV antenna. "Anyway, I don't have to rent it to this person on a permanent basis. They've only paid rent for the last two weeks of the month."

Jury went on as if she hadn't spoken. "You see, to me a woman can be attractive for reasons other than the physical. What you fail to see is the effect of intelligence and spirit on physical beauty. I've seen women *you* might consider absolutely *dowdy,* but who had so much of a spiritual quality that I wouldn't have minded spending the rest of my life with them." Jury was leaning back, staring up at the ceiling, wondering where he'd ever seen her.

"Who's talking about the rest of your life, anyway?" Carole-anne now had the rest of the month to worry about. She bit her lip, stood up, said, "I've got a phone call to make."

"Oh?" Carole-anne wasn't on the phone. "Aren't you going to use mine? As usual?" Graciously, he swept his arm towards the instrument.

"No, I'll just go down to Mrs. W's." She shoved her feet into her black mules. "Back in a tick!" This she called from beyond the door.

Jury sat there smiling until he dozed off.

38

"Are you telling me, Jury, the man killed three people for a bogus peerage?"

"No. For money and revenge—the two best motives, other than love. Anyway, it wouldn't be the first time murder had been committed for a title. And the title, incidentally, is hardly bogus. 'Absolute Master of Maryland and Avalon, Baron of Baltimore,' Jury quoted. " 'Avalon settled by colonists that were taken over by George, First Lord Baltimore, which was then abandoned, and later restored to Cecil, Second Lord Baltimore.' Then Charles, Third Lord; then down to Frederick, where title died, or became a title de jure, if that's what you—"

"Oh, stop gibbering, will you?" Racer sniffed, ran his thumbs beneath the lapels of his jacket. The suit was new. He sorted through half a dozen faxes, hit the intercom and demanded of Fiona that she produce the rest of the fax pages from the commissioner's office that had been coming through just before he left for his club. "I saw it with my own eyes, Miss Clingmore!" There was only the answering hum of the machine; Miss Clingmore did not respond. Racer jiggled the switch and repeated her name. No answer.

Jury cast his eye around the freshly decorated office. New carpeting, fresh paint. But not even the gentler diffusion of the new indirect lighting system could soften the purpling-over of the chief superintendent's complexion.

It could and did soften the cat Cyril, however. While Racer was barking into the intercom, Jury was checking out the new continuous concave lighting and noticed a burnished copper tail hanging over the edge of the ceiling molding up there on Jury's right. The tail twitched lazily. The rest of Cyril was apparently lying on the ledge built all around to accommodate the tiny halogen lights, the molding added to hide the ledge.

"What's so funny?" Racer's head jerked up from the intercom that he had been trying to shake into submission.

"Nothing. Nothing at all. I was just admiring the new decoration. Very attractive."

"And pricy. Don't worry—it came out of my own pocket, in case you think I'm dipping into public funds." Racer smirked. Stopped smirking. "What about this Tate Gallery business? ME seems to be waffling on the cause of death."

Jury was surprised by this. "It was a stroke, I thought."

"Perhaps." Racer was trying to look inscrutable, not succeeding. "And this old kraut who wanted you on the case. You've seen her?"

"Sergeant Wiggins is there now."

"Wiggins? It was *you* she wanted."

"*I* intend to see her. You forget, I'm on leave."

"You just had leave. A policeman's life isn't one long holiday, Jury."

A tap at the door and Fiona stuck her head in. "There's Mr. Plant on the line; wants to know when you'll be by for him."

Jury turned round. "Tell him in an hour—no, make that two. I have to go home and pick up some stuff."

"Right-o."

"Miss *Cling*-more!"

But Miss Clingmore had shut the door, and just hard enough to cause a stirring of fur above the well of the ceiling molding.

39

"I don't *know* what she's done with it, old sweat." Marshall Trueblood's whisper was fierce. "I coaxed her with money; I bribed her with gin. Oh, of course, she took both—don't think she didn't take *both*—and then she denied ever seeing it: 'Ah don't know what y'mean, dearie. Ah niver seen nothin' like that, I niver.'" Marshall did a fair rasping imitation of Mrs. Withersby's gin-slurred voice.

The subject of this discourse between Trueblood and Melrose Plant was now sitting across the saloon bar in front of the fireplace, occasionally lifting the small hearth broom to sweep back the ashes, availing herself of whatever Cinderella possibilities she found in her position. Prince Charming (in the person of Melrose Plant) had already brought her a double gin and moved her cleaning bucket to the other side of the fireplace.

"Go on," urged Marshall Trueblood, "have another look." He gave Melrose a little shove to send him on his way.

Melrose rocked back into his sitting position and returned the whisper with an equally fierce one of his own. "Look: all I know is, it was in the bloody bucket! I could hardly rummage through it, could I?"

"What," asked Richard Jury, setting the three pints on the table, "are you two on about?"

"Oh, nothing," said Marshall, draping his Armani-clad arm along the windowed alcove behind them.

"Oh, nothing," echoed Melrose, returning to the *Times* crossword he'd propped against the dusty plastic peony meant to decorate the table.

Jury looked from one to the other. "Uh-huh. I'll be back with the sausages."

"What sausages?" they both asked of his departing back.

Said Plant, returning to the point, "You didn't search properly. I've been gone for almost a week; you must have had an opportunity to look through that bucket. By now she's slopped it out. The damned notebook's floating down the Piddle!"

"Don't blame *moi*." Trueblood clapped both of his palms against his seafoam-green shirt. "You're the one that stuck it in the bucket. And she doesn't slop it out because she damned well doesn't *use* it. Withers doesn't *work*, for God's sake."

They both looked, both fuming, in the direction of the slatternly subject of this argument. Her bucket was presently stashed beneath the fireplace chair opposite, as far from herself as she could get it. She was fondling an empty glass and smoking the cigarette she'd filched from Marshall Trueblood.

"I'm not buying her another drink. That's what she's waiting for. Blackmail, that's what it is. Fortunately, she can't read. . . . What's he doing?" Trueblood was watching Jury.

He was handing Mrs. Withersby what looked like a water tumbler full of gin. Now he was actually offering her a plate of sausages, stabbed with toothpicks. Dick Scroggs had lately decided to lay on some "happy hour" food. Holding the plate, he sat down in the chair opposite Mrs. Withersby. They chatted merrily away for some few minutes.

Disgruntled, Trueblood lifted his pint, said a vague "Cheers," and then said, "The superintendent would talk to the statue of Nelson in Trafalgar Square."

"And it would answer," said Melrose.

"All that work," said Marshall. "It was *so* good. How can we ever duplicate it?" He tossed the pen he'd been scribbling with down on the paper and sighed.

"Still arguing?" asked Jury, who set the plate of sausages on the table and sat down.

"We're not arguing."

"We're not arguing."

"Writing something?"

"No."

"No."

They both shook their heads.

"Thought maybe I'd take a walk and look in on Vivian," said Jury. "Before she leaves for Italy. *Again*. The whole thing's ridiculous." He looked at Melrose. "She could be persuaded to stay here, I'm sure."

Said Melrose, "Haven't we been trying to for years?"

"Well, you've never given her a good enough reason to break off this silly engagement, have you?"

Mrs. Withersby, having had a taste of the good life in the shape of gin and sausages, was shuffling up to the bar where the plates had been laid out, Dick Scroggs having left it temporarily to replenish happy hour provisions.

Melrose Plant watched her wavering progress across the room for a moment, and then excused himself.

Although Jury was talking to him, Marshall Trueblood was more interested in Melrose Plant's lingering before the hearth. Pretty soon, Melrose sat down in the chair vacated by Jury and appeared to be tying his shoelaces.

Mrs. Withersby left the bar, paper plate full of sausages and puff pastry, and returned to her chair, detouring long enough to launch a verbal attack across the room at (Jury thought for a moment) him and Marshall. But he discovered in the next moment the invective was directed at the face in the window behind Trueblood, outlined in the winter vines of the rosebush—the face of Lady Ardry. The face disappeared. Agatha was no longer popular with Mrs. Withersby, for she was once again writing letters to the editor of the *Bald Eagle* and working up a sweat in front of the town council in her attempt to "erase the blight" (as she put it) of the row of cottages, once almshouses, along the farther bank of the Piddle River. These cottages housed the Withersby clan. The Withersby clan, Melrose had often said, was large enough and ancient enough to have its own tartan.

Mrs. Withersby had switched affection from Her Ladyship (the instigator of this plan) to His Lordship, Melrose, who believed in championing the underdog, largely with strong drink.

Agatha came through the doorway in a dust of snow and made quite a show of ignoring Mrs. Withersby before she demanded a schooner of sherry from Dick Scroggs, who started putting the plates of food under the counter when he saw her.

In the meantime, Melrose had come back to the table looking pleased with himself and giving a nod to Trueblood, and Agatha was delighted with her news.

"They're moving into Watermeadows!" she announced.

Jury asked who "they" were.

"Oh, God," said Marshall Trueblood. "The WEMs."

Jury frowned. Who the hell were they?

"Week-End Man. Didn't Melrose tell you they'd leased the Man with a Load of Mischief? I'd so much rather see it fall into ruin and disrepair. How do you know, Agatha? About Watermeadows?"

"Mr. Tutwith himself told me. The estate agent. They're taking Watermeadows instead of the pub."

"I don't think so, aunt," said Melrose. "I definitely heard they were planning to restore the pub."

"Well, you're wrong."

That settled that, and Jury asked, "What happened to Lady Summerston?" He had liked the old lady who owned Watermeadows. Looking away, out of the window, he thought of that summer; he wondered if there were an age when memories were a solace rather than a torment.

"Oh, she still owns the place. They're only to be tenants."

"I can't see anyone leasing a place like Watermeadows as a weekend retreat," said Melrose.

"My dear old fellow, you do not understand the WEM psychology. That's just the sort of place they *adore*. Come down from London on the Friday; on the Saturday you pull on your wellies, get the dogs, and take the snaps in front of the Range Rover; then you run up to London on the Sunday and there you are! Show your friends the pictures and turn them green with envy."

Agatha said, "*She* wants a large dining hall and *he* wants to garden—"

"Bluhhh," said Trueblood, simulating sickness. "God, but I loathe men who like to garden. They're always wandering around in their oilskins and thick shoes going on about compost and spouting the Latin names of flowers."

"I can think of sillier pastimes," said Jury, with a level look at Trueblood, who raised a sculpted eyebrow. "You didn't at all mind Lady Summerston and Hannah Lean. Indeed, I seem to remember you made quite a little money off your wares."

"You don't seem to understand. They were *not* weekend people. It's a whole different sort of thing. Don't you know the WEMs are invading the provinces? Taking over whole villages—"

"You make it sound like Long Piddleton's going to have a Night of the Living Dead." Jury noticed that Plant had called Trueblood's attention to something beneath the table. He rose. "Well, I'm taking a little walk. Look in on Vivian, maybe."

Agatha, who had risen to make her way to the bar, said, "They've taken six months' lease. To see if it suits."

Both Trueblood and Plant looked at Agatha. And then at each other. They smiled.

"What are you two grinning about?" asked Jury.

"Nothing."

"Nothing."

A little snow was falling now, slowly, tiny flakes, far apart. Outside the Jack and Hammer, Jury stopped by the window in the embrasure of which they had been sitting.

". . . couldn't have missed it," Trueblood was saying.

"Well, you did. It was right there."

"Put it away," whispered Trueblood. "Here comes Agatha back."

Jury shook his head in wonder and looked down the High Street to see the local postman trundling along on his bicycle, stopping first at Jurvis the butcher's, then at Miss Ada Crisp's across the street.

The elderly postman Jury had run into once or twice—run into almost literally, since the man could hardly see. Abner Quick was old as the hills, deaf as a post, and blind as a bat. People were always getting the post wrong, getting other people's and having to take it round to the addressees themselves. Agatha, of course, had made it her mission to rid Long Pidd of Abner Quick, but she hadn't been successful. Actually, receiving another's letter and therefore having to go round to that person's cottage was more an occasion for an extra cup of tea than for complaint. And if one didn't care for a cup with the addressee, one had only to wait for Mr. Quick to come round later or drop it off at the sub-post office and let the postmistress deal with the problem.

At the moment, Miss Ada Crisp was standing by her door reading one of the envelopes Abner Quick had chosen for her hand to receive and looking terribly upset by it. She looked up, saw Jury directly across the street, and waved him over.

"Hullo, Miss Crisp." She looked horribly worried. "Can I do something for you?"

"It's that Mr. Browne who owns the Wrenn's Nest." She looked off down the pavement to the corner. Then her pale eyes looked up at Jury, miserably. "Says he's going to send me a summons."

"Summons? Why on earth would he do that?"

"Wants me out, that's why. Wants my shop."

She stood there with her biscuit-colored eyes and hair into which the gray melted like the new-falling snow and wrung the end of her coverall apron. "I've been here forty years, Mr. Jury. That *person* only came three years ago and thinks he owns the village. All he does is make trouble. He keeps saying he wants to 'expand' his business. Now, I ask you—whatever does a little village like this need with a huge bookshop?"

Jury read over the document, which was indeed a legal summons. He was sure complaints about Miss Crisp's premises ("public nuisance") were without foundation, but, of course, the idea was undoubtedly to attack her nerves, not her reason. It was infuriating. It was also unfortunately the provenance of the law to find a basis for baseless allegations, so that any fool, anyone seeking redress or revenge, could bring a lawsuit. Jury looked off down the street for a moment and smiled.

The smile seemed visibly to shore her up, to lift a weighty burden from her thin shoulders.

"Not to worry, Miss Crisp. Perhaps I'll just stop and have a word with Mr. Browne."

"Oh, *would* you? I'd be ever so grateful."

Jury turned, as he walked away, and called back, "Remember the pig, Miss Crisp." This was a reference to the lawsuit Agatha had brought against the butcher, Jurvis—or, rather, against Jurvis's plaster-of-Paris pig.

Miss Crisp laughed and waved.

Inside the Wrenn's Nest bookshop, three people stood in line while Theo Wrenn Browne stamped a book and admonished the first of the three, a little girl, who waited in silent humiliation on the opposite side of the counter. She had left chocolate fingerprints on one of his rental books, and he was threatening to keep the deposit. The two adults behind her tried to look away. She ran out with her book.

The Current Books for Rental shelves had been started largely as competition for Long Piddleton's tiny but adequate library. It was unusual for a village the size of this one to have a library at all, and the villagers had been just proud until Theo Wrenn Browne had determined to demonstrate its needlessness. He himself supplied the latest crop of bestsellers, thereby putting a considerable dent in the library's patronage. For the library had to wait for its books, whereas Theo Wrenn Browne could get his immediately, weeks before they were even reviewed. It wasn't money but misery—other people's—that motivated him.

While words like hard coin fell on the next borrower's head, Jury read the sign setting out the lending rules. Deposits were required, and there were different rates for different days and for different books. An accountant would have a hard time juggling this information, but when a person wanted a new book, a bestseller, or one by his favorite writer, well, he'd put up with a lot of nonsense, even the excoriating comments of Theo Wrenn Browne.

When the last borrower had left, his book stamped (his days numbered), Theo Wrenn Browne called out an enthusiastic greeting.

Jury smiled his hello and said, "I see you've started up a new line of business here."

"Ah, yes. Public service, you know." He enjoyed a martyred sigh. "Our library is so behindhand, Mr. Jury. I keep telling the council that."

"Didn't know there was a council."

"Oh, yes. Long Piddleton's got a lot of problems. What I'm pushing for now is for us to compete in the Prettiest Village in England competition. I don't see why it always has to be the Cotswolds—Bibury and Broadway and those places—do you? Northants doesn't have to be always thought of as industrial. I'm trying to change our image. What we need is good PR. Attract more tourists, that sort of thing. I think, you know, we're beginning to attract Londoners."

"Too bad. I was wondering, Mr. Browne, if you might have a copy of *Bleak House.*"

"Dickens? I'm sure I do. Come along back here."

Jury thought, as he followed through the shelved books, it was a shame that the Wrenn's Nest had to suffer the waspish presence of Theo Wrenn Browne. It was a lovely shop: black beams, polished floors, cushioned window seats, nooks and crannies. And an extensive collection of antiquarian books along with the recent ones.

"Here we are. You like Dickens, do you? Well, one *does.* Honestly, the *tripe* that people come in and buy. I have to *stock* it, you know. Dreadful thrillers, idiot mysteries. Genre stuff. God. Well, I'm in *business,* aren't I? I can hardly set myself up as the arbiter of taste and refuse to sell Danielle Steel. Finally, I had to stock Joanna the Mad's books. My customers were going to Sidbury and even all the way to Northampton to get hold of them. Rubbishy romances." He shuddered pleasantly and handed down the copy of *Bleak House.* "But at least I'm glad to see you're reading Dickens."

"The Dickens isn't for me; it's for an acquaintance who's thinking of bringing a suit. I thought he should get a taste of what the law's like." Jury riffled the pages. "I've had a lot of dealings with civil suits, and I can tell you, I wouldn't, for love nor money, ever get involved in one."

Theo Wrenn Browne brought his neat little hand to his mouth. "Oh?"

"Last person I knew did it lost everything—bank account, job. . . ." Jury shook his head and sighed. "This is fine. I'll have this."

Theo Wrenn Browne coughed nervously. "But surely, if one is *justified . . .*"

Jury gave a short, astonished bark of laughter. *"Justified?* What difference does that make? Most recent case I know of was a prominent shopkeeper in Piccadilly. He'd got people living over him, woman and her brood of six kiddies, that made his life a misery. Not only was there screaming and shouting the whole day long, but the kiddies managed to get into his shop at night and take things, mess things up, create havoc. The poor fellow tried to get them off the premises and went to court. He was at it for three years, had to pay out so much money to the solicitors and so forth he lost his business, finally. Now he's on the dole. Terrible."

Both of them had been looking up at the ceiling, and Jury shook his head sadly, as if the kiddies who figured in this tale of woe had materialized in the elegant private apartments above, where Theo Wrenn Browne read the latest rubbishy romances.

"Jarndyce and Jarndyce, Mr. Browne," said Jury as he paid for his book and left Theo Wrenn Browne a wiser, if paler, man.

* * *

Across the wine-brown stone bridge, the cottages, sub–post office, and Betty Ball's bakery clustered on three sides of the green. Although Vivian's house was far too large to be a cottage, that was how she referred to it. According to the note Sellotaped to the door, she would return shortly.

Jury walked across the green, now with its sugar-coated layering of snow, to the bench by the duck pond and sat down.

He thought about Jip. Jip with her specter aunt and her strange story. From his pocket he took the old snapshot and studied it. He felt saddened by this little girl. Perhaps he could help her. He could try, certainly.

Then he thought of Jenny Kennington and felt a kind of content. He must go tomorrow or the next day to Stratford to see her. He sat back and watched the ducks sheltering under the overhanging branches of a blackthorn bush. The last time he had sat on this same bench had been over ten years ago; he'd been sitting here with Vivian.

Ten years, a decade ago. Was it possible?

The little pond wore a skin of rime, melting now in the unseasonable warmth of late-January sunlight. Two ducks bobbed sleepily beneath the overhanging branches of a small willow trailing its tiny leaves across the pond's surface. Jury sighed and rose and thought that a cup of tea and some biscuits in Betty Ball's tearoom wouldn't go amiss.

The bakery was behind him, across the road that split at this end of the bridge and straggled around the green where he'd been sitting. The bakery was on the bottom floor of three levels, and the tearoom at the top, which made it a long climb for a cup of tea or coffee, but Betty Ball apparently liked to keep the floor between for some purpose of her own. Perhaps she lived there. Or perhaps she had, like Carol-anne, plans.

Jury took a table in an alcove so that he could look out onto the village below. He could see most of it, all the way to Plague Alley, where Agatha lived, even while he was sitting down. If he stood, he could see all of the nearer part of Long Piddleton. So with his cup of tea and a muffin, he stood there sipping and munching and looking out. This posture gave him quite a bit of childish pleasure, for he imagined his view of the village to be godlike from up here, and he liked the sense of omniscience even if he couldn't, godlike, participate in the omnipotence. It was fun seeing the village from this perspective, a miniature village, where he could now retrace his steps simply with his eyes.

He saw Trueblood and Melrose Plant emerge from a door on the other side of the bridge, undoubtedly the Jack and Hammer. They walked in the direction of the bakery. Occasionally they stopped to discuss something, and once appeared to be engaged in what looked like an argument, with both assuming various postures and gestures of irritation or impatience. On the other side of the bridge, they headed off to the right, and Jury noticed that Melrose Plant was carrying a large brown envelope. They passed several houses on that side of the duck pond and then stopped before the sub–post office. Plant started into the post office with the parcel, but Trueblood pulled him back. Then they more or less huddled, Trueblood moving off a little and gesticulating with the usual Trueblood theatrics, waving his arms in the air as if he were conducting the London Symphony Orchestra, pointing across the bridge with a batonlike finger. Trueblood then walked back and forth, looking here, looking there. As Plant simply stood there, he walked away some hundred yards, apparently saw something, for he ran back, and then both of them leaned against the whitewashed Tudor building housing the post office and its stores, smoking cigarettes, and looking as casual as any couple of delinquent schoolboys waiting to be busted by the headmaster.

Jury had finished his carrot muffin and his cup of tea without even realizing it; now he reached back over the table to pour himself another cup from the pot, milk from the jug, and feel around for the muffin plate. And he did all this pouring and muffin hunting without taking his eyes from the little drama proceeding below.

Abner Quick had appeared now, having bumped over the brown bridge on his bicycle and come to rest in front of the post office. Melrose Plant and Marshall Trueblood greeted him in comradely fashion, and Abner went on into the post office, presumably to collect the second batch of letters for the day and get down to the business of misdelivering them.

Soon he came out with another batch of letters and circulars and so forth, and while he was fixing the pouch to the bicycle, Melrose Plant dropped his own package in the snow at his feet. Trueblood was engaging Mr. Quick in conversation while Plant did this, and when Abner Quick was wheeling his pouch and himself away from the curb, he was stopped by both of them, Plant reaching down to pluck the package from the ground and Trueblood then handing it over with a clear direction (Jury presumed) and pointing at what must be the addressee.

Now, since Abner Quick could get about with any success at all only because he'd committed the village to mind like a book of braille, Jury pretty much knew that this little ruse of Plant's and Trueblood's was necessary to ensure that the package would arrive at its proper destination.

Richard Jury had not spent over twenty years at Scotland Yard only to find himself stumped by what this destination was.

He stood there eating a third muffin and drinking a third cup of tea while he watched Abner Quick pedal his bicycle up an alley, be lost to view, return, stop here, stop there, and make his way all round the green while, at the same time, Plant and Trueblood were over by the pond throwing snowballs that simply feathered apart without landing anywhere as they doubtless waited for delivery to be made.

It was not long before he could make out the figure of Vivian, all the way on the other side of the humpbacked bridge, coming along with her string bag, no doubt filled with little paper parcels done up by the butcher, Jurvis. Vivian, in any event, could be seen for a country mile because the sun was out and when it shone on her red-brown hair it turned the color of Graham's sherry.

Plant and Trueblood saw her too and stopped popping the pond with weightless snowballs and made quite a fuss of waving and calling. Vivian waved back and opened her gate and went up her walk.

Jury saw he had eaten three muffins (and he disliked carrot muffins) and drunk three cups of tea. Now he thought he would like to be on hand at Vivian's house. He paid his bill and in addition had the thin little waitress pack him up a box of muffins. ("We've only got the carrot to-day") and tie it with string. With this offering, he ran down the stairs to the green.

Mr. Quick had just plopped his bike down in front of Vivian's as Jury greeted Plant and Trueblood heartily enough, but saying he was in a hurry to take Vivian her muffins—for tea, Jury shouted, having passed them as they stood with snow on their gloves. Did they want to join Vivian and him?

No. Jury was quite certain they'd want anything but.

Mr. Quick's bicycle was now weaving along a little lane farther down, his mail pouch lighter by at least one parcel, if the one he drew from Vivian's box was any measure.

He held it up with her other two letters and waved the lot at Melrose Plant and Marshall Trueblood.

"*What* are they doing out there? Oh, thanks," said Vivian, taking her letters and her parcel from Jury, and returning her gaze to her front window. It had started to snow—not much, just a flurry, but the flakes were drifting down.

"Thought you'd like some muffins." Jury held up the white box.

"Betty Ball's?" She smiled.

"Carrot. I hate carrot muffins, and I've eaten three."

"Oh, I like carrot." She was obviously lying. "Want some tea?"

"No. I had three cups."

"One per muffin. Interesting." She had opened and discarded the envelopes of her letters or bills. "What's this, then?" She frowned a little, looking at the front. "It's from Italy. Venice." She brought the parcel up close to her eyes, frowning. "You know, these stamps look—odd. Not properly franked."

"Oh?" Jury tried to sound indifferent.

She opened the envelope, took out a black book. *The* black book. She leafed through it, frowning all the while, then shook the brown envelope, peeked into it. Nothing. "What is this?" She looked at the black leather binding, flipped through the pages again, shook it. Nothing.

Jury watched her, rocking on his heels.

Vivian was perplexed. "It looks like a diary, with dates and all. Aren't you going to sit down, for heaven's sake?"

Jury murmured some acquiescent thing or other and moved over to the window.

Vivian held it up, above her head at arm's length, as if the fall of light from the chandelier might penetrate the murky depths of the black book. "Listen to this: 'My own dearth is as nothing—' "

" 'Death,' not 'dearth.' "

Vivian raised her eyebrows. "Oh?"

Jury shrugged. "Well, 'My own *dearth* is as nothing' doesn't make any sense. . . ." His voice trailed away as he looked everywhere but at her.

She smiled. "I expect you're right." She turned over the envelope, looked again at the stamps, at the postmark, at Jury. "Aren't you wondering what this is? You don't seem curious."

"Curious? Of course I'm curious. I just don't want to pry into your affairs."

"You don't?" Vivian was looking through the window. "That would make a change," she said sweetly. "What in heaven's name are they doing over there—playing at Statues?"

It was true, Jury saw when he came to stand by her: Plant and Trueblood were standing stiff as statues, their eyes on the house. He sighed.

"I've got the distinct impression over the years that none of you want me to marry Franco."

"No! Where would you ever have got that?"

She read a passage, giggled, and handed him the book. "Memoirs, I take it. He's had a busy old life. Look at them; they're throwing snowballs."

Irritated with her acceptance of this nonsense, her sangfroid, he commanded: "Don't go. It's ridiculous to go."

Her look at him was inscrutable. "Actually, I've taken a house there on a short let. It's on the Grand Canal. Quite beautiful."

"What?" He actually grabbed at her shoulder, shook her.

But it didn't dent her composure. She clasped her hands behind her and sighed. "Oh, I expect I'm trying to believe I'm free."

"Free?"

"Haven't you ever felt . . . stuck? In your life, in your work?"

Without really thinking about it, Jury lay his arm across her shoulders. "Yes—*oh*, yes."

"The trouble is, one begins almost to enjoy it. The stuck-ness." Here she cast a glance around the comfortable room. "The same chairs, the same faces. The daily routines, the same friendships and estrangements. It all becomes so familiar. And so safe—too safe; I feel hemmed in, like the little pond over there. I feel like the ducks drifting on the water. Oh, it's not unpleasant at all; perhaps that's the trouble. Are they"—she nodded her head towards the green, towards her two friends—"seducing those ducks with bread crumbs over to the edge so they can—?" She shook her head. "Idiots."

But Jury wasn't paying much attention to the idiots, for he was thinking of what she'd said. "I like the way you put that, Vivian. The same faces and friendships and estrangements. Maybe that's the best of it." He thought of his Islington digs, his office at New Scotland Yard. Then he laughed.

"What's funny?"

"Oh, it's just a song that used to be popular. 'Is that all there is?' the singer keeps asking about life. Finally, when the house burns to the ground, she's still singing 'Is that all there is?' Nothing's ever enough. I mean, once it was, but the more you get—like money, like success—the more you delude yourself into thinking you need. Because once it *was* enough." He picked up the book. "So much trouble."

She took it. "Yes, so much trouble."

"And if you were a duck, you'd have just got a snowball in your face."

She nodded. "Idiots."

Dreamily, they stood there.

40

"Pour vous!" Theo Wrenn Browne raided his stockpile of foreign words and phrases for an appropriate one to accompany his act of placing a long-stemmed rose on the table in front of Diane Demorney. *"Une rose parfaite."* In case this candy-wrapper French was too much for them, he smiled round at the others and translated: "One perfect rose."

Diane Demorney stuffed the stem into an empty bottle of Plant's Old Peculier. "Next time, make it one perfect Rolls, would you?"

"I told you," went on Joanna the Mad, whose remarks on the asininity of writing had been interrupted by Theo Wrenn Browne and his rose, "any ass can write a book. Don't take that personally, Melrose. Just hack it out." She danced her fingers along imaginary typewriter keys to simulate the art of hacking.

Melrose felt a twinge of anxiety. He had been having a delightful time with his mystery ever since the flight back to London; what concerned him now, though, was that he was beginning to take Smithson a little too seriously. He also found that he enjoyed writing round the village—in the library, or in Betty Ball's bakery over morning coffee, or even on that bench by the duck pond. And he liked walking with his notebook under his arm and his dog, Mindy, somewhere at his heels, tossing sticks that Mindy never fetched. He hoped he was not becoming ill; he certainly knew he was not becoming a writer.

Nonetheless, there were fringe benefits to the writing life. Not only was it keeping Vivian in England, it was also keeping Agatha out of Ardry End and Richard Jury out of London. Jury was, at the moment, over by the fireplace, joining the Withersby person in a pint.

"Gin Lane, chapter seven. 'Smithson stood, deeply perturbed—' "

"Hold it, old sweat! I don't remember seeing chapters two through six," said Marshall Trueblood.

"I thought the title was *The Opal,*" said Diane Demorney.

Said Melrose, "I haven't typed up those chapters yet." Hadn't written them yet, either. He wanted to get to Smithson's ruminations. " 'Smithson stood, deeply perturbed—' "

Vivian asked, "Yes, but what about *The Opal*?"

Trueblood was worrying the end of his tangerine scarf. "Isn't 'Gin Lane' a set of Cruikshank engravings?"

"Trust Melrose to steal whatever he can," said Agatha.

Was the Algonquin Round Table like this? Melrose read:

—deeply perturbed, and suddenly remembered the time that had shown beneath the shattered glass of Lord Haycock's pocket watch.

Theo Wrenn Browne gave a stagy sigh. "Good God! What a cliché!"

"Shakespeare was never afraid of a cliché," said Melrose, trying to think of one of Shakespeare's.

Smithson realized that one thing or the other had happened: either someone had changed the hands of the clock against the wall, or changed the hands of the pocket watch. The butler had commented that both of them kept impeccable time.

Melrose adjusted his glasses and continued.

Smithson hadn't noticed Nora slipping in through the French windows—

Joanna the Mad asked, "Don't you think it might be better to name his wife something else? There's that Nora and Nick, you know. Awfully famous. Especially as she's always drinking champagne and loves hats."

"Yes. That's just a typo, there. It's supposed to be Norma." Melrose made a little stroke with his pen.

Norma was wearing a simple black suit, snug at the waist, and a clever little red hat, ringed with black feathers.

"Do you have a light, darling?" She moved towards Smithson, a cigarette plugged into a red lacquer holder.

Smithson lit her cigarette and asked her why she was here.

"I was simply wondering about the clock. Do you think Church would bring me a champagne cocktail?"

"And what made you think of the clock?" Smithson summoned the butler by pulling the tapestry bellpull beside the fireplace.

Norma sat down. "It's fairly obvious, isn't it?"

"Always is in stories." Richard Jury had drifted over, leaving Mrs. Withersby to talk to herself and probably think she was still talking to the superintendent. He drank his pint, leaned against the wall at Melrose's elbow.

Melrose wished he'd go away—not back to London, just back to the fireplace. He wasn't sure he wanted a policeman listening to what Smithson was doing.

But before Norma could finish, Church appeared with an iced bottle of Dom Pérignon and some biscuits. She thanked him.

"Where's Chloe?" she asked, pouring champagne over a bitters-soaked sugar cube.

"In the car. What's 'obvious'? Tell me."

Norma sipped, smoked and thought. She had a subtle mind; it was difficult to get her to give a straightforward answer. Nora's—I mean Norma's—attitude towards language was intensely deconstructive; words were lies. Not deliberate lies, of course, but the mere choice of one word, in its denial of other words, cancelled out meaning. Smithson thought solving cases was a science; Norma thought it was an art. She said, "Have another word with that guard at the gatehouse. I feel something's wrong there."

"Lord!" said Theo Wrenn Browne. "A gatehouse? How original!"

Joanna said, "You'd kill for a gatehouse, Theo—you'd draw and quarter your old gran for a gatehouse. Go on, Melrose."

Smithson crunched along the gravel of the serpentine drive towards the stone pillars of the entry.

With his knuckles he tapped on the glass partition behind which the guard was deep into what appeared to be an old edition, a very large black book with a cracked binding whose title Smithson couldn't see. It was thick with dust; when he snapped the book shut at the sound of Smithson's voice, dust motes swam in a slanting ray of sunlight.

"Yes, sir?"

"A few more questions, Charles. When His Lordship stopped here at the gatehouse on the Thursday night, you say he checked the time with you?"

"That he did, yes, sir. Took a lot of trouble about it, too. Made sure he'd got the time spot-on to the minute, he did. Looked at his own watch—it was a Rolex—and asked me what time I had, and I said 'Nine-oh-two.' 'That's all right, then,' says he; 'that's just what

my Rolex says.' Then he tells me to check the wall clock up there to make absolutely sure"—here Charles nodded towards the big white clock above him—*"because, see, it's got to be right as it's linked to the alarm system. I says 'nine-oh-two' and His Lordship repeats it a couple of times, and—"* Charles heaved with laughter—*"I don't guess anyone's about to forget the time after checking all that lot, right? But His Lordship, he still says that the clock time looks more like nine-oh-three to him, and I says, 'Well, of course, ain't we been chatting here for thirty seconds, at least, so it's actually nine-oh-two-and-one-half.' Then he puts his ear down to his car radio and says, 'Well, that must be right, the news is just coming on.' Now, I know what you're thinking, sir. Lord Haycock died at nine-twenty-five and you're wondering when Mr. Gabriel left, and I can tell you it was nine-oh-two-going-on-three."*

Smithson thanked Charles, who, he noticed, when he looked over his shoulder, had rescued the black book from its place behind his chair. Had he hidden it?

Norma was still drinking champagne. She nibbled on a biscuit as Smithson told her what Charles had said. She looked all sparkling interest—

"Looked *what?*" asked Trueblood. " 'Sparkling interest'? Must be all that champagne. Probably drank a magnum." He had his gold nail file out, whisking it across his ring finger.

"And," put in Diane, "that's an absolutely dreadful ensemble Norma's wearing. I'll be happy to write that part for you."

"Thank you." Melrose read on:

"But if it was nine-oh-two, why did the housekeeper mention the church bells pealing the quarter-hour when she brought in the drinks?"

Norma gave her husband a tiny smile. "Church bells keep notoriously bad time, my love—"

Diane interrupted. "That, of course, was the flaw in the Sayers book."

"What are you talking about?" asked Joanna. "Her bells weren't telling the wrong time. It's irrelevant, anyway."

"I didn't mean *that*. But this detective of hers, Lord somebody—"

"Wimsey," said Vivian. "Lord Peter Wimsey."

"He did all of this bell-ringing for hours and hours and obviously knew when the bells rang. Still he goes monkey-climbing up to the tower, *knowing* what happened to whoever got killed. Well, I've forgotten the plot, but you get the point."

> "*It's not the bells, love, it's the* radio," *said Norma.*
>
> "*What?*" *Smithson was perplexed.*
>
> "*The car* radio. *Gabriel never listened to the radio, only to his digital tapes!*"
>
> "*My God! You're right! He's obviously lying!*"
>
> "*Ah, but who's lying, my love?*"
>
> *They were interrupted by the door's bursting open. A young woman wearing a twin set and tweeds and a cashmere shawl strode in. She seemed upset.* "*You're Inspector Smithson? I'm Lord Haycock's stepdaughter, Imogene.*"
>
> "*Have some champagne, darling,*" *said Norma, with a sunny smile. Norma was never flustered.*
>
> "*A bit early for me, thanks. I stopped to have a word with Charles. He said you'd been asking him a lot of questions about Gabriel checking the time. I know what you're thinking!*"
>
> "*You do?*"
>
> "*Yes. You think that because Gabriel was checking the time that he wanted to be sure Charles remembered exactly what time he left and that it was before my stepfather was murdered.*"
>
> "*That was the furthest thing from our minds, darling.*" *Norma poured another glass of champagne.*
>
> *Pouting, Imogene said,* "*People always question gatekeepers in mystery stories.*"
>
> *Smithson and Norma laughed. The detective said,* "*This is real life, not one of your mystery stories.*"

A sound came from Jury. Melrose looked round. Jury's expression was impassive, as he leaned there and drank his beer.

> "*He's always been obsessed with time!*" *exclaimed Imogene.* "*Ever since he was a child. Anyway, he* has *an alibi! He was with me the entire evening!*"

Dick Scroggs had come to the table to deliver fresh drinks. "What's she on about then?" He rolled the toothpick around in his mouth and didn't stay for an answer, but returned to the bar and his *Bald Eagle.*

Vivian said, "She's in love with Gabriel so she's going to lie for him."

"No, she isn't," said Melrose calmly.

They all, to a man, stared at him.

"Wait a minute," said Joanna, "at the beginning we *saw* Gabriel kill Lord Haycock."

"True, old bean. Remember, you said it was one of these inverted mysteries," said Marshall, stashing his cuticle scissors.

Melrose capped his pen and looked smug. "It's inverted-reversed."

They all looked at one another and then at Richard Jury, who merely shrugged his shoulders.

Theo Wrenn Browne turned away in disgust and Agatha babbled something about the story's being a cheat.

Vivian was truly baffled. "But Melrose, we *saw* it—where Gabriel was murdering Lord Haycock."

Smugly, Melrose said, "You mean you *thought* you saw it." Give them a taste of Maxim. Then he sat back and looked up at the ceiling, thinking, happily, how nice it was, writing mysteries. *Gin Lane* was a wonderful title.

Diane Demorney had, of course, given up on the inverted reversion from its inception. She said, "*The Opal* was a better title. This is supposed to end in Morocco."

"It doesn't. It's called *Gin Lane* because . . . because it ends up in Shoreditch. Or Whitechapel." He added, "Maybe."

Uncommitted to any ending, and certainly to any part of any city, not setting it in Morocco was as good as not setting it anywhere else. Melrose ate a pretzel and stared happily over towards the fireplace, in front of which Mrs. Withersby was weaving and discoursing on her own time and into her own ear. My, but writing was freedom! Looking ceilingward again, he felt he was floating up there. He had never realized before how liberating writing a mystery was, and he wondered why Polly Praed was eternally complaining about its demands and constrictions and how one had to check facts and on and on and—

"This Smithson works at Scotland Yard?" asked Jury.

Oh, hell, thought Melrose, leaving the ceiling and landing hard on the floor. He sighed. Here comes the droning part.

"I just wondered why his wife was hanging around. It doesn't sound, if you don't mind my saying it, very authentic."

Melrose shut his eyes against this intrusion of so-called reality.

"—especially," Jury droned on, "with that cat. Chloe?"

Melrose snapped to attention. He'd got Jury there! "What about that cat in your chief superintendent's office?"

"Well, yes. But I don't carry it around in the squad car, do I? Cyril wouldn't go along for the ride, anyway."

Diane said, as she tapped her blood-red fingernails against her glass,

"Oh, aren't you being a bit particular, Superintendent? I rather like Norma. If she could dress with a touch more chic."

Dick Scroggs was calling the superintendent to the telephone, and Jury walked over to the bar.

"Someone named Macalvie," said Scroggs.

"*Mac*alvie." Jury corrected him and took the receiver.

"I've been trying to get hold of you for a week, Jury," said Macalvie, without preamble.

"I was out of the country. What do you want?"

"Well, it's what *you* want. You want a job. So come to Exeter and help out."

"It's funny, Macalvie, but I'm not a freelance cop."

"You're bloody on holiday, you said so."

"Right. So what do I want with some damned case in Exeter if I'm on holiday?"

"Well, agreed no one wants some damned case in Exeter, including me. I could use some help—"

Jury nearly dropped the receiver. Macalvie asking for help?

"—but since I can't find any, I'm asking for you. Hold on—"

He turned away from the telephone to argue with one or another—or perhaps all—of his subordinates, and in the interim Jury had time to read a paragraph of the gardening column in the *Bald Eagle* and to reflect that Macalvie was much like Norma: police work (the divisional commander seemed to think) was an inexact science at best. Macalvie did not believe that an accumulation of discrete facts necessarily added up to anything. He had to grasp the gestalt of the problem. His lengthy silences at a crime scene made some people who didn't know him assume he'd gone to sleep on his feet.

"It's this tapiser." Papers crackled; from a distance came the muted tap of typewriter keys.

Jury brought his mind back from the petunia border and asked, "This *what*?"

"Tapiser. One of the ladies who does, you know, *tapestry.*" The impatient tone told Jury that should be perfectly clear. "That's where she collapsed, right in front of these rondels."

"Rondels?"

"Embroidered cushions. Very artistic, very historic. A big deal in the cathedral."

"So what was it—her heart?"

"Could be. ME isn't sure what caused it."

Jury frowned. "You're saying she dropped down dead without apparent cause?"

"That's what the ME's saying. Of course, he carries a spanner and pliers in his black bag, so consider the source. I'll tell you the details when you get here."

Jury shook his head, returned his gaze to the flower border. "Macalvie, I'm sorry, but I don't get it. An accident in the cathedral and you're calling—"

"Why're you calling it an accident?"

"Why am I—? Macalvie, I'm not there, remember."

"Obviously. That's the point." From somewhere came a sudden crash, and Macalvie turned from the phone to yell at someone. Noises off went with Macalvie. "Devon and Cornwall constabulary needs a few good men," he said, back again.

"But you'll settle for me."

"Right. See you." Macalvie hung up.

Jury shook his head, returned to the table and told the assembled company about this tapiser collapsing in front of the Exeter Cathedral rondels.

"It's the Stendhal syndrome," said Diane. "Go on, Melrose, with your story. *I* love it."

Melrose sighed. "You seem to be the only one, Diane."

"No, she isn't," snapped Vivian. "I think it's wonderful. Certainly better than *this*." She smiled and waved the black notebook.

Trueblood brought the front legs of his chair down with a thud. Melrose gaped.

"I couldn't imagine what it was, at first. And then I remembered." She looked round the table, seeming to savor her bit of suspense; her eyes lingered on Marshall, then on Melrose.

"Remembered what?"

"Yes, what?"

"Franco's cousin. I hope you don't mind, Joanna—"

"Mind what?"

"Well, you see, the cousin is a writer; he was writing this first novel, and I happened to mention I knew you and—" her little laugh was as insincere as the grasping of Joanna's hand—"well, he asked if perhaps you'd help him."

Plant and Trueblood stared across the table at one another.

Theo Wrenn Browne declared, smirking, "Joanna is not very helpful in that department."

"Oh, really?" Joanna returned the smirk. "I certainly am if one shows any promise *at all*. What's it about, Vivian?"

"Apparently, it's to do with a bank robbery. In the Middle Ages."

Trueblood gagged. Melrose adjusted his spectacles and leaned closer to Vivian.

Vivian continued. "It's a peculiar situation. And why an Italian would choose San Francisco as a setting . . ." She shrugged, shook her head over the wayward writing habits of Italians.

Jury slugged back half a pint of beer and choked.

"A *bank* heist in the Middle Ages?" Joanna looked thoughtful. "Why not, considering my own—"

Vivian read: " 'They carried the poor creature into the bank vault—' "

" *'Dank* vau—*'ouch!'* " Trueblood leaned down to rub his shin.

Melrose looked owlish.

Jury looked away.

" '—and the pile of bills—' "

" *'Peal'*—'peal of *bells'*!" Trueblood stopped; he bit his lip; he smiled.

Vivian ignored him, saying, "Well, the handwriting's rather grungy and I can't make it all out. And Dono never could spell. But it seems that the robbers kidnap the bank teller and shove her in the vault. Anyway, I hope you don't mind having a look at it, Joanna." Vivian rose. "I have to go pack. Ta." She wiggled her fingers and was out the door.

Jury was convulsed with silent laughter.

Plant and Trueblood looked hopelessly at the little black notebook.

The silent laughter overflowed as Jury said, "So take *that*, mates—" he pounded his pint on the table—"and the horse you came in on!"

Acknowledgments

My sincere thanks to Jeff Jerome, curator of the Poe house on Amity Street; William Addams Reitwiesner, genealogist, and his help with the intricacies of entitlement; Maria Wrzesinski for the excellent *copie*; and the Perrys for the NFL updates.

   . . . and I assure my friends and students at Johns Hopkins University: I have never once met a Vlasic there. Or a little Vlasic.